# CHAPTERS

# PART I

# The Backwind

# 1. CIRA

The whole adventure was, as always, Cira's fault. A servant girl determined never to learn her place, she took every opportunity to lead her friend Jordan astray. This was an improper state of affairs, for Jordan was the son of the lord of the Galea Estate, the largest land holding of the Backwind County. According to social etiquette, he ought not to associate with a girl of such lowly station at all, much less be her best - indeed only - friend. But Lord Falric, like Cira's own mother, an otherwise ferocious woman who could beget terror with a single raised eyebrow, had given up trying to teach Cira simple virtues like silence and decorum. Instead, he had learned to tolerate, and at times even appreciate, her mischievous influence on his son.

Cira and Jordan had been inseparable for all that they could remember of their respective eleven and twelve years. Attempts to encourage Jordan to widen his friendship circle had been unsuccessful. While Lord Falric knew his son to be intelligent, articulate and - albeit selectively - enthusiastic, he was all of these things only with Cira. It was as though the boy came to life in Cira's presence; on occasions when she was absent - usually on account of being bribed, manipulated or even blackmailed into performing the work expected in her role as a servant - Jordan lapsed back into his natural introversion. Having been embarrassed at a number of social events by the unexpected shyness of his sole son and heir, Falric now tended to overlook what he politely considered to be

Cira's more *colourful* personality traits. He allowed her free access to his son, his son's education and, outside of classes, largely left the children to their own devices.

This was not always a good idea.

On this particular bright autumn day, Cira and Jordan spent the afternoon class plotting a grand adventure. This was done by way of notes slipped under the nose of their tutor Master Adamant, an elderly gentleman whose snout practically deserved geography all of its own. Rumour had it that Aethon had been sighted the previous afternoon, and such a claim clearly required investigation. The earliest sightings of the black and gold unicorn dated back centuries; countless stories of his exploits circulated the county districts. Luckless hunters recounted tales of how Aethon had led their *grandfathers'* grandfathers in merry chases across Leaverness. Although the ancient forest was geographically uncertain at the best of times, it was said that a man could pursue Aethon for a week in a straight line and never find the centre, much less far side, of a stretch of wilderness no more than four days ride across on the map. By the foolish, he was hunted for his flowing golden mane and tail; for his golden hooves and horn; and for his extraordinary beauty, which outshone that of any mortal horse. By the wise though, he was hunted without intent to capture, but for the sheer adventure of the chase. For there would never be any other chase ever like it, and it was also said that Aethon could lead one to their destiny. Or as Cira would say, Destiny, with requisite capitalisation. It was in such worthy spirit that Cira and Jordan intended to pursue the fleet unicorn on their sturdy, stocky ponies.

Afternoon astronomy class was normally a highlight of the week for the children, for it was held in the Astronomy Tower, which was the scholarly Lord Falric's pride and joy. The literally breathtaking journey up sixteen flights of draughty, barren stone stairs was well worth the arrival. The view from the circular turret was a spectacular one across Leaverness. From this height, the great forest seemed to own the whole horizon, if not swallow the world. It was to this window that Cira always ran to first, where she would hang out over a dizzying height and gulp in the bracing air. Jordan meanwhile would take a few more sedate steps across the flagstones, and then just look *up* to where all the known stars shone down upon him from the ceiling. The fresco was one of visionary detail, with silver lines dainty as spider webs tracing out the Dancing Bull, the Wyrd Wizard and the Duck Billed Owl, along with the more serious constellations such as Aethon the Unicorn himself, the All-Sky Falcon, Aksaya the Eternal Mother, the Dark Lady Shivaia and Brynir the Cursed. On this day though, even Jordan ran straight to the window, almost threatening to topple Cira out as they both squeezed their torsos over the pale stone parapet. On this day, even their favourite class of the week dragged - brightened only by Jordan's talent for finding Master Adamant's nasally distinct profile in any given constellation - and when finally it was over, the children ran straight to the Galea stables.

The crisp early autumn air nipped at the skin, reddening their cheeks as they rode forth on frisky ponies. Their first objective was to evade local detection, and this they achieved by skirting the Backwind village, with its many curious eyes and wagging tongues. As the Backwind was all they knew they thought little of it, oblivious to the quaint charm of its thatched cottages covered in fading rambling roses, set higgledy-piggledy into rolling hills, and surrounded by stonewalled pastures of emerald green. In no time at all the quiet village and grazing pastures of the Galea Estate fell behind them and they set the ponies into a joyful canter through the open, trackless expanse of the forest fringe. The leaves of the deciduous trees were starting to change colour from the top down, so that they were crowned in glorious reds and golds. Winter was harsh in the Backwind, bringing biting cold temperatures with deep winter snows, but though the children dreaded that season, they adored the natural beauty of the autumns that preceded it.

Soon their primary objective, the search for Aethon, was almost forgotten in the thrill of the ride, as was often the case when Cira and Jordan rode out together. Though Jordan was short for his age and afflicted with the most extraordinary coverage of freckles over what can only be described - despite all his objections - as sweet, cherubic cheeks, and Cira was not a boy at all, they imagined themselves to be knights. Lord Falric had raised the children on stirring chivalric tales, usually featuring the legendary knights of the Order of the Coeur. The versions of the stories Falric told tended to be of a more swashbuckling nature than was entirely truthful though and so he was recently, and regretfully, realising that this current obsession of the children was entirely of his own making. Even the fact that Cira was of the female persuasion, when the venerable Order had a proud history of discriminating against women, was considered only a minor obstacle in their all-consuming fantasy. After all, Cira was a tomboy of such determination that people often forgot that she was a girl at all. This pleased her enormously, because she had long since concluded that it was boys and men who had all the fun, and she was determined to share in as much of it as possible.

The sun was making a determined plunge towards the horizon by the time the ponies pulled up at the Bridge, blowing tangles of silver smoke into the chill air. They were uneasy now: a sentiment shared by Jordan. His grey-blue eyes widened as he took in the moody expanse of Leaverness. Miles into the forest, the tallest trees reached so high as to make an artificial horizon, one that caused the dusk to draw in early across the Backwind. Night, too, overtook the dusk faster here than anywhere else, as the dark heart of Leaverness seemed to absorb even the light of the setting sun.

'Sir Jordan, dost thou consider thyself stout of heart?' Cira demanded, challenging his hesitation.

'Sir Citar, I admit to...perilous qualms?' Jordan hazarded, less comfortable with ye olde worlde language, but at least remembering to use Cira's adopted boy-name. Sir Cira was hardly going to wash as a manly knight title, after all.

'Aye, and be not ashamed that thou art so, good knight, for true courage is that which stands firm in the adversity of fear,' Cira opined. 'But be ye more afeared of yonder grave forest, or thy father?'

She paused.

'Thy father? Thoust's father?'

'*My* father, and yes, nothing in even Leaverness

worries me more,' Jordan groaned, and given the nature of the forest, that was really saying something.

'Oh I don't know,' Cira mused thoughtfully, dropping all affectation. 'There are things out there that make Adamant look like a kicked puppy even when he's in an apoplectic rage,' she said, nodding meaningfully to the dense forestland ahead. 'And *that* makes your father look like a pussy cat.'

'It's his disappointed face,' Jordan said, his own face contorted with remembered guilts. 'Those accusing eyes, that hurt expression, like I've let him down...'

'No-one does Disappointed like your father,' Cira conceded. 'My mother just smacks me and sends me to bed without my supper. Perhaps she should have a word about parenting with Falric?'

Jordan shot her a doubtful look, only to find her smirking at his expense. He laughed, cautiously; she grinned and slapped him playfully on the shoulder. Well, he was fairly sure it was *intended* to be playful, as he froze his expression on its way to a pained grimace. With Cira, even playing tended to be a full-contact sport.

'Right. So Aethon was seen towards the Scratchthorne. That's a half hour in. I reckon we've got just over an hour's light, so we'll just have a quick look around and then nip back before we're even missed.'

Cira fixed Jordan with an authoritative glare, one perfected through years of getting what she wanted.

'Do ye accept our mission, Sir Jordan?'

'Sir Citar, I do, but I charge you with returning us before the lighting of the lamps,' the would-be knight cautiously agreed. Cira nodded: it was a reasonable condition. The Bridge, which had no other name but a definite capital B, was an antique wooden structure, but sturdy as stone and built with pegs as thick as a man's fist. Protective runes, rumoured to be of the language of the long dead Phaedrans, had been deeply carved back when the blackened wood was young. Circular lanterns of thick misty glass rode along the length of the guardrails. These were lit on dusk every night without fail, and had guided many grateful travellers from Leaverness to safety after dark. Cira and Jordan were forbidden from crossing the Bridge without Lord Falric, who, aside from his famous Disappointed Face, had come up with a number of other hitherto effective threats, including loss of privileges - eating, speaking and most effective of all, riding - to enforce this law. This was not an exercise in draconian authority: Falric was the foremost authority on Leaverness, which is to say that he knew just how dangerous the forest girding his estate was. It did not forgive, it did not forget and it certainly did not forewarn.

Perhaps this explains why, to Jordan, the Bridge represented the last vestige of civilisation: he saw it as a grim-faced sentry guarding a borderline where danger and safety - the unknown and known - met. In a way, the Teine river itself was just such a border, separating the forest fringe - which was technically part of his father's land - from the wilderness of the forest proper.

But through Cira's eyes, the Bridge was an invitation to adventure, a gateway between the mundane world of the Backwind and the literally magical unpredictability of Leaverness. She took a moment to enjoy the thrill of disobedience before turning to Jordan to give him a challenging *I'm game if you're game* look. While he tried to arrange his nervous features into a look of suitable enthusiasm, they were both distracted by a flash of movement in the forest.

A dark shape paused, some hundred yards ahead, obscured by a screen of foliage.

Jordan felt a hand shoot out and clutch his wrist.

'I saw black,' Cira breathed.

'I saw gold!' Jordan murmured.

Their eyes widened, and so saw clearly as proud Aethon jumped out from behind his brush screen, struck out at the air with one front leg as though to demand the children's attention, and then wheeled on powerful hind legs to canter away, his tail held high behind him like a golden banner.

For a moment, Cira and Jordan and even their ponies remained frozen in awe of the magnificent unicorn. He really was spectacularly beautiful with his fine boned face, shining gold mane and tail, golden legs, glittering horn and glossy obsidian coat. To Cira's surprise though, it was Jordan who recovered himself first. He kicked his grey pony forward and with a wild whoop, set off across the Bridge in pursuit. Cira's bay pony leapt forward too, his iron shoes echoing loudly as he bounded across the aged wood. Their faces flushed with excitement, the two children rode out of the safety of Lord Falric's lands and into the wilds of Leaverness.

Aethon, it seemed, held little regard for the established tracks of the forest. This was of no concern to the unicorn, for he appeared to navigate his way effortlessly through the undergrowth that bordered his flight, almost as though Leaverness itself made way for him to pass. The children however were forced to crouch low over the necks of their ponies to avoid the slapping and stinging of the branches that reached for them from all sides. Between ducks and dives, Cira found herself squinting ahead to see whether Aethon's hooves were actually touching the ground; while the ponies struggled along, the dark beauty moved so effortlessly across the variously solid, slick and boggy terrain she wasn't at all convinced. More than once her pony almost slipped his footing and each time her heart leapt to her mouth. Cira had seen men maimed by falls from horses, but adrenalin trumped any instinct of self-preservation. And so she rode on and on, but the ever present threat of death or severe injury distracted her from noticing something terribly important: that there was something almost hypnotic about the way Aethon weaved in and out of view, always keeping exactly the same distance ahead of the children. It was like he was teasing them.

Or luring them.

In what seemed like no time at all, Cira and Jordan had unwittingly chased the fleet unicorn through many miles of forest. They had leapt logs, splashed through rivers, skirted ravines, sprayed turf on tight turns through mazes of brush and bramble and flown over open clearings. As both the ponies and the light flagged, it became harder and harder to see Aethon, so that by the time Jordan reined in his blowing pony, the children had no idea when their quarry had disappeared completely. Jordan's round face was still split with a huge smile though when Cira reined her tired mount in next to his.

For a moment, they just stared at one another, lost in the enormity of what they had done.

'We crossed the Bridge...' Jordan panted.

'We chased Aethon!' Cira breathed.

'But...now we're in big trouble...'

Jordan's grin faded first as reality weighed in on their situation. Two pairs of wide eyes scoured the dense woodland around them. The shadows of Leaverness seemed to claw inwards towards them irrespective of the direction of the ailing light, leaving them huddled in a closing ring of darkness.

'Cira?' Jordan asked, his high voice harsh in the unnatural silence of the dusky forest. 'On a scale of one to ten, how much trouble would you say we're in?'

'Let's say, seven and a half?' Cira hazarded with forced cheer. She could see the fear rising in Jordan's eyes. 'Don't worry Jordo, the ponies will know their way home.'

And the next moment that was pretty much all the ponies were thinking about, because something massive and fast and shadow black was exploding from the undergrowth ahead and hurtling straight for them. Cira and Jordan managed only strangled cries of horror as their ponies lurched violently left and right, peeling off around the creature's furious charge. Cira hadn't even the time to see what it was that chased them, but between the two targets, it was her that it chose, wheeling laboriously before crashing along savagely in the wake of her pony's frantic flight. Some small voice in her head expressed relief that her imminent maiming guaranteed Jordan's safety; the rest of her brain shut down in a blind terror exceeded only by that of her mount.

They were careening through the forest without a trail to be seen. The pony awkwardly leapt at logs, threw himself over mossy boulders, swiped Cira under low lying branches and slipped in unseen puddles as he fled the racing wall of darkness on his heels. Cira rode the nauseating plunges, slides and corkscrew turns with grim determination, dimly aware that it was no longer a matter of *if* she fell but *when*. Hot stale air intermittently coursed over her back from whatever hellish creature pursed her.

A dangerous lurch from the pony left Cira falling forward over his shoulder; as he miraculously regained his footing, she was thrown back to the saddle. Struggling even for breath, she tried to look forward again but cried out as she turned her face straight into a cutting clout of tree brush. Tears welled in her stinging eyes, almost blinding her, but as her head turned back, she saw the darkness taking a flying leap at her. Hairy legs built like tree trunks propelled airborne black death, all gaping maw and one vicious intent. A primal scream ripped itself free from Cira's throat and then she was gagging under a blast of hot, rank air. She heard the snap of sharp teeth then the rib-crushing pull of her coat across her chest as it was hauled back; and because she was holding the reins with a vice-like grip, she unintentionally pulled her pony's head up too. His exhausted legs finally lost their footing and he slid in the muddied ground, catapulting Cira from the saddle. There was a surreal moment in which she simply hung in the air as her trajectory accepted bids between the sideways jettison of the fall and the backwards wrench of the creature's strong jaws. A prolonged ripping sound settled the matter; cold air rushed onto Cira's exposed skin as layers of cloth tore from her back, and then the ground was rising to meet her. She tried desperately to twist away from her pony's legs in the free-fall before impact.

Cira slammed down across the backs of her shoulders, the impact jarring the length of her spine. Paralysed by shock, unable even to breathe, she found herself face to maw with her doom. Just a foot away, ready to pounce down upon her, was something with eyes intelligent enough that it might have started as a man. But a man that might have been cursed into the form of a wolf; a wolf that had grown beyond all proportion; and that some fool mage had tried to remodel as a bear. But a bear that needed horns to gouge the eyes from its victims and teeth the size of spearheads, set in jaws powerful enough to rip a swarthy man's head from his body. It was raw untamed fury and malice and rage, and frozen in its furious, predatory gaze, for the first time, Cira knew that there was nothing, not a thing at all, that she could do to save her own life. Her body refused to move, leaving her only able to stare, almost hypnotised, into the eyes of the wretched monster, feeling a visceral despair wash over her -

- and then something brown and white and whistling shot between her and the incoming death.

'Brynir!' it shouted, and a blood and mud-matted paw swatted at these newcomers: an audacious boy and his brown and white skewbald coloured pony. The pony wheeled on his hind legs, his front hooves singing right over the vicious swipe, and he landed like a coiled spring, ready to explode into movement again at any moment. The boy held his pony's mane in one hand - for there was no saddle or bridle to be seen, only a rope around his mount's neck - and a long, slender staff in the other. On the top of the staff a collection of iridescent gold, purple and green feathers danced, and these he thrust towards the face of the beast, drawing its attention from the frozen Cira.

*Brynir?*

Brynir *the Cursed?*

The constellation from the night sky and Falric's astronomy tower?

Cira mentally filed the creature's identity, and the identity of her saviour, as important items to return to, and looked around for the only other thing that immediately mattered.

While Brynir had turned on Cira, Jordan had found himself in another struggle altogether: this one against his petrified pony, who'd had more than enough of this lark and was rocketing home at breakneck speed. This route was parallel enough to Cira that he could hear the beast's crashing pursuit over to his right. Jordan wanted to direct his pony towards Cira, but although the reins cut into his hands, even through his gloves, he could not steady or turn the terrified animal. Terror hot-wired his body too, but for Jordan, the fear was not so much for his own safety. He was a timid boy indeed, but under that gentle exterior beat a strong and loyal heart. Jordan's only concern was for his best friend. He would not  could not  leave her to die. Born of desperate panic, Jordan finally found his backbone. He kicked his stirrups free, gritted his teeth and, hoping for the best, ambitiously bailed on his one-way ticket home - via an overhanging branch.

It had seemed a good idea at the time.

*Ooooomph.*

Pain exploded through Jordan's chest, shoulders and arms as all his forward momentum met a resolutely stationary object. His winded body dribbled down the branch into an undignified huddle on the ground, but he refused to accede to its demands to remain there. He struggled unsteadily to his feet and forced himself into an unsteady run towards the sound of the scream Cira had given when she had looked back and seen what pursued her. He had to thrash through undergrowth to cross the distance between them, but he did it in time to see Brynir drag Cira from her pony. While he pumped his burning legs and his breath rasped from his fright-tightened chest, he could see that his rescue attempt would be too late. The malformed creature was looming over the fallen Cira, poised and ready to strike. Jordan tried to scream out because it was all he could do, but breathless from his fall and run, he had no air even for that. The hoarse wheeze died on his lips though when he saw the jigsaw-patterned brown and white pony leap forward into harm's way, and Jordan almost collapsed to his knees with relief when he realised that Cira was being defended. Even if it was only by a small under-dressed boy with a couple of feathers on a stick.

And this was Lien, although there was no time for introductions just yet.

# 2. Lien

'We have to help him!' Cira panted to Jordan, as he staggered to her side.

'Really?' Jordan wheezed, helping Cira scramble back to her feet. 'He seems to be doing perfectly well on his own – '

He broke off under assault from a sharp elbow, but Cira couldn't really argue. The newcomer *was* doing rather well for the moment, though only because his pony was so light-footed in relation to the sheer mass of the monster.

'Jordan, he called it *Brynir*,' Cira whispered, her eyes still locked on the boy and pony as, like one fused entity, they slid and spun, danced and weaved their way around their opponent. Under any other circumstances Cira would have been thrilled to learn that such a nasty piece of local folklore actually existed. Meeting the subject of many a gruesome legend in the flesh, in his own domain, was another matter entirely though. Folk had seen Aethon for a hundred years or more and lived to tell the tale. If Brynir the Cursed had been seen in the last century though, no-one had lived to tell the tale of what they saw, and Cira could well appreciate why. He was a weathered warrior, battered and scarred, his ears torn, his nose once savagely cleft across and knitted back together in a rope of scar tissue: this was a fighter who had been thrown down and crushed and risen again regardless.

It quickly became apparent though that the boy was not making any attempt to *attack* Brynir: the pony's nimble moves simply fulfilled defensive positions. Concerned that this did not seem to be a way to send the beast away, Cira's fingers closed around a large, satisfyingly sharp ended rock in the mud beneath her feet, before hefting it with a grunt towards the great shaggy head.

It was a good shot: she caught Brynir right across the temple.

It was just a terrible idea.

The wolf-bear creature roared furiously, swinging his scarred head in pain. Hot scarlet blood sprayed across the forest boy's startled face and light vest. Distracted from his efforts, he neither flinched nor at first understood what had happened. Sighting Cira's wild, triumphant expression though, his face darkened.

'No!' the boy shouted, kicking his pony forward between the children and Brynir, as if to protect the *beast* - which was surely unthinkable, not to mention unnecessary. Brynir was far from grateful; instead he made a ballistic swipe with a massive paw that was set with claws like stained ivory tusks. Cira watched in guilty horror as the boy was slammed from his mount. His brown and white pony - the bravest friend a troublesome boy could ever ask for - pivoted neatly to land such that his fallen rider was safely protected between his front and back legs. He would have fought Brynir for his rider's life too, had the beast not now turned his attention upon this new declaration of war. Cira's guilt swiftly froze into new terror as the monstrous creature advanced on her, the blood from the wound collecting in one mad eye and weeping down his long snout like crimson tears.

'Perhaps he was doing fine on his own after all?' Cira

babbled as Jordan gripped her arm so tight his nails dug in through her jacket. Brynir snarled, and it was a chillingly guttural sound. He flattened his ragged ears back against his skull, giving him an unexpectedly elongated, almost serpentine appearance; and indeed his head snaked disconcertingly as he seemed to consider his options. With Brynir's hulking form stalking closer, Cira could not see the extent of her would-be saviour's injuries, or whether he was even alive or dead; and then she had no time to wonder at all because Brynir was crouching and launching himself forward and she and Jordan were diving away for their lives.

Their lives they kept; Cira however screamed at the searing pain lancing through her right leg as one huge paw caught her in her retreat. Her knee twisted sickeningly as a claw gouged through her calf, before being wrenched equally brutally back out. Once she'd finished screaming, she gasped for breath as her body tried to process the shocking sensations. She looked desperately at what Brynir was doing next; he was swinging back towards the boy, who was shouting for the monster's attention while hauling himself back to his feet. His right hand clutched at a series of rips torn through his light vest. With evident difficulty, he managed to remount, just in time for the pony to wheel away from an angry swipe. This target now fleeing, Brynir fixed his attention back on Cira and Jordan.

Something flung itself over Cira's sprawled body, shooting new hot pain through her twisted knee; she cried out again, but it was only Jordan, sliding them both a few inches over the slick ground and out of harm's way as Brynir made a second pass at them. When Cira managed to look back up again, she first refused to believe what it was her eyes told her, but Jordan left her no choice.

'He's not leaving us?' he cried, his weight bearing down heavier on Cira as he realised they were alone - alone against a monster he'd thought no more than a fiction with which to idly threaten delinquent children. Cira too sagged in despair, fighting back tears of fear and pain, the cold sludge seeping through her clothes as she sank into the churned mud. But then her gloved hand met something hard. Something long and wide and flat.

'On your knees,' she muttered. 'We're not dying here in the mud, Jordo.' He nodded, stiffly pulling himself off her.

'Get behind me. Wrap your arms under mine. When I say, heave up with everything you got. Understand?' she asked, forcing her uninjured leg up into a low kneel that almost made her cry out again at the pressure it pushed through her right knee. But baulking at her own suffering was a luxury she did not have, for Brynir was on the attack again. Cira held her breath, held her shout, held her ground. She felt Jordan's arms snake under hers, and his hands clasp in front of her chest; she could feel his rigid fear. She almost winced under a rancid draught of monster's breath, but only tightened her grip. It was only when she could see herself reflected in the fathomless black depths of Brynir's eyes that she shouted for Jordan to pull. He did, immediately and with strength and speed born of adrenalised fear. Cira grunted as, with their efforts combined, she hauled the object from the mud and in front of her face, ducking her head to the side so that, at first, she didn't know what it was, this object that saved their lives.

A shockwave travelled down her arms, rattling even her teeth, although not so badly as it did to Brynir as his head crashed into a hard slab of steel. He howled in pain, falling back. It was only a brief reprieve though as he shook his shaggy head, enraged but not undeterred. It was long enough for Cira to see that it was a knight's shield she had thrust aloft - a shield now slightly dented by the high velocity impact of Brynir's skull.

'Hah!' she yelled triumphantly, thrusting the shield at Brynir again and again from her awkward half kneeling position. But instead of making another attack, the beast instead sat back on his hindquarters with an almost exasperated air.

'I think he's tiring, Jordan!' Cira called, confidence rising. Brynir may indeed have been tiring of the situation, but he was far from physically tired. He was carefully watching Cira's awkward thrusting pattern of defence, and then simply swiped the shield out of her hands with one massive, perfectly timed paw.

'Heeeeeey - *oh* - ' Cira gagged under the putrid breath as the wolf-bear-thing padded forward, pushing her back into Jordan's arms. It was an almost comically incongruous act from a wild creature that had now been trying to kill them for several minutes. What was he doing? Playing with them?

Brynir gazed upon them, and snarled, a chilling sound that raised all the hairs on the back of Cira's neck. She felt despair wash over her.

This was it. With her injured leg, she could not run.

But Jordan could.

'Jordan, run!' she hissed over her shoulder.

He only hugged her closer.

There wasn't truly time for anything else anyway.

Like so, eyes screwed closed, they waited for the final blow: the tear of cruel teeth or claws, whatever it would be that would bring the end -

- but they felt only the harmless *whoosh* of something very large - say the head of a nightmare monster - sweeping by close overhead, and a passing rush of hot foul air from the snarling mouth of just such a creature, accompanied by two triumphant shouts. Jordan too shouted out, but in relief, and Cira opened her eyes to see Brynir caught in a tug-of-war between a vine lassoed around his sensitive nose and now *two* grinning boys sitting on the back of the dancing brown and white pony.

'…we're…dreaming…right…?' Jordan managed.

'Dunno about dreaming, but I think we're saved,' Cira breathed, spellbound by the unreal sight of the boys wrangling the monster. The battle was not won though: Brynir was stronger than the combined strength of the boys and their trusty steed, and started to drag the pony through the mud, even as he tried to widen his legs and resist. Brynir was also intelligent and cunning, and as they leaned all their weight and strength against him, he unexpectedly leapt *forward* with a snarl. As the tension on the vine released, the pony's braced back legs suddenly slid under him and he landed on his quarters, with the boys, who had already been leaning back, tipping off his back and onto the ground behind. The first boy landed on the second, who bellowed, but they both swiftly recovered their wits enough to roll away from the pony's back legs as he scrambled to his feet to escape Brynir's incoming attack. The beast turned next to the first boy, who was still on the ground, and snarled viciously, his head held low. The boy leaned forward to get back to his feet but as he did, Brynir - his mouth still held shut by the vine lasso - threw his head up, catching the boy on his long snout. He was flung up and back through the air like a rag doll, landing hard on his back. He was too winded to move initially, allowing Brynir to leap forward and pin him down with one huge paw. The second boy ran over, shouting wildly; Brynir took his paw off the winded boy to also knock the second to the ground. He then turned back to the first boy and raised a paw over his exposed body, his enormous claws extended.

Cira couldn't breathe as she watched the monster preparing to kill their rescuer.

And then... something changed in the boy.

Cira never discussed it with Jordan after, because she thought she must have imagined it. But as Brynir's claws descended, the boy rolled out of the way and up to his feet, but not with the alert grace he had previously displayed. Instead, it was with a menacing aggression that surprised and unnerved Cira. As Brynir's head snaked back towards him, the boy deftly spun to the right, swept up the trailing rope and vaulted up onto the shaggy back. He turned Brynir's head back into his own left flank. With his muzzle now firmly trapped shut by the tightened vine, the beast could not even roar his rage as the unfair leverage dragged his whole body around, until he was facing away from the children. Although her eyes were fixed on this, Cira did notice in her peripheral vision that the second boy looked as surprised at this turn of events as she felt. And he did not look impressed by his companion, but...concerned. Cira then realised the first boy was speaking into one of Brynir's battered ears. She strained to hear, but could only gather two things: it was a language she did not understand, and the tone was deadly serious. It was not all what she expected of him.

'You getting a word of that?' Cira whispered to Jordan. He slowly shook his head.

'That's not any language I've ever heard,' he murmured back. But just then, there came one word they did recognise. From the tone and context, Cira guessed it was a name and was being used as a threat.

*Sky.*

If it was indeed a threat, it was a good one: Brynir ceased his struggle. The boy on his back maintained the pressure on the vine nonetheless, his face cold and hard, his eyes hidden by hair fallen across his face.

*'Lien!'*

The second boy was next to Cira and Jordan now, his tone sharp, reprimanding. Lien paused, then said something to Brynir - from the tone, Cira assumed a warning - then drew a small knife from his belt. Cira gasped as she thought he might stab the creature with it, but he only cut the noose around the long muzzle before slipping to the ground. Brynir's body remained motionless but his huge head swung around to fix the three watching with a baleful look. Then, with a last resentful snap in Lien's direction, Brynir the Cursed turned and stalked defiantly away until he was swallowed by the forest shadows.

Cira and Jordan collapsed with relief into each other's arms.

'Jordo, we're alive!' Cira almost cried, hugging her best friend tightly.

'I was so sure we were a goner,' Jordan agreed, hugging her back, then pulling away a little as he realised that she was crying. For as their adrenaline levels dropped, the pain in Cira's twisted knee and wounded calf returned with an intensity she had never experienced before. Choking back tears, she finally looked down at the back of her right leg, still in its awkward kneeling position, and they both saw the bloody tear through her leather knee-high riding boots. Brynir had gouged her calf to the bone. The sight of the gruesome wound made them both briefly light-headed, so Cira was grateful for a distraction: an initially hushed discussion between their two saviours was now breaking out into a shouting match. Neither Cira or Jordan could understand what was being said, but it appeared the second boy was refusing to do something the one called Lien wanted him to. The second boy forcefully shoved the first in the chest. Lien gasped and bent double; the second immediately jerked his hands back as though stung, to see that one was printed with blood.

'L-lien?!' he stammered, his eyes puzzled as Lien carefully stood back upright. His friend briefly surveyed the torn and blood-streaked tunic, then roughly tugged it up, ignoring Lien's protests, to inspect the four claw marks Brynir had raked across the boy's chest when he had been wiped from his pony's back. The dynamic between the two boys shifted completely as the second boy now berated Lien, who just laughed weakly back at the aggressive show of concern. Eventually they seemed to arrive at some kind of truce, if not agreement, and turned together to Cira and Jordan.

The second boy looked suspicious while Lien - paler now but somehow still cheerful - gave them a friendly wave. He could not have been more different from the way he had just sent Brynir packing.

'Hello,' Lien said, smiling, and Cira briefly considered this be a fluke of similar greetings shared by their two languages, until he followed up carefully with 'Pleased to meet you,' in her own tongue.

'You speak our language!' she said, genuinely surprised.

'I do, a little,' Lien replied, then with a sidelong glance to his friend, added, 'but he does even less.'

The second boy clearly knew enough to understand what had just been said, and shrugged dismissively.

'I am Lien, and he is Bravo.'

'Well – thank you both so much for saving our lives,' Cira said gratefully, knowing even as she said it that such a sentence didn't nearly cover what the boys had done for her and Jordan.

'You were *amazing*!' Jordan chipped in, finally finding his tongue.

Lien beamed; Bravo remained impassive, bordering on sullen. He clearly didn't share his friend's enthusiasm for meeting strangers.

'Was that *really* Brynir the Cursed?' Jordan asked, eyes wide, still in awe of the two boys.

'Yes,' Lien said, clearly puzzled by their amazement. 'You are deep in Leaverness, you are in his lands.'

The way he said it, like an obvious statement of fact, made Cira realise there was something far more foreign about these boys than just their language. They were perhaps worlds apart from the children of the Backwind. She also realised, from the curious tilt of his head, that Lien was wondering why she was still kneeling in the mud. He extended an arm to help her rise. She hesitated a moment before taking it, and with a deep, determined breath, let him help draw her to her feet. To her shame though, she whimpered and sank back down as her right knee buckled under her weight.

'You are hurt?' Lien said worriedly, stepping forward in unison with Jordan to support her. From Bravo she was sure she heard a put-upon sigh.

'It's not so bad,' Cira lied through gritted teeth, 'I've twisted my knee and just…cut…my calf.'

But she was already being closely examined. Lien, clearly concerned at what he saw, called Bravo over and they argued briefly again in their own language. Unlike herself and Jordan, these boys seemed unfazed by the sight of bloody injuries; they were not in agreement about what needed to be done about it though.

'It is very bad, very deep,' Lien eventually announced gravely. 'Must be cleaned, soon.'

'But she'll be okay? When it's cleaned?' Jordan asked anxiously. Lien looked briefly to Cira, then back to Jordan, with a slight shake of his head.

'It is very bad,' was all he said, but both Cira and Jordan were sure he knew more than he was saying. Lien and Jordan took her, one a side, and hoisted to her feet, so that she was standing on her left leg and leaning heavily against Lien. Even through the wave of nausea that passed over her, Cira dimly noted the strength and power in the forest boy's slight frame as he took the majority of her weight, and in the way he steadied her, with only the slightest gasp at the pain the effort of doing so must have caused him. When he was satisfied that she would remain standing this time, Lien transferred her to lean fully against Jordan, and pulled his tunic off. Cira and Jordan winced at the sight of the bloody tears down his torso, and before

Cira realised what he was doing, he started ripping it up at the back.

'Wait, you need that - !' Cira protested, but too late. Ignoring her protests, Lien knelt down and started tightly binding her right calf, right around her boot. She gasped in pain at the pressure.

'To slow the blood,' he grunted as he worked. When he had tied off the makeshift bandage and discarded the sorry, bloodied remainder of the tunic, he made a quick examination of her throbbing right knee. When she yelped at a light pressure he applied, he sat back on his heels, a troubled look on his face.

Bravo snapped something to Lien, glaring at Cira and Jordan as he did. Lien stood slowly, carefully considering his translation before delivering it.

'Bravo says Avenelese should not be in the Falseweald,' he said carefully, struggling a little with the unfamiliar language.

'Dangerous. *Foolish,*' he added with emphasis, because neither Cira nor Jordan looked remotely chastised. They were too busy looking shocked.

'This is the *Falseweald*?' Cira managed. 'That's - that's impossible! We came from the Backwind what, half an hour ago?'

She glanced to Jordan to check she wasn't crazy; he nodded his urgent agreement. They had both studied the great forest on Lord Falric's maps and knew the Falseweald was a good two day's ride from the Bridge. There was no *way* they could have possibly ridden into that darkest, most dangerous part of the forest during their chase of -

' - Aethon,' she breathed. 'We were following Aethon,' she explained, louder, to the two forest boys. She'd always thought the stories about Aethon changing the geography of the forest were exaggerated but there was no other explanation. At the black unicorn's name though, both boys looked tense.

'*Chevaliers!*' Bravo almost spat the word, like it was poison.

'Who, us? No!' Cira said.

'Not chevaliers?' Lien clarified hopefully.

'Not chevaliers *yet* – ow ow ow my *foot* – ' Jordan interjected, immediately regretting it, although perhaps not as much as Cira, who really shouldn't have moved that leg, even to shut Jordan up.

'Course we're not chevaliers *at all!*' Cira assured the boys with brittle brightness as she painfully shuffled her right foot from Jordan's toes. 'I'm a girl, after all.'

They remained blank.

'Only boys can become knights,' Cira explained slowly, watching Lien carefully for understanding. It came, along with puzzlement.

'I know, I think it's stupid too,' she agreed heartily, and, having organised her balance, thrust a hand forward to Lien. 'I'm Cira.'

Cira shared a puzzled sideways glance with Jordan as Lien watched the hand cautiously, a worried expression forming on his face. As he clearly had no idea of what to do with it, she dropped it, embarrassed.

'And I'm Jordan,' Jordan broke the awkward moment, automatically starting to extend a hand too, but catching himself just in time.

'Lien, I'm sorry about – ' Cira started, indicating shyly in the direction of the bloodied claw marks along his chest. He glanced down indifferently and shrugged, and she realised, now that he was standing still and topless, that he bore several scars crossing his body, as well as a thin black line circling his right arm at the bottom of a well-defined shoulder muscle. A tattoo? Cira had only ever heard of tattoos on adult men, never on children. She glanced to Bravo and saw he had the same marking, with a second, slightly thicker band below it. Lien's skin was an olive brown, like hers, against which the black ring did not stand out. Bravo's skin was a pale white, making the contrast between ink and skin colour more evident. They were both lean and muscular, much more than any boys Cira knew from the Backwind. Despite his father's best efforts to develop some muscles on his slight frame, Jordan looked positively scrawny next to these mysterious Leaverness boys. Their rough hide trousers also looked like nothing worn by the folk of the Backwind and beyond, and their light sleeveless tunics were grossly inadequate wardrobe for the fall season, especially next to the warm tops and jackets Cira and Jordan wore.

'Brynir is very angry,' Lien said simply, then looked reproachfully to Cira. 'And you made him angrier.'

Cira flushed, and looked down from his curious, searing, emerald eyes.

'I was just trying to help – ' she muttered.

'Yes,' he agreed. 'But this is Brynir's land. It was not the way. But you are strangers here. You were not to know. Aethon led you a dance, yes?'

It was true. Lien might as well have dumped a bucket of ice water over Cira; meeting Jordan's eye, she saw he was experiencing the same sudden dread realisation. Lengthening fingers of shadows were closing in and they were far from the forest fringe, from the safety of the Bridge and the Galea Estate. As Cira glanced around, she realised she didn't even know which way the fringe *was*. She was completely lost. The ponies would be arriving home riderless by now –

– no, wait, they were in the Falseweald. They were two days from the Backwind.

*Two days*.

Lord Falric would soon realise they were not coming home and would be panic-stricken, rallying a search party to find his only son…and she was pretty certain she knew who would be blamed for his disappearance.

'We are *so* far from home,' she said, suddenly overwhelmed by the reality of their situation. Exhaustion was beginning to set in, along with a chill as the cool dusk air bit into her damp, muddied clothes. She could not even walk, even if she knew which way to go.

'We are *so* dead,' Jordan echoed.

'Dark comes. Not safe for you here,' Lien agreed, also glancing around -and also, Cira noted, shivering a little. Bravo noticed as well, and immediately pulled off his own tunic to hand to his friend, leaving himself topless. Lien hesitated, looking down at the vivid claw marks etched down his chest.

'I've washed both our blood out of it before,' Bravo grumbled, but kindly, in their own language. 'But we need to get your wounds cleaned too. How do we get rid of these two?' and he threw the two frightened children another annoyed look.

'Get rid of them? Bravo, we have to get them home,' Lien protested as he gratefully pulled the tunic over his head. 'They chased Aethon, they'll never get back alone, and Cira is badly injured.'

'Lien, they're from the Backwind, it's *two days* to get

them to their home, and we can hardly take them to ours,' Bravo argued, astonished at the suggestion. 'And they've *seen* us. You know how much trouble that gets us in!'

Lien stared at his best friend.

'What are you thinking then?' he asked, reluctantly. He didn't want to hear the answer he suspected was coming.

'We tell them the way and we leave them to it, obviously,' Bravo said in the exasperated tone of an adult speaking to a difficult child. 'Two problems solved.'

Lien just stared again, then shook his head in disbelief at the casual way his friend was implying they should let Cira and Jordan die in the forest.

'Bravo, they're *people,* not *problems,*' he said eventually. 'You can go home, but I'm taking them back.'

'In your condition? Lien, you're injured too, you've already started to bleed through my top,' Bravo snapped. 'You're not thinking sensibly. Listen, you go get the ponies, I'll deal with these two.'

Out of the corner of one eye, Lien saw Cira and Jordan holding one another in the dusk, lost and frightened and waiting for their fate to be decided by two bickering boys.

'No, Bravo,' Lien said. He whistled to his pony, who had been grazing nearby but now amicably ambled over.

'Is everything…alright?' Cira asked, glancing anxiously at Bravo's stony face.

Lien flashed a bright smile he hoped might be reassuring to the two children.

'I will help you home,' he said. 'It will be crowded, but Jest is very strong,' he added, stroking his pony affectionately, and Cira and Jordan understood then that Bravo would not be coming. They had gleaned as much from the boys' argument: Bravo was clearly opposed to helping them. Cira's heart swelled with gratitude to Lien for having their backs, even as she wondered what it was about them that made the other boy so very angry.

Lien stepped to the far side of his pony and gently guided him into a side step that brought him to an arm's length from Cira. As she wondered in sudden panic how she was going to mount with her right leg unusable, Jest obediently followed the next instruction: he carefully folded his four legs under and away from Cira and eased himself to the ground, so that his back was right in front of her. Grinning at her wonder, Lien joined Jordan to awkwardly part-boost, part-slide her onto the pony's back. She tried so hard to keep a brave face but couldn't stop the gasps of pain as the boys guided her right leg over and around Jest's withers. Lien held her reassuringly at her elbow and waist though as he clicked for Jest to stand. The action of a horse rising from the ground is enormously jerky but the pony moved mercifully slowly, so that with Lien's support, the pain was almost bearable.

'Good?' Lien asked Cira as she leaned a little forward, forcing her breath to remain calm. She felt sick, but nodded mutely.

'It will hurt. But it is better you are in front.'

He grinned - again that playful, boyish grin - then went to vault up further back on Jest. He got no further than throwing his left leg forward before gasping himself in pain.

'Lien - ' Cira cried out, turning to try and help him, but Bravo pushed forward, his scowl impossibly deepening as he legged his injured friend up. Lien took the boost gratefully, then slid forwards so that he was seated directly behind Cira. His face was paler with pain, but he still smiled warmly as he turned to offer a hand to Jordan. The boy stared helplessly from Lien's hand to Jest's short back, mostly hidden by the two children already on board. Jest too looked back a little worriedly, and as he did, Bravo's bay pony, who had been grazing nearby, started to pointedly rub his face on his rider's back, pushing him forward.

'Bank!' Bravo admonished the pony, then realised all eyes in the clearing were fixed upon him. He grimaced.

'Lien – ' he started, warningly, but was cut off by the high shriek of a large bird of prey majestically sweeping through the clearing. The flyover was so unexpected and fast that Cira didn't quite have time to identify the species, but it was enormous, and its passage left Bravo blanched and Lien grinning.

'There you go, Bravo,' Lien said triumphantly to Bravo in their own language, 'Sky will guide us a faster route to the Backwind.'

'Lien, this means Sky *knows* we let these two see us!' Bravo hissed.

'Then we will already have to face him, whether now, or after helping them home,' Lien shrugged. 'And we will have to ask them to promise not to tell anyone.'

'And you trust them to do that?'

Lien glanced at the two drawn, worried faces, then nodded back to Bravo. For although he had only just met Cira and Jordan, he did trust them.

While Bravo still looked uncertain, Cira picked up on the familiar word from earlier.

'Sky…that's what you said to Brynir,' she said, looking searchingly to Lien. 'Who – or what – is Sky?'

Lien pointed up upwards to where, far above them, a giant falcon hung in the dusk expanse.

'*That* is Sky,' he said, awe at the magnificent bird

lighting up his face. He turned back to the other three children. 'He is also Bravo's grandfather. I think he will see us a short way to your home.'

'But that's a – a falcon,' Jordan said, confused. 'How can a falcon be someone's grandfather?'

'The same way a unicorn can change a path to lead you far from home,' Lien smiled.

Bravo caused a moment of consternation for the other three as he initially stalked away from them. But he went only a few steps past his pony before bending down and pick up Lien's long staff, which had fallen when he was thrown from Jest. The iridescent feathers were now limp and muddied, but Lien beamed when Bravo threw it to him. Completely unmoved by Lien's gratitude, Bravo vaulted onto his pony and reluctantly offered an arm to help Jordan up behind. He then immediately squeezed Bank into a canter, eliciting a yelp of surprise from his unprepared passenger, who grabbed Bravo frantically around the waist. Cira turned an anxious look back to Lien as Jest shook his head, keen to follow his friend. She had ridden bareback, but never without reins, and never with one leg pulsing with an exquisite pain which would be exacerbated by every stride the pony took

'Hold the mane and rope, and I will hold you,' Lien said. 'We must ride fast to beat the night, but Jest will look after us,' he promised.

Just as Lien had found himself trusting her, Cira now found herself fully trusting him. He tucked his staff under his right armpit and gently placed one hand at the top of each of her hip bones.

'Okay?' he asked, his breath warm on her right ear. She nodded, mutely, preparing herself for the ordeal ahead.

'Good,' he said, and she could feel the smile in his voice.

'We go,' and he softly squeezed Jest's sides.

As the pony set off forward to follow Bank, Cira inadvertently gave a little shriek as she slid and bumped painfully forward onto Jest's bony wither. She had ridden bareback before but tended to sit further back, which was not possible with two aboard. Jest's coat was still sweaty from his earlier exertions, but on the plus side, he was warm beneath her, and Lien warm behind her and her torn jacket: two sources of heat welcomed by her cold, stiffening body. It took a couple of arduous minutes for Cira to find the best way to balance with only the rope and base of Jest's mane to hold, and only one leg to grip his sides. She noticed, to her chagrin, that Lien seemed perfectly balanced, even when steadying her whenever she lurched dangerously one way or the other. Soon enough though, despite her pain, she felt the familiar thrill of riding as the forest flashed by.

'Okay?!' Lien called cheerfully from behind her as Jest caught up with Bank, steadying his pace as he fell in behind the bay pony.

'Yes!' Cira replied, and this time, a smile formed around the word, for it was true. Her right leg was killing but dammit, she was going home, and on an incredible pony with an amazing, mysterious forest boy holding her steady and laughing as the ponies raced their way towards the Backwind, following a - magical? - grandfather falcon. Although, having run that line of thought to completion, Cira then considered she might be entering a delirious state.

As the track widened and Jest drew up abreast with Bank, she looked across to see how Jordan was managing. In stark contrast to Lien's generally upbeat joyful disposition, Bravo still looked angry, or at the very least, annoyed. But that might have been because Jordan was still having to hang on to him to stay mounted. She flashed her best friend a reassuring smile, which, after a brief pause, he returned, and she saw him visibly relax a little. She had no doubt he was thinking about the trouble they would face at home, but even Lord Falric's Disappointed Face beat being dead - or left for dead - in deepest, darkest Leaverness.

For Cira and Jordan, the ride back to the Bridge was completely different to the ride away. On the way out they had chased the setting sun; on the way back they were being pursued by falling darkness. On the way out, Leaverness had pushed in upon them, even as it opened up for Aethon. On the way back, it treated Jest, Bank and their young riders as it had the unicorn. This was self-evident when they galloped on wide tracks, but even when Jest and Bank veered off on side tracks, guided always by the flight path of the great falcon above them, there were no branches slapping in their riders faces, and the ponies remained calm and sure-footed on the varied terrain. The wind chill factor was rising, but the effort of moving smoothly with the ponies, combined with the warmth of their co-riders' bodies, meant both Cira and Jordan found themselves immune to the now bracingly cold air.

Cira soon lost sense of time, finding Jest's regular strides hypnotic, and without needing to be in charge of the riding, she let her increasingly discombobulated brain start flagging up more items on the growing list of discontinuities from the evening's events. She remembered the term Bravo and then Lien had both used to describe herself and Jordan: *Avenelese*. The term referred to both citizens of Avenel and the language of that city and its empire, but a man could get his face pulped in the counties for using it so generally. Avenel might technically rule the Backwind and its surrounding counties and indeed most of the continent, but the city was physically a good week's ride around the far side of Leaverness and psychologically like a foreign country. The boys clearly had a better grip of the unpredictable geography of the forest than the world around it.

While she was mulling on who the boys could be and where they came from, Jordan worked out what Cira's brain had been refusing to see. As Bank and Jest galloped parallel again, he tried to tell her silently what he had realised. On the third time - Cira was a good lip reader but the gathering darkness and bouncing of the ponies complicated the process - she finally understood.

*They're from the People!*

Cira frowned: they *couldn't* be - could they? But then...while at first glance the idea was wild, it also made a certain amount of sense. For all the tales told about them, little was actually known about the reclusive Leaverness tribe. Stories did tell of their ritual tattooing practices, and of course they had their own language, and they were said to have a special way with animals. Some of them performed magic with an energy they called "espréi", but the easiest way to identify them was by their skin. They were unnaturally pale, like bone. This was why her brain hadn't made the connection: Lien's skin was a similar olive brown to her own. He could be a boy of the Backwind. Bravo's skin *was* white though, and that was rare. You saw all colours in the cities and counties, just not white, with very few exceptions. These exceptions were almost always associated with what Falric called "the Old World", and the People were *definitely* of the Old World. But yes, everything else about Lien and Bravo aligned with Jordan's hypothesis: their clothing, their tattoos, their language, their way with their ponies - that alone was far from normal - and their intimate knowledge of Leaverness and even one of its most dangerous denizens, Brynir. But if both boys were truly from the People, how had Lien, clearly an outsider, come to be living with the mysterious, secretive tribe?

But Cira did not have a lot of time to ponder such questions, for her thoughts were slowing, and her body becoming heavier. During a dangerous lurch to the right, from which Lien immediately steadied and righted her - holding her a little more firmly from that point - she dully noticed that right side of his hide trousers were now soaked a deep crimson colour. *That's a lot of blood*, she thought curiously, not understanding that it was her own, seeping from her wounded right calf.

Lien too noticed the gradual changes in Cira's body: she was not balancing as well, her reactions were becoming sluggish, and he was having to correct her seat more and more often. Unlike Cira, he understood about the consequences of blood loss. He was himself having to concentrate hard to keep his own body and mind focussed on the tasks at hand and not on the pain from the four wounds raked down his chest, but in his ten years he had already seen and experienced injuries that Cira and Jordan would faint at the mere sight of. And so, despite the whipping wind in their ears, he started firing off questions to try to keep her awake and alert. He asked about the Backwind, of which he knew nothing more than the name; Avenel, which he expected to be tyrannous and repressive; the Order of the Coeur, which he assumed was a brutal organisation that conditioned men for murder; houses, for the idea of permanent structures fascinated him; and why they rode their ponies with saddles and metal bitted bridles, items he considered redundant if not cruel. He seemed to expect everything from Cira and Jordan's world to be full of savagery and violence, and was genuinely surprised by Cira's slow but defensive counter-intelligence.

Had Cira not been injured of course, Lien would have been unable to get a word in edgeways, for she would have had enough return questions to cover the true two day ride back to the Backwind, much less the magical falcon-led shortcut. But as it was, she was having to concentrate very hard just to answer his questions. One question of her own kept hovering at the edge of her growing brain fog though, and she finally managed to slip it in between Lien's friendly interrogations.

'What…what did you say…to Brynir?' she asked, finding the words difficult to force out.

'Oh. I don't know,' Lien said, derailed by the question. Cira looked back questioningly, bringing her right cheek against his warm chest.

'I don't remember. It was very…intense. I just said - uh - what came to my mind,' he said, failing to keep his tone light. Cira was not satisfied, and sensed the boy was hiding something from her, but although Lien's questioning had kept her awake and talking for the half hour it took them to ride the two days' distance from the Falseweald, she was desperate to close her eyes and slip away from the pain. She felt lightheaded but her body was so heavy. As soon as they spied the bridge lanterns ahead - mere diffuse spheres of light in the distance - Cira fully slumped into Lien's chest. His left arm encircled her to hold her safe as she succumbed to the deep fatigue that had been gnawing at her. She found her final thoughts to be melancholic. The Bridge meant safety, but also signified the end of something magical, something surreal; of experiences that, Cira dimly realised as she slipped into unconsciousness, may never be repeated again.

Jest and Bank were also tired by this time, and so on sensing the relief of their riders, gratefully fell back into a walk, blowing hard steamy mist into the night air as they approached the Bridge in single file. Their ears pricked and rotated anxiously though as they picked up the distant sound of dogs barking, iron shod hooves ringing against stone and loud voices. The sounds reached the children shortly after, and Bravo stiffened immediately, his seat asking Bank to stop.

'It'll be a search party, for us,' Jordan explained. Bravo shook his head.

'No more,' he said, and these were the only words he had said in the language of the lands surrounding Leaverness. As Jest stopped next to Bank, Lien just looked helplessly down to Cira, unconscious in his arms. Jordan gasped at the sight.

'Cira!' he cried out. 'Is she - ?'

'She needs help, *now*,' Lien said. He looked to Bravo.

'Stay. Jordan can walk. I must ride Cira,' he said firmly.

'Lien - ' Bravo started to argue, but stopped at the

sound of a shout on the other side of the Teine.

'Sir! There's something there, across the river!'

'Lien, we *can't* be seen!' Bravo was begging now, in their own language, fear clear in his face. 'Tell them!'

Lien turned to Jordan.

'Jordan, you must *never* tell *anyone* you saw us,' he said, and Jordan was surprised at how serious the normally jovial boy had become.

'But…how do we explain…?' and he waved his arms to indicate the entirety of their adventure in a grossly insufficient manner.

'You be the hero,' Lien said urgently. He was running out of time; two horses were galloping across the Bridge now, their hooves drumming against the old wood. 'You chase Aethon, you fight Brynir, you survive. You make a good story!'

He grinned desperately, waiting for Jordan to look like he was onboard with the idea. Jordan chewed his lip: he was a terrible liar.

'I'm not a hero like you, Lien – ' he started but was swiftly cut off by Bravo pushing him off Bank. He landed awkwardly on the damp grass.

'Then make Cira the hero, okay?'

Lien's wide emerald eyes implored Jordan to agree. Reluctantly, the boy did with a small nod. Lien almost sighed with relief.

*'Jordan? Cira?!'*

The shout came from the rider of the first horse, who held a brush torch out ahead, the better to see the dark shapes ahead he could only otherwise just make out. Jordan looked up to Lien, eyes wide.

'That's my father!' he said. Lien nodded.

'Ask him to stop,' he ordered. Jordan gulped, and blundered forward from the screen of bushes that less than two hours before - hours which might as well have been a lifetime - had barely concealed Aethon from two excited children looking for an adventure.

'Father!' he called, his voice thin but cutting through the night like a knife.

*'Jordan!'* Falric's voice almost cracked, choked with the fear of a father who thought he had lost his son.

'Father, stop, please!' Jordan continued, almost sobbing as he stumbled forward, waving his arms frantically. Reluctantly, but obediently, Falric reined in his black horse and waved the rider behind him to do the same. The sounds of the larger search party were coming closer.

'Jordan - are you alright? Where is Cira?'

'I'm okay father. Cira is injured,' Jordan yelled across the yards separating them. He looked back anxiously to Lien and Bravo, unsure of what to do next. Bravo shot Lien a warning look.

'You stay. I look like them,' Lien said, and knowing he shouldn't, but also knowing he must, he urged Jest forward, out of the forest fringe, and into the furthest reach of the torch light of Lord Falric and his stable master, Tomas.

From the perspective of the two men, the staggering relief of finding Jordan alive quickly turned to fear at his request they stop their approach. Both immediately jumped to the conclusion that a trap of some kind was afoot: that Jordan had escaped the forest but brought something dangerous and cruel with him. Falric's right hand had immediately gone to his sword hilt and his heart was hammering hard in chest as he watched his son glance back, as though for permission - *from who?* As the foremost authority on Leaverness, he knew better than most what terrible things might have been lurking behind the screen of bushes from which Jordan had emerged.

But perhaps one of the last things he might have expected to reveal itself though was a brown and white pony, on which Cira was slumped, unconscious, and held protectively by a boy only around the age of his own son and who, at first glance, could have been a child of the Backwind. But as he processed all the details of the scene, Falric took in the unusual details as well: the lack of saddle and bridle, the unseasonably light tunic, the long staff, and the child's evident anxiety.

'Cira,' the Tomas gasped. 'What's he done to her?'

Like everyone on the estate, the stable master frequently ran afoul of Cira's mischief, but would sooner harm himself than see harm set upon the girl. He too put a hand to his sword.

'Wait,' Falric breathed, reading the scene. The boy did not seem threatening. If anything, he looked afraid of them, and like he was guarding Cira.

'Do you mean the children harm?' Falric called to the approaching apparition.

'No father, he helped us,' Jordan cried, now shoulder to shoulder with Jest and clearly unafraid of the pony or his rider. 'But Cira - she needs help, it's really bad,' and now Jordan finally *was* crying at the sight of his best friend collapsed into Lien's arms. Lien stopped Jest several yards from Falric and the stable master.

'Your father, alone,' Lien said quietly to Jordan.

'Just you, father, to take her,' Jordan called.

Tomas went to protest, but Falric ordered him away to head off the search party. The stable master was evidently unhappy about the instruction, but obeyed, turning his horse to canter back across the Bridge.

'My father will keep your secret,' Jordan assured Lien. 'He will. He's a good man. I promise.'

Lien nodded and waited for Falric's horse to reach them. The man's eyes were wide, questioning, taking in every detail he could see in the light of his torch. Including the tattoo ring around Lien's arm, and blood-soaked trousers.

'What has happened to her?' Falric asked, hoarsely, dismounting to wrap Jordan into a spine cracking hug.

'She has hurt her knee, and has a bad leg wound,' Jordan mumbled from the depths of his father's chest.

'She has lost blood. Too much. Needs help now,' Lien added urgently. Falric released Jordan immediately and approached.

'Oh Cira, Cira…' Falric repeated quietly to himself as Lien released his grip so that the girl could be slid over Jest's left side. Cradling her in his arms, Falric looked back at the nervous boy and now saw the four lines of blood that had long since seeped through Bravo's borrowed tunic.

'You look like you need help yourself,' he observed. 'We will take care of you too. Come,' he ordered, turning back to his horse. He easily pushed Cira up in front of the saddle, swung himself up and then reached down to draw Jordan up behind the saddle.

Lien and Jest though did not move.

'Lien…?' Jordan asked, his voice small, hoping the boy would come but knowing he could not. Falric looked swiftly between his son and the strange child in front of him.

'I can see I owe you a debt,' he said to Lien. 'Please, allow me to repay it. We have a good doctor.'

'I cannot come. But please, tell a different story,' Lien replied. 'Tell your friend too,' he added, nodding in the direction of the Bridge, but knowing with a sinking feeling it was too late. Tomas would have reached the rest of the search party by now, and while he would have stopped them crossing the Bridge to see Lien themselves, he would also have told them all about the boy who bought the children back from the forest.

'I think I understand. Thank you,' Falric said, bowing his head to Lien. 'Be safe,' and he turned his horse, to get Cira home to the care she needed.

'Lien?' Jordan called out, looking back as the black horse cantered away. 'Another time?'

'Another time!' Lien called back, smiling. 'It was fun!' he added, although quietly, to himself. He knew the injuries to Cira's calf and knee meant she might never walk properly again, which dampened his enthusiasm. And he knew there would be severe repercussions from his actions this night.

He had no idea just how severe though.

Lien thoughtfully watched Falric's horse clatter back over the Bridge, taking Cira and Jordan out of the dangers and magic of his and Bravo's world, and back to the safety of their own. A world he could no longer remember, but was told he had once been a part of. In fact, Cira, Jordan and Falric were the first people he had seen who looked like him. This realisation gave him a strange feeling in his stomach; but once Falric's horse had disappeared from sight and sound, his shoulders slumped forward. Lien finally allowed himself to feel the more urgent pain and weariness he had been forced to shrug off since Brynir had swiped him from Jest. He didn't even hear Bravo riding over until Jest gave a tired but friendly whicker to Bank.

'Do you think Sky will show us a shortcut back?' Lien asked, glancing up to the sky with a rueful smile.

'I bloody hope so,' Bravo sighed. 'You're such an idiot, Lien.'

The boys were seen standing there together by two sets of eyes that night: those of the falcon, a blacker shadow in the endless night sky above; and those of Tomas, the stable master. He had stopped the larger assembled rescue party as ordered, and told them that the missing children had been returned by a boy; but then turned back to quietly guide his horse to the bank of the Teine. He rode until he was adjacent to where to where the boys murmured to one another in a language he could not understand. As though to help him see better, the full moon emerged from behind clouds to bathe them in soft silver light, just for long enough for him to be sure of what he was seeing.

One of the boys now noticed the falcon hanging far above, backlit by the revealed moon, and with evident relief, they turned their tired ponies back into the forest. They were quickly swallowed by the darkness from which they had come, and the stable master pondered on what to do with the information - and suspicion - he now harboured.

That night was the last time Lien would see Jordan and, in a way, the last time either of the Leaverness boys would see Cira. At least, as they knew her then.

Two days later, muddy, exhausted, their reins long since snapped and saddles scratched beyond all repair, Cira and Jordan's ponies finally found their way back to the stable yard. All the way from the Falseweald.

# 3. Lady Beckworth

Cira's injuries initially postponed, but ultimately averted any disciplinary action against the children. Even the famous Disappointed Face was absent, for Lord Falric's features were otherwise preoccupied with various expressions of concern. It was obvious to everyone that the lion's share of any bollocking belonged to Cira, but it was also apparent that she was being punished enough by the consequences of the great adventure.

She was crippled.

The calf wound, savagely deep and wide, was problematic in itself. But it was the tearing of the tendons and ligaments of her right knee that prevented her from being able to take a single step unaided. It was a devastating plight for a courageous girl with grand dreams of the chivalric life.

Cira had a lot of time to think as she rested in the weeks after returning from Leaverness. She was upset and angry: at herself, at Brynir and at the world at large. She was especially angry at Lyschiva, He Who Destroys, for taking so much from her. She begged Chal'Om, She Who Creates, to heal her leg and allow her to continue her life as planned. Life was so unfair to women and now all her plans to keep up with Jordan - riding, sword fighting, hand to hand combat, jousting, joining the Order - were impossible. She felt like she was being punished for wanting to escape a traditional woman's life by being brutally forced back into it.

She could also see that Jordan, Falric, her mother and all the other staff of the Galea Estate were sad and fearful for her. Everyone's behaviour changed: they all treated her with kid gloves and she hated it. She wanted *something* to feel normal again, but it seemed impossible to return to her former carefree self. Cira once imagined herself as two people, pre- and post-accident Cira, to have a conversation with her earlier self. But in doing so, she realised that as much as she wanted to undo the injuries, she could not warn herself not to chase Aethon. She could not tell herself to miss out on that extraordinary ride behind the beautiful unicorn; on discovering Brynir the Cursed was real; on fighting for her life with her best friend; and on meeting Lien. And Bravo, obviously, but…mostly Lien.

She *would* tell herself not to throw that damn rock though. That rock made Brynir hurt both Lien and herself. But how was she to stand by while the creature attacked them? She had been certain Brynir was going to kill them.

Although, when she replayed the whole scene in her mind, she remembered how, when she and Jordan had finally been helpless, Brynir had *not* attacked. He had *played* with them. His behaviour just before Lien and Bravo had roped him had made no sense.

*Would* he have killed them?

How could she ever know?

And then it was in a conversation with Jordan, several weeks after the accident, that Cira finally found her way, more or less, back to her former self. In an unusually honest moment, Jordan told her that she had used to be upbeat and fun-loving like Lien, but was now brooding and bad tempered - like Bravo. He asked her whether that was a permanent change. The subtext was glaringly obvious: had he swapped his Lien for Lien's Bravo?

Cira was floored by the question, and at first thought it unfair: she had just been through a serious trauma, after all. Jordan had only bruises and sore ribs, how could he possibly understand? She sulked for a day, over which she eventually conceded that he had a point. They had not laughed together since the accident. She had changed, so he had changed too, and it wasn't for the better. She realised that even though it was hard to imagine laughing again, she wanted to see Jordan laugh. Which meant she had to *make* Jordan laugh.

And so Cira tapped back into her pre-accident self. At first it was just an act, being her old self again, but as everyone else's behaviour around her started to normalise, she began to feel better. The more upbeat she acted, the more upbeat she felt.

If she had to choose between being like Lien or Bravo, there was no way she was going to be like the boy who would have left her and Jordan to die in Leaverness.

By request from Lien and Jordan, Falric had invented a story for the search party about what had happened to the children in Leaverness. He explained that they had gone for a ride, got lost and then encountered a bear. The bear spooked their ponies and wounded Cira's leg after she fell. They had been rescued by a boy from a nearby town, who had ridden Cira home on his pony, but had not wished to be identified, because he was forbidden from being in Leaverness alone and feared he would be beaten for disobeying his father. This, Falric told Cira and Jordan, was the only version of events they could ever speak of in front of others, even Cira's mother. Flavia found nothing suspicious in the story, but then, she was much more preoccupied with the consequences of her daughter's injuries than the cause.

It was more than a month after their adventure before Cira was permitted to resume her studies with Jordan. On the first day she returned, Falric himself unexpectedly took their last session of the afternoon. Lessons with Falric were not unusual, for no tutor possessed the education of Jordan's father, and he loved imparting knowledge to the children. But the last minute announcement made them both uneasy. Falric had not pressed them fully on what had happened yet, beyond an attack by Brynir and rescue by Lien and Bravo. He had not wished to subject Cira to the traumatic memories until he felt she had sufficiently recovered herself from the ordeal. And with Cira constantly under the watchful eye of her mother, the children had not yet had a chance to talk privately about anything, much less about how much they could - and should - tell Falric, when the time came.

The uneasiness was, however, somewhat offset by the thrill of learning that the lesson would be held in Falric's private study. It was his scholarly sanctum and was usually forbidden even to Jordan. Cira had never been inside.

She entered slowly. She had no choice, still struggling with the wooden crutches Tomas had made for her. Even so, she relished pausing just inside the heavy oak door to inhale deeply. The study was more of a small library and smelled of old books, leather furniture and smoke, with a sweeter lingering tang she could not identify. All four walls were covered floor to ceiling with bookshelves, and all the shelves were full of beautiful, thick, leather-bound books. The study also contained a table covered in maps; a heavy brass telescope; an elegant drinks cabinet, within which exquisite bottles blinked and winked in the light of glass mounted pillar candles; and Falric's huge, ornately carved wooden desk. Falric softly closed the door behind them and then pulled back one of the two leather chairs he had positioned across from his desk. This was to allow Cira to - carefully, and painfully - lower herself down into it while keeping her bad knee straight. Falric leaned her crutches against the side of the chair before settling himself down on the other side of the desk. Both children felt drowned in the adult-sized chairs and dwarfed by the desk: a problem not helped by the piles of books, papers and lamps that covered its aged surface. Noticing the way that the children were sitting up as straight as possible to peer over these obstacles, Falric stood to clear the contents of the centre of his desk to the sides, before sitting back down to observe them closely over steepled fingers.

Cira and Jordan watched him back apprehensively, both wondering whether they were finally getting into trouble. Eventually, after stretching the silence just a little too long, Falric spoke.

'Jordan. Cira. I hope enough time has passed that you feel ready to tell me everything that happened in Leaverness. I will ask you a series of questions, and then, when I am satisfied, you may ask me any questions *you* have. I will answer to the best of my knowledge, and that shall be your education for this afternoon.'

The children glanced uncertainly at one another, both wishing they could have had a private conference first in which to agree a game plan.

'Neither of you are in trouble,' he said, observing the silent transaction. 'I believe the punishment has, if anything, exceeded the crime,' he added, nodding sombrely towards the crutches propped up against Cira's chair.

'Actually, sir, the punishment could have been much worse,' Cira said, her voice unusually thin. She cleared her throat, embarrassed at the sound, and tried again. 'What I mean to say is that we nearly died a number of times.'

'I have no doubt of that,' Falric replied seriously. He knew well how many things might have easily killed two children in the forest: some by intent, some by accident, some simply by their nature.

'Why did your ponies take so long to make it home?'

Again, the children glanced to one another, their eyes mutually asking *how much do we tell him? How much will he* believe?

'Do recall that I am well versed in the idiosyncrasies of Leaverness' geography,' he reminded them patiently. It was true: everything they knew of Leaverness, they had learned from Falric.

'Recall also that I am aware of preceding sightings of Aethon, and of his...how shall we say...*special* abilities.'

Cira nodded briefly to Jordan, indicating he should begin.

'Father, we too had heard of the sightings of Aethon, and went to find him. That was *all* we set out to do, I promise,' Jordan said.

'And Aethon showed himself to you?' Falric surmised.

Both children nodded.

'Just across the Bridge, sir – there he was, immediately. It was like – it was like he was waiting for us to see him,' Cira said, realising this even as she said it.

'Indeed,' Falric said. He pushed his chair back to peruse a bookshelf as he continued.

'That is often the case with Aethon. He is the stuff of legends, as you well know. The thing about legends is that they seem to like playing silly buggers with us mere mortals.'

Falric drew out a very old, red, leather-bound book with gilt decorations on the spine and corners of the front cover. Cira couldn't quite catch the title as he opened it to flick through its yellowed page. Falric found the page he was looking for, and held it up open for them to see. He had chosen a page showing an illustration of a beautiful black unicorn with golden horn, mane, tail, legs and hooves, standing over a pool of water. What drew the children's wide-eyed attention though was the unicorn's reflection.

It was not that of a horse.

It was the reflection of a shaggy, sinister, wolfish creature.

'Where did Aethon lead you?' Falric asked, noting the children's reactions to the drawing

'He led us to the Falseweald,' Cira said. True to his word, Falric was unfazed by the geographic impossibility of this claim. He knew that when it came to Leaverness, the taller the story, the more likely it was to be true.

'To Brynir the Cursed,' Jordan said slowly, staring at the unicorn's reflection. Cira realised that from Falric's perspective, standing above the book, the picture would be of Brynir, with Aethon as his reflection.

Falric slowly sat back down, laying the book down on

the desk, open to the disorienting illustration.

'Before we continue, I want you both to make me a promise: that you will never chase Aethon again,' Falric said, deadly serious.

The children shared startled looks: how could they promise such a thing?

'Swear to me you will not do so,' Falric insisted. 'At least - not while I live. You may chase any destiny you like once are you old like I am.'

'You are not old, father,' Jordan said earnestly.

'Flatter me not, Jordan: only swear to me.'

Slowly, reluctantly, the children agreed they would not chase Aethon again. But Cira had her fingers crossed under the table.

Somewhat mollified, Falric leaned back with a creak of his old leather chair.

'Thank you. Now: we continue. How long did you chase Aethon for?' he asked.

'We thought we had an hour's light. It was not yet dark when Brynir attacked us. I don't think it was more than a half hour, to be honest,' Cira said, thinking back on it.

'And how did you know you were in the Falseweald?' Falric asked. 'Perhaps you should start at the beginning.'

And so they did. At first the story came in fits and starts, but eventually it all came tumbling out as the children finally had a chance - the first since it had all happened - to really *talk* about their experience. Falric was a very receptive listener, only occasionally prompting for clarity or further information. He did not rush Cira when she faltered while recounting how she was injured, or Jordan when he had to take over the story solo after Cira had passed out. Cira explained the different personalities of Lien and Bravo, and how she was sure Bravo wanted to leave them to die in the Falseweald. When Falric asked for a detailed description of each of the boys, the children paused again.

'I saw only one of them - Lien, I assume?' Falric asked, and the children nodded.

'You say they were of the People. But Lien could not have been *born* of the People?'

'I don't think so, sir. Bravo surely was - he was white as chalk - but Lien could have come from the Backwind,' Cira agreed cautiously. She knew from Falric's pensive expression that this was significant, if not dangerous. She just didn't yet understand why.

'Or Avenel,' Falric said lightly, but there was a tell in his voice that Cira latched onto.

'You know who he is, don't you?' she demanded, before, remembering her place, adding a hasty *sir* to cover her tone. Falric couldn't help admire the acuity - not to mention audacity - of the girl.

'Lien asked you to keep the truth of your adventures secret, and I will explain why he might have done that. To the best of my knowledge, plus some educated guesswork,' he said. 'Lives are at stake - foremost, that of Lien himself.'

And Falric proceeded to tell them a story: one tall enough to be true.

He took Cira and Jordan back a decade - which was nearly the whole of their lives - to when the last king of Avenel ruled sovereign over the lives of tens of thousands, including everyone in the Backwind and surrounding counties. Du Romeau was a conqueror king, overseeing the most successful expansion of Avenel territory in its long history, from a vast kingdom into an empire. He more than quadrupled its land size and citizenry with a combination of stick and what he considered carrot: after crushing resistance with his knights and infantry, Du Romeau sent in engineers and educators to "modernise" towns and cities and forcibly replaced local languages and bartering systems with the language and currency of Avenel. Whether the conquered wanted such changes, or considered them a fair trade for their sovereignty, was irrelevant -the king rolled them out across the continent as aggressively as his armies regardless.

Du Romeau's Knight Operis was a champion amongst champions: Sir Lindahl, a common man who had challenged the law of birthright that governed entry to the Order of the Coeur. Lindahl was particularly good with the negotiations that always took place before subjugating new territory, to the point that his knights were not always needed. When they were, he minimised collateral damage and forbade the sacking of significant buildings or harm of women or children. Which was not, Falric hastened to add, to put a picturesque sheen on what was essentially a decade of constant invasion and occupation; but it was true that King Du Romeau and Sir Lindahl tried to put an air of respectability upon their warfare. And wherever Lindahl and his men went, they returned victorious.

This period was romanticised within Avenel as a Golden Age of both the city and chivalry...until it was brutally ended by living embodiment of chivalry himself. For one night, for reasons unknown, Lindahl murdered Du Romeau: his close friend, benefactor and king. In one inexplicable act of violence, the collective dream of Avenel's majesty came crashing down. Overnight, the love of a nation for their champion soured to a bitterness of equal proportions. He had been a strong ally of the People, and rumour had it that their leader, Sky, had helped Lindahl escape Avenel. Knights of the Order of the Coeur retaliated by scouring Leaverness for Lindahl and the People, driving the tribe into the deep and dangerous heart of the forest where no other man dare tread, and not one had been seen since.

Until Cira and Jordan had met Lien and Bravo.

A moral and political darkness fell across Avenel, a proud city stripped of her two finest men, and this shadow only deepened when Du Romeau's queen and infant son disappeared also, leaving no heir for succession. An advisory council to the crown, the Council of Voltanna, was promoted to being a caretaker governing collective to hold the empire together. But as its powers grew, so too did opposition to the monarchy from advocates of more progressive forms of government – a movement largely led by members of the Council itself. The Avenel of today still thrived and maintained its empire, but was internally bound up in a power struggle between the institutions of the monarchy – including the Order of the Coeur – and the Council of Voltanna, which was capitalising on the political vacuum left by an empty throne. A throne they wanted kept empty, if not eliminated altogether.

The children were enthralled by these political shenanigans. They had previously only known an abbreviated and highly simplified version of the story. But there was still more.

'Several years ago, the Council of Voltanna announced they had learned that Du Romeau's wife, Giselle, and their son, had died shortly after their disappearance, slain by bandits during their flight from of Avenel,' Falric continued. 'Obviously as it had occurred years earlier they were unable to produce bodies as proof, but they claimed to have extracted a confession from one of the killers. Thus the official line was that heir to the throne was dead, and as Du Romeau's brothers had both died without children, the direct royal line was ended. However, the Order was not convinced. A sacred divination to Mama Aksaya was performed by the knight Sir Bane, to ask whether the heir lived.'

'Aksaya, the Eternal Mother?' Cira interrupted, thinking of the constellation painted on the ceiling of the Astronomy Tower.

'The same, keeper of truth and secrets,' Falric agreed.

'What is she? Essene?' Cira asked.

'Who cares what she is, what did she *say?*' Jordan demanded. Falric smiled at their different objectives: Cira wanted all of the detail, while Jordan only wanted to get to the end result. He decided to indulge Cira, for he loved sharing his knowledge, and especially on such a fascinating subject.

'She is Essene. She may even precede Essene, for all we know. She is ancient, and powerful, and manipulative. For Sir Bane to ask a truth of her was…very brave. To get a truth from Aksaya, you must enter a formal Arrangement with her, in which you agree to perform an act on her behalf in return. But you do not get to know what that act is, until after she provides the truth, by which time, it is too late to refuse. Goodness only knows what Bane had to give, or do, to ask his question.'

Cira was impressed at the courage of a man who would enter such an agreement; Jordan did not give it a second thought.

'So? What was the answer?' he begged impatiently.

'Mama Aksaya appeared before members of both the Order and Council and said that Du Romeau's wife and child are alive, of course,' Falric said, a twinkle in his eyes.

'Where? Did she say where?' Cira asked.

'Well, Aksaya did not consider that a *truth*, but a *secret*. To ask her a secret, you must agree to trade one of your own. But Aksaya decides which one, and when she takes it, you don't even know you gave it.'

'So…you forget your own secret?' Cira asked, wide-eyed.

'Yes. For you Cira, for instance, Aksaya might take the secret of what happened in Leaverness. You would forget Aethon, Brynir, Lien and Bravo. It would be like that entire afternoon and evening never happened for you.'

Cira's mouth made a silent "O" of amazement.

'Legend has it there is a place hidden deep inside Leaverness called the Forest of Secrets, and it is there that she stores the secrets she takes. They also say a man can forget his whole life, if it is based completely on a single secret that Aksaya takes. I would expect Sir Bane to be a man of many secrets, and can appreciate he might consider trading one, even for the exact location of the heir, to be too dangerous. And the main point had been proven anyway: the Council of Voltanna was trying abolish the monarchy completely, and now could not. For the word of Mama Aksaya is truth, and she said Du Romeau's heir lives.'

Cira was busy connecting the dots.

'You think Lien is Du Romeau's son!' she said excitedly.

Jordan gaped.

'*We* were rescued by the future *king* of Avenel?' he

breathed, thrilled.

'Isn't this good news, Sir? Isn't this what Avenel has been waiting for? The return of a king?' Cira asked, frowning now as she kept connecting the information she had. 'Why would we be keeping this secret?'

Falric looked troubled.

'Well. This is where it gets...complicated. Firstly, in full disclosure, that is only my educated guess. Lien may *not* be Du Romeau's son. He appears to be around the right age, but never underestimate the power of a good coincidence. Secondly, Sky helped Lindahl escape after murdering the king. If the Order of the Coeur, who are desperate to restore their king, found out that there was an Avenel boy being hidden in Leaverness by the People, the right age to be Du Romeau's son...what do you think they would conclude?'

'That Sky stole their heir,' Jordan said quietly.

'Exactly. Personally, I don't think that is his style. Sky is renowned for being calm and wise; stealing the heir of Avenel would hardly be *wise*. But you can see how it would look. And then what do you think the Order would do?'

'They would hunt down the People and...and have revenge upon them,' Cira said, finally understanding Falric's apprehension.

'Exactly,' Falric said. 'I daresay many of them would enjoy it, too,' he added bitterly. 'So Lien would feel responsible for the slaughter of those who raised him. Thirdly, I have to ask you: how do you think the boy of the forest you met would fare in Avenel? In even the Backwind? You have told me of the many questions he asked, Cira – he comes from a completely different world.'

The children could not argue with any of Falric's logic.

A heavy silence fell over the three; Cira felt like this knowledge was a terrible weight to carry.

But Lord Falric had not yet finished.

'And there's one more thing we need to consider,' he broke the silence. 'This is where it gets dangerous, for Lien. If the Council of Voltanna found out a boy who might be the heir to the throne was alive and living with the People, what do you think *they* would do about it?'

'Same as the Order, surely?' Jordan asked. Dear sweet Jordan, who did not have a malicious bone in his body.

Cira, who had only piggy-backed into his privileged life, and therefore understood human nature a little better than her best friend, slowly shook her head.

'No. The return of a king would end their power,' she said. 'They would not want him found.'

Jordan looked appalled at the unspoken implication. He looked to his father, who nodded agreement with Cira's assessment.

'It's true, Jordan. If the heir was ever found, and returned to Avenel, he would effectively usurp their authority. So it would be in their interests to ensure that he is not found - or at least, not found *alive*.'

'That's so... *evil*.' Jordan eventually managed.

His father shrugged.

'I am afraid these are the realities of power,' Falric said simply. 'I wish I could tell you that this sort of politicking belongs only in Avenel, but you will both encounter it - admittedly on less grandiose scales - throughout your lives. There will be many times when you need to decide whether to do what best serves *you*, or least harms others. And I hope you will be able to make good, just decisions.'

'We will, father,' Jordan assured him fervently.

'I know you will, Jordan,' Falric said fondly. 'Now, what questions do you have for me?'

'Is Sky a falcon, or a man?' Cira asked immediately. 'Because it was a falcon that led us the short route back from the Falseweald, and the boys said Sky was the falcon but *also* Bravo's grandfather, which seemed - well, strange. And Brynir was afraid of his name, I think.'

Falric nodded, smiling.

'I know only rumours of Sky, of course. I myself have never met any of the People, though I have tried many times to find them. You are both enormously privileged to have done so,' Falric added, almost enviously. 'But yes, the legends say he is a powerful shaman and can shape-shift, favouring the shape of a golden falcon.'

'Legends?' Cira frowned. 'How old is he?'

'I do not know,' Falric shrugged. 'What I *do* know is there have been stories of Sky leading the People for hundreds of years. Now whether that's one man, or a hereditary title passed down from man to boy, I can't tell you. But I would very much love to find out,' he added, eyes bright at the prospect of unlocking such mysteries.

'Now, what of you, Jordan? What would you like to know?'

'Father, why would Lien and Bravo be in trouble for helping us?' Jordan asked after a thoughtful pause. 'Bravo was so angry at Lien for wanting to help us.'

'Ah good question,' Falric said, nodding approvingly. 'The People are famously reclusive by nature, and so little has ever been known about them in Avenel. After Lindahl killed the king though, and Sky helped him escape, they fled, and disappeared. I would assume the adults of the People counsel all the children against being seen at all; I would guess further that they know how dangerous it would be for Lien specifically to be seen. Regardless of whether he is Du Romeau's son, there are plenty who would persecute them for "stealing" any child of Avenel or the counties.'

'*If* they could find them,' Cira chipped in.

'Quite.'

'If Lien knew how serious it was to be seen though, why would he have helped us? And revealed himself to you?' she mused further. 'I mean, if our roles were reversed and I knew being seen by the People meant the death of everyone on the estate, I'm not sure I'd go gallivanting around fighting Brynir to save two of them.'

'You would have let Lien and Bravo die, if our roles were reversed?' Jordan asked her, amazed.

Cira shrugged.

'I dunno Jordo. That's a pretty serious consequence.'

'Perhaps he doesn't know the *why*, only the rule?' Falric suggested.

'And maybe Bravo *did* know, and that's why he was so angry about helping us?' Jordan added. Cira blinked: that had not occurred to her. That certainly threw a different light on Bravo's behaviour.

'Or he simply couldn't let two people die, whatever the risks,' Falric countered. 'You see, we can guess all we like, but it's only guessing. Be careful, children, of making assumptions about other people's behaviour without knowing the full situation.'

Something had been bothering Cira for the last couple of minutes, and she finally realised what it was.

'Sir - if Lindahl and Du Romeau conquered so much of the continent, did they conquer Leaverness? And the

People? I mean, the forest is right on Avenel's doorstop, so to speak.'

'Leaverness is neutral territory,' Falric said. 'Has been since the founding of Avenel. There is an ancient contract between a founder of the city called Cobi and, believe it or not, a man called Sky.'

'He is *so* old!' Cira breathed.

'So it would seem,' Falric smiled, then sobered.

'I heard a rumour though - and I stress it was only a rumour - that Du Romeau was competing with the Immortalis Imperator Kyronus – '

' - with the what?!' Cira asked.

'*Who*, not what. I know it's a mouthful though. The Immortalis Imperator Kyronus. He conquered almost a whole continent, as Du Romeau almost had with this one. The rumour I heard is that Du Romeau wanted to match Kyronus' achievement, and then he would title himself Imperator Du Romeau. But he had to conquer Scyros and Leaverness to achieve that. And died before he could do either. But! These are histories for other days,' Falric hastily wrapped up, seeing the children's eyes widening at all of these new names and places and intrigues. He sat back, flexing his interlaced fingers until his knuckles cracked.

'For now, there endeth the lesson. I thank you both for your honesty, and trust you to keep what we have discussed secret between only the three of us. Absolutely *no-one* else can know about Lien.'

The children nodded seriously, but then Jordan was struck by a thought.

'Father, what about Tomas? He saw Lien too,' he asked worriedly.

'I have spoken to Tomas. He is a good man. I believe

we have come to an understanding on the matter,' Falric assured his son.

Tomas, the stable master, was indeed a good man, but also a good monarchist, deeply loyal to Du Romeau and the crown, and this was where he was presented with quite the dilemma. Before settling in the Backwind for a quieter life, he had worked in the vast stables of the Order of the Coeur in Avenel, and he knew what most folk did not: that the heir lived, and the Order was actively seeking him out. Tomas had listened to Falric's explanation about the boy who rescued the children being a Backwind lad, who would be in trouble with his own father for being in Leaverness, even if he had saved the son of the Lord of the county. This was a reach already; but he had also seen Lien with Bravo, and the moonlight had shown Bravo as a ghostly white figure next to Lien's brown skin. And Tomas had been a horseman all his life and knew of no lads of the Backwind who rode around without saddles and bridles.

Tomas was sure Falric must have seen all of this as well, but said nothing of it. He was sure the Lord had his reasons, and was aware that the Order would send knights to Leaverness if they found out about an Avenel boy living with the People. But what he wanted most was to see a king back on the Avenel throne, and he thought that more important than protecting the People. And it did not even occur to him that it might harm the very boy in question.

He ruminated on his decision through the autumn, until it was too late to ride to the city. But when the winter snows had passed and the tracks were safe to traverse once more, he requested leave to visit family. Instead, he rode to Avenel, where he had a quiet word with the knight he most trusted with his information. He was uneasy as he rode back to the Backwind, but told himself that his first duty was to king and country, and therefore he had made a good and just decision.

* * * * *

There were three important visitors to the Backwind in the spring. First there was much excitement in the village when word got around that Lord Falric would be hosting Lady Selene Beckworth at the Galea Estate. Lady Beckworth was the notorious and powerful backbone of Avenel society. She was a force to be reckoned with politically as well, often clashing with the Council of Voltanna. These clashes were generally resolved discreetly though, because she could blackmail almost all of the most honourable gentleman on the Council, thanks to her very specific business interests. She was also allegedly Falric's aunt; a claim that had made good sense when he was a young man and she a woman in her prime thirties, but less so now that he was in his forties and looked much older than she. While the rest of the world aged, Selene remained youthful and glamorous, and somehow, absolutely no-one ever noticed.

Falric had written to his aunt in the winter, when it became apparent that Cira's calf wound was not healing as it should. In fact it was barely healing at all, and he was deeply worried about it, though he tried to keep his fear from both the parchment and the children. The letter had looked innocuous enough: just general chat about the estate, the season, the last harvest, and of course the near-death experience of Jordan and his best friend who, incidentally but very sadly, might never regain the full use of her right leg.

Lady Beckworth had immediately sent a return letter saying that a visit to the Backwind was overdue, and that she would come as soon as the roads were safe to travel by carriage. This was followed in the spring by a letter advising to expect her in three to four days from receipt, which would be around five days after being sent by the express post system. Coach mail took nearly a fortnight between the Backwind and Avenel, while premium bags were galloped in relay across the Avenel Empire and covered the same distance in less than half the time.

The preparations required to present the manor to the standard befitting such a visitor threw almost everyone on the estate into a frenzy of work. The only residents of Galea who were not concerned were the children. Lady Beckworth had visited her nephew three times previously in Cira and Jordan's memory and they always enormously looked forward to her arrival. They knew nothing of her formidable reputation, only that she was fantastic company: irreverent, mischievous and also very generous, always bringing them thoughtful gifts.

This visit was no exception. Lady Beckworth arrived in a grand four-horse carriage with a butler, driver and extravagant embraces for her "favourite nephew". She insisted, as she did every time, that Jordan and Cira call her Selene, told them how enormously they had grown since she had seen them last, and produced gifts. Falric was delighted to receive a port the children later learned was fantastically expensive; Jordan a lustrous silver shield with the Galea coat of arms emblazoned on it; and for Cira, standing awkwardly on her crutches, Selene had bought an archery set. The bow was lighter and shorter than Cira had seen previously, and the arrows had bright blue fletchings. Just before the fletchings, a single thin black line encircled each shaft. Cira stared at the rings a moment before her brain worked out why it had flagged them as significant: they reminded her of the thin tattoo line that had encircled Lien's right arm. She threw a questioning look to Selene, who was otherwise occupied examining her injured right leg while making concerned noises.

'We will look at this tomorrow,' she announced, standing up and giving Cira a wink. Cira and Jordan looked to one another immediately, eyes widening with hope. Months after their foray into Leaverness, Cira was still in a tremendous amount of pain and like Falric, feared her calf wound was unnatural and might never heal.

Lady Beckworth spent the afternoon first with Lord Falric and then Cira's mother. This was another unusual breach of traditional etiquette, but it had been Selene who had suggested Flavia join the Falric household many years earlier, and the two women had always been very close. In the evening, Falric hosted Selene and other minor aristocrats of the Backwind and surrounding areas for a lavish dinner in her honour. It was of course yet *another* breach of social protocol for Cira to be seated with Jordan at such an event, instead of working as serving staff with her mother. Eyebrows were raised and tuts tutted, but as always, everyone was far too polite to make a direct comment. Cira always felt odd being included in such events while her mother managed the running of the dining service, but she was also enormously grateful to be able to join in. She knew she really ought to have been working in the kitchen, neither seen nor heard by the guests. Jordan meanwhile always had a better time with Cira at his side, and Falric was able to enjoy himself without worrying about his son retreating into the kind of shyness that made busybodies gossip. And Lady Beckworth, as always, delighted in the company of the two children much more than that of the other guests. She quietly told Jordan and Cira outrageous stories of the knights of Avenel, in between telling the more mainstream news and carefully curated gossip to the adults of the table.

The next day Lady Beckworth appeared at Cira and Flavia's cottage early in the morning with a large leather bag. Cira was sitting at the small kitchen table, her right leg propped up on another chair.

'Selene - ?!' she started, before clapping a hand over her mouth upon seeing her mother frown at her improperly familiar use of their visitor's first name.

'*Lady* Beckworth, what a - surprise - ?' she stammered.

Selene laughed, a light, tinkling sound.

'Dear Flavia do not look so horrified, I told Cira yesterday that she, like Jordan, may call me Selene,' she said breezily. 'As must you, when we are out of earshot of all those stuffy nobby folk. I do get so bored of "Lady this" and "Lady that", and enjoy a little more familiarity among friends from time to time.'

'Thank you, Selene. But I do feel it is important to encourage Cira to employ at least a *touch* of decorum,' Flavia said pointedly. 'Her special treatment on Galea will not be extended beyond the estate, after all.'

'This is true,' Selene agreed. 'But let us worry about that another day. I think it is of more immediate importance to teach Cira *bear* etiquette. Cira, what do we *not* do with bears?'

'We do not wrestle with bears,' Cira said, trying to keep a straight face but unable to in the face of Selene's mock seriousness.

'That is correct! In fact, we do not go *near* bears. But since it is done, let us have a look at the consequences. I am afraid we will need to remove all the bandages to inspect the wound.'

Cira blanched. She dreaded the changing of the bandages around her calf. It was a hideously painful process - even more painful, she had decided while biting on a cloth to stop herself from screaming, than the actual goring itself. And it wasn't due again for another two days.

Selene caught her expression.

'I'm sorry Cira, but I *will* need to see it to see what I can do. Falric tells me that both the wound and the knee are proving - problematic - to treat.'

'Neither improves,' Flavia sighed. 'The doctor has done all he can. The wound is not infected, but still, it does not heal.'

The doctor had actually suggested cauterising the wound, and if that did not work, amputating the leg. Flavia had refused both, but she could also see that Cira could not live her whole life with her calf gouged open.

Cira lay on her front on her bed while Flavia carefully helped Selene remove the bandages. The girl was determined not to cry out in front of their guest, but could not hold back the tears that welled in the corners of her eyes as the final pad was removed, pulling off muck and scabbing with it. The wound smelled terrible, even though there was no infection. Flavia brought over warm water as requested then hovered around anxiously as Selene produced from her bag a clean cloth and bottle of what Cira soon painfully learned was alcohol. With no fuss at all, Selene began to clean the wound. It was huge. Brynir had gouged wide and deep, right to the bone, which by now should have been hidden by regrowing tissue.

'What kind of bear did you wrestle with?' Selene finally asked, sitting back to survey both the mess that was Cira's calf, and the girl's face. Selene's stare was challenging; Cira was desperate to tell the truth, in case knowing it was Brynir would better inform Selene how to treat her. But she could say nothing out loud.

*It wasn't a bear, it was Brynir the Cursed. It is not a natural wound!* she tried to say with her eyes. She had no idea whether Selene understood, but suddenly the Lady broke the lengthening silence with a bright smile and cheerful announcement.

'Well I'm sure I will have just the thing, *somewhere* in my bag of tricks.'

Selene washed her hands carefully, then started digging through the leather bag. Cira watched in amazement as she lined the kitchen table with more items than could possibly have fitted into the bag they came out of. Cira noticed that while her mother looked bemused, she did not appear surprised at the physical impossibility of the display before them.

Selene eventually made a happy exclamation upon finding a jar of what looked like a greenish grey mud.

'This is the one,' she announced, holding it up triumphantly. 'I must warn you, it smells utterly dreadful, but then, so does the wound, so not to worry.'

Selene daubed a clean cloth into the jar and then

applied the ointment liberally to the wound. It did indeed smell terrible, acrid and fermented, but to Cira's astonishment, the wound almost immediately began to feel less painful. The sickness she always felt during bandage changes began to recede.

'What *is* that? It's amazing!' she asked, awed. Flavia shot a desperate but hopeful glance to Selene, who smiled.

'It's a secret home remedy of mine, enormously powerful if I do say do myself. If anything can heal this wound, that'll do it.'

She held up her hands though as Cira's face lit up.

'Don't get too excited yet,' she warned. 'We won't know for *sure* for a few days if it's doing the job.'

Cira's face fell a little.

'*However*, if it does work, it should ensure your calf will heal pretty much back to how it was before you so rudely interrupted the peaceful afternoon of an innocent bear.'

'*Innocent* bear?' Cira protested hotly.

'They only attack if *provoked*,' Selene said calmly, but there was an inflection in her tone and sharpness in her eyes that made Cira wonder whether Lady Selene Beckworth knew more of the truth of the matter.

'Your knee is another matter though,' Selene continued, prodding the inflamed joint. This time Cira did squeak in pain.

'This, I am afraid, there is no secret balm for. Flavia, I will show you how the knee should be strapped. Cira, I can give you another lotion to reduce the pain and swelling of the joint, and with the right strapping and *extremely* good behaviour on your part, the knee will improve. With your calf healed as well, you will regain some use of your right leg.'

Cira looked appalled; Flavia resigned.

'*Some* use?' Cira asked, weakly.

'This is a much better prognosis than you had prior to my treatments,' Selene said. 'The wound was not...natural. It might never have healed. The strapping will allow your knee to bear weight again. However, I have seen many knee injuries like this, and I am afraid it will never be the same again.'

Cira's face fell again, but Selene continued relentlessly.

'One bad step, one bad fall, one bad twist, and you will tear the ligaments and tendons again. You must understand this. This knee will always be fragile. You will have to take *extremely* good care of it for the rest of your days. *Do* you understand?'

Cira nodded, numbly.

'What *will* I be able to do?' she asked, quietly.

'You will be able to shoot,' Selene said. 'With strapping, you *will* be able to ride again. On that which Lyschiva destroys, Chal'Om creates. You will be able to become a *very* good horseback archer. The bow I gave you is not a normal bow, it's a horse bow.'

Cira's eyes widened at this – she had never seen a bow like it before, and now understood why

'You will be able to continue your education. You will be able to be Jordan's best friend. You will be able to help your mother on the estate. You will walk unaided,' Selene continued.

Flavia looked relieved at all this good news. Cira was relieved that she would walk and especially ride again, and she liked the idea of being a horse archer. But she had wanted more.

She had dreamed of so much more.

As though reading her mind, Selene looked upon her sternly.

'You will not, however, be able to dress up as a boy and run away to join the Order of the Coeur with Jordan,' she said firmly. 'Do you understand, Cira?'

Flavia looked first astonished, then laughed uneasily, assuming it was a joke. It was, after all, a ridiculous idea.

Cira avoided both women's eyes and nodded mutely.

'Good!' Selene said brightly. 'Right, let's re-dress this wound and see how we do, shall we?'

Lady Beckworth left the Galea Estate two days later, satisfied with her patient's progress. Cira's calf had *finally* started to heal. The vile smelling ointment and strapping method Selene taught Flavia both made a huge difference.

Before she left, Selene had a private meeting with Lord Falric in his study; the second of her stay. During the first, he had told her the fabricated bear attack story he and the children had agreed on. During the second, she had more information and she wasn't afraid to use it.

'That was no bear that attacked Cira,' she opened, settling into one of the deep leather chairs in Falric's private study. She gave him a challenging look.

'I have seen wounds like that, but not for a very long time. And I know Aethon was sighted in the counties in the autumn. So tell me, nephew: how did two children of the Backwind escape from Brynir the Cursed?'

Falric maintained a very solid poker face, but his right eye did twitch slightly at the last three words.

'The three of you have lied uniformly to me. I will be generous and assume there is a very good reason for this, but I assure you, Falric, you do more harm than good in hiding the truth from me. It is very likely that I can help.'

Falric's poker face faltered.

'I can also keep making educated guesses.'

Falric briefly struggled with himself, but found himself unable to lie to his aunt. He told her the truth of what had happened to Jordan and Cira in Leaverness - reluctantly at first, but increasingly confidently as she listened gravely. She correctly predicted sections of the story before told, and validated his concerns.

'You are right to keep all of this secret,' she said when the tale was done. 'As always, you show outstandingly good judgement, my nephew.'

But instead of showing pleasure at the praise, Falric looked uneasy.

'Speak freely, Falric,' Selene said.

He took a steadying breath.

'You have demanded truth from me. But you have not always been honest yourself,' he said. It was true, but also a sensational accusation to make against one such as Lady Selene Beckworth.

'I do withhold information. But for the same reasons you initially lied to me,' she replied calmly. 'To protect the concerns of others.'

'You came here because of Cira,' he said.

'I did,' Selene agreed. 'Obviously I enjoy seeing you and Flavia and escaping from the bustle of the city. It does one so much good to take in the country air. But I did need to see if I could help her. You were right to tell me about her injuries.'

Falric cocked his head to one side as he considered his next question.

'Forgive me, Selene, but are you this concerned for the

welfare of all the orphaned infants you deliver to their aunts to raise? Who was Cira's true mother - or father - that she is so important to you?'

Selene also carefully considered her reply.

'Most of what you and dear Lady Falric suspected about Flavia and Cira are correct,' she said finally.

Falric's eyes widened.

'Cira is not even Flavia's niece, much less daughter?'

'She is not.'

'Flavia knows this?'

'Of course. She has no siblings,' Selene shrugged.

'But Cira knows nothing of it?'

'Correct, and this is for the best for everyone involved. In all the most important ways, Flavia is her mother.'

'And Flavia…she worked…for you? For your - business?' Falric asked, awkwardly.

'She did,' Selene said. 'She fell pregnant, and she wished to keep the child and leave my employ, of which I was completely supportive. But she had a tragic, late miscarriage. In her grief, she wished to leave Avenel and start a different life. When I heard you had a vacancy in your household, I saw a perfect solution for you both.'

'I thought that she was sad, when she arrived,' Falric reflected. 'She was happier when Jordan was born, but even then, there was a tinge of sadness in her love for him. I don't believe I saw her truly happy until you brought Cira here.'

'Indeed. When I found an unexpected infant in my care, I could immediately think of no-one better to take her to. Even better, you had Jordan, just a year older, to raise on Galea. Again, another perfect solution presented itself to me.'

'Why did you both lie about where Cira came from?' Falric said.

'Flavia was your head of household. It was hardly convenient for you to have me ask her to raise a stranger's child. You are a good man though, who I knew would not refuse to allow her raise her own niece,' Selene said.

Falric went to argue that she underestimated him, but on consideration, let the protest slide off his tongue. It was true. In hindsight, having the two children growing up together had been a compilation of blessings, but Lady Falric had been dubious about the head of their household adopting an infant a year younger than her own. When Falric lost his beloved wife to illness a couple of years later, Flavia had gravitated naturally into an additional parenting role for Jordan. She could not ease the aching loneliness Falric felt, but she had filled a maternal hole in his son's life. And her daughter - of sorts - had become his son's best friend.

The memories stung, so he changed tack.

'Then who *is* she?'

'She is Cira of the Backwind. She is Flavia's daughter, Jordan's best friend, and I am acting as her secret godmother. I have no children of my own, Falric, it is not for me to raise a child. But if I could have, I would have raised Cira. So yes, she is important to me.'

Falric waited, but Selene's confession appeared complete.

Except that he was certain it was not.

'And?' he pressed boldly.

Selene smiled.

'What a wily old fox you are. I have told you some secrets, but they are not *all* mine to tell. You will find out all things in their own time. And until then, I must beg more patience, discretion and secrecy on your part.'

Her exquisite right eyebrow remained lifted, awaiting his answer.

Reluctantly, he finally nodded.

'I am, as always, your faithful servant, Selene,' he said, a little too formally.

She beamed, instantly melting his frustrations.

'It's going to be a good secret when it comes out though, isn't it?' he asked hopefully.

'Oh my dear Falric. It's going to be the *best*.'

# 4. The Red Knight

Lord Falric decided there was definitely something supernatural about his aunt's ointments. In the weeks after Selene's visit, after months of no progress at all, Cira's calf suddenly healed unnaturally well. Large gouge injuries from animals were not unknown in a village on the edge of an infamously dangerous forest, and to the best of everyone's knowledge, Cira's calf muscle should not have been growing back in the way it was. Every bandage change showed rapidly increasing tissue mass though, and a month later, Flavia announced -to her own disbelief as much as that of others -that no further bandaging would be needed. Falric asked to see the miraculous calf himself and inspected it closely, first on its own, then next to Cira's other leg. They were identical in size and shape, and but for the broad pale scarring on the right one, it was impossible to imagine that back in the autumn Brynir had made a bloodied crater of it.

Cira would have liked very much to be trying out her healed calf by running amok with Jordan and riding her pony; she was prevented from doing so though by her knee, which was healing more slowly, in a natural manner. Flavia had carefully followed Lady Beckworth's strapping instructions, and after consulting experts in Avenel, Selene had also posted a design for a brace for Tomas to make. Cira hated it: it was an awkward contraption that rubbed painfully in places, and while it ensured she could not twist her knee to set back its recovery, it made it impossible for her to run, jump or ride. However, all the adults explained to her at length - and repeatedly - how important it was to allow the knee to heal fully: she was, Falric improvised, "buying" future years of running and riding with this time of patience. If she rushed, she might have even more trouble with it than already expected. This was a concept Cira grudgingly understood, and as she planned to have much running about and riding ahead of her, she paid her dues, albeit reluctantly. She did find herself becoming desperately envious however whenever she saw anyone else - and especially Jordan - on horseback. She kept this to herself though, maintaining her bright and breezy public disposition.

Nonetheless with the calf bandaging completed, Cira was permitted more mobility, on the condition she did not ride, run, jump or make quick changes of direction. With the chilly grip of winter fully surrendered to bright glory of spring, the late afternoons tended to find the children once more taking every opportunity to play - albeit carefully - outside.

On one such afternoon they were play-fighting with make-shift wooden swords in the stable yard. Cira couldn't do much in the way of fancy footwork but that certainly didn't stop her waving her weapon around with great aplomb. They considered themselves to be "training" for their heroic destinies in the service of a king they would cunningly find a way to restore to the throne - without anyone dying, obviously. But given that neither had any formal training or natural flair for sword play whatsoever, it amounted to little more than much shouting, enthusiastic grunting and frenzied clashing across the flagstones until either one of the children - or their swords - gave out. Cira's splintering sword was only a few more blows from the casualty list when she saw an unexpected shape out of the corner of one eye. Distracted, she messed up her parry; Jordan's ballistic overhead strike shattered Cira's sword into two jagged sections. She was too occupied with the object of her distraction to be concerned though. Jordan had only a moment of triumph before following Cira's gaze. Seeing a stranger leaning on the yard tie-up rail, his bay horse quietly tethered next to him, Jordan faltered, mid-gloat.

At first glance the man was not actually the children's main interest: it was his horse that bedazzled them. He was the second largest they had ever seen. In fact the word "horse" seemed grossly short change for an animal like this; "charger" leapt immediately to mind, along with a mental footnote never to get in the way of his full gallop - he could flatten a child without even noticing. His coat was an immaculate burnished red and his hooves were wider than Cira's hand with fingers fully spread, yet he was finer and more majestic than any of the heavy workhorses of the Backwind. It would be unthinkable to harness such an animal to a cart or dray.

The charger's rider watched the children with interest. Over cream breeches and knee-high leather boots he wore a tunic of deep scarlet, a more beautiful garment than even Lord Falric's finest attire. A mane of dark hair shot through with grey tumbled over rugged square-jawed features. There was something intrinsically majestic in his bearing: something you couldn't quite put your finger on but *felt* the moment you looked upon him.

'He looks like a king,' Jordan breathed. Having never met one, he had no idea what a king actually looked like, but if he had to guess, he would guess one looked a lot like the visitor.

'He's a knight. Has to be,' Cira whispered out of the side of her mouth.

Jordan's face lit up with awe.

The man who looked like a king but had to be a knight beckoned the children forth with one gloved hand.

'How do you talk to a king or knight?' Jordan panicked quietly. 'You're much better at all this ye olde world stuff, Cira, you do the talking.'

Cira was not certain that knights actually spoke with *ye* and *thou* outside Lord Falric's enthusiastic storytelling, but she supposed there was only one way to find out. She and Jordan came shyly forward. Close up, the stranger was even more impressive: given the breadth of his body under his tunic and riding jacket, it was evident that he was muscular and powerful. Measured across his shoulder span, he was nearly twice the man Falric was.

'Good day, Sir…?' Cira offered, trying to sound respectful but not awestruck. As his face showed no indication of whether it was indeed a good day or not, she felt some follow-up was required. 'May we be of some service to ye?'

The corners of the probably-knight's eyes crinkled with amusement.

'To *you*. Service. Us, to you?' she rambled, desperately glancing to Jordan for help, of which he was exactly none.

Now the corners of the knight's mouth were definitely twitching towards a smile.

'Oh bother it, you know what I mean,' she sighed, surrendering the polite air she had no idea how to use anyway.

'I do indeed,' the stranger said in a voice Cira considered *thrillingly* deep.

*'He sounds like a king too,'* Jordan whispered, far too loudly.

'A king? Me? I am afraid I must disappoint you. I am but a humble knight. Sir Bane, at your service,' the not-king-but-confirmed-knight said, bowing his head slightly. Cira furrowed her brow: she knew she'd heard that name, and recently.

'However, I come looking for a boy who *could* be king,' Sir Bane continued. He directed this last statement straight to Jordan, whose face lit up for a moment before Cira's heel grinding against his toes brought him back to reality.

'Don't know any could-be-kings, Sir,' Jordan managed painfully, rewarded with the release of his toes.

'You must be Jordan,' Bane said, full of charm, 'and you must be Cira?'

That temporarily stalled even Cira.

*'He knows who we are!'* Jordan whispered, happy enough to die right there and then, fully satisfied in life.

'You're the knight who summoned Mama Aksaya,' Cira said suddenly, as the thought hit her tongue before her brain could filter it. Bane looked first surprised, and then his eyes narrowed curiously.

'Now why would two children of the Backwind know that, I wonder?' he said, and Cira knew she had screwed up.

'I am now convinced you can indeed be of assistance to me, and the great city of Avenel,' Bane continued silkily. 'I hear you had quite the adventure in Leaverness?'

'We have frequent adventures in Leaverness, Sir,' Cira said quickly.

'Tell me about your most recent one. I'm assuming it is the reason you're wearing that contraption on your knee, Cira,' Bane said.

'Well we went for a ride and we got lost and we ran into a bear which scared our horses so they threw us off and while we were on the ground it attacked Cira but a boy from a nearby town saved us and took us home and that's absolutely all that happened!!' Jordan narrated briskly, sticking perfectly to the script with only a mild lack of punctuation and the addition of a few extra exclamation marks and a gasp of air at the end.

'And that's *absolutely* all that happened…?' the knight asked, one eyebrow raised sceptically.

'Pretty much sums it up, Sir,' Cira agreed, nodding in unison with Jordan.

'You didn't meet anyone else out there?'

'Just the boy who saved us. He wouldn't tell us his name though, because he wasn't allowed to be alone in Leaverness, and he was afraid of being beaten by his father,' Cira said. 'Sir.'

'He must have been very brave, this boy, saving you from a bear,' Sir Bane said thoughtfully. 'How old was he?'

The children paused a moment: no-one else had asked them this.

'About our age I'd say,' Jordan hazarded, looking to Cira for support.

'Might have been. Might have been older though. Much older. It was getting dark,' Cira mused unhelpfully.

'And how old would you both be?' Bane asked politely.

'I'm twelve and Cira is eleven years old,' Jordan said, proudly.

'Eleven and twelve, fancy that,' Bane said. 'Tell me,

have you ever come across anyone else in your adventures in the forest?'

'In Leaverness?' Cira said, a picture of polite surprise. 'No-one else from the Backwind is foolish enough to venture out there alone.'

'What about someone *not* from the Backwind?' the knight asked.

The children shook their heads.

'What about some-one *from* Leaverness?' Bane pressed.

'*Ohhh,* you mean the People?' Cira looked to Jordan. 'Never seen any of them, have we, Jordo?' she asked. He shook his head emphatically.

'Nope, I don't know anybody who's seen anyone from the People,' he concurred.

They smiled with strained innocence.

'I have seen them,' Bane said, his tone less casual now. 'Best you keep it that way. They'd have a pair of children like you for breakfast.'

'I heard they're very peaceful,' Cira said, meeting and holding Bane's gaze.

'Have you now? Perhaps you shouldn't believe everything you hear,' he said, his tone cooling. And then he smoothly changed gears, producing a warm smile once more.

'It is of no matter,' Bane said. 'But from what I've seen, I think perhaps I can help you.' He nodded to their battered excuses for swords. 'Would you permit me the honour of teaching you some real swordplay?'

This was how Lord Falric found the three of them: one of the greatest knights of the Order of the Coeur with a dodgy wooden sword in each hand, simultaneously sparring with both children while coaching them on the most basic points of swordsmanship. Cira and Jordan were having too much fun to clock Falric's approach and so they missed his deep frown, for he had re-arranged his face into a more civil expression by the time he drew close. The knight, on the other hand, saw everything, and expected nothing less.

'Sir Bane, I am honoured. But also puzzled: what brings the Red Knight to my humble estate, so far from Avenel?' Falric asked cordially. 'It is hardly where I would expect to find one of the Five.'

The children shared an astonished look: *one of the Five?* Cira looked at Bane again with eyes anew: his towering frame, his movement quick and light despite his mass, his regal bearing. Indeed, he could be no ordinary knight, but she would never dare dream to meet one of the Five, the King's elite Guard. Only the greatest of men were honoured with the mantle of the Red, Blue, Green or Gold Knight, and it was the greatest of even those who became the Knight Operis, and rode under the royal purple banner.

Cira and Jordan were now even more awed than they had already been, which was quite a lot to start with. They knew from epic stories and poems that the Red Knight was typically a man of great charisma, one who embodied the spirit of the phoenix, the element of fire and was represented by the symbol of a candle. He was the summer, the south and the noon. The Red Knight was a coveted position, and here and now, Sir Bane was he - which made him, in short, the closest the children had ever been to a living legend. Aethon notwithstanding, of course.

Now practically glowing in their eyes, the Red Knight

strode to Falric with feline grace and removed one glove to shake the Lord's hand. Cira squinted to see his signet ring: a silver band embossed with a ruby flame.

'Lord Falric.'

Bane closed the shake in a vice-like grip; with no hope of competing, Falric settled for a defiant bearing to hide the immediate loss of feeling from his right hand.

'I have come to hear stories of Leaverness,' Bane said. 'I understand you are the expert on such matters, and that the children here have had - interesting - adventures there of late.'

What Falric thought was *So. Word of Lien has made it back to Avenel.*

What he said, however, was 'I am your humble servant, Sir Bane,' though with a pointed lack of subservience.

'And are you likewise a humble servant to the Avenel throne?' Bane asked so lazily that Falric felt the hair pricking on the back of his neck: he felt like prey trapped by a lion enjoying playing with its dinner. One of the Five would not have ridden the many days between Avenel and the Backwind to sit around chatting about the beautiful, rare and fearsome flora and fauna of the forest. And more important than Falric's loyalties would be those of Sir Bane, for the lord knew that if the Red Knight was a monarchist - which he had surely been when he had taken the risk of summoning Mama Aksaya - he would pluck Lien out of Leaverness without hesitation or concern for his welfare, or that of his surrogate family. And that was by far the better option for the boy. For if, in the years since he had consulted Aksaya, Bane had switched allegiance to the Council of Voltanna, the inconvenient discovery of a potential heir in Leaverness surely meant his presence in the Backwind would be to ensure that the boy was never seen again.

'I was a faithful subject of King Du Romeau, and am now obedient to the Council of Voltanna,' Falric said, striking out for neutral ground.

'As are we all, my lord, as are we all. The Council has done a commendable job holding the empire together. However, searching for Du Romeau's heir continues to be a pastime of the Order, and all crown loyalists,' Bane said conversationally. In the expanding, suggestive silence, Falric grappled over how best to take the hanging bait.

'If I see sight or sound of a prospective heir, you will be the first person I inform, Sir Bane. I doubt that you will find him in the Backwind though. And I apologise for your wasted journey, for if there is a particular story you seek about the lost heir, I am afraid there is no-one here who can tell it.'

Bane considered the man and two children before him.

'Perhaps I have been misled,' he said, looking from Falric to Jordan, who, unlike his father, was a terrible liar, and whose face was a picture that might not have quite have said a thousand words but certainly covered all of the important ones. Falric, following the knight's gaze, made a mental note to start developing his son's poker face.

'I would not consider a ride to the Backwind wasted, however.' Bane glanced around at the neat but, by Avenel standards, quaint stable yard. 'It is such a charming region,' he said graciously. 'And besides, times are quiet in Avenel at the moment.'

'I have heard many stories of unrest from the city,' Falric countered warily.

'Political unrest,' Bane sniffed. 'Quiet waters that run

deep, for certain, but knights, it would seem, cannot slay monsters who wear the faces of gentlemen.'

Bane stared pointedly to where tips of Leaverness' trees reached over the stable rooftop and towards the darkening afternoon sky.

'Times are changing, Lord Falric, and we must all decide whether we are willing to change with them, or not. There are many in the city now who would consider it - how shall I say - *unfortunate* if something were to disrupt the course of that change. Something say, from the past. Something that was lost, that they feel perhaps should not be found.'

Meeting those searching, azure eyes, Falric knew they had failed to protect Lien.

'And what of you, Sir Bane? Are you an ambassador of these changes?' Falric asked. He had to know on which side the knight stood.

'My Lord Falric, what use is a knight of the crown with no king to serve?' Bane asked seriously. 'I know you have told the children that I invoked Mama Aksaya to find out whether we were searching in vain. Since she told me that the heir lives, I have never stopped searching, and I shall not, until he is found and restored to his throne. So if you do hear anything I might consider relevant, I fully expect you will send word to me with due haste.'

Jordan stole a side glance to his father; he considered the move subtle, but it was glaringly obvious to Bane. Falric's face remained studiously blank though as he agreed he would, and offered the knight lodging in the manor before his return to Avenel. He was now at least convinced Bane would not kill Lien, but he knew the boy's future, and safety, was very uncertain.

*****

There was one more unexpected visitor to the Galea Estate as a result of the children's adventure following Aethon. She was Lien's honorary aunt, and she rode into the Backwind over the Bridge from Tauron'Est, an ancient Phaedran fortress deep within Leaverness, where she had been visiting the People. She had spoken to Bravo and Lien and then conferenced privately with Sky over what to do about the boys' well-meaning, but dangerous, actions in the Falseweald. Lien was by this time long since recovered from his battle with Brynir, but for his own scarring to remember the adventure by. Unlike the doctors of the Backwind, the People knew how to deal with wounds left by the claws of creatures such as Brynir, and Sky had ensured Lien's wounds were treated appropriately from the outset.

Lien and Bravo had not exactly been in trouble on their return home that night, but had an amazingly similar conversation with Sky to the one Cira and Jordan had with Falric, resulting in a cover story wherein they too ran into a bear and certainly neither saw nor were seen by any children of the Backwind. Sky doubled down on his blanket explanation that none of the People must ever be seen by outsiders, and left any more specific explanations for Lien's aunt, the woman who had brought him to them a decade earlier with the unprecedented request they raise and protect an outsider child. There were many among the tribe who had objected to the idea, and were still uneasy about Lien's presence, all too aware of the dangers the boy - himself blissfully unaware of - presented to them.

Cira and Jordan were in school when Falric, working in his study, felt a pricking at the back of his neck. He had a sensitivity to espréi that was rare in mortal folk of the new world. He didn't understand that though, and so simply considered himself to have a sixth sense for what he considered the magical and supernatural. Apprehensive at the feeling, he closed the manuscript he was working on, fetched his coat and strode in haste out to the stables, just in time to see the great black stallion Erebus enter the yard. Falric suspected Selene Beckworth's ointments to have unnatural origins, but he *knew* Erebus was not a natural horse. It was difficult to explain how being in his presence made people feel, but Falric had decided that Erebus was not "a" horse; he was more "the" horse. Like the ultimate horse, the king of horses, he represented complete horse-ness. As always, all the estate horses and ponies had already sensed his arrival: every head was hanging out over the stable doors, all ears keenly pricked forward, all eyes on the big stallion. Where most horses would trot, Erebus effortlessly floated into the yard in a flashy, elevated pace the professional trainers called the *passage*. It took years for trainers to achieve the passage in normal horses; the black stallion passaged naturally, entirely by his own choice and with effortless flair. He wore an ornate bitless bridle and deep black saddle with elegantly engraved leather saddle bags strapped behind. The bags would have taken up most of the back of a normal horse, but looked perfectly in proportion on him.

His rider beamed when she saw Falric. He beamed back.

'Areté!' he greeted her warmly as she lightly dismounted.

'Falric!' she returned with equal warmth, extending her right arm. Where Selene was an enthusiastic hugger of good friends, Areté was greeted in a warrior's way: forearm to forearm, firmly clasping one another at the elbow. She wore a deep purple leather and brass armoured bodice and gauntlets over a full-sleeve tunic, dark brown leather trousers and black knee-high leather boots. A sword was strapped in a scabbard on her back. Her rich auburn hair was gathered in a loose plait over her left shoulder, and her blue-green eyes shone with good nature. But for her skin...she was pale as the moon. Before encountering Bravo, Cira and Jordan had met only one white person in their lives, and that was Areté.

'It is so good to see you, old man,' she continued happily.

'Likewise. It has certainly been too long,' Falric replied, still smiling. Areté had that effect on people: she had a contagious lightness about her.

'The children will be delighted to see you.'

'And I them, but it is with you that I must speak first,' she said, with a slight incline of her head towards Tomas. The stable master was standing at the entrance to the stables, pitchfork in hand and eyes wide as he beheld Erebus.

Falric nodded his understanding.

'Tomas, would you be so kind as to take Erebus, and tell the children there's a special visitor in the stables when he is settled?' he called to his stable master. The pitchfork immediately disappeared out of sight and Tomas eagerly approached.

'It would be my honour, sir,' he said, clearly besotted with the black horse. He gave Areté a respectful nod as she handed over the reins, then turned his full attention to his new charge.

'Who's a good boy, Erebus? Who wants the finest bran

mash with extra molasses?' Tomas fussed the stallion as he led him away, his usual slouch abandoned as he proudly led the greatest of all horses to his stable. Areté gave Erebus an affectionate clap on his hind quarters as he followed Tomas away, but the horse was oblivious, already playfully frisking Tomas' pockets for carrots or sugar.

'You've made Tomas' year,' Falric observed.

'Era tends to have that effect on horse lovers,' Areté smiled. The children would squeal with delight when they saw him and easily spend the whole afternoon clambering all over him and plaiting his mane and tail. Areté always rode away on the best turned out horse in the Backwind.

'Have you come from far?' Falric asked, noting the big horse had barely broken a sweat.

'From Tauron'Est,' Areté replied as they headed to the manor house.

Falric paused his pace and raised an eyebrow. Tauron'Est was deep in Leaverness, within a secret valley that had a miraculously milder microclimate in even the coldest months of winter. Only the People knew of it, and it was the only permanent structure they used: a partially derelict fortress built before even Avenel. Areté had described and drawn parts of it for Falric, but it was not enough: he was desperate to one day see it for himself. This news also confirmed his suspicion that Areté was not here on a social call, but business, and he knew what business that would be.

After greeting and taking tea with Flavia in the manor drawing room, Areté and Falric retired to his private study. Knowing the topic would be serious, Falric offered the port Lady Beckworth had gifted him, which Areté inspected with bemusement.

'A gift from Selene?' she guessed as Falric poured the thick ruby liquor.

'Indeed,' he said, surprised. 'She was here just a few weeks ago.'

'I bet she was,' Areté said, taking a cautious whiff of the port. It was eye-wateringly strong, but one sip proved it to be smooth and sweet on the tongue: a truly remarkable liquor.

'Only the best from Lady Beckworth,' she said, savouring the finish. 'Have you had any other unexpected visitors?'

Falric's face sobered.

'Yes. I am afraid I suspect Tomas has done us a great disservice,' he said. He knew only Tomas, who had seen Lien with his own eyes, could have reasonable suspicion of the cover story, and so the word that had reached Sir Bane could only have come from the stable master's lips. Whether directly, or second hand, the consequence was the same.

'I see. He was with you when Lien returned Cira and Jordan to you?' she surmised.

Falric nodded.

'You have not spoken to or dismissed him though?' Areté asked curiously.

Falric looked conflicted.

'You have to understand, Areté, that Tomas is a good man. He's loyal to me, but he's loyal foremost to the crown. I myself considered whether I ought to go to Avenel to tell of what I saw.'

'I do understand,' Areté said, sipping the port again thoughtfully.

'But - *is* he though?' Falric asked suddenly, taking the plunge. He had to know the truth.

'Is who what, Falric?' Areté asked, a mischievous twinkle in her eyes.

He glared at her.

'You know what I mean. Is Lien *him?* The prince? The heir to the throne?'

'What did Selene tell you?' Areté asked, trying to hide a small smile.

'Nothing helpful,' Falric said darkly, expecting the same from his latest visitor.

'Lien is not the son of Du Romeau,' Areté said calmly. Falric's pessimism switched immediately to astonishment: he had not believed for a moment that he would get a straight answer out of her. The astonishment then switched to disbelief at what that answer had been.

'He's *not*?!' he managed, stunned.

Areté shook her head.

'I was so sure,' he said, shaking his head and slumping back in his chair with a heavy sigh. '*So* sure.'

'You did the right thing keeping him secret though,' Areté said, serious now. 'You are not the only one who will be certain they know who he is, and even if he is not, will try to fake him onto the throne anyway.'

'Is it really just a coincidence then?' Falric asked, frowning. 'An outsider boy around the age of the missing heir just...turning up with the People?'

'Do you think Aethon leading Cira and Jordan to Brynir was a coincidence?' Areté countered.

Falric considered what he knew of the unicorn and the cursed wolf beast. He thought of the picture he had shown the children.

'No,' he said slowly. 'Aethon is linked to Brynir. I don't know how, or why, but I'm sure.'

Falric dropped another figure into the mental calculations he was running.

'Leaverness is - extensive,' he said.

'Enormous,' Areté agreed.

'And Jordan and Cira were taken an impossibly long way in.'

'The Falseweald is certainly a few days ride from the Backwind.'

'And knowing Leaverness as you do - which is better than I, and I know it better than most - what do you consider the odds that these two children were led impossibly far by a unicorn, to meet a monster, from which they were saved by two other children, when there cannot be more than a hundred children in the entire, and we agree, *extensive*, forest?' Falric asked.

'I would call such odds astronomical, and consider that a generous appraisal,' Areté replied evenly. 'But let me remove all speculation that we are dealing with coincidence. Do you know how Lien and Bravo came across Cira and Jordan in their time of desperate need?'

Falric shook his head.

'They *also* followed Aethon that afternoon.'

Falric stared.

'There are powerful forces at work here, Falric, and we do not yet know if they conspire for, or against, the children,' Areté said.

'But - that's not fair. They are *only* children,' Falric protested.

'And we can only protect them as best we can. Now, tell me of your other recent visitations.'

As Falric told of the visits of Lady Beckworth and Sir Bane, Areté worked her way through the first glass of port and then a second.

'Bane will be searching for Lien now,' she said grimly. 'He will be convinced he has found his heir, and he is very persistent.'

'Can he find the People in Tauron'Est?' Falric asked anxiously.

'No, he won't be able to find them at all. Sky and I took care of that after the persecutions following...all of that bad business in Avenel. However, that protection doesn't help when Lien goes showing himself to people, so I'll be having some stronger words with him about that. But I conclude - and reluctantly - that at this point, merely protecting the children will not be enough. We will also have to prepare them whatever all of this may be leading to.'

'And how do we do that?' Falric asked.

'I understand Jordan has...chivalric ambitions,' Areté said.

'Of course he does, all boys do - in fact they *both* do - but Areté, you know he doesn't have the disposition for it. And he'll never let himself be separated from Cira. Who would be twice the knight he would, if we're being honest,' he added ruefully.

'I know. But - allow them to indulge the ambition. Train them in martial forms and sword play. We do not know what they may be facing, but we can at the very least give them a fighting chance - so to speak.'

Falric tried to stare her down but her gaze was unyielding.

'I'll see what I can do,' he sighed.

Areté returned to the stables, where Cira and Jordan were indeed all over Erebus, although in Cira's case, not literally, and her disappointment was clear. Tomas was keeping a close eye on the children to ensure Cira did not take off her brace and try to get on the black stallion. He knew Erebus would not harm the girl, but the shape of a horse that large was not conducive for repairing her knee, and he had warned her of such.

Cira and Jordan's faces lit up anew when they saw the visitor. They excitedly told her everything they had been up to since she had visited last, well over a year ago, sticking obediently to the script regarding their Leaverness adventure, for they had no idea of Areté's connection to the People or Lien. Falric noted some new embellishment around their meeting with the bear, which, in this version, they had withstood magnificently until Cira's injury. Areté listened with great interest and agreed with all the adults that Cira's knee would need to be looked after. But she slipped a folded note into the girl's trouser pocket with a sly wink. Later, when she was alone, Cira read it in astonishment.

*Dear Cira*

*When you are allowed to ride again, burn this note at midday, and then ride to the Bridge at midnight.*

*There you will find someone who may be of assistance to you.*

*Consider the price carefully before proceeding.*

*Tell no-one.*

Cira thoughtfully folded the bottom of the note up, seriously considering telling Jordan about it, when she realised there was writing on the back-side bottom as well.

*Not even Jordan!*

She laughed quietly - Areté was always a step ahead - and did indeed keep the secret to herself, even though she was desperate to share it. She actually felt terrible keeping something so exciting from her best friend.

Months later, when the brace finally came off and she was permitted to carefully ride again, Cira burned the note one afternoon in her cottage hearth as instructed. That night she lay determinedly awake in her bed, dressed in her riding clothes. It was now summer, and the evening would be mild for a sneaky midnight jaunt. The time until half past eleven - measured on a candle clock, and which she expected to pass excruciatingly slowly - actually passed like no time at all. With great excitement she padded quietly out of the cottage and walked to the stable yard. She wanted so much to run there, but did not. Could not. She could now walk unaided, and she could ride with strapping, but she still could not run or jump or twist and she was always painfully aware of how weak her right knee was.

Might always be.

To her astonishment she found Erebus in the stable yard, waiting quietly for her by the mounting block, tacked up in his beautiful saddle and bitless bridle. Unable to believe her eyes and her luck, she carefully made her way to the highest step on the block, which made even Erebus relatively easy to carefully lift her fragile right leg over. His saddle was like nothing she had ever sat in, it was so deep and comfortable. It should have been much too big for her, but it felt like it was holding her in place. Not that she expected Erebus would put a foot wrong. As soon as she was settled, thrilling at this new view of the yard from such a height, the black stallion set off at his huge trot. Cira gasped a moment, first at the enormous bounce of his strides but also expecting the sound of his hooves striking the cobbles to bring Tomas running from his room above the stables. But Erebus made no sound until he had cleared the village and settled into a smooth canter, his hooves now making thick *thud thudding* sounds on the hard ground. His long black mane streamed back into her chest and face in the wind generated by his speed. Cira couldn't stop grinning as the horse effortlessly travelled the distance to the Bridge in just a few minutes - which was the only disappointment, as she would have loved to ride him for hours, for *days*. She wondered how she would ever be satisfied riding even her beloved pony again after these mere minutes on Erebus.

To Cira's delight, the stallion did not stop at the Bridge as expected. He only steadied his pace to a trot to cross the old structure, before falling back into a canter on the other side. The ride would continue! But - into Leaverness. A bright full moon had bathed the Backwind and forest fringe in silver light, but once Erebus entered the forest proper, darkness closed in. Cira had not been into Leaverness since the night with Aethon, and felt a flutter of anxiety under her breastbone as she remembered the last time she had been out here in the dark. She trusted Erebus, and Areté, but her breath shortened nonetheless.

After only a few minutes further canter though, Erebus entered a moonlit clearing. In the centre stood a woman, or at least something that looked like a woman. The figure was spectral. Deathly white skin highlighted luminous amethyst eyes, dark lips and a mane of wild black hair. She was beautiful, for certain, but there was something deeply cold in her beauty, thrilling and frightening all at once. She wore a silver necklace of the crescent moon and was wrapped in a cloak that seemed to be made of a hundred swirling swatches of blacks, greys, purples and blues.

But the trepidation Cira felt at the sight of this wild apparition was not shared by Erebus. Quite the opposite in fact: the black stallion trotted straight to her, and contentedly rested his head into her open hands with a deep, relaxed sigh. It was a gesture of affection beyond what Cira had even seen him show even to Areté, whose horse he was. She felt there was a different, and perhaps deeper, bond between Erebus and this woman. The mysterious figure initially ignored Cira completely in favour of stroking the horse's long black face.

Eventually, the pale face and purple eyes looked up.

*Cira. Welcome. Do you know who I am?*

Cira flinched as the words arrived straight in her mind without leaving the woman's lips, or entering her own ears. They arrived with a primal chill - or was it a thrill? - down her spine. She couldn't speak. She wasn't even sure if she *should* speak. Could the figure read her mind as easily as she could speak into it?

*I am Shivaia.*

Again, the words - or rather, the meaning of the words, it was hard to tell - arrived directly in Cira's brain. Her eyes widened. Shivaia, the Dark Lady! Here was another of the constellations of the fresco in Falric's astronomy tower come to life. She was going to have a lot of questions for him tomorrow.

*I will have need of your services.*

Now Cira stared dumbly at the haunting, impassive face below her. This seemed unlikely: how could an immortal being need *her* services?

And then, with the same suddenness and clarity with which Shivaia's words appeared in her mind, she decided herself that none of this could be real.

*You think this is a dream.*

Cira started, again, realising her mind had been read. But she nodded anyway.

*Does this feel like a dream?*

Cira considered. The cool midnight air on her cheeks felt real. The supple leather reins in her gloved hands felt real. The radiating heat of Erebus, the tilt of his deep comfortable saddle as he bent one back leg into a resting position, the spill of his mane onto her thighs: these all felt real. And the sequence of events of the evening had been fundamentally logical - even if unfathomable - unlike a dream.

She met the amethyst eyes. She could not bring herself to nod.

Shivaia seemed satisfied.

*I offer you an Arrangement. For services you will do for me in the future, I will grant you a favour now.*

*How far in the future?* Cira wondered.

*That is not in my power to foresee. Do you understand the terms of an Arrangement?*

Cira shook her head.

*It is an unbreakable pact between two parties. It can work in one of two ways. One party can seek a specific boon – or favour – of another, which will require them to perform a boon in return. Or one party can offer a boon to another, which will also require a boon in return. In both cases, there is no disclosure of the nature of the return favour.*

*That doesn't seem fair*, Cira thought.

*An Arrangement is not intended to be fair. It is not a frivolous bargain.*

Cira recalled Falric's explanation of the "act" Sir Bane would have to perform for Mama Aksaya in return for finding out whether the heir lived.

*That was indeed an Arrangement. It is particularly dangerous to enter into an Arrangement with 'Mama Aksaya though.*

*Are you less dangerous?* Cira wondered.

*I am. I am even willing to disclose the return boon, for you are only a child, and it is I who have come to you. But for this concession, there will be a condition to the favour I do for you.*

*What is it that you want from me?* Cira thought.

*When you take the name Citar, I will require you to seek out and, whatever the dangers you encounter, ally yourself to and protect the Mandala.*

*When I take the name of Citar? I will become a knight?!* Cira practically shouted internally, she was so elated.

*You will require this Arrangement for that to happen, and later to seek out Praxidice. When the time comes.*

*Who is Praxidice?! How will I know when the time comes?*

*You will know.*

*And what is the Mandala?* Cira asked, trying to drag her attention from the excitement that she would become a knight with Jordan. She searched her memory for any reference to the name but found none. Was it a person? An Essene? A title?

*Lord Falric is yet to complete your classical education. Prompt him on this subject.*

Shivaia held Cira's gaze with her beautiful, cold eyes.

*Cira. Do you wish to enter into this binding Arrangement with me?*

*You can heal my knee?* Cira asked, not daring to hope.

*I can.*

*Then yes! Yes please! I wish to enter this Arrangement!*

It was that simple to change her life, her future, her destiny.

Shivaia nodded and walked to Erebus' right side. She placed her hands on Cira's damaged knee. Her touch was glacial, even through Cira's thick riding trousers. The girl stiffened involuntarily; the spectral figure lifted a gently reprimanding eye brow. Cira exhaled, forcing herself to relax. Shivaia closed her eyes, concentrating. Cira gasped aloud as a series of contradictory sensations ran through her knee: alternating hot and cold, like she was between fire and ice. Her knee was burning then freezing in turn. Shivaia ignored her gasps and twitches, instead impassively holding her knee lightly between her hands for what seemed like an hour. It was probably only a few minutes but all of them were exquisitely painful. Cira bit her lip eventually to distract from the pain; and then it was over, as suddenly as it started.

Shivaia released her knee and stepped back, stroking Erebus again.

*Your knee is healed.*

Cira rapidly blinked back the tears that had formed in the corner of her eyes. She was shaking. She kicked out her right stirrup and cautiously straightened her knee.

It did not hurt.

'Th-thank you,' she stammered, finally able to use her voice again. The pain had been the worst she had ever experienced - worse than the bandage changes - but if her knee was healed? That was literally life changing. Cira would exchange a lot more pain for that. She roughly wiped the tears away.

'Thank you! Thank you so much,' she said, the gratitude she felt now evident in her voice. 'I mean I don't understand all of this, but – thank you!'

Cira found herself almost lightheaded with joy. She and Jordan would be knights! Wait until she told Jordan about all of this this! Now they could play and fight as normal, they could start their knight training –

*I said my favour to you was conditional.*

Cira froze. She had completely forgotten that. To be honest, she hadn't really paid attention to it.

*You may tell no-one that your knee is healed.*

Cira gaped as her plans were punctured.

'I don't – I don't understand,' she started. Surely she could tell Jordan –

*Not even Jordan. For as long as you are Cira of the Backwind, you will act as though your knee is still damaged. In front of others, you will train only in the ways you are permitted. You will wear the strapping Lady Beckworth prescribed for you.*

Cira stared. Cira of the Backwind? What did that even mean? And such a pretence – it would be so *boring* to pretend to still be injured –

*If you do not do this, Cira, you will learn that what is given, may also be taken away. An Arrangement is a sacred pact. You entered willingly.*

*But I didn't know what the condition would be!* she thought bitterly.

*And if you had thought to ask, would you have refused*

*to have your knee healed?*

Cira pulled herself together. Of course she would not have refused.

*Erebus will return you home.*

The black lips broke into a gentle smile.

*I will ask him to take you on the scenic route this time, that you may enjoy your ride.*

Shivaia gave Erebus a last affectionate pat on the neck while Cira tried to organise her thoughts and mouth into words. Which words though? The questions she had? More thanks she felt she ought to give? But the black stallion was already turning to leave the clearing and then breaking into his rolling canter. Cira automatically gathered the reins but knew she would not need them. She took her attention to her right knee, discovering that she was able to close her leg right around the big barrelled horse without any stiffness or discomfort. A wild smile escaped her lips: she was healed!

Erebus did indeed take her on a thrilling, scenic route home, galloping through Leaverness and circling the moonlit counties around the Backwind, before dropping her home just before the sun rose. She slid the long drop from his high back, marvelling at the way her right knee bent naturally to absorb the impact without any pain at all. As Erebus rubbed his face along her chest she dug around in a pocket for the sugar she had bought for her own pony. The stallion slurped it up gratefully before turning to canter out of the yard. Again, his hooves made no sound. And without any pain or limp, Cira jogged joyfully back to her room in her mother's quiet cottage.

The next morning Cira was woken by her mother, who told her they were both needed over at the manor house as soon as possible, for the estate had been ravaged by an unexpected and violent overnight storm.

'The front hit around midnight, I don't know how you slept through it,' Flavia said as she quickly prepared gruel for their breakfast. 'I checked on you twice, you were completely under. Why did you waste a clock candle? You know they are expensive. And *why* did you go to bed fully clothed?'

Cira blinked, confused. She had ridden Erebus out at midnight. There had been no storm.

She cautiously straightened her injured knee in bed – and still felt no pain.

She got out of bed, stepping gingerly onto her injured leg, and found it was still completely healed. She almost ran to the window to see the world outside, but heard the Dark Lady's warning ringing in her ears.

*You may tell no-one that your knee is healed.*

Cira immediately proceeded to limp appropriately to the window, from which Flavia had already pulled back the shutters. Sure enough, she could see vast puddles and fallen branches that could only have been caused by a serious storm.

'I didn't hear a thing,' she said slowly.

'Must have been quite the dream you were having. I heard you cry out once,' her mother said, serving up the gruel with honey.

~

It was more than a week before the children had a class with Lord Falric again, a week within which Cira flicked through every book she could lay her hands on, searching fruitlessly for any reference to the mysterious Mandala and Praxidice. She sat restlessly through an hour of Falric educating them about the dangerous plants of Leaverness, until finally, at the end, he asked whether either of the children had any questions. Cira's hand shot up so fast that it practically took one of Falric's eyebrows with it: he had not expected any urgent questions about poisonous plants.

'Sir, what is the Mandala?' she asked with forced nonchalance, realising she had shown too much initial excitement.

Falric frowned deeply at the question, fixing Cira with a curious look.

'The Mandala? Where did you hear about that, Cira?' he asked after a long pause. Jordan too looked curiously at Cira, for she had not mentioned the name to him either, and it was unlike her to keep anything to herself.

'In a dream,' Cira said promptly. She had thought long and hard about how she would explain the origin of her question, and unable to come up with any convincing lie, had decided to tell the truth. She had such a rich imagination she was certain she could get away with it.

'I dreamt that I met Shivaia, and she told me to find the Mandala,' she said boldly.

Both father and son stared at her in complementary puzzlement: Falric that she could have had such a specific dream of things she should know nothing about, and

Jordan that she had not told him of the dream.

'I mean I didn't think anything of it at the time,' she continued, with an innocent look to Jordan. 'I'd forgotten about it, to be honest, it just came back to me now.' She shrugged. 'You know how dreams are. I don't even know if the Mandala is a real thing! But if it is, I figured you would know, Sir,' she continued, now turning her attention to Lord Falric. He met her gaze steadily for a few long seconds, then seemed to accept the explanation with a short nod.

'Well. That is the question. Is it real, or is it not? I've never met anyone who has encountered it,' Falric said. 'But then, I had never met anyone who had encountered Brynir until you two blundered into him,' he added wryly.

'But what *is* it?' Jordan asked.

'I'm honestly not sure, Jordan,' Falric replied. 'I'm not being obscure, I promise. So I will tell you what I know, and then you can decide what *you* think it is.'

Falric sat back in his chair, a thoughtful look on his face as he decided how to proceed. The children leaned forwards in theirs, rapt by this unexpectedly thrilling turn in what had been an otherwise standard botany lesson.

'It is said that the Mandala appears only in times of great crisis. It selects people - no, that's not right.' Falric tapped the side of his face with one restless index finger as he sought the right word. 'It *uses* certain people, just one at a time, to further its interests. I've heard it can only use people of one hereditary line, but I've never found anyone who knows what the origin of that line is. I've also heard people of that line have tried to end it, to prevent any of their ancestors being…used.'

'So it's…an evil spirit?' Cira pressed into Falric's pause.

'No,' Falric said slowly. 'Not *evil*. I would

say…necessary. It only appears when there is an evil to be defeated. But its own power is rooted in darkness, and this is what it gives to the person it uses. To its avatar, you could say - the person it chooses to act through.'

'So it's *not* evil, but it uses evil to fight evil?' Cira asked.

Falric considered this simplified synopsis of his laboured explanation.

'I guess you could say that, Cira. I mean it's not quite right. It is said the Mandala has saved the world from evil many times. But always at terrible cost to its avatars. Sometimes they cannot balance the power it brings them, and they are overwhelmed. Often they are killed in whatever battle it takes them into. Being chosen by the Mandala is essentially a death sentence, and this is why members of the family of one who has been chosen try to ensure there are no more heirs to the line. It is not a fate you would wish on your children, or your children's children.'

'Gosh, that's terrible,' Jordan said.

'For that person, yes. For the rest of us? If there's a terrible threat to the world, it makes sense to sacrifice one person to Mandala to drive it back. Unless that pawn is someone you love. But it is not a force you ever want to encounter. And Cira, whatever your dream said, do *not* try to seek it out. You do not want to have anything to do with it, and the person it inhabits.'

Falric was deadly serious. Selene's opinion that the children were being manipulated weighed heavily on his mind, and this prophetic dream of Cira's troubled him greatly.

'Well - I guess it was just a silly dream,' Cira said with forced cheer. No matter what warnings Falric gave, she had no choice but to seek and ally herself with the Mandala. She had entered an Arrangement.

*Whatever the dangers*, Shivaia had said.

'And anyway, there's no great evil afoot, is there? So there's no need for the Mandala to be about,' she added, trying to lighten the mood.

'Hopefully there is not,' Falric agreed, but he remained serious. 'You will recall my tales of the Black Knight of Avenel?'

Both children nodded. They loved the stories of the Order and its legendary knights. The Black Knight was not of the Order though; rather, he had been a shadowy figure who had worked counter to it on occasion.

'There are some who say that he was an incarnation of the Mandala, and his sword was Reviere, the Sinless Sword. It is a legendary weapon that only the Mandala can wield, and only in a just cause.'

'The Mandala comes with a magical sword? That's so cool!' Jordan said, brightening immediately.

'So...what happened to the Black Knight?' Cira asked, distracted even from the idea of a magical sword by the possibility of the Mandala - *a* Mandala? - being found.

'He disappeared,' Falric said.

'When?' Cira asked, her face falling.

'Around ten years ago,' Falric said, leaving the girl to do the maths herself. She did, immediately.

'When Lindahl killed King Du Romeau,' she said slowly. Falric nodded. Cira frowned.

'But - Du Romeau was a good king. He was, like, a famously good king,' she said, puzzled. 'He was not a great evil. So why would the Mandala be present then?'

'Du Romeau was aggressively expanding the Avenel

Empire through warfare and conquest. Conquered countries would well have considered him evil. Alternately, perhaps the role of the Mandala in that time was to stop the murder of Du Romeau.'

'Well it failed!' Jordan said.

'And that would make Lindahl the great evil?' Cira said.

'There's a logic to that, I concede - except that that to my knowledge, Sir Lindahl was the best of knights.'

'But he killed the king,' Cira objected.

'The *good* king,' Jordan chipped in, for good measure.

'Who was hated by many of the peoples he conquered. And now you can see why nothing is as black and white as you would like, children. And why it is so hard to understand what happened in Voltanna that fateful night. There are so many great mysteries of this world, and as much as I wish I did, I do not have all the answers. Like you, all I have is a great many questions.'

'You have more answers than us though. What can you tell us about Shivaia? And Praxidice?' Cira asked, daringly. Falric raised an eyebrow.

'Did you meet Praxidice also in your dream?' he asked.

'Who is Praxidice?' Jordan asked, saving Cira from either a lie or a truth too far. She know Falric was getting suspicious now.

'Praxidice, the Dark Witch, is very dangerous. She will grant certain gifts, such as a glamour, to aide someone in the pursuit of revenge. But the gifts come at great cost - I should imagine, greater cost than any satisfaction gained in the vengeance. Shivaia, the Dark Lady, is her sister. Less is known of her. But she communicates through dreams,' and here Falric gave Cira a pointed look.

'So Cira's dream was true?' Jordan asked, awed.

'It may have been,' Falric said. 'But even if it was, please heed my warning. Both of you: steer clear of the Mandala and these dark, dangerous forces.'

*****

Throughout the following three years, Cira and Jordan never spoke of the Mandala again, though Cira thought about it all the time. Falric's warnings weighed heavily upon her. She knew that Arrangements were intended to be expensive, and she was hugely grateful for the healing of her knee - even if she couldn't show it - but she worried about what the ultimate cost would prove to be.

They spoke often though of Lien, Bravo, Aethon, Brynir and Sir Bane between themselves. Although they had met Sir Bane only briefly, like Lien, the knight had left a lasting impression on them. Cira and Jordan decided that it was their destiny to help the Red Knight restore Lien, the presumed lost heir, to the throne of Avenel, bringing about a glorious second golden age of chivalry. For their efforts, they would be rewarded by themselves becoming part of the King's Five Knights. Cira would be the Green Knight, who had the spirit of the earth-bound stag, was represented by a ring and represented the north, the sunrise and the spring. Jordan would be the Gold Knight, who had the spirit of the sky-born eagle, was represented by rings and represented the east, the sunset and the autumn.

In a way, they each developed an infatuation of sorts: Jordan with the Red Knight and the idea of chivalry; and Cira with Lien and the idea of him as a lost prince, growing up within the enchanting mysteries of Leaverness, ignorant of his supposed birthright.

The memories of both the knight and boy took on lives of their own in the children's fertile imaginations, gradually transforming into heroes far removed from the truth of their real-world counterparts. Jordan's imagined Sir Bane was the role model he now aspired to, supplanting even his beloved father.

Cira's memory of Lien, meanwhile, developed a very special private place in her mind. She often found herself remembering the way he had held her onto Jest as he took her home; how safe she had felt encircled in his arms. This imagined Lien ruined the chances of any of the local lads as she grew more mature and striking in her teens, for who in the real world could compare with such a strong, selfless and brave boy? Much less the man he would become! If it was true that Aethon led people to their Destiny, and he had led Cira and Jordan to Lien, then it seemed clear to Cira that helping Lien *was* their Destiny. He would make Leaverness safe for them, and one day, they would make Avenel safe for him, as they restored him to his throne.

She thought she understood how stories worked.

As they grew older, the friendship between Cira and Jordan deepened but was uncomplicated by distractions such as love, for they were both devoted to their shared dream of becoming knights. These dreams, however, had no bearing on reality. While as the son of a regional Lord, Jordan would be permitted by birthright to enter the Order, Cira had no natural way in. She would have to firstly be male, secondly have an aristocratic sponsor, and thirdly earn the right through passing the Commoners Trials...and these had been banned since the common man Lindahl had killed his king. Further, Jordan, like everyone else, still thought Cira's knee was damaged, and was quietly concerned. Cira obediently maintained the strapping Selene had prescribed and in front of others, partook in only the activities she was permitted. And as foretold by Selene, she became an extremely skilled horse archer, able to hit even moving targets from a flat gallop on her pony. But horse archery was not a chivalric skill, and Jordan began to realise their shared dream was going to have a painful reality check in the future.

Cira alone knew her knee was not an issue and pretended not to notice Jordan's moments of uncertainty. She continued trying to solve what she considered her only real problem: how to pass herself off as a boy. The only progress she made was with Areté, who was also the only person into whose confidence they had entrusted their plans. It wasn't even as though they went to tell her their secrets; she just had a knack for asking the sorts of questions that led them to unintentionally overshare. Areté took their plans seriously, though she was as direct about the problems as the possible solutions.

The only way that Cira could safely pass herself off as a boy to join the Order, she told them, would be through a glamour. This was a magical spell that, in its most basic form, changed people's visual perception of the wearer. Mid-level glamours could change the visual *and* physical perception of a wearer, while the most advanced spells could do both of those things and also deflect basic associations between the person others saw, and the person they truly were. With this kind of glamour, Areté explained, Cira could not be perceived as anything *but* a boy, and basic connections to her past that might be noticed, would be as quickly forgotten.

'The first I would not recommend, it is much too dangerous,' Areté said. 'You would be seen as a boy, but anyone who, for instance, actually touched your body, might notice an incongruity between what they saw and what they felt. The second solves that problem: their perception of touch would match what they perceived they saw.'

She paused thoughtfully.

'Although that can lead to *incredibly* awkward interactions, because perception is *not* reality.'

She clocked the children's puzzled expressions.

'Not that you would need to worry about such things for a few more years,' she hastily added, before continuing.

'To be safe, you would need the most advanced glamour. No glamour is completely foolproof of course – you would break it yourself if you told anyone outright who you really were. And someone who knew you very well as Cira could potentially work it out if there were *lots* of tells. Something as obvious as having the same knee injury could, for instance, give it away for someone who really deeply thought about it.'

Cira gave Areté a searching look: it was she who had sent her to Shivaia to heal her knee, after all.

Areté gave nothing away though.

'Where would one acquire such a glamour?' Cira asked.

'Well. Such a thing is not acquired easily. The only ways I know are to go to Mama Aksaya, or Praxidice. The first I would forbid outright. The second is also risky, but also very specific. You may only approach Praxidice for vengeance.'

'Only?' Cira pressed.

'Only,' Areté confirmed. 'And let us hope that you never need to seek the sort of vengeance Praxidice can help you with.'

'So...there's no way for Cira to get the glamour she needs?' Jordan asked quietly, feeling traitorous for even saying it.

'There is no *desirable* way, no,' Areté replied slowly. 'But that is not the same as no way at all.'

Cira meditated on the conversation as she lay in bed that night. Shivaia had said she would one day be Citar of Avenel, and that she would require assistance from Praxidice for that to happen. The Dark Lady had also forced her to pretend to still have the knee injury. Had Shivaia known, years ago, that in the future, Cira would take a glamour from Praxidice? And that the knowledge that Cira was crippled would throw off any suspicion that the chevalier Citar was really a servant girl from the Backwind? And...if she took a glamour from Praxidice...what vengeance would she be seeking? What could happen that would be so terrible?

Over time, Falric's fear that the children were being manipulated by larger forces faded. He had more immediate concerns for them: he could accept that his blooming son wanted to become a chevalier, instead of staying on the estate, but he knew that when the time came, Cira would discover her fate was to stay in the Backwind and be wed, with children of her own in her near future. Jordan would not be wooing women or being wedded off until he was a young man, and then to a woman more the age Cira was now approaching, and by then would be past. He wondered more and more often whether he had done the girl a grave disservice by allowing her the freedoms he had. A girl who expects nothing more than to work, be wed, have children and continue to work would surely be more accepting of her fate than a girl allowed to live and fight and dream like a boy. When he did, on occasion, recall the children's adventure with Aethon, and his subsequent conversations with Selene and Areté, he would find himself hoping that actually there was a more exciting destiny ahead for Cira, for she was not at all suited to the mundane life that otherwise awaited her.

Falric also suspected, and worried, that although Jordan's confidence had grown enormously over the last years, he drew much of it from his constant companion, and that severed of that source, he would not find the training of the Order of the Coeur to be of his expectations or even ability. He quietly hoped his son would instead decide to stay on the estate and grow into the gentle but noble successor Falric was sure he could become.

Three years after Cira and Jordan had followed Aethon into Leaverness, in the early summer, Areté disappeared, although, due to her nomadic nature, no-one would realise for some time.

Soon after she did so, Aethon was again sighted near the Galea estate. No longer children but teenagers now, and well into their training regime for entry to the Order, the intrepid duo again took chase. Jordan had forgotten their promise to his father never to seek Aethon again; Cira had planned all along to seek both the unicorn and the

Mandala, and she was determined to take any opportunity to meet Lien once more. She was certain they would find him - or he would find them. She rode out with a light heart, ready to meet her prince again.

She thought she understood how dreams worked.

Again the ponies returned frightened, exhausted and riderless. But this time they returned first.

The dogs led the search party to the body of Jordan.

They never found Cira.

# PART II

# LEAVERNESS

# 5. Prince Rupert

Sir Bane did indeed scour Leaverness for Lien and the People in the years following his visit to the Backwind. But neither he nor his knights caught as much as a glimpse of their quarry, and for good reason. That reason was called Areté, and Bane knew she needed removing from the picture if he was to make any progress. He had his contacts, and found one whose goals coincided with his. Plans were made, and executed.

Shortly before Aethon lured Jordan and Cira back into Leaverness, on a bright and hot early summer afternoon, Areté and Sky were settled on a broad branch of the last borealus tree left in the forest. The borealus were breathtaking giants of the Altican botanical world, around which a great deal of fascinating and surprisingly accurate folklore existed. It was true, for instance, that they were sentient, which made their rarity doubly tragic. Their wood was a unique, gorgeously mottled deep scarlet which varnished up a treat. It was very difficult to cut but never aged or even burned, making it a highly prized commodity. It was frequently found in the oldest grand buildings of Avenel, and furniture made of its wood was near priceless.

This particular living treasure had escaped the slaughter of its fellow specimens, by generations of Avenel woodsmen, only because they could never find it. Although it could be seen from the highest towers of

Avenel itself, and from any high vantage point within the vast forest, this ancient borealus was the subject of a very intelligent befuddlement charm. Someone who meant the tree no harm might be able to find it with a compass and reasonable sense of direction, *if* it wanted to be found. No number of compasses, maps and careful planning could lead someone with commercial interests anywhere near it though. The whole affair was a favourite challenge of the Avenel Royal Guild of Science, who were determined to prove that logic and science would win the Battle of the Borealus against the charm. Their interest was purely academic, for they had nothing to gain by the felling of the giant; the tree still eluded their most carefully laid plans though. Borealus hunting was now akin to rainbow hunting, but could be done on all days in all seasons, which was much more convenient. Just how the befuddlement charm had come to exist, however, was a secret the People guarded closely.

But it was from the heights of this gracious old sentinel that the two people responsible for its safety were arguing, in the comfortable way that only very good friends can.

'Then it is time to take Lien to Avenel,' Sky was saying. 'Past time. He will get his first facial tattoos soon. You will either have to deny him the rituals, or use a glamour after that process begins.'

'I can't deny him the Kia'Oro,' Areté said pensively.

'I'm aware,' Sky replied dryly. 'The later you take him, the greater the risk.'

'The risk of what?'

'The risk that you will not be here yourself to take him,' Sky said.

Areté held his gaze.

She blinked first.

'You think I have made a mistake,' she said.

'You of all people understand the dangers of entering an Arrangement,' he said calmly.

'I haven't fully entered it yet,' Areté said.

'But you will, and it could be anytime,' Sky countered. 'And one who is wise - and I am renowned for my wisdom - would guess sooner rather than later.'

Areté considered, and nodded.

'I will take him then.'

'When?' Sky asked.

'Tomorrow,' she said.

Sky nodded approvingly, then paused, listening carefully.

'Actually, you might want to hold off for a few days.'

Areté raised an enquiring eyebrow. She could hear nothing untoward.

'It seems the chevaliers are on manoeuvres today,' Sky explained.

When Areté showed no surprise, he slowly frowned.

'But you already knew that.'

Areté grinned innocently.

'And you've told the children,' he sighed.

The children of Avenel and its surroundings counties grew up on a prodigious diet of half-truths and wild exaggerations about Leaverness, which its indigenous tribe encouraged wherever possible. This is not to say Leaverness was safe for a general afternoon's jaunt - far from it, it could be deadly to those who did not respect and understand its moods and its rare and unpredictable flora and fauna. But it was also an abundant and beloved home to those who did, so its dangers were a matter of perspective.

The People had a similarly fearsome reputation amongst those they called "outsiders". Few outsiders could tell you *exactly* what made them fearsome though, since all they really were was different. They were what Falric would call "of the Old World," and so their skin was white, which outsiders saw as unnatural. They had their own language, which shared little in common with the languages and dialects of the rest of the continent. The ancestral memory of the People stretched back far beyond that of the written histories stored in Avenel, yet was preserved only within oral tradition. They knew how to manipulate *espréi*, the energy of the world, in a fine art which others called magic. Few outsiders could even *experience* espréi, much less do anything with it, and so considered the art and its practitioners with suspicion.

But none of this was exactly fear-inducing, and so parents being interrogated by their children as to *why* the People would get them if they didn't go to bed; *what* the People would do to them; and why being in bed made them safer in the first place anyway, tended to fall back on tales of the ridiculous, only helping to propagate this strange mythology. Meanwhile adults caught trying to explain to a sceptical and less gullible teenager tended to fall back on clumsy attempts to implicitly elicit the answer from the questioner themselves.

'The People? Oh, they're just...well, you know.'

And most tended to agree that they did know, even if they didn't. It was as if the subject made people almost supernaturally stupid, and not that a spooky flair to the legend would be unexpected. The People knew how to keep to themselves.

Of course the People were quite capable of being fearsome, just not in the "eating babies for supper" sort of ways that your average folk could understand and communicate easily to small children who won't eat their greens. But on the whole, they had much better things to do with their time than terrorise the children of Avenel and the counties that surrounded both the city and its neighbouring wild forest.

At least...that was the case with the adults. Because, for all their aura of enigma, sacred ancestral duty and generally antisocial tendencies, the People still consisted of perfectly normal adults who bore perfectly normal children. And these were as perfectly mischievous as children anywhere else in any world.

Every summer the new intake of chevaliers, the young knights-in-training of Avenel's chivalric Order of the Coeur, were sent out into deeper Leaverness. This was casually termed "manoeuvres", but in reality, acted as a character-building rite of passage, like an institutionalised version of pushing the new kids' heads into the chamber pot. This was the time of year when an amazing number of newly accepted chevaliers would suddenly fall ill, be urgently called home or find their horses mysteriously lame; thus the actual convoy that made it to the forest only ever represented a modest portion of the entire group.

Terrorising the chevaliers had, for many decades, been an established and respectable practice of the youth of the People, who had little love of the dangerous men the boys would become. It had stopped with the death of King Du Romeau and subsequent persecution of the tribe, before cautiously resuming, without any tacit approval from Sky, a few years ago. It was nominally considered as a stealth exercise: it was absolutely forbidden for any of the participants to be seen. While Areté, an honoured friend to the People, would never be caught openly encouraging such frivolities, she did recognise an educational opportunity when she saw one, and had been known to provide occasional constructive advice - usually delivered in the form of sheer harmless speculation, within casual earshot of a half dozen mischievous children - about how best to exploit the vulnerabilities of young men, in armour, on over-sized highly strung horses, who were unable to easily remount unaided. Her suggestions tended to be imaginative and while inconvenient on the part of the chevaliers, were never particularly cruel.

This year only twelve boys had made it into Leaverness, of which only eleven were first year chevaliers. The new boys were always escorted by someone who had ridden the manoeuvre the previous year. This was an unpopular role, and this elder boy's general bravado in the face of his underlings had gradually dissipated upon entering the deeper forest. The bruises from his last excursion to Leaverness had long since faded, but so too had his naïve aspirations of returning to Avenel that afternoon *on* his horse.

The teenage boys uneasily watched the twelve delicate pairs of long, furry ears shooting forward and back and rotating from side to side, as the horses tried to interpret the unusual whispers of the trees, caused by a small horde of children and teens running through the forest around them. Not on the forest floor though: no, this chase consisted of an athletic series of delicate runs and nimble leaps along the sturdier forest branches in the forest canopy, all of which was having a distinctly unnerving effect on the equines below.

As the children and teens of the People paused in the trees above to confer on how best to hatch their cunning pig-related plan - sourced from idle speculation by Areté the day before - Lien looked around to find the inevitable audience. No-one would logically expect to be watched from the top arbour of the borealus, above where even the lithest climbers would dare to ascend; which is exactly why Lien looked there first. He was too far off to see the faces of watchers, but he knew of no-one else they could be but Areté and Sky. He grinned to himself, before turning to the others, who were waiting impatiently with palpable anticipation.

'We must choose the trophy,' he whispered.

'The sword of the leader,' Bravo announced.

'We did that last year, Bravo.'

'S'right. It's traditional. We always take the sword,' the boy insisted.

'But it's uninspired,' Lien argued. 'It's just a useless weight of metal. What does Sky want with that? Let's do something new this year.'

'Thank goodness,' chipped in one of the girls. 'I vote we nick the grey horse. Sky would like a horse like that.'

Now it was Bravo's turn to be exasperated.

'What would Sky want with a chevalier's horse? They're far too heavy to run like his Horse.'

'And besides, Sky doesn't really need a horse at all,' Lien, font of all wisdom, added. The smallest of the boys was impressed at the apparent knowledge of his elders.

'Is it true then?' he whispered. 'Can Sky fly?'

'It's none of your business, even if he can,' snapped Bravo, glaring at Lien, who shrugged him off with irritating cheer. Sky's many abilities were gradually revealed to the youngsters over various ceremonies on their way to adulthood, meaning not all the children had the same information as the teenagers.

'Of course he can. How else do you think he got up there?' asked the purveyor of all secrets, with a sly wink, pointing up high in the borealus.

'Oh, well spotted, Lien!' said Areté, practically radiating pride. 'I know esprći is a terrible drag for him, but I do believe it has forced him to be smarter with his other senses.'

'That's another thing we need to talk about,' Sky said.

'Later, Sky. We can't possibly let him get away with being such an unbearable smart-ass,' Areté deflected him. 'Let us make a fool out of him together.'

'What's to see?' Bravo demanded, glaring first at his friend and then at the borealus. He disapproved of Lien revealing secrets that were not his to share.

'Right there, with Areté. On that...branch...wait a minute...'

'Which very empty branch would that be, idiot?' Bravo demanded.

'They were *there*...'

'Next thing you'll be telling us that he transformed into that falcon, I suppose?' asked Bravo, giving Lien a very hard look that dared him to disagree. Lien glanced back where he had seen Areté and Sky only moments earlier. The falcon, a large, brilliantly golden plumed bird, gracefully landed just there. When it came to Areté and Sky, Lien knew well that he only ever saw what they wanted him to. As Sky returned to man form after the other children had lost interest, and Areté ceased looking remarkably like a leafy branch, the boy knew they wanted him to know that he had not been wrong, but that he had been too cocky. Suitably chastised, he turned back to his scornful companions.

'Had you going though, didn't I?' he said with a wry grin.

'I s-say, s-settle old g-girl?' said the first knight-in-training, nervously, to the highly-strung grey mare he rode. He was a tall boy, at that most awkward time of adolescence when his limbs refused to organise into a matching set. He was sweating profusely under his helm, above which sat a glorious deep purple royal feather. His position at the front was something of a joke on the part of the other chevaliers, who had insisted that the prince amongst them ought to be permitted the place of honour at the top of the single file. The jury was still out on whether Prince Rupert had been too good-natured, too shy or simply too stupid to object. The eldest chevalier, who ought to have led, was instead safely ensconced in the centre of the line. Having visited the forest the year before he knew better than to be caught at the front or back.

'You going to ask that horse what to do, or tell it?' this unpleasant eldest asked, enjoying Prince Rupert's discomfort as his mare pranced, neck taut, eyes bulging.

'I d-don't think we're really g-getting along, to b-be honest,' Rupert confessed, tugging anxiously on the reins. 'I d-don't know why my f-father sent me this h-horse. There are p-plenty of qu-quieter ones in the yard.'

'Maybe he wanted to make a man out of you,' the boy behind him said, over his shoulder, bringing chuckles from the rest of the line.

'I'm s-sorry? I didn't quite c-catch that?' Rupert called, politely.

'I said, maybe they wanted to make a *man* out of you,' the boy repeated, this time spitefully loud and said forwards so that Rupert could hear. Rupert flushed, but forced his concentration to the path ahead. The comment, though cruel, was actually correct. Rupert's father was the King of Mayana, a modest kingdom that had been conquered and subjugated by King Du Romeau over a decade earlier. Du Romeau allowed compliant kings of his new territories to retain their thrones, but under the auspices of the Avenel Empire. It was not uncommon for the sons of those kingdoms to be sent to the Order of the Coeur for training, and Rupert's father had indeed sent his eldest to Avenel to see whether the Order could, in his own words, 'make a man out of a monkey'; or, and perhaps more agreeably, kill him in the course of the training. This was not an unusual outcome and would clear the way for the king's second, and much more suitable son, to become the heir to the throne of Mayana.

'Just as well we're not nicking that grey horse, look at it prance like that. It's only got half a brain,' one of girls in the trees laughed.

'More like its rider's only got half a brain, look at him, the royal twit,' Bravo replied.

'Royal?' Sindhe, the object of Bravo's attentions, asked.

'Uh-huh. It's the purple feather. Sign of royalty. Not of

Avenel itself, cos their king's dead, but he'll be from royalty elsewhere,' Lien explained, pleased to have a chance to redeem himself. Bravo, however, had seen an opportunity to impress Sindhe.

'Then that's what we'll get. A royal feather. For Sky.'

'But what use has Sky for – ' one of the boys began, but Lien cut him off.

'It's a sign of honour. He doesn't need to need it, or use it, or want it. But it means something. It's got *significance*.'

Lien caught a look from Bravo that had not yet decided whether it was suspicious or pleased that they had agreed, for once. He shrugged it off.

'Everyone has to have a good idea once in a while…' he said dismissively, before impulsively dropping the act with a genuine grin. Bravo's expression remained frozen for a moment before softening a little.

'Come on,' he said gruffly, 'we've got to a see a pig about some horses.'

Automatically, the other kids looked to Lien for affirmation. It would not have mattered which of Lien or Bravo had spoken first; one was always cross-checked against the other.

'Um, yeah. What he said,' Lien agreed.

The youths sped gracefully through the trees to spring the trap ahead.

'Seen any ghosts yet then, Your Highness?'

It is a cruel but common practice for those who are frightened to channel their fear into the mockery of others. All the teenagers were worried now, and the more worried they became, the crueller they were to Prince Rupert.

'I've h-heard that there are n-no gh-ghosts in L-leaverness,' the prince stammered, desperate for conversation; anything to distract him from the jigging and jogging of the grey mare.

'No? Then what do you expect sends horses bolting home without their riders every year?' the next demanded. 'The People?' and they all laughed in unison.

'I h-heard that it's the o-other ch-chevaliers. L-last year's boys. It's tradition, you s-see. The first years c-come out here, and the second years s-s-spook them. Next year, it'll be our t-turn.'

'Well I'm a second year, you idiot, and I'm still here,' snapped the eldest.

'M-m-maybe they just didn't t-t-tell you?' Rupert stammered, stung.

'And maybe you're just a big, sad joke. Your father probably put on you on that flighty mare to get you lost out here, so he won't have the embarrassment of one day making you king of whatever crappy kingdom you come from,' said the second year viciously. His escalated hostility stemmed from Rupert voicing an embarrassing suspicion he had already come to on his own. Having rarely ever caught sight nor sound of the People, the superstitious folk of Avenel had come to the logical conclusion that Leaverness must be haunted by beings of a spiritual persuasion. But there is always a small minority cursed with too much intelligence to be properly superstitious, and it was these who tended to wonder at and champion the inconsistencies of the theory. The eldest was brighter than he let on, and suspected that the annual dumping of first years in the forest was indeed an elaborate prank played by older chevaliers. He was wrong, of course. Others who suspected more natural explanations had noted there was a seasonal regularity of the spirits: the chances of being properly haunted in Leaverness seemed to be significantly higher in the summer. This was, not coincidentally, also the time of year the People inhabited the forest reaches nearest Avenel. There was also the matter of the trophy hunting. For the last few years, one of the young victimised chevaliers would lose an item. It was usually a sword, and not always the best or most expensive weapon, but the boy in question could never explain how or when it disappeared.

Back in the borealus, Areté and Sky watched as further dissent broke out in the ranks of the tribal youths, who had assembled in the clearing that was to become the site of the trap. Lien dealt with the current debate by shoving Bravo, who was clearly railing against taking orders. Moments later, the two were transformed into a rolling, kicking, punching, spitting, testosterone driven ball of waving limbs. The other kids gathered around, egging them on.

'Do you remember when he was a sweet, shy boy?' Areté asked fondly.

'He is certainly blooming now,' Sky replied dryly.

'You're his father figure, it's your job to knock a few corners off him,' she reminded him.

'I assure you, it would be like moulding water into a sculpture.'

The chevaliers were approaching the clearing.

'How long until they hit that clearing, do you think?' Areté asked, enjoying the anticipation.

Sky assessed the two parties.

'I would say around – twenty seconds.'

Areté nodded, and started counting at fifteen. By ten, Lien and Bravo were disengaging. By seven, they were sharing a very serious "to be continued" stare. By four, the clearing was miraculously empty, and by zero, the horses were reluctantly entering the silent space, fully expecting something terrible to happen.

'They're good.'

'A little too good.' Sky did not sound impressed. 'One day, they will miss the mark.'

The youth of his tribe were gathered, out of sight, around a makeshift cage in the under scrub. The cage rocked and attempted to squeal. The kids muffled giggles.

'He used to be perfectly good with espréi, you know,' Sky said.

'*Must* we have this conversation right now?' Areté protested. 'We're just getting to the good part.'

'Yes. We must. You are going to have to tell him. To warn him.'

Areté sighed.

'You are over-protecting him. He will not thank you for it, in the end.'

'But he won't hate me for it right now, either. And he can enjoy…you know. Being a teenager,' she said, with an illustrative wave to the clearing below.

'He has the right to know where he comes from.'

'Lien does not belong in Avenel. There are too many who would exploit him.'

'Yet he will not always be satisfied here with the People, either.'

Areté stared glumly out over the forest, her good mood dissipated.

'You need to prepare him,' Sky pressed her.

Below, a look of intense mischief on his face, Lien prepared to release the wild pig they had so carefully trapped that morning.

'He's still so... innocent...' Areté objected.

Bravo shoved Lien one. Lien shoved him back.

Sky fixed Areté with a sceptical look.

'Alright, alright. I already said I'll take him to Avenel, and we'll see what he thinks,' Areté surrendered.

As Lien opened the makeshift wooden cage, Bravo shooed the pig out. It was a pygmy pig, utterly adorable and desperate to be reunited with its family. It shot into the clearing, squealing as its little legs propelled it straight into the line of horses, practically underneath the forelegs of Rupert's tightly coiled mare.

Several things happened all at once.

The horses scattered in one spectacular moment, rearing and shying in an explosive arc away from the now screaming pig, which veered sharply right. Surprised, Areté suddenly recognised the tall boy on the grey mare, and Sky spoke just two words, although they, in effect, said ever so much more.

*'Prince Rupert.'*

Areté's face locked into an expression of intense concentration as the armoured boys crashed to the ground left, right and centre - all but Rupert, whose horse dropped suddenly back to the ground, as though severely reprimanded. For a moment the mare stood taut and motionless, while Rupert scrambled to re-seat himself; then she leapt into a flat bolt, her rider clinging on for dear life, his feathered helm slipped to a jaunty angle, partially obscuring his sight.

'I am not sure that your efforts have been entirely successful,' Sky politely noted.

'Don't be silly. Rupert will be just fine now… oh.'

Seeing the trophy feather disappearing at a great rate atop Prince Rupert, Lien ignored the exciting carnage unfolding in the clearing, racing instead to his waiting pony to take up the pursuit. Not about to surrender the agreed trophy, Bravo quickly followed suit.

'Damn those boys. What could they possibly want with Rupert? They can trophy any old sword,' Areté snapped.

'You're going to have to stop those two, before they do something we will all regret,' Sky said.

Areté nodded, and gave a high whistle. Far below the borealus, an answering whinny heralded the immediate arrival of Erebus.

Lien was now getting too big for his beloved Jest but the skewbald pony was nonetheless famously sure-footed on even the most hazardous of terrain - often to the great distress of elder members of the People, when subjected to the pair's hair-raisingly nimble gymnastics. The boy trusted Jest implicitly, and the pony invariably rewarded this faith with an almost acrobatic ability to extract his rider out of the frequent tight spots Lien effortlessly landed them in. Now, Lien lay low over Jest's brown and white mane, guiding the pony with the lightest of shifts of his body as they shot down the forest paths on the trail of Rupert's flighty grey mare.

They were not alone for long though, for what Bravo's leggier pony lacked in agility, he made up for with an extraordinary turn of speed. Bank surged up to the left of Jest, attempting to force the lighter pony right off the track.

Lien left the footwork to his mount and set about sabotaging Bravo himself. The two boys fought hand and nail, sliding about perilously on the slick, bare backs of their ponies, until Lien, almost unseated by a low branch that broke over his shoulder, enlisted the offending piece of wood as an impromptu weapon.

While Lien and Bravo were having a jolly old time shouting at and wrestling with one another, the net result for Prince Rupert was a terrifying flight past, over and painfully through the brush and branches of the forest, apparently pursued by the vengeful spirits of Leaverness. If not for the wind whistling in his poor ears, the pounding hoof beats of his panicked horse - not to mention the thudding of his own heart - and had he understood the language of the People, Rupert might have realised that the loud curses of said verbose spirits actually went something like this:

'You don't really want the feather for Sky anyway, admit it!' (Lien, smartly rapping Bravo's knuckles with his stick).

'What are you talking about? What else would I want it for?' (Bravo, reaching for Lien's left leg, to lever him off Jest).

'To show off to Sindhe, of course!' - (and here the conversation took a very mature turn) - 'Because you *luuuuuerve* her,' (scoring Lien a double shove: one to the heart, one to the shoulder).

'I do not!' (On the defensive now, Bravo slid around Bank's left side to pick up a stick of his own from the track). 'I mean, not like that!' (Re-seated, he made a strike at his enemy). 'Besides, you're just jealous!'

'What is there to be jealous of?' (Lien, dropping off the right side of Jest to avoid the stick strike, his legs momentarily touching down to the racing ground below, before immediately vaulting back to the relative safety of the pony's narrow back).

'None of the girls are interested in you! Because you're from *Avenel!*' (Bravo, viciously blocking and parrying the oncoming blows).

'So's your father!'

'But I don't *care* about that!'

'What's that supposed to mean?'

'It means I don't secretly want to *go* to Avenel!'

At about which point, flushed with embarrassment at this unspoken truth, Lien lunged all the way across the dangerous, surging chasm between Jest and Bank. Bravo was wise enough to choose that moment to bail out, swinging elegantly up onto an overhead oak bough. Lien didn't even bother to savour the victory, vaulting from Bank straight back onto Jest before he swung the pony off onto a side track.

With the sounds of the spirits falling behind them now, Rupert tried desperately to rein his horse in. But despite her exhaustion, her brain and nervous system were still resolutely locked in flight mode, with thousands of years of instinctive self-preservation overriding the pain inflicted by a terrified boy hauling on the bit, or the waning strength of her own legs. Rupert could do nothing more but desperately clutch onto her slick, foaming neck for dear life. He was so convinced that the end was nigh that his panic-stricken brain had kicked into slide-show mode, passing his entire life in front of his eyes not just once, but twice, the second time in reverse. He didn't explicitly notice it at the time, what with the imminence of his demise, but there was a gaping hole in his memories, a conspicuous blank where something important ought to have been.

All of a sudden, a monstrous figment burst out from the scrub to the left, a furious child spirit astride a small but furiously snorting brown and white pony. Partially blinded by his helmet, still slipped forward on his head, Rupert shouted in fear as his mare lurched right to evade the intruders, but they stuck like glue to the grey horse's side. Above the rising panic ringing in his ears, the prince suddenly felt his helm being roughly hauled off, dragging his head to the left with it. Sheer survival instinct saved him, as his fingers locked like claws around the sweat-soaked, stiffening leather of his reins, steadying him even though his head was pulled around to face his attacker.

As his eyes were finally freed of the tipped helm, Prince Rupert beheld an unexpected sight: not a monster or a demon as he imagined, but a boy, only a year or two his junior. His face, streaked with sweat, dirt and even blood, was contorted into such a wildly triumphant expression as to assume a genuinely fearsome aspect. Ever so briefly, their eyes met and locked, and as they did, Rupert knew for certain that this was no apparition, for he saw the other boy's expression swing wildly from elation to alarm.

As quickly as he had appeared, Lien wheeled Jest left and was gone.

Tearing free of the path into the forest proper, barely skirting trees and boulders, leaping creeks and scrub, Rupert's grey mare forged on almost blindly until finally one foreleg buckled and gave way. Horse and armoured rider came crashing down in a sudden, violent heap. Rupert instinctively tried to roll clear of the mare's lethal, thrashing legs, but caught a square blow to the chest, denting his breast plate into his ribcage. Lurching free of her heavy burden, the mare scrambled to her legs and charged off once more, head down in an attempt to buck the saddle and wildly swinging stirrups off.

Not far down the track though, she unexpectedly stopped.

Lien allowed the blowing, exhausted Jest to walk out, as he examined the helm and its stunning, iridescent, but now also bent and mud splattered purple feather. His thoughts were no longer of the victory earned over Bravo though, and the adrenaline from the mad chase had sharply cut out, leaving only a growing cold dread. He had let Bravo wind him up too much, and he had gone much too far. Feeling sick, he wondered whether his prize was worth the potential risk he had placed the People - *his* people - in.

Whatever Lien's own conclusion, according to Bravo, the answer was indisputably "no". Lost in his worries, Lien was knocked clear from Jest as Bravo swung down like a wrathful god from a branch above.

'Did he see you?' the boy shouted furiously.

'Wh-what? No!' Lien objected, struggling to rise, the wind knocked from his chest.

'Can you be *sure*?' and now Bravo was hauling Lien back to his unsteady feet.

'Yes! He didn't see me, alright! Relax, Bravo,' Lien said, pushing the other boy back. 'I know the rules.'

Bravo glared.

'And besides, that boy was so scared, he won't remember anything but soiling his own pants. And only that once he's taken them off.'

Bravo roughly hauled Lien close again, his eyes wild with rage.

'You *did* let him see you!'

Some distance off, in serene silence and upon crushed daisy grasses, Prince Rupert lay perfectly still on his back. He was slipping away as his dented chest-plate pressed through the broken ribs that should have protected his lungs, but were now fatally unable to draw enough air. His sight, and indeed whole world, were contracting as a buzzing darkness closed from the outside in. *Now* he remembered the blank gap in his memory. He felt something cold and cruel trying to slip into his consciousness - *back* into his consciousness, actually. He somehow knew that whatever the eerie thing was, it belonged to him, it was what belonged in the blank space in his memory. He mentally recoiled from its whispers because they were of pain, screams and violence. He wanted to leave his broken body behind and flee the growing susurration, but even as he thought that, he realised it was not his body the secret wanted to enter. It wanted to get into his mind, into his soul, and so he could not escape its pursuit. His lungs were expelling the last of their precious, spent air, and the tunnel of light that was the physical world was collapsing. He tried with every ounce of strength he didn't have to fight against the encroaching cold dark…

*'… Rupert … '*

A warm, loving, familiar presence approached the edge of his retreating consciousness, giving him an anaemic flash of hope - but it was too little, too late.

*Hello, Rupert.*

Rupert started. He was still on his back, and now fully surrounded by darkness, except for a purple glow and silver smoke rising around him.

*You may stand.*

Rupert's hands shot to his ribs, where just a moment ago his armour had been crushing his lungs. But he was both uninjured and unarmed. He was in his favourite blue shirt and brown trousers. He scrambled, confused, to his feet, and beheld the pale apparition before him.

'H-hello…?' the prince stammered. 'Am I d-dead?'

*Not yet.*

'Oh. C-can I n-not d-die?'

*We are about to find out.*

Rupert never felt the hands that loosened his armour, cutting away straps that would not release immediately, to rip the crushing chest-plate away from his collapsed lungs. When he did not resume breathing, Areté swore furiously and sat back on her heels. And only then did she realise where they were. She looked at the boy at her feet, and the tree under which he had fallen. Eyes narrowed suspiciously, she glanced at the grey mare, who had meekly followed Erebus back. She now stood with her head down low, a picture of exhaustion. Areté felt the mare's espréi, and found nothing untoward. Which meant it had to have been Leaverness, not the horse, which had brought Rupert to this place. Areté knew Leaverness very well, almost better than anyone; but it still kept its secrets, even from her.

She considered her options. Sky had been right: the

trap would be closed sooner rather than later. But even so, this was much sooner than she had anticipated.

She sighed, closed her eyes and made a triangle shape with her right hand, index and middle fingers raised.

In doing so, she called in a favour.

A favour that would change everything.

As Areté swung the outcome of Rupert's fight against death, Lien had found himself in what might have been a fight for his own life against the cold rage of his best friend. Bravo's temper was terrifying to behold, and it had taken all of Lien's agility, cunning and comedy to finally draw out the anger and replace it with mere bullishness. This was a safer place for both of them, and playfulness had finally returned to their battle.

'Yield,' Bravo ordered.

'I'm not done yet!'

Bravo paused a moment, taken aback by the sheer audacity of the statement.

'How are you not done? What is there possibly left to do? You're tied to a tree!'

It was something of an understatement. Lien was suspended by his ankles, wrists bound and dangling below his head.

'Untie me and I'll show you a thing or two!' the defeated insisted. The victor just stretched out his aching back and dropped to the grass, massaging his right shoulder ruefully as he surveyed his own handiwork. Bravo too was aware of how dangerous his temper was, and was aware that had he not been fighting Lien, he might have severely hurt or killed another opponent. He was confused, ashamed, and a little frightened of himself.

'You just wait ten minutes. You'll be bored and wanting to cut me down!' Lien called, trying to pull Bravo out of the downward spiral he could see coming.

'Actually, you might be surprised how long I can enjoy watching you spinning about up there like a slaughtered boar,' Bravo replied, still scowling. He turned to try on the hard-won helm that Lien had torn from Rupert's head, stopping sharply.

'What happened to the feather?!'

'Feather? What feather?' Lien asked innocently. 'Cut me down, Bravo, and if you've lost it, I'll help you look for it.'

'Why you – '

Lien's lazy spin robbed him of the joy of Bravo's irate expression, but he found himself instead face to face with Areté. Also hanging upside down. Lien's blood flooded brain couldn't quite read her inverted expression but it didn't look friendly.

'Hello, Lien.'

'Areté! Lovely day, isn't it?'

'Where's the feather?'

'What feather?'

'Okay, let's not play this game. I know where it is.'

'Oh. Then you would know I can't exactly reach it at this point in time. However, if you were to help me down…'

Areté obliged. Lien fell several metres to the ground, landing with an impressive and painful whump on his left shoulder.

'What was that for?' he yelped, pushing his way out of the loosened vines. Areté played hard but always fair, and he smarted from both the emotional and physical impact of the fall.

Areté dropped down lightly beside her wayward ward,

and delicately extracted the feather from his trousers.

'Oh, you can't give that to Sky now...' Bravo objected, appalled. Areté gently blew on the damaged feather, which rippled back into immaculate condition under her warm breath.

'A boy nearly died for this feather, Lien,' she said quietly.

'He never did. He's on a fast ride home, is all.'

Areté lifted her eyes to meet his. He saw purple flecks in her irises, almost the same amethyst hue as the feather, and equally beautiful. But Lien didn't think he had ever seen her as serious as she was now.

'His horse was terrified, and tripped and fell, kicking him in the chest. That was your fault.'

An awkward pause fell upon the clearing.

'The feather was for Sky,' Lien said, eventually.

'Was it worth it?'

Lien was silent.

'Will he be okay?' He asked eventually, his voice small.

'He will now, and my friend Lady Beckworth will ensure his full recovery,' Areté said. There was something in her soft tone though that made both boys' blood run cold.

'What did it cost you?'

It was Bravo who asked the question that Lien could not. The boys knew that all consequential magic came at a cost, though the price was variable. If Lien winning the feather had almost cost the prince his life, but for Areté saving it, it was a very expensive feather now indeed. Powerful magic was required for life, or death.

'I had a handy favour to call in,' Areté said, flashing a smile that didn't quite make it to her eyes. She knew that, in saving Rupert's life, she had walked into an open trap and closed it upon herself.

She was also suspicious. Leaverness had shown Rupert's fleeing grey mare an unnatural path to Mama Aksaya's Forest of Secrets, a place almost impossible to find by intention. In a vast tract of a million trees, the mare had fallen so that Rupert had landed at the foot of the very tree that held his secret.

To save his life once before, he had changed his life, in that exact place, by giving up a secret he could not live with.

And that had been Areté's idea, too.

Areté spent the rest of the day and the evening with the People, listening as the children told a greatly embellished tale of the afternoon's exploits to the adults. Lien and Bravo presented Rupert's royal feather to Sky, but without the bravado one might expect of the two boys, and the old man received it with equal uneasiness. He alone knew about Rupert seeing Lien, and what Areté had done to save the prince.

After the evening meal, Areté laughed and danced around the bonfire with the tribe, showing not a care in the world. She hugged both Lien and Bravo in her usual manner, but her farewell with Sky was silent and somber. And then she rode Erebus slowly back the place where Rupert had fallen.

She arrived at midnight, and was met by the shimmering, translucent, psychic projection of a young woman. She wore round gold rimmed glasses over bright blue eyes; a white shirt under a burgundy waistcoat with stars picked out in glittering gold thread; a grey woollen knee length skirt; and flat black slip shoes. Her head was crowned with several inches of bright green hair, currently swept to one side and tucked neatly behind an ear.

'I didn't expect to be having this conversation so soon,'

she said, looking Areté up and down curiously. Though they appeared around the same age, centuries separated them and they made an incongruous couple: a fresh-faced young woman with styled and coloured hair in luxurious aristocratic clothing; and a suspicious, ancient woman with a loose auburn plait spilling over a battle-worn armour bodice.

'You and me both, Callista. Please allow me to complete the transaction with Cosmos,' Areté replied, her usual warmth absent. A momentary expression of disappointment flashed across Callista's face, for she had more to say herself, but she inclined her head and then closed her eyes. When they opened, Callista was gone, replaced by someone - or something - else entirely.

The most obvious change was the bright golden eyes, but Cosmos wore Callista's entire body differently. The woman's youthful face somehow looked older and sharper, and where Callista had a relaxed demeanour, Cosmos stood more erect: a little broader, a little taller. More masculine, Areté realised; though she suspected Cosmos had little need for gender.

ARETÉ. I HAVE SAVED A LIFE ON YOUR BEHALF, AND SO YOU HAVE WILLINGLY ENTERED THE ARRANGEMENT I OFFERED YOU.

Cosmos' gracious voice - heard directly in Areté's head - was deeper, and their cadence slower, than that of Callista.

'Yes. I am now in your debt,' Areté agreed warily.

Cosmos smiled the beautiful, translucent face they wore.

DO NOT WORRY SO. IT IS SUCH A SMALL THING I NEED OF YOU.

'You do not trade such a favour as saving a life for something small,' Areté said. 'That is old, powerful magic, and must have cost you as greatly as it will now cost me.'

IT WAS EXPENSIVE TO ACQUIRE, IT IS TRUE. BUT I BELIEVE IT WILL BE WORTH THE INVESTMENT.

Cosmos smiled encouragingly.

DESPITE YOUR FEARS, I NEED ONLY A LITTLE THING. BUT FIRST, I HAVE A CURIOSITY I HOPE YOU WILL INDULGE.

'Of course.'

I SHARE CALLISTA'S CURIOSITY.

Cosmos' projection pushed their glasses back over their green hair, sweeping their fringe back, and lent forward to inspect Areté in an exaggerated fashion.

I OFFERED YOU A VERY SPECIFIC, VERY VALUABLE, VERY RARE FAVOUR: THE ABILITY TO SAVE A LIFE. ANY LIFE. AND I CAN THINK OF FEW LIVES WORTH THE RISK OF PLACING YOURSELF INTO AN ARRANGEMENT WITH ME. BUT YOU SURPRISED ME, ARETÉ. YOU CHOSE TO SAVE THE LIFE OF A TEENAGE BOY OF NO NOTABLE CONSEQUENCE OR ABILITY – A TALENTLESS PRINCE WHOSE OWN FAMILY WOULD BE GRANTED A FAVOUR BY HIS DEATH. AND THUS WE ARE HERE, WITH YOU WONDERING WHAT ENORMOUS THING I MIGHT ASK IN RETURN, AND I DO NOT AT ALL UNDERSTAND WHY.

'All lives are important, Cosmos.'

COME NOW, ARETÉ. IT IS NOW IN MY POWER TO PUSH YOU INTO THE DARKNESS. TO REQUIRE YOU TO DO THE WORK OF SCYROS. TO ASK YOU TO MURDER AND TO MAIM; WHICH WE BOTH KNOW YOU ARE VERY CAPABLE OF DOING. I CAN ASK ANYTHING OF YOU. I FIND IT HARD TO BELIEVE THAT SOMEONE AS DANGEROUS AS YOU WOULD SO LIGHTLY PUT YOUR ABILITIES INTO THE HANDS OF ANOTHER – ESPECIALLY ONE YOU HAVE NO REASON TO TRUST.

Areté met and held those clear, bright gold eyes in a steady gaze. She had known it was a trap. It could be nothing else. But sometimes you had to step into the trap, to see who the hunter really was.

'It is my belief that whatever game you are playing, Cosmos, however carefully you have planned it, you are in turn being played by someone - or some*thing* else - more powerful altogether. Had Rupert fallen anywhere else in Leaverness - anywhere else on all of Altica - I would have used only the methods available to me to try to save his life. And when I could not, I would have held him in his death, and then grieved. But that it was Rupert who fell just here in the Forest of Secrets, I could not ignore. That you had come to me just weeks ago, with the offer you did, in time for what happened today, I could no more leave him dead than I can refuse the favour you will ask of me now. We are just role playing, you and I.'

HOW DREADFULLY DRAMATIC.

Cosmos raised a fine eyebrow.

WHAT A WOEFULLY HELPLESS WORLD VIEW YOU HAVE, ARETÉ. WHILE I ASSURE YOU THAT I WOULD LOVE TO BELIEVE THERE IS AN OVER-RIDING ORDER TO OUR LIVES, I AM AFRAID THERE REALLY IS NOT; WE LIVE AT THE MERCY OF CHAOS. OR WE CHOOSE TO DETERMINE OUR OWN ORDER.

'And what order do you seek?' Areté asked.

NOW THAT WOULD BE TELLING. BUT I SEE ONLY ONE TRUE OBSTACLE TO MY GOAL, AND SO THIS IS THE FAVOUR I HAVE EARNED FROM YOU. I NEED TO KNOW WHO – AND WHERE – IS THE MANDALA.

Areté let the words land, and sink in, and then almost laughed with relief. This provoked a disapproving look from Cosmos, but Areté just shrugged helplessly.

'You have made an enormous gamble on nothing, Cosmos, for this I cannot tell you,' Areté said, and it was the truth. 'The Mandala is hidden under a glamour so strong even I cannot find it. It is Praxidice you needed to ensnare in an Arrangement, not me.'

Cosmos studied Areté closely, and she felt the cool brush of their espréi against her own. She deflected it effortlessly but frowned momentarily at the vestigial familiarity of the contact.

Cosmos, noting this, turned on a distractingly winning smile again.

I AGREE THEN THAT YOU CANNOT TELL ME WHERE THE MANDALA IS RIGHT NOW. BUT THE CURRENT HOST, EVEN IF HIDDEN, WILL DIE IN THEIR TIME. I AM PLAYING A LONG GAME. CALLISTA IS VERY YOUNG, AND I AM SO VERY PATIENT. IF YOU CAN TELL ME WHERE THE MANDALA WILL GO NEXT, THEN OUR ARRANGEMENT WILL BE CONCLUDED.

These words sobered Areté immediately. She briefly considered whether it was a change in favour - which, under the terms of such agreements, she could refuse - but she could see it was not truly. The request was still to find the Mandala, no time frame had been specified.

She swung from relief to despair in just two simple questions, for this information was indeed in her knowledge.

Areté gave a bleak smile.

'Well, that is another matter entirely,' she said. 'I do know. But I cannot tell you.'

CANNOT? OR WILL NOT?

'It is the same, in this case.'

Cosmos digested this thoughtfully.

YOU UNDERSTAND THE COST OF REFUSING TO GRANT MY FAVOUR? OF BREAKING THE ARRANGEMENT?

'Of course I do.'

DO YOU WISH THE OPPORTUNITY TO EXPLAIN TO RUPERT WHY HIS LIFE WAS SAVED, ONLY TO BE TAKEN AGAIN? OR SHALL I RESTORE HIS DEATH IMMEDIATELY?

'There is no need to annul your favour. I forfeit my life to you, instead,' Areté said.

I CANNOT SIMPLY KILL YOU, ARETÉ, AND NOR DO I WISH TO.

'I did not offer my death, Cosmos.'

SO YOU OFFER...YOUR FREEDOM?

'I do.'

Cosmos had offered the Arrangement to Areté knowing only one of themselves or Bane would get what they want: information, or Areté out of play. It was their preference to get the result *they* wanted though, as quickly as possible, even though time was not strictly of the essence.

I COULD HAVE ASKED UNSPEAKABLE ACTS OF YOU, AND THESE, I BELIEVE, YOU WOULD HAVE DONE. I COULD ASK STILL, ASK YOUR PERMISSION TO CHANGE MY FAVOUR, AND YOU COULD RETAIN YOUR FREEDOM.

'I permit you to change the favour,' Areté said, hope jostling against the dread of what Cosmos might ask instead.

Cosmos' next smile was cold though.

AH BUT ARETÉ, I CANNOT. WHICH IS TO SAY, I WILL NOT. THERE IS JUST ONE TRUE OBSTACLE TO MY PLANS. ONLY ONE. AND IT IS NOT YOU, ARETÉ, IT IS NOT EVEN YOU. NOR SELENE, NOR COBI, NOR KYRE, NOR SKY. NOT PRAXIDICE OR SHIVAIA OR EVEN MAMA AKSAYA. LYSCHIVA AND CHAL'OM SHALL NOT BOTHER THEMSELVES TO GET INVOLVED. I BELIEVE I CAN HANDLE ALL OF YOU, GIVEN TIME. NO, THERE IS ONLY THE MANDALA WHO IS A RISK TO ME. BUT AS I SAY, I AM PATIENT. YOU WILL NOT GIVE IT AWAY NOW, BUT I THINK, GIVEN TIME, EITHER YOU WILL LEAD ME TO MANDALA, OR IT WILL COME FOR YOU. AND TIME IS SOMETHING WITH WHICH WE ARE EQUALLY BLESSED TO AN EXCESS. LET US TEST BOTH OF OUR PATIENCE.

And so it was that Areté did not get to take Lien to Avenel after all, or tell him things of his past that he would, in time, need to know.

*****

Hours earlier, as Areté had chided Lien, a warm, damp snuffling woke the fallen Rupert. He gasped as something enormous and wet slurped in his ear, and forced his eyes open, expecting the worst. Cavernous nostrils blew hot breath across his face, and the boy shuddered, panic rising, before his brain kicked in and waved a white flag. No monster ever had grass-sweetened breath like that.

'I *hate* horses...' Rupert groaned, experimentally rolling first onto his side, then into a half sitting position. His battered - though no longer broken - body objected strenuously, and the big black horse promptly flattened him back down while attempting to use him as a personal rubbing post.

'Geeeerrrrofit!'

The boy tried to push the horse away, before realising it wasn't his. The grey mare was standing quietly a few yards off, head low, snapped reins hanging between her legs, looking for all the world as apologetic as a horse can. The animal that had woken Rupert was a larger, heavier boned charger, with a shiny coat of the deepest obsidian black. Even to someone who disliked horses as much as the prince, he was magnificent.

Rupert's body though was less so, objecting vehemently to his attempts at movement. His bruised ribs ached and he could barely move his neck, which seemed locked permanently to the left, the direction from which the devil child had pulled off his helmet. His armour, he soon discovered, was strewn about, apparently torn free in haste. Coaxing some movement into his numb fingers,

Rupert clumsily fumbled his breastplate straps toward his locked neck for closer inspection. They had been cut clean through.

'You didn't do this, did you?' he vaguely asked the black horse. It just gave him an expectant look.

'You are lovely, and look very clever, for a horse,' the fallen boy started, almost drunkenly, 'but sadly, it would appear that I am broken.'

The horse remained apathetic.

'Look,' Rupert proceeded to spell it out, as though the horse might understand. 'You are up there, and I am down here. Our relative positions do not coincide.'

And then something entirely ridiculous happened. The horse doubled carefully at the knees and hocks, folding his long legs safely away from Rupert, so that his back was right up next to the boy. Rupert stared.

'I absolutely don't believe that just happened,' he murmured groggily, head fogging again as consciousness began to slip away. The horse snorted, almost crossly now, and threatened to roll back over the boy.

'Okay, okay, I got the message,' the prince groaned, wrapping his arms about the thick black neck and proceeding to painfully drag himself onto the horse's wide back. Ever so carefully, the horse gathered his legs below and hoisted himself back to his feet.

'You're naked...' mumbled Rupert as he started to pass out again. His last thoughts were to wish he had a saddle or reins or anything at all but silken mane to hold onto.

The arrival of Prince Rupert in Avenel alone, severely injured, unconscious, on the back of an unsaddled horse, without his armour, and hours ahead of his horse-less colleagues, caused much excitement in itself. The magnificence of the horse that he returned on - followed docilely by the grey mare - caused even more. All the way from the city gates people tried to catch the black stallion, but he had allowed none to touch him and he wore no bridle to be caught by. Throngs of adults and children fell in behind the black and grey horses and followed them in an excited crowd to the gates of the Voltanna, the fortress that was the home of the Order of the Coeur. There Sir Bane, believing himself to be facing Erebus, requested permission of the horse - out loud - to take the unconscious chevalier to the Order's infirmary. The black horse allowed Bane to approach, unwrap Rupert's rigid fingers from his silken black mane and slide the boy down into his arms. As he did so, Bane realised this horse was a little shorter and a thicker set than Areté's black stallion. When he had gone to the stables later to see the miracle animal up close, Bane discovered he had a small, perfect white star under his thick black forelock. This was not Erebus indeed, but the likeness was remarkable.

Lady Selene Beckworth took on Rupert's initial and most critical care, which included extensive diagnostics, straightening his neck out and treatment for severe concussion and broken ribs. The Order Infirmary staff were shocked by her unannounced arrival in Voltanna and dared not argue, even though the lady was not widely known for her medical skills. They could not fault the results though, as the prince recovered far better than expected.

Sir Bane visited Rupert at his bedside during his lengthy convalescence, politely asking him about everything that had happened in Leaverness. He especially focussed on what had happened once Rupert had been separated from the other chevaliers. Rupert explained that the horses had been frightened by a screaming creature - though it was hard to tell in the moment, as he never saw what spooked them, only heard its cries - and that his mare had bolted and fallen and that he remembered nothing else until he was woken in Avenel, hours after he had been pried from the back of the black horse. This was not strictly true of course, but Rupert was cautious about giving inexplicable and potentially delirious recollections to anyone, much less a senior knight.

Bane asked what had happened to his armour; Rupert said he did not know. Bane asked if he knew whose horse he had ridden back on; Rupert said he did not. Bane asked if he had ever seen a horse similar to it; Rupert hesitated before replying, as a faint memory stirred. He couldn't quite catch a hold of it though, so he shrugged it off and said he had not. Bane asked if Rupert was *sure*, and whether he needed to think harder. Rupert did so, himself curious about the elusive memory, and caught a little more of it. He had been tutored for...a season? A few months? No, more. He had been tutored by - a man? No, a woman. His only female tutor. A tutor who rode a big black horse. The associations with her were confused, but not negative. Rupert decided he must have been very young, too young to fully remember, and told Bane so, and that he felt a headache coming on. Perhaps a relapse of his concussion.

Bane was fascinated by the Rupert's struggle. While outwardly agreeing with the boy that he might simply still be concussed, the knight was inwardly considering how intrusive he dared to be. They were alone, after all.

Deciding he dared quite a lot, he placed his right hand over Rupert's head. Rupert blinked at the unexpected move and went to pull back, but Bane gripped his head and acted quickly on his gamble.

From Rupert's perspective, he lost just a few seconds of time. He had been startled to find Sir Bane's hand on his head, and then felt like a bucket of ice water had been thrown over him. But in what seemed just moments later, the knight was asking, with concern, whether he needed to lie down. The headache had turned into a full migraine with shocking speed and Rupert now felt like he might be sick; which he promptly was, to the side of his bed, noisily and to his great embarrassment.

From Sir Bane's perspective, he spent a good few minutes rummaging around in the prince's mind. He did not possess the skill to access any memories that were not already lined up for Rupert's own perusal, but Bane could easily and vividly see all the key details the prince had omitted. He saw the wild child giving chase, and the fear in Lien's face when he realised that he had been seen. Bane experienced the rib crushing kick to the chest that should have been fatal. He felt the hands that cut off Rupert's armour and heard the voice that said his name. And he knew the voice. Rupert had no idea of what happened next though, until being woken by the black horse, and so Bane could learn nothing further either. But he now had the important information he sought.

Bane should have ended the intrusion into Rupert's mind at that point, but he was intrigued by the prince's confusion over the memory of the tutor. He looked further, and found a peculiar emptiness that, on its edges, distorted other memories. The only memory that was active and available to Bane was the one Rupert had been looking for himself: that of a big black horse and his rider. His female rider. It was a confused, damaged memory. Bane cautiously felt his way around it, and he too felt queasy, although nothing like the prince shortly would be. But he was certain of three things: that Areté had history with the prince; that she had helped him after his fall; and that the horse Rupert had ridden back on had her fingerprints all over him.

Bane left the infirmary satisfied and thoughtful, and called upon his uneasy ally Callista to confirm his suspicions.

For his part, Rupert was certain that he had been dying after the kick in the chest. He couldn't quite shake the feeling that he should still be dead: that his continued life was a mistake. He often woke in cold sweats after dreaming of the terrifying chase through Leaverness, reliving the sight of the pursuant devil child, and how his eyes had switched from wild to - what? Fear? Could something so fearsome have also been afraid of Rupert?

Rupert had not told Sir Bane about the child, or the way he had been awakened and collected by the black horse, because they were preposterous details, and he had not wished to end up being more mocked than he already was as standard. Bane's son would soon be joining the Order and struck Rupert as a cold and perhaps cruel boy. He would not want Tryst to end up with any socially compromising ammunition which to make his life in Avenel even more miserable.

But Rupert had, for now, forgotten two important things from the incident in Leaverness, and his forgetting had shielded them from Bane's investigation. The first was meeting Shivaia on the borderline between life and death.

The second was the cold, eerie secret that had tried to wind its way back into his memory as he had lain dying in the Forest of Secrets. He was not to know, but when he had survived, the secret had returned obediently to the tree within which it had been securely bound many years earlier - and by his own, now forgotten, request.

Once Rupert was released from the Order's infirmary, he and the black horse became inseparable. Although there was nothing to suggest the prince actually had legal ownership of the horse he named Lord Jorge, Jorge possessed an acute attitude of ownership towards the young prince. This was proven by the best efforts of several horse thieves and thugs, who had painfully discovered firstly that the black horse was himself disinclined to be parted from Rupert, and secondly that the prince had family connections to organised crime. It was one thing for the family to plot to dispose of their unsuitable heir to replace with his younger brother, but that didn't mean anyone could just go around stealing his property. Jorge meanwhile was ill-tempered to anyone who showed anything less than respect to the prince, while also unaccountably patient with his young charge's clumsiness, awkwardness and fundamental cowardice. One might go as far as to say Rupert only made it into his second year at the Order because the horse ensured he excelled in their mounted training, even as he struggled in all other areas.

~

Eyebrows were raised throughout the Order though when, a year later, Rupert was selected for the role of second-year escort for the next Leaverness manoeuvres. The thought occurred to a few of the more cynical knights that Rupert's father had made the request himself, in the hope that this time the forest would actually succeed in eliminating his embarrassingly hapless son and heir. But the truth was that the instruction came from the Red Knight, Sir Bane, whose son, Tryst, would also be on the ride, and had been given very specific instructions.

Rupert himself was appalled to learn that he would have to escort the first years on the very exercise that had almost killed him the year before. He had but two consolations: he knew Jorge would ensure no harm befell him; and he knew at least one of the chevaliers on the trip would not give him a hard time. This chevalier was merely indifferent to Rupert, as he was with everyone, where the others were anywhere from mean to outright vicious.

He had made it into the Order through the recently reinstated Commoner Trials. He no longer believed in dreams, but in vengeance. His patron was Lady Selene Beckworth, and his name was Citar.

# 6. Bravo

By the summer of Rupert's second visit to Leaverness, the consequences of Areté's disappearance a year earlier were rippling out across the people and places she had protected. Jordan had died; Cira had sought Praxidice to demand vengeance against Brynir, and had joined the Order as the boy Citar; Sky had moved his tribe deeper into the forest, away from Bane's roving knights; and Lien had started having nightmares.

The summer itself had descended early, assaulting the Avenel plains with spiteful temperatures. Even in the shaded depths of Leaverness it was too hot for mischievous spirits to do what they did best: havoc remained conspicuously unwreaked across the wilderness bordering the plains. The children of the forest retreated to the rivers, splashing about in lukewarm water before collapsing to bake on the banks. The adults of the People relaxed. Sky alone remained uneasy, sensing the current order unravelling around him, and made yet another unusual departure from Leaverness.

A week into this unprecedented early heatwave, the oppressive conditions had defeated even Lien and Bravo, whose usual combined ability to attract trouble was fast approaching a magnetic quality. If trouble could be bothered to seek them out on this day though, it would find them only by their lean, bare legs - one pair naturally brown, the other lightly tanned from white - dangling over a broad branch within the lower echelons of the forest canopy. The bark was warm against their sprawled bodies, but the odd breeze managed to infiltrate the dense foliage, cooling the permanent sheen of sweat on their skin.

While Lien looked as peaceful as his best friend, the stillness of his body belied a chaotic mind where worries chased one another around, jostling for pole position. One thought ran in reverse though, almost unnoticed in the clamour of the others; in a bid for notice it skipped lanes, causing a spectacular pile-up. Lien's worries collided into and over one another, scrambled back up and stood to reluctant attention to the rogue idea.

It demanded consideration.

Eventually, Lien capitulated.

'You're good with dreams, Bravo,' he ventured with general admiration, fishing to gauge his friend's mood. Bravo typically oscillated somewhere between angry-suspicious, angry-defensive, angry-sarcastic and angry-aggressive. This led most people to assume he was simply angry all the time, but Lien knew better. He automatically filtered out the anger altogether and that was why he knew Bravo was rarely as angry as he seemed: he simply faced the world with pre-emptive antagonism as a matter of habit.

Bravo reluctantly rolled his head to the side, fixing Lien with a baleful glare.

'You waking me up to make a point, Lien, or just a statement of the obvious?'

Good result: Lien knew from the merely minor inflection of anger, leaning more towards petulance, that his friend was actually quite pleased with the implied compliment.

Time to lay bait.

'Good enough to catch a night-mare?'

Bravo considered.

'Those bad dreams are getting worse,' he said eventually, acknowledging the hook.

'Yes.' Lien tried to keep his tone casual, which told Bravo how serious the problem was. 'Do you think it's possible?'

'I don't think it's ever been done, they're difficult creatures, and dangerous too,' Bravo mused, too thoughtful to even snap. He caught himself with a dismissive, 'Though Sky would be the one to ask.'

'Sky's not here.' Lien fed out line. 'But you are.'

'Hah,' Bravo said, turning an interrogative stare back on Lien. 'And say we could catch one. What would you do with her? Ask her politely to stop?'

'Ride her back to the source of the dream,' Lien said, as though they were talking about the weather and not something absolutely outrageous.

Bravo paused a moment, before bursting into serrated laughter.

'And you're worried about how to *catch* her? Lien, no-one can ride a night-mare, I'd swear it true.'

'Well if no-one's ever caught one, how would they know?' Lien argued, but only briefly: far from being twisted in his usual sneer, Bravo's face softened absently as his mind went to work on the idea.

*Hook, line and sinker…*

With luck, Lien wouldn't have to convince him further: competitive to a fault, Bravo would already be starting to convince himself of the merits of the challenge.

'Look, Lien, I can try to go to Aurebos for you, you

don't need the messenger when you can go straight to the source,' he finally offered, although reluctantly because while a practical solution, it lacked the attractive impossibility of Lien's proposition.

'You don't understand,' Lien said, rolling upright as he became more agitated. 'I don't think she's coming from Aurebos. It's always the same mare, I'm sure of it.'

'You think someone's captured a night-mare for the exclusive use of torturing you?'

Bravo had a snide follow-up reality check ready, but let it die on his lips when he saw Lien's expression. "Fantasist" and "naïve" were both terms Bravo would comfortably use to describe his best friend, but paranoid he was not. The look on Lien's face suggested he'd thought long and hard about what he was suggesting.

His faced begged: *help me.*

Bravo sighed, rolling up to sitting also.

'Look, there are a number of reasons why that is impossible,' he began patiently. 'One of these is that it's almost impossible to see your own night-mare. It's like this: you sleep, the mare delivers the dream, and then she doesn't hang around. You're entering the dream or nightmare *as she leaves*. By the time you wake,' he snapped his fingers loudly, 'no night-mare. She's long gone.'

Now that Bravo was on a roll, he was quite immune to the heat, absently wiping trickles of sweat weaving their way down his right temple. Lien however was puzzled. He *was* seeing the ghostly apparition every time he surfaced, sweaty and shaking from the nightmares she delivered. The dapple-grey mare with her obsidian black legs, mane and tail and an unknown sigil painted in red upon her hindquarters. Before his wild, staring eyes, she'd dissolve into coils of silvery smoke as she galloped away to the darkness that was her realm.

He *was* seeing her.

Or… was he only *thinking* he saw her…?

'Tell me about the dreams,' Bravo invited, perhaps hoping to tease some sense from Lien's evident suffering. 'They're always the same?'

'It's awful,' Lien shuddered. 'It's hard to explain. You have to understand that if I tell you, it doesn't sound so bad. So when I tell you, don't *see* what I'm saying. I need you to *feel* it.'

And then he tried to explain the nightmares.

There was only really one, so if Lien was losing his marbles, he was doing so in a deeply unoriginal manner. As with all dreams, he had no memory of entering the nightmare; he would just be there. And "there" was inside someone else's body.

'Whose body?' Bravo asked.

'Well I didn't know at first,' Lien explained, agitated now. 'I see through their eyes, you see. So I can't see who I'm seeing, if you follow.'

'Yes you can, you just need to find a reflection.'

'I can't move the body, Bravo. I'm in there, but I have no control. And…'

He paused.

'And…?' Bravo prompted, curious. Lien could talk the hind leg off a donkey. All this posturing and sighing was out of character.

'And I'm often tied up. Chained, usually. At least, the person I'm in is chained. It's all terribly uncomfortable.'

And that was an understatement if ever there was one.

The wrist and ankle manacles bit and chafed on raw skin while stiff muscles wasted under lack of movement.

'Can you see their hands? Any clue there?' Bravo pressed, intrigued now.

*Yes, they are hands I thought I knew well, but how could I be sure?* Lien thought miserably.

*I didn't want to be sure.*

*That these were hands that carried me as a baby, picked me up as a child, tended my cuts and bruises as a boy. That these were the hands that showed me how to light a fire, to calm a frightened horse, to write in the language of Avenel.*

*I wanted them to be any other hands but these.*

These were all things he thought.

'Yes. They're a woman's hands,' was all he said though.

This caught Bravo by surprise.

'Anything else?'

'I'm - she's - starving. Beaten. Bravo, she is in so much pain. More pain than I think I can endure, and I *feel* it, it's my pain too. When I wake, it's still there, just for moments, but it makes me ill. Sometimes it's not so bad. Sometimes it's worse than bad.'

The pain wasn't even the worst of it though.

'What else?' Bravo pressed, reading Lien's expression like an open book, as only he could.

'She's so unhappy. Sometimes she is sad. Sometimes she feels despair. Sometimes she is angry. So angry. It's like...well, it's hard to explain...?'

Lien grappled for the words, but failed to find any adequate. He looked instead to the resident expert.

'It's like a furious knot in the centre of yourself, a knot that's actually made of miles of rope wound so tight it's just the size of a fist and it pulls at your whole body, dragging it inwards until it seems you must either collapse in on yourself or blow up completely, at which point every one of those ropes will snap and you will be free and there will be nothing in the world that can stop you from expressing every ounce of rage you've got trapped down there,' Bravo offered.

Lien digested this over several long seconds.

'Yes, exactly like that,' he eventually agreed. 'Is that really how you feel all the time?' he added cautiously, not sure if he wanted to know the answer.

'Not all the time,' Bravo said simply as he lay back down again.

'Oh. Well, that's good,' Lien offered.

'The rage is like a pulse in your brain,' Bravo said dreamily. 'The pulse of your soul.'

'And who is the least angry person you know?'

'Trick question, right? It's obviously you. I don't even know how we're friends, if I'm honest.'

'Okay, the least angry after me.'

Bravo considered a moment. He found an answer, but before he could say it, his face froze. He sat bolt upright.

*They're a woman's hands…*

'Oh no…'

'Listen, last night – '

'Can't be!' Bravo cut in.

'I said *listen* to me – '

'There's no way. You said you don't know who it is, anyway.'

'I said I *didn't* know. Until last night. Because last night…' Lien trailed off. It was difficult to explain. He was only a passenger in a body enduring violence at the hands of persons unknown. A body that had, in last night's act of torture, had its head forced into a bucket of grimy water. But before "his" face had broken the surface and Lien had woken, soaked but only in his own sweat, in his own body - before that, he had momentarily glimpsed the reflection of face he wore in his nightmare -

' - and that's why you woke up screaming,' Bravo finished quietly. Everyone had heard. Bravo had claimed responsibility at the time because he didn't think Lien actually capable of speaking, and he was no stranger to nightmares and night terrors himself. He had not pressed Lien about the dream at the time. He had known that his friend would talk about it when he was ready.

'She needs me, Bravo. She's the one who's sending the dreams, has to be.'

'Look, Lien…if someone's managed to trap Areté, what do you think *you* are going to be able to do about it? I mean you've heard the stories they tell about her. Things that exist to terrify are terrified of her.'

'That's why I need you,' Lien said earnestly, shuffling a little closer.

'Who you need is Sky. Therefore what you have to do is wait until he's back in Leaverness,' Bravo said in a tone that warned against argument.

'Wait? Knowing that she's in danger, that she could die - '

' - she's not going to die, Lien. That's one of the advantages of being immortal.' Bravo thought about that a moment. 'As far as we know,' he added, less confidently.

'There has to be *something* we can do!' Lien wailed. 'Something *you* can do!'

Bravo raised one eyebrow at the telling inflection.

'You can do dream magic. *You* can use espréi.'

'Well there's no need to be so defensive about it. We all can.'

*Except for me*, thought Lien.

Bravo's face reflected the same realisation.

'I mean, it's not my fault that you're… you know…'

'Useless?' Lien finished sullenly.

'Avenelese, I was going to say.'

'Which is the same thing.'

'Not in your case,' Bravo said firmly. 'So you're a little - brown. Well, very. And you have no natural talent for magic that anyone's been able to find - '

' - not helping, Bravo - '

' - but we've bought you up properly, and that's the important thing.' He tapped his temple. 'You might look like you're from Avenel, but you think like the People, and that's what matters, right?'

Lien shrugged. As a child, he had actually shown modest talent for connecting to espréi. But that had changed when he had met Brynir.

Lots of people, as he understood, could *feel* the energy of the world. But to be able to do anything with it you had to be able to open your soul eye. Your two standard eyes see the physical world, while your soul eye sees the energetic world. To the uninitiated, early attempts to open the Soul Eye felt like being blinded: too much light pours in. Sky would say that first you are blinded, and then you spend your life learning how to see again, see anew. See the espréi that is everywhere in the world around you. And once you can see it, you can learn to interact with it.

In his tenth year, Lien had started to feel a - a darkness, a somber and cold presence, whenever he had tried to open his soul eye. It was supposed to fill him with light, but instead, a shadow rose up within him any time he tried to open his third eye. This put him off trying, and he had initially blamed it on his heritage, as that was easier and safer than telling the truth. It was also a narrative that had been readily accepted by the tribe: folk from Avenel didn't even know the soul eye existed, much less how to find and open it. And then, when he had faced death at the paw of Brynir, Lien had heard an eerie voice in his head.

**LET ME.**

He hadn't had time to even think about it. Brynir had been about to kill him, so he had opened his soul eye, and felt the darkness rush into his mind, and into his body, and then he had...watched himself deal with the beast. It had been a little like his dreams of Areté, in that he was a mere passenger, but inside his own body. He had only fully come back to himself to find Bravo demanding what he had done. And he'd had no idea what to tell him.

Bravo's unknown father was also from Avenel, but his mother had been a daughter of Sky, and like her, he had a talent for dream magic. He could already astroplane and had successfully found his way to Aurebos, the dreaming realm - the collective consciousness of all peoples and all stories, a place of darkness that lay beyond the path of the rising moon. Even more impressively, he had even found his own way back again. Lien could think of only two people he could ask to help with a dreaming problem, and with Sky away, that left only Bravo.

'Will you help me?' Lien pressed again.

'I am sure I can come up with something brilliant, but only if you shut up and let me think about it for more than a minute at a time, Lien!' Bravo grumped, his fingertips kneading his temples now. The look of intense concentration on his face defied any further interruption, so Lien flopped back on the wide, warm tree branch. The fretful kicking of his hanging legs gradually subsided as he allowed himself to become lost in the hypnotic splendour of the upper canopy, where searing sunlight danced through the dome of leaves. A trouble shared was indeed a trouble halved; Lien felt confident his friend would find a solution. He would never admit it of course, but he considered Bravo the brains of their small party.

Eventually Bravo sat up again.

'Tell you what. I'll stay up tonight. See if I can't meet this mare of yours, and then at least we'll have somewhere to start,' he said.

Lien grinned, heart swelling with gratitude. Bravo was difficult, tempestuous and often unnecessarily aggressive, but he was also a brilliant best friend.

*****

The two boys were close in age, with Bravo just a year older, and they had grown up united in the knowledge that they were pariahs within the tribe, even though they had not always understood why. They knew more now, though there was still much to learn. They were both orphans: Lien was a complete outsider, a boy from Avenel who was brought to the People by Areté as an infant; and Bravo's father had also been an outsider from the city. Lien's skin was a light olive brown; Bravo was as white as his mother and the rest of his tribe.

Lien's backstory, as told by Areté, was painfully incomplete.

Areté had been drawn by screams in Leaverness to find his mother being attacked by two men trying to take her child. She had been unable to save his mother but had saved her infant son from the men. Suspicious about why they had wanted the child, she had then taken him to Sky for protection until she could find his family. But she claimed she had never found them, and so he had stayed in Leaverness, an outsider raised by the People. Lien had always accepted the story as told, and in fact parts of it were even true; Bravo was beginning to harbour suspicions about the finer detail though. Bravo also knew what Lien did not: that his presence was a danger to the whole tribe.

What neither of them knew was that to convince the People to adopt Lien, Areté had joined Sky in creating a powerful obscuration spell which meant the tribe could not be incidentally found. It did not, of course, obscure anyone showing themselves to outsiders, as Lien and Bravo had done in saving Cira and Jordan from Brynir; or Lien had in chasing Prince Rupert to steal his feather and helm. But the charm had otherwise done its work, diverting any outsiders in Leaverness around the People, and frustrating even academics like Falric, who meant them no harm.

Bravo meanwhile pieced his backstory together more gradually. For most of his life, he had understood that his father was an unknown outsider and his mother, Endora, had died from complications of his birth. It was much later that he had learned that his father was a knight. While it was historically common for women of the People to have children with outsider men - at least, prior to the obscuration charm - being fathered by a knight was particularly offensive, especially given the persecutions that followed the death of King Du Romeau. As the son of, of all things, a knight; and having, as he felt, caused the death of his mother, Bravo believed his existence was a terrible error, and this discoloured his entire outlook on life.

Sky adored and protected his grandson as best he could, but even he could not completely protect the boy's heart. And the protection he gave frustrated Bravo further. When he was twelve, Bravo had begged Sky to tell him the truths he sensed were being withheld. Sky told him only that his questions would be answered as part of his Kia'Oro trial, the ritual through which teenagers of the People transitioned into adulthood. He could choose to learn the truth then if he wished.

Sky counselled caution, but knew Bravo would never be satisfied until he knew the truth.

Even if he liked the truth significantly less than the mystery.

* * * * *

That night, Bravo kept watch over Lien as promised. The boys had chosen to stay away from the main camp, so they could have more privacy. The night air and earth were still warm after the baking heat of the day, and Lien fell asleep in just his shorts. Bravo settled into a tree above where he could watch without disturbing his friend - or the nocturnal visitor, should she come.

Just after midnight his patience was rewarded by the approach of phantom galloping hoofbeats, a sound experienced in the body, not by the ears. Night-mares can only be heard by the sleeper whose mind they are approaching, but as Bravo was connected with the dreaming realm of Aurebos and was expecting her, he too felt the drumming of her hooves. The night-mare was as described by Lien: a young dapple-grey with black legs, mane and tail, and she did indeed have a sigil painted in red - with what, he wondered? - on her quarters. The sigil was similar to the sign of Aurebos. Similar, but not the same, and he felt sure he had seen it before. He committed it to memory to investigate later.

The night-mare slowed to a floating trot and then a walk as she approached the sleeping boy. She came to a full stop over Lien, dropped her nose to his temple and breathed the nightmare, a silvery mist, into his temple. At that point, she should have galloped back to Aurebos to collect and deliver another nightmare, but she did not. She stayed. She looked, to Bravo, to be watching: but whether she was watching Lien dream, or watching *over* the boy as he dreamed, he could not tell.

The nightmare took hold quickly: within short minutes Lien started to tense, his head jerking side to side as though he was trying to shake something off. A sheen of sweat accumulated at his brow and he started to gasp. This worried Bravo, but he knew the dreams were very vivid, so he waited, although he was now tense himself. Everything so far had been wrong about this dream encounter, so he was willing to bet the normal rules may not apply. Indeed, Lien's gasping soon became more desperate. His body started thrashing at some unseen opponent and the blood vessels of his reddening face began bulging. Bravo realised something else had changed: his friend was not getting any air in. The finale of the nightmare happened so fast: in the seconds it took Bravo to shin down the tree, Lien's thrashing subsided into shuddering.

As he landed on the ground, Bravo momentarily froze when the night-mare fixed him with a long, expectant look. He felt seen. Not just by the mare, but by something else. Something that looked through her huge, black eyes.

He threw himself back into action.

'Get away, you're killing him!' Bravo yelled at the horse, waving his arms wildly. She shied and galloped away, but Bravo had no time for her – Lien had now stopped moving completely. He was deathly still. Bravo knelt down to put the side of his face above his best friend's mouth, dread rising as his fears were confirmed: there was no breath.

'Lien!' Bravo shouted, slapping the still, limp boy. 'Wake up! Lien! You have to wake up!'

He slapped Lien again, and again, harder each time, and almost sagged with relief when the boy finally woke, gasping. Lien's lids opened but his eyes were rolled alarmingly up in his head, so that he was initially blind. He tried to cry out, but didn't have the air for it. Disoriented, he flailed wildly with his arms, still trying to fight off some unseen threat. Bravo caught his arms wrapped him in a tight hold.

'It's okay Lien, you're okay, you're safe now,' Bravo said, his voice shaking. He realised he was trying to reassure both of them. As Lien's sight returned and the sound of his best friend's voice punctured his panic, he ceased fighting, instead falling slack in his friend's arms while he focussed on drawing ragged breaths.

'Bravo? Wh-what happened?' Lien panted eventually, weakly pushing himself out of Bravo's arms into a sitting position. He could see fear and relief chasing one another around Bravo's face.

'You had a nightmare. Lien, you almost died – you

weren't *breathing!*' Bravo said, voice still unsteady. Lien's hands went to his throat.

'Yes…I was being…well, *Areté* was being strangled,' he said hoarsely, as he remembered the nightmare.

'No Lien, you were *also* being strangled. These aren't just nightmares in your mind. Just listen to your voice! It's like you're living them as well - like they're really happening to you.' Bravo exhaled deeply. 'I've never heard of anything like this. And the mare? You're right, she's not coming from Aurebos. She's wearing a different sigil.'

'The mare! You saw her?' Lien asked, the words painful on his ravaged throat. 'So you believe me?'

'Lien, I just watched you get strangled and nearly die in front of me in your sleep. I believe everything you've told me,' Bravo said seriously. 'We need to work out who's sending you these dreams, and where Areté is, and then we need to free her, before whatever's happening to her kills one - or both - of you.'

Lien gave an exhausted but relieved smile: he was sure that with Bravo's help, the two of them could find and rescue Areté.

'Thank you, Bravo,' he rasped gratefully. 'And thank you for staying awake to watch over me.'

'And for slapping some sense into you when you tried to die on me,' Bravo grunted. Lien lifted a hand to his stinging face.

'Is that why my face is burning?' he asked accusingly.

'You bet. You better not scare me like that again Lien.' Bravo shifted from kneeling to squatting and with a stick from the tree, proceeded to make two drawings in the soft loose dirt.

'This is the sign of Aurebos, which you thought you

saw on your night-mare,' he said as he completed the first. 'And this is the sigil she actually wears,' he added as he finished the second.

'Well to be fair, they're pretty similar,' Lien said, squinting over Bravo's shoulder to see in the darkness.

'They are indeed. Whoever is sending her is clearly connected to the dreaming realm.' He considered something else. 'She looked at me, you know. She looked at me as though to tell me I needed to help you. She knew you were in danger, and she knew I was with you. But I felt like I was being seen by something else too - something that was looking at me through her eyes.'

Lien frowned, struck by this description, for it reminded him of his "darkness". It was like a dark energy, which he had initially thought was outside himself and trying to get in. He thought that instead of touching espréi, he was touching some sort of inverted version of it. But over time he began to realise that it was not outside of him at all. It was *inside,* even though he only encountered it only when opening his soul eye, or when he was in danger. In such moments, it would rise up, and he would feel it looking *through* his eyes. This, he now reflected, was not unlike how he dreamed through the eyes of Areté - and sounded disturbingly similar to how Bravo described the presence he sensed inside the night-mare.

Lien knew the darkness wanted to take control of him, though it had done so only once, and only because he had been so far out of his depth that he had no choice. So he had let it deal with Brynir.

Did his night-mare have the same force inside her?

'Lien? What are you thinking?' Bravo asked curiously.

Lien blinked.

'Oh – that we should, uh – we should name her!' Lien said, scrambling for something safe to say. He couldn't bring himself to tell even Bravo that he had a shadow living inside him.

'Who? The night-mare?' Bravo asked.

'Yes. I mean, we'll be talking about her a lot, it will be much easier. She's beautiful, isn't she?' he added, his tone brightening for the first time.

Bravo cautiously nodded his agreement.

'What do you want to call her?' he asked.

Lien closed his eyes to think back on the mare. He knew, instinctively, that she did not mean him harm. She was merely the messenger. That said, he wasn't so sure about the motives of whoever was *sending* the dreams.

'I think she's a Shah,' he finally said.

Bravo nodded his agreement.

'Then Shah she is.'

The boys lay down next to each other and slowly fell each into a fitful sleep. Bravo was sure Shah would not make two visits in one night, but did seriously wonder how he would ever sleep again knowing Lien might die next to him during a nightmare. Lien meanwhile was haunted both by the horrific experience of being strangled, and a nagging worry: if he might have died, but for Bravo waking him up, what of Areté? It was true that she was considered immortal, but she had once told him only the Essene were truly immortal. She described herself to him as 'ageless', which was not the same at all.

Lien worried all of the next day.

Shah did not come that night; Bravo stayed up for hours in case she did though, and eventually fell asleep, exhausted, just a few hours before dawn, but with one hand draped across Lien's back, so that any dream thrashing would wake him.

Shah did not come the next night either, or the one after that or the one after that. She had not always come every night, but the frequency and intensity of the nightmares had, until now, been increasing. Bravo, now napping in the afternoons after staying up as long as he could every night, suggested that he might have spooked Shah when he'd chased her off. Or that whatever was sending her now knew he was waiting for her. Lien agreed both were possible, but they needed Shah to return if they were to catch her. And he needed her to return, so that he knew Areté was still alive. Sleep had become a frightening experience for Lien since the nightmares had started, and especially now that two of the dreams had caused him real harm in the physical world. But he was now also frightened by the nightmares *not* coming. And so every night, even though he knew he might never wake up, he prayed desperately to Shah to bring him a nightmare.

By the time a week had passed since the last nightmare, Lien was fighting the growing fear that Areté had died that night - that he had failed to save her. He would not - could not - give up hope though. Every night, he went to sleep forcing himself to believe Shah would come.

But still Shah did not come. Their next visitation was not from the night-mare, but from Prince Rupert, leading the first-year chevaliers - including the mysterious boy called Citar - into a very real nightmare.

# 7. CITAR

'We've gone far enough now, haven't we Rupert?' asked Shiloh. The boy was slouched in his saddle, his helm pushed back, looking ready for an afternoon kip. They were around three hours into Leaverness itself, and well off the established trails that ran through the safer, outer reaches of the forest. Rupert had been instructed to follow compass directions for the ride out; it was common for Leaverness to mess with compasses further inside though, leaving the boys to work out their own way back home. They ought to have travelled much further than they had in the time now passed, but it was too hot to push the horses hard.

They were currently walking on a single file path surrounded by dense forest and foliage. They were deep in shade, but even so, it was only getting hotter, and it was difficult to imagine anything frightening or horrific happening in such bright, summery conditions.

'C-couldn't agree m-more! J-job well d-done b-boys, we've m-made it into the f-forest, had a jolly ci-civil s-stroll, shall we call it a d-day now?' agreed Prince Rupert, technically the esteemed leader of the party. A year on from his first encounter with Lien, Rupert was still tall for his age, yet for all his ungainly lankiness, still over-mounted on the small mountain that was Lord Jorge.

'Don't be so wet, Rupert. It's barely noon, we should head further in,' said Tryst, casting the older boy a challenging sideways glance. Rupert tugged anxiously at his sweat-soaked necktie.

'It's w-well w-warm, T-tryst. Think of the h-horses.'

Lord Jorge lazily flicked a grateful ear.

'The horses are fine. Bored, even. I don't see why you should have enjoyed all the fun last year,' Tryst said.

Rupert paled.

'I h-hardly call being ch-chased by the s-spirits of the f-forest over r-ridge and vale "f-fun,"' he protested.

'You were pale as a sheet when you came back, as I recall. My father had to practically pry you off Lord Jorge,' Tryst needled.

'Although you've still never adequately explained how you ended up on Lord Jorge in the first place,' Shiloh said pointedly.

'Or why you gave the horse such a daft name,' Tryst added quietly. Every chevalier - and indeed knight - was envious of Jorge, and felt it a cruel irony that such a remarkable animal was wasted on the hapless prince.

'If we m-meet any more s-spirits of the f-forest, I'll be sure to let you t-take the l-lead, T-tryst,' Rupert floundered, trying to deflect attention from awkward questions about his horse - questions he was quite unable to answer. 'Sh shall we take a v-vote?'

'You're the leader. You make the decisions,' Tryst said with infuriating reason. Rupert looked to the rest of the party for help. This year's group was embarrassingly small, comprising of Rupert escorting just four first years. Just after news got around about who would be leading the ride, an amazingly timed stomach bug took out of the majority of the first years. The only four who able to join the manoeuvres were mouthy Shiloh, cunning Tryst, silent Ben and Citar - who was, of course, Cira. Poor Cira, who had chased Aethon again to find adventure and Lien, only to find violence and tragedy. Who was so traumatised by the death of her best friend that she had fled Leaverness and the Backwind both, to seek vengeance on Brynir from Praxidice. Who had had more than her fill of princes and stories and dreams, and now wanted only revenge.

As Areté had recommended, she had gone to Praxidice for the strongest glamour available, one that made her appear as a boy, and which deflected basic associations with her past. If anyone took the time to describe her, they might so do as a slender, fine featured, even pretty sort of a boy. But even if they did that, they would then not give her appearance a second thought, and they would certainly never think of her as feminine. And as Shivaia had foretold, she was no longer the lamed girl servant Cira of the Backwind, but the sound and strong boy chevalier Citar of Avenel.

But the reality of joining the Order and becoming a chevalier was far removed from the glorious dreams she had shared with Jordan. It was bittersweet, painful, and only a route to the retribution she craved: revenge on Brynir. It was also incredibly hard work and, in the absence of her best friend, desperately lonely.

When Lien came across the line of chevaliers he did not see Cira, for he was as much subject to the glamour as anyone else. He saw only another chevalier, whom he wanted to see dumped from his horse along with all the others. If he *had* known Citar was Cira, he might have begun to understand the mechanics at work around the two of them. As it was though, he initially considered his unexpected rendezvous with the chevaliers coincidental, even though Aethon was again the agency through which they met.

Lien had been out on Jest alone while Bravo took an afternoon nap - after another fruitless night of waiting on Shah - when he had come across the unicorn. Aethon was all shining obsidian and gold and breathtakingly beautiful, standing patiently in a forest clearing. Lien knew it was no accident: when one finds Aethon, you can be sure he was waiting to be found.

Lien had a way with all animals, as did all the People, but he had a particular affinity for horses. He had slipped off Jest and approached Aethon slowly, speaking in the language taught to him by Epona, the tribe horse whisperer. The unicorn had shown no sign of fear but waited, stock still, until Lien was a hand span away from his outstretched nose and wide, flaring nostrils. Lien made no attempt to touch his fine boned face or glossy black neck, but shared a couple of deep breaths, nose to nose. Lien had not seen Aethon since the unicorn had led him to Cira and Jordan four years earlier, and was elated to be this close to the mighty creature. He could have stood there taking in every detail of the unicorn for hours, but Aethon had ended the engagement with a sudden snort and shake of his head, before turning tail and leaving the clearing at an invitingly steady canter. Lien had grinned, and whistled Jest over, the heat of the day forgotten by both boy and pony: the game was on. They just didn't yet understand what - or whose - game they were playing.

The chase had lasted around twenty minutes and Lien had quickly understood where he had been led: into the path of the chevaliers. He had jumped off Jest and shinned up a tree to watch their advance, immediately noting three things.

The first was their number: a record low, in his experience.

The second was the big black horse at the front of the line, which bore such a striking resemblance to Erebus that Lien's heart skipped a beat as he thought momentarily that he had found Areté.

But no, for the third thing he noticed was the horse's rider: a lanky boy with a royal purple feather in his helm.

Lien leaned back against the tree trunk, suddenly light-headed as he realised that this was the boy that Areté said he had almost killed the previous year, but for her saving his life. As his brain connected the rider, horse, Areté's reprimand and Bravo's intuition that her interference had come at a cost, Lien felt a vice-like cold tighten across his chest, shortening his breath into shallower gulps. Areté had not returned to Leaverness since that day, and Lien's intuition was now screaming that the reason was to do with the nervous boy below. That it was Lien's own actions a year before that had sealed her fate.

Lien waited for the grip on his chest to loosen and the pounding of blood between his ears to subside. When he felt more in control, he took a few deeper breaths and then proceeded to catch up with the chevaliers, who had continued to ride on while he recovered himself. He noticed now that the boys were in much lighter armour than he had ever seen before, and he briefly wondered whether this was also his fault.

Which, of course, it absolutely was. After several years of gleefully watching the youth of the People cause the chevaliers' horses to unceremoniously dump their riders in clanging heaps on the hardest available forest surfaces, Areté - being an egalitarian of sorts, therefore advising both sides - had long since provided constructive advice to the Order about not sending out their youngsters out on summer time manoeuvres to Leaverness in plate iron. Her suggestions had met with a certain degree of resistance from senior knights, some of whom had endured the humiliation themselves and considered it character building. But the deciding factor was Prince Rupert, and therefore was indeed Lien's fault. The precise events surrounding his traumatic, near fatal experience of the previous year were still a matter of conjecture, but falling off in even the light chevalier armour is no joking matter when seriously injured and separated from one's fellows. When Rupert was announced as the second-year leader to the new intake, it seemed foolish to tempt fate a second time. Character building was all very well, but killing off the heir of one of the empire's constituent kingdoms, even by accident, and even when that accident was potentially being engineered by dirty politics from the heir's own court, was deemed by wiser heads of the Order to be an unnecessary risk. After all, Prince Rupert - an awkward and uncoordinated boy - was not only an accident waiting to happen, but also a boy who happened upon accidents much too often.

Consequently this year the chevaliers had been permitted to waive their usual training armour in favour of a more practical type of armament: just helms and chain mail shirts, with nothing at all to protect their arms or legs. This was somewhat cooler for the boys - a blessing given the relentless attentions of the sun - and while chain mail was still damn heavy, it also meant they would not be so easy to unseat, and more likely to get back up on their horses if they still fell off anyway. Had the youth of the People been preparing tricks to play, they would have needed to be laid more carefully this year.

But this year there were no tricks prepared, for Sky had expressly forbidden even stealth contact with outsiders. Additionally, the summer heat had arrived early, and so too had the chevaliers, and Lien had only discovered them via the machinations of Aethon. He knew he absolutely must not be seen by them, but he also knew the unicorn must have led him to them for a reason. He was torn about what to do, and initially wished Bravo was present to consult, before realising that had he been, Bravo would have dragged Lien as far away and as fast as possible.

And he knew that was the sensible and safest thing to do.

But Aethon had led him there. There was something of his destiny in meeting Cira and Jordan three years ago, and something of his destiny in encountering these chevaliers now.

Hoping desperately that he was making the right decision, Lien began to quietly follow along in the canopy to hear what was being said, and to try to understand why the unicorn had brought him here.

'Well for what it counts - and I'm as shocked as anyone to be saying this - I'm with Rupert,' Shiloh was saying in response to Rupert's suggestion of taking a vote. 'Let's not tempt fate. The spirits of the forest are clearly far more sensible than us and staying somewhere cooler today. I say we head back to Avenel and be the first chevaliers in years to come back *on* our horses.' He glanced at the prince. '*Conscious* and on our horses.'

Shiloh looked at Citar, who was next in line, and whose fine features were narrowed thoughtfully. She promptly derailed the conversation, as she was often wont to do. She had a strong suspicion about what had happened to Rupert last year and wanted to investigate.

'I don't believe the chevaliers are harassed by spirits of the forest.'

A short silence met this bold statement. Tryst looked amused.

'I s-say, C-citar, that's a bit l-left of f-field. Of c-course they are. W-well known f-fact. I have myself s-seen them, after all,' Rupert objected politely.

'And what exactly did you see, Rupert?' Citar challenged the prince.

Above the chevaliers, Lien froze; he did not trust Rupert not to inconveniently try to explain his embarrassment with the truth. He knew it would bode badly for the People if it were to become known that they were responsible for the many accidents the chevaliers and even knights of the Order experienced in Leaverness.

'Well, I d-didn't *e-exactly* s-see them. It was more a f-figure of s-speech. They are s-spirits, after all. Perhaps it would be m-more correct to s-say that I *experienced* them.'

'I don't deny that you experienced something, but I think it more likely to have been the People than anything more mythical,' Citar said.

'The People are history, the Order ran them into the ground years ago,' Shiloh said dismissively.

'They're still out here,' Tryst said, gazing around thoughtfully, before turning to Citar. 'But I think it's a stretch to imagine they hunt chevaliers to spook their horses every year. Do you really think that they have nothing better to do with their time?'

Lien thought on that a moment, and decided that most of the youth of the People really would be unable to think of anything better to do with their time than haunt chevaliers.

'I heard that last year the horses were frightened by a pig,' said Ben, his deep, quieter tones cutting through the banter. It was the first time he had spoken in an hour, and the other boys glanced around in surprise. All but Tryst, who turned to Rupert, delighted.

'Is that true, your very highness? A *pig*?'

Rupert blushed, and mumbled something vague.

'Well there you go,' Citar grinned. 'There's nothing even remotely supernatural about a pig. That was either very bad luck, or more likely, someone having a laugh at your expense.'

'It wasn't *j-just* a p-pig!' Rupert snapped, rallying what little backbone he possessed. He immediately regretted the short outburst though - as did Lien, above him. But as Tryst grinned and leapt promptly on the admission of said pig - 'Aha! His Royal Highness squeals at last!' - both boys briefly thought Rupert's statement had escaped further scrutiny. Citar, however, observant as ever, ensured this was not the case.

'Then what else was it?' she asked, cutting through Shiloh and Tryst's enthusiastic snorting and squealing.

Rupert stalled. He had never breathed a word of what he had experienced during that bizarre forest chase the year before, maintaining that he remembered nothing, and suspected this was not the right audience with which to break his silence. And besides, what was he to say? That he thought he had been chased by a devil-child, smeared in blood and dirt and mounted on a wild pony? When even he could not be sure of what spectre he had seen?

Above them, Lien listened with bated breath, wondering whether he was about to be given away. He could not allow the tall boy to tell the others of his existence. Perhaps this was why Aethon had led him here: to stop this boy from telling the others about seeing Lien last year?

He carefully watched Rupert's indecision.

'Come on Rupert, you can tell us,' Tryst coaxed, picking up on Citar's curiosity.

'Yes your highness, do share your secret with us all! Or I'll deck you one tonight in your sleep,' Shiloh chipped in, unhelpfully.

Rupert's face was screwed up with agonised indecision.

He opened his mouth.

Lien swiftly shinned down the tree to ground level.

Rupert began to speak –

– and from ground level, Lien made a commendable imitation of the shrill squeal of a pygmy pig and viciously shook the bushes all around before legging it back up into the high branches again.

Rupert turned his attempted explanation into a terrified yelp as all the boys shot to wary attention, their horses waking up sharply, heads thrown high, skittery all of a sudden. But when a conspicuous lack of pig followed the sound, it was Tryst who mockingly laughed first.

'The spirits are among us!' he announced loudly to the world at large. He leaned over, cheerfully belting Rupert on the back. 'I think we have indeed solved the mystery of the forest, your highness. Chased by wild pigs.' Tryst shook his head in mock sympathy. 'Could have happened to anyone.'

Rupert spluttered slightly under the other boy's enthusiastic assault, grateful nonetheless that he'd been saved from further interrogation regarding the now debunked spirits of the forest. Just to be certain, he decided to derail the conversation completely.

'I h-heard th-that the Order are about to re-replace the M-marked M-men,' he offered. It was an entirely unsubstantiated claim, having been overheard from stable boys who talk all manner of nonsense, but one absolutely guaranteed to draw attention away from his own misfortunes. It was also, by sheer chance, absolutely correct. As this news brought the desired rustle of excitement from the other boys, Tryst threw the prince an appraising look.

'Finally. It's about time Lindahl and Kai were replaced,' Ben said. For the first time, his dark eyes ceased to restlessly roam the forest, settling on his companions instead, to their general discomfort.

'Not if you believe they are still alive,' Tryst said. All eyes now turned to him: his father had been the Red Knight while Lindahl had been the Knight Operis, before Lindahl's great betrayal and downfall. If anyone in the group had valuable intel, it would be Tryst.

'Someone would have heard from them by now. It's been well over a decade. Kai might be dead in a ditch, but a man like Lindahl does not just disappear,' Shiloh countered.

'He might well be among us. Lindahl had the contacts and resources to get a glamour,' Tryst said. Citar blinked in surprise, while the other three boys all frowned in various depths of disbelief.

'C-come on now, T-tryst, there's no such th-thing,' Rupert said, signing off with a slightly nervous laugh.

'You tell yourself that,' Tryst shrugged. 'But I'm telling you, he could have been in Avenel all this time and we'd never know.'

'Surely we could work it out then?' Shiloh said, warming to the idea. 'We just need to do a list of knights and gentlemen who have arrived in the last fourteen years or so and dig into their pasts.'

'You can't guess or deduce, that's the point of a glamour,' Tryst said.

'Depends on how good the glamour is. With the weakest ones, we could work it out. But with the strongest ones, the suspicion just…slides off,' Citar, the resident glamour expert, agreed.

'So they say,' she added quickly, realising it might be unwise to give away her knowledge. 'I mean, I don't think they're real either.'

Tryst raised an eyebrow at her clumsy backtrack.

'This is correct,' he said. 'Even if we somehow managed to work out which knights or lords had arrived in Avenel since Lindahl killed the king - and there would be many - he wouldn't be on that list. Or if he was, we'd discard him, without even knowing why.'

'He could even be here as a woman,' Citar said, only realising it herself as she said it, and loving the idea.

'Lindahl, the First Knight, a *woman*?!' Tryst roared with laughter.

'M-my b-bet would b-be Lady B-beckworth,' Rupert said, grinning.

'And what inside information do you have on Lady Beckworth, your very highness?' Tryst asked, waggling a suggestive eyebrow.

Rupert flushed.

'N-nothing l-like that, T-tryst! S-she h-helped m-me l-last y-year,' the prince stammered. 'A-and is a f-friend of m-my f-father.'

'What *sort* of friend of your father?' Tryst teased, enjoying the Rupert's embarrassment. 'Many wealthy men are *very* good friends of Lady Beckworth.'

'N-nothing t-to do w-with - w-with - y-you k-know w-what,' Rupert dug himself deeper into trouble, and Lien deeper into confusion.

'With *what*, pray tell?'

'With being an outstanding pillar of Avenel society,' Citar cut in. 'Not to mention my patron,' she reminded the boys. Rupert threw her a grateful look; Tryst a sour one.

'You're no fun, Citar,' Tryst complained. 'But if we must be sensible, let us return to the topic at hand. Just where did you hear this nugget of information, your very highness?'

'J-just - s-stable boy ch-chatter,' Rupert said vaguely.

'Interesting. Because I overheard something very similar. And that Lindahl and Kai's replacement will be Areté once more,' Tryst said.

At the sound of that beloved name, which sounded so foreign in the pronunciation of the Avenel language, Lien almost slipped from his aerial travels in surprise. Heart pounding, he steadied himself as the conversation below continued. *This* had to be why Aethon had led him here.

'And just where did you hear *that,* Tryst?' Citar demanded.

'Just...stable boy chatter,' Tryst said lightly, mockingly mirroring Rupert's earlier response.

'He'll have heard it from his old man,' Ben said, bored. Tryst gave a short, humourless laugh.

'You've met my father, Ben. He's not exactly the sort to sit down and tell his son state secrets.'

'Bet you eavesdrop on him all the time though,' Shiloh said. 'I mean, I would.'

'But that's absurd. How can Areté be declared the Marked Man? She's a woman, for one thing. You'd have to call her the Marked Woman,' Citar objected.

'And w-what respectable m-man would bring down a w-woman for the sake of p-promotion?' Rupert asked.

'Areté is always the Marked Man in the absence of a really decent outlaw,' said Tryst, who would definitely bring down a woman for a promotion. 'It's just almost always been Lindahl and Kai in our lifetimes.'

'When you say "always", how along are we talking here?" Shiloh asked. 'I mean - I'm fifteen and Areté looks *fantastic* for even thirty.'

'She is immortal, Shiloh,' Citar said, one eyebrow raised at the question. '"Always" as in "forever".'

*Ageless,* thought Lien, from above. *Ageless, not immortal, and not the same thing.*

Shiloh though was deeply impressed.

'I thought that was just nonsense urban legend!' he exclaimed.

'I wonder if that's why she hasn't been to Avenel in so long?' Citar mused. Above, Lien held his breath, hanging on every word. 'If I didn't know better, I would say that Lady Beckworth is concerned.'

'No fun to make it too easy,' Tryst shrugged. 'Has to be a real challenge to find the Marked Man. Or, as the case may be, Marked Woman.'

'But finding Areté wouldn't even be the most difficult part,' Citar said. 'Beating her in combat - *that* would be the really difficult part. Has anyone ever captured her?'

'Kai did, years ago. That's how he got into the Order. He failed the Commoner Trials, so went after the Marked Man. Marked *Woman*,' Tryst added, with a sarcastic glance at Citar.

'And then he *became* a Marked Man himself?'

'Yeah, if you'd failed the Trials, you would have had to go find him to get into the Order, Citar,' Shiloh grinned. 'And then get yourself kicked out a few years later, of course. Now, seriously, can we turn back already? I am swimming in my own sweat here.'

As the conversation below dissolved back into an argument about whether they should turn back, Lien let his mind focus on more pressing manners. Of first importance was that the chevaliers knew Areté at all - although even as he thought that, he realised that his surprise was foolish. Areté only visited the People, so it made perfect sense that she might also visit Avenel. But of more concern was the confirmation that others too had noted her absence, and that her good friend Lady Beckworth was concerned about her welfare.

As long as Lien could remember, Areté had come every year to Leaverness. It was what he looked forward to most in all the seasons, which was really saying something from a boy who lived a life full of exciting change and adventure. While the majority of the People remained in Leaverness around the year, fluid groups migrated through the year between the forest and three other tribal strongholds. Partnerships were brokered through these adjoining tribes - Bravo, for instance, was still denying his fixation on Sindhe, a girl their age on her second visit to

Leaverness. For the last three years Lien and Bravo had been included in the migration, and so they had spent crisp autumns on the expansive, wild plains of Osai, followed by chill winters spent in the protection of the Mirror Mountains, which gave way to mild early springs spent along the coasts of the Sea of Sighs, before surrendering to the glory of summer and the annual return to Leaverness. But in all this, it was still the appearance of Areté every summer that Lien most looked forward to. If you could set a calendar by the migrations of the People, you could set a clock by the arrival of Areté. Only this year, that clock would be wrong, and so Lien had thus far found this to be a summer season of discontent.

Lien was drawn from his thoughts by a cascade of shouts below him. Lord Jorge had unexpectedly come to a full stop, bringing the rest of the line to a bumpy stop behind his ample hindquarters. The boys in the queue shouted in agitation as their mounts, now jammed in dangerously close, swished their tails and stamped warningly at the horse behind. Five heads rose up on taut necks with ears pricked keenly forward.

'Jeez Rupert, would you kick that nag of yours?' Tryst snapped, before being distracted by his own horse starting to anxiously half rear.

'What's going on with the horses?' Shiloh asked as their mounts - practically sleepwalking mere moments earlier - all started to snort and shake their heads, now restless to take off.

'I d-don't k-know,' Rupert stammered, unnerved by the usually unflappable Jorge's sudden change in behaviour. 'Oh - there's s-something ahead,' he added, trying to work out what he was seeing between the trees.

'Black and gold?' Citar called forward, voice tense. Rupert shot a surprised look back.

'Y-yes,' he confirmed, 'H-how did you k-know, C-citar?' he asked.

Citar's eyes narrowed.

'It's Aethon,' she said, her heart suddenly beating so fast it made her breath catch. She'd had a feeling, and she had wanted so much for it to be true.

'It's what? Talk sense,' Shiloh demanded, yanking angrily on the reins of his snorting, plunging horse.

'Aethon is a unicorn,' Tryst said steadily, fascinated at Citar's reaction.

'That's just a stupid story. There's no such thing – ' Shiloh started, falling silent as the black and gold unicorn stepped out into full view ahead of them.

' – as a unicorn?' he finished lamely, his statement skewed into a disbelieving question. Aethon held his beautiful head high, watching the chevaliers with a piercing intensity. Their horses all nervously settled, cautiously watching the unicorn back.

'W-what d-does it w-want, C-Citar?' Rupert asked, his voice a high squeak.

'Aethon wants only one thing: a chase. And that's exactly what he's going to get,' Citar said grimly, and kicked her horse forward around Lord Jorge. Aethon wheeled with a rear and set off at a canter, his tail held banner high behind him.

'C-citar – !' Rupert objected, fighting to hold back Jorge, who wanted to follow.

'Well, I've never chased a unicorn before,' Tryst said cheerfully, releasing his reins to allow his horse to follow

Citar, pushing past Jorge.

'Yah!' Shiloh yelled, kicking his horse past Jorge too, and closely followed by Ben, still silent. Rupert looked around helplessly for a moment before also, reluctantly, releasing his reins to allow the foaming Lord Jorge to join the chase.

As soon as he'd seen Aethon's reappearance, Lien had whistled for Jest, who had been following along below and far behind at a sedate walk. Jest quickly cantered the distance to Lien, unnoticed by the five boys, who were entirely focussed on the unicorn. When the boy called Citar took off on the chase, Lien slid swiftly down the smooth, warm bark of the tree he had been in and dropped lightly onto his pony's back. He was deeply curious about the chevalier who had known Aethon. There had been something...*personal*...in his interest. Lien wanted to get a closer look: could this boy be Jordan? It was many years now since they had met. A deep anxiety was growing in Lien's stomach: there was something really off about this whole situation. Aethon bringing him to the chevaliers, the presence there of Rupert and now the reveal that one of the boys knew - and wanted to chase - the very unicorn which had brought Lien to them?

Jest meanwhile needed no urging to pick up the chase, setting off at a gallop after the larger, faster horses.

Cira of the Backwind had twice chased Aethon with a pure, innocent excitement. On the first occasion she had met Lien; on the second, she had lost Jordan. But today, the excitement Citar of Avenel felt came from a completely different, and much darker, place. Cira had disguised herself as the boy Citar to learn to the skills she would need to have vengeance on Brynir for the death of her best friend. While she had not yet learned enough to make her significantly more dangerous to him than one year earlier, she was not going to miss this first chance to have her revenge. This time she was not an unarmed girl on her pony. She was an armed chevalier on her horse and she was *mad*.

Even though Citar's horse Adagio had long strong legs, Aethon kept the same teasing distance he had from her beloved stocky pony all those years ago. He was always just in sight, his shining gold tail blinding when caught by the odd rays of sun piercing the forest canopy. Citar ignored the helpless cries of Rupert and excited whooping of Shiloh from behind her: her focus only wavered when, in a clearing, Tryst's bright chestnut horse drew up apace next to her.

'Not your first chase, Citar?' Tryst called over the rushing wind in their ears. Citar clenched her jaw but did not reply.

'You know we're going dangerously deep into Leaverness with no idea where to find water?' Tryst continued. This time Citar just shrugged. She honestly didn't care. She didn't care if she never came out of Leaverness today.

'I don't care. Turn back if you want,' she called back, voice hard.

'Well, we've lost Aethon, so might as well,' Tryst called, starting to rein his panting horse in. Citar looked immediately back ahead, but could see so sign of Aethon either. She kicked a resistant Adagio on for another minute to be sure the unicorn wouldn't reappear before letting her blowing horse fall gratefully back to a walk: he was now alone, the other chevaliers having all reined their horses in behind Tryst. Citar drew Adagio to a halt, and swore loudly. The obscenity bounced around between the trees and was even heard by the other chevaliers behind her.

'Wh-what was th-that about?' Rupert asked, exasperated at the whole debacle. 'N-now we're t-totally lo-lo-lost!'

'And the horses will need water, soon,' Tryst said seriously, stroking his mare's foaming neck.

'That unicorn made Citar totally flip,' Shiloh said, loving the drama. 'Who knew he was so mental?'

'It certainly did,' Tryst mused thoughtfully as Citar came back into sight: a tight, angry figure hunched on her horse.

'Want to explain what that was all about then, Citar?' Tryst asked.

'Yeah, you got us all in trouble now!' Shiloh added.

Citar shot them a dark, furious stare.

'You didn't have to follow,' she snapped. The boys were all startled by the depth of emotion being shown by their usually congenial colleague.

'C-come now C-Citar, we c-could hardly l-leave you,' Rupert parlayed uncertainly.

'Well you should have!' the girl barked back.

'And how did you expect to get back if we had?' Tryst asked with infuriating reason.

'I didn't *want* to go back!' Citar exploded, a year of pent-up grief and guilt finally breaking out of her. 'I wanted to chase Aethon and find Brynir and then I wanted make him pay for – ' but Citar broke off, her brain finally wresting control of her mouth from her emotions and trying not to land herself in even more strife.

'Make him pay for what?' Tryst asked, eyes narrowing.

'What would you care, Tryst?' Citar asked bitterly.

'Oh I don't *care*, Citar. But I'm curious, and I know a thing or two about wanting revenge,' he said, with distant smile.

'You got any idea who - or what - Brynir is?' Shiloh quietly asked Ben, as they waited a few meters back, slouching on their tired horses.

'Brynir the Cursed,' Ben rumbled unhelpfully.

'...which is...?' Shiloh prompted, when it seemed no more information was forthcoming.

'A story used to frighten children with,' Ben said.

'Well I thought unicorns were made up until we met one this afternoon,' Shiloh shrugged. 'Which, I will add, was very awesome. I mean, apart from the whole "getting lost in Leaverness" thing.'

'Brynir is not a story you want to meet.'

The darkness in Ben's tone and eyes drained Shiloh's cheer.

As the chevalier Citar, Cira had further piqued Lien's curiosity with her knowledge of Brynir. He heard her emotional outburst to Tryst, and was now having his first encounter with the effect of her glamour. Chasing Aethon to meet Brynir...Citar's story reminded him of Cira and Jordan. But this chevalier was not Jordan, he was now certain, and could *not* be Cira, because Cira was a girl, and the chevalier was clearly a boy. Lien wanted to ask Citar about these claims, but literally as he thought this, he felt a slight headache coming on, and his mind changed tack. He forgot how interesting Citar's outburst was, and focussed instead on the growing dread gnawing at his stomach. He knew something terrible was about to happen, and that he mustn't get involved. That he must *not* do anything that might reveal himself to the chevaliers. But then, why had

Aethon also led him on the chevalier's merry dance? Why had the unicorn presented him with this impossible quandary? Was he only there to stop Rupert from giving him away earlier, and to gain information about Areté? Should he now leave? But then what had Aethon led the chevaliers to?

He wished that Bravo might now arrive and drag him away, for he could not otherwise bring himself to leave, even though he suspected he ought to.

Waiting anxiously just out of sight of the boys, Lien first heard, then saw, what destiny Aethon had led to the chevaliers to. As he did, he wished it were Brynir after all. Brynir the Cursed he had managed once before.

Well, his darkness had.

But this, he could not manage, and he did not want to meet his darkness again.

He wished it were anything but this.

'You boys look hot.'

Despite the heat, the lazy growl sent a chill down Lien's spine. Jest threw his head up so fast he almost smacked his rider between the eyes. They both knew that voice. Lien's eyes sought its owner through the trees, and found him entering the clearing, addressing the chevaliers. Although only his face and hands were visible beneath the shabby grey seer's gown he had always worn, Saul looked ancient - grizzled and scarred by the tyranny of far too many unforgiving years. Lien knew all too well though that the old man's age and gaunt frame belied terrific strength, and a terrifying secret. He remained bolt upright on Jest, frantically running through options. He could go to the People for backup - but he had been far from camp when he met the chevaliers, and Aethon had led them further; and besides, no-one else in the tribe would want to expose themselves to outsiders, even to save helpless chevalier teenagers.

He could try to tell Saul that Sky was nearby, to warn him off his fun, but Saul was a master liar and would see through Lien in about the same space of time he needed to take the throat out of the nearest boy. And how could he communicate with Saul without being seen by the chevaliers? Lien wished Areté and Sky had been a little more specific about *why* he could not be seen by outsiders. That would help guide a decision in which the stakes were literally the lives - or brutal deaths - of the five boys walking into a deadly trap.

Rupert started at the sudden appearance of the haggard stranger. Saul had been standing quietly to the right of the group for some time, but even the most observant soul would not have noticed him until he was ready to be seen. Rupert's fright was not allayed by Lord Jorge pinning his ears back suspiciously, then trying to back up into Shiloh and Ben's horses, which were standing just behind him.

'Dammit Rupert, *control that horse!*' Shiloh bawled at the prince, before directing an equally ill-tempered 'And who the hell are you?' at Saul, the most dangerous thing there was to be found in all of Leaverness. The battered old man approached, peering up at the surly teenager from under his hood, apparently amused by something only he knew. Under the scrutiny of that cold stare, made more disconcerting by the perfect liquid black of Saul's irises, Shiloh felt like something small and furry being looked over by a wolf: being measured and found wanting. As though he were not even worth the effort of the hunt.

The boy felt riled.

'I know your secret,' Saul whispered, so quietly and so close to his horse's shoulder that only Shiloh heard.

The chevalier blanched.

'Just an old man, passing though,' Saul said to the group, louder now, though in a voice that sounded like it didn't get much use. Not out of a human shaped mouth, at any rate.

'I don't get company much in the forest,' he continued. 'I'm heading to a spring ahead. Perhaps you'd like to water yourselves and your horses.'

As he said this, Saul drew the bottom half of a circle in the air with the index and middle finger of his right hand. The gesture meant nothing to the chevaliers but Lien felt the espréi ripple out across the boys below him. He suspected it was a calming or dampening effect, but couldn't be sure.

Having completed the spell, Saul reached out to clap Lord Jorge on the neck; the horse bared his teeth and angrily struck out with one foreleg. Saul had already anticipated the move though, and neatly stepped out of harm's way, an unpleasant smile about his lips. Rupert was too shocked at his horse's unusual behaviour to even attempt a reprimand.

'Nice horse. Spirited. But you might want to show him the whip a little more,' the old man said mildly. Jorge snaked his neck forward ready to bite; Saul calmly delivered a ringing slap across his sensitive nose. Rupert hastily half leapt, half fell off Jorge and grabbed his bridle before hostilities could escalate, while stammering an awkward apology.

'Do control that beast of yours, your highness,' Tryst sighed, before turning back to the stranger, wisely addressing him with far more respect than had the quietened Shiloh.

'Sir, we are indeed hot, geographically challenged and short of water. We would be pleased to accompany you to the spring,' Tryst continued with a cursory glance around to see if his fellow chevaliers objected. Largely, they did not: Shiloh still looked oddly pale but seemed compliant; Citar grimly hopeful, for she had an unpleasant suspicion about Saul, the kind that would please only the suicidally inclined; Ben was watching Saul with narrowed eyes but knew they needed water; and so it was only Rupert who chewed his bottom lip anxiously. The prince also searched for some sign of hesitancy from his colleagues, but could also see that there was none. Quite aside from Lord Jorge's warnings, he could think of nothing more stupid than following a distinctly unsavoury looking stranger in Leaverness.

'You k-know, I think w-we're quite a-alright if it's all the s-same – '

'Shut up and get back on your horse, Rupert,' Tryst commanded sharply, before turning another polite expression to the monster standing in man-form before him.

'What may we call you, friend?'

'You may call me Saul,' said the leader of the Cuán, with an equally polite smile. 'Please, this way.'

Even with Rupert remounted, Lord Jorge baulked, clean refusing to move. The other horses filed past him one by one, and Rupert dug his heels hard into his mount's sweat flecked flanks, while trying - without success - to look completely unconcerned.

'I'll, er, bring up the rear, shall I?' he muttered to himself; but still, even when he was being left behind, Lord Jorge would not move. He stood rigid, head high, legs braced wide.

'You coming, Rupert?' Citar called, reining Adagio in to look back.

'I...uh...I just n-need to...I'll j-just be a m-minute. C-catch you up,' Rupert called. Ignoring the blend of curious and hostile stares from the departing chevaliers, he dismounted again, standing helplessly at Jorge's head. The horse had never put a hoof wrong for him thus far, and he was torn between the embarrassment of being unable to control his mount in front of his peers, fear of getting left behind, and the sickening certainty that Jorge was right in refusing to follow Saul: the certainty that Jorge was saving his life, but in doing so, preventing him from helping his fellow chevaliers.

Citar hesitated only a moment longer before shrugging and turning to follow the others. The marvellous Lord Jorge was keeping his helpless rider out of danger, and danger was exactly what she was looking for. And there was something sinister and familiar about Saul. She couldn't quite put her finger on it, but she couldn't shake the inexplicable feeling that they had met before.

And she disliked him immensely.

'Well come on then old chap, I know you always look out for me, but I can't see how leaving me all alone out here is helping,' Rupert helplessly complained to Jorge, his stammer mercifully gone in the absence of the other boys. 'I agree he was a most objectionable sort but aaaargh-

aaaargh-aaaargh-aaa – '

'Sshhhhh!!' Lien hissed, waving both hands in a way that only made him seem more alarming, but Rupert obediently froze mid *aaaargh* nonetheless. That meant he was standing next to Jorge with his mouth open like an exotic flycatcher, while his eyes tried their best to pop out of his head and all the blood fled his face. Having anyone appear upside down from a tree next to you, while abandoned with a belligerent horse in Leaverness, was bad news; for that anyone to be the wild child who had almost killed him a year earlier was all too much for the prince's delicate disposition.

'Breathe,' Lien ordered, worried the petrified boy might expire at any moment, which would be most unhelpful. As he swung down from the tree, Rupert did so in a relieved gasp, which meant he was able to make another try at strangled screaming.

'Not going to hurt you!' Lien insisted.

Rupert rethought and settled for a mortified 'Y-you…?!'

'Yes! Me!' Lien said cheerfully, though his expression fell as Rupert took this as confirmation that it was time to get the hell out of there. With a surprising turn of speed, the lanky boy tried to remount Jorge in an attempt to escape the demon boy - but the horse neatly stepped to the side, leaving Rupert to crash down in an undignified tangle.

'Smart boy!' Lien laughed, stroking Jorge's sweat-streaked neck. The black horse wuffled back at him affectionately like an old friend - an interaction completely opposite to the one he had just shared with Saul. Rupert suspiciously watched this exchange from the ground, reluctantly mollified by Jorge's approval. He even cautiously accepted Lien's offer of a helping hand to get back up.

'S-so you're n-not d-demon then? Only I'm s-sure you n-nearly k-killed me l-last y-year,' he added pointedly as he staggered back to his feet, dragging the slight boy down under the weight of his chainmail as did so.

*I'm sure you nearly killed me last year.*

Lien stiffened.

*A boy nearly died for this feather, Lien.*

He remembered Bravo's question to Areté.

*Will* you *be alright?*

Lien's chest clenched. He had screwed up last year, and Areté had paid the price. It was his fault that she was gone. He had suspected it for a while, but now, he was certain. Her suffering was his fault. Was that why he was being sent the nightmares? To share the consequences of his foolish actions?

'I s-say, are you a-alright?' Rupert asked, watching Lien with concern.

Lien shook his head to clear it: there was work to be done right now. He would have to do his worrying and self-flagellating later.

'Yes,' he said, casting his mind back to the conversation before his unfortunate epiphany. 'And I'm not dangerous. Not to you, anyway. Well, not *this* time, anyway,' he added, with a rueful smile.

'W-well J-jorge l-likes you, and he's n-never wrong,' Rupert said, grudgingly nodding towards Jorge, who was now demanding a hard scratch behind his right ear from his apparently new best friend. Lien obliged, looking thoughtfully at Rupert as he did. The boy's espréi was a mess. He was obviously stressed and anxious about the current predicament he was in, but even under that, there was a taut and permanent fear that presented as a disconcerting quiver in his energy. And in his stammer. Lien couldn't help but reach out his own espréi to touch that of Rupert.

'W-why are you s-staring at me l-like t-that?' the prince asked, eyebrows knitting together in worry. Lien ignored him, but closed his eyes and *felt* the connection. Lien was still able to feel and read espréi, even since the emergence of his darkness. But to try to *use* the energy - that was a risk. But a risk he found himself willing to take.

He closed his eyes and felt for his soul eye. He opened it just a fraction, just enough to see and try to breathe calmness into the other boy's aura -

*- and his darkness stirred -*

Lien's eyes shot open. Rupert was staring at him anxiously.

'What are you doing?' he asked, but with more confidence now.

And no stammer.

Lien grinned.

'Nothing, sorry, I was just thinking of - of what to do about your friends,' he said, pushing the darkness back down.

'Yes! Jorge has just saved me from this most dodgy sort of fellow,' Rupert said. 'I am sure he's leading them quite astray. My friends that is. Though "colleagues" might be a more accurate description - '

'Not just astray. To lunch,' Lien said.

'Lunch?' Rupert asked, perking up. 'Well that's not so bad then - '

'It is when your friends *are* the lunch.'

'Oh.' Rupert blanched. 'Good heavens. What are we

to do?'

Lien tapped the side of his head. 'I have a plan.'

'Excellent!' the prince cheered.

'But you have to do it.'

'Oh.'

Rupert gave Lien an imploring look. 'I really don't think that's a good idea, you see I'm absolutely disaster-struck. Last time I was in Leaverness I nearly died and – ' he broke off. Lien was blushing also.

'Well, you know. You'd better have a jolly good explanation for it, too,' Rupert added sharply. Lien nodded.

'Later, yes. Now: we face the Cuán.'

'Later – what?! Did you just say...you didn't just say the Cuán, did you...?! Say you didn't just say the *C-cuán* – '

While Rupert suffered a nervous breakdown at the prospect of facing the sort of monsters that made hyenas look like recommended pet material, Citar was suffering an inconvenient attack of conscience. On the one hand, she was absolutely certain Saul was leading the chevaliers into a trap, but it seemed that this time, Aethon's trap was not Brynir, which was frankly disappointing. But there would nonetheless surely be some sort of fight, and she knew four chevaliers held better odds than three. Strangely, she could think clearly of all these things, but she could not feel the concern she was sure ought to accompany such conclusions.

On the other hand, she *was* worried about the idiot prince, and because she could feel that emotion, and only that emotion, it ate at her. Rupert had been in the Order a year longer than her, and so prior to today, she had encountered him only in passing and by reputation. But she couldn't shake the feeling that she ought to look out for him. As she pondered her dilemma, she realised there was something of Jordan in Rupert's fundamentally gentle and good nature. Certainly he was much more spineless than Jordan, but watching Rupert struggle in the aggressive and competitive world of the Order made Citar realise that without her - and perhaps even *with* her - Jordan would have been unlikely to have enjoyed becoming a chevalier. Perhaps that was why she felt a certain responsibility for the prince; perhaps that was why she reluctantly held her horse back until she had dropped, unnoticed, out of the file. Unnoticed by all but Saul; as she prepared to turn her mount back down the path, she caught the corner of his hard, black eye. And the corner of his cruel smile.

She trotted Adagio back the way they'd slowly come, but drew the horse into a shocked halt when she first caught snatches of a conversation between Rupert and another voice. A voice deeper than she remembered, but she remembered it well nonetheless. A voice she had dreamed of for years. A voice that belonged to someone who had let her down, and let Jordan down. Let Jordan die. And when Jordan had died, Cira had learned that dreams were not reality. She had turned her back on three years of dreaming of Lien and became Citar, a chevalier who didn't want or need to put a prince on a throne. She became a chevalier that just needed to find and kill Brynir the Cursed.

She could barely breathe for the confusion of emotions that voice triggered in her, but this quickly slid to a completely different confusion as she listened in. The voice was raised in argument with Rupert; specifically, Rupert was babbling while Lien was trying to rationalise his panic. This logic was based on the supposition that Rupert having a mere *medium* chance of dying slowly and painfully was better odds than those currently facing his fellow chevaliers; Rupert's counter-argument was that *any* odds of dying were lousy so please count him out, thank you so much.

'You are a chevalier, fighting is what you do!' Lien objected.

'I never *wanted* to be a chevalier, and although I put up with a bit of fighting here and there, I draw the line at dying!' Rupert insisted, practically head-to-head with Lien now – although in their case, head-to-just-under-shoulders would be more accurate. When they noticed Citar reining her horse in, the two boys ceased glaring at each other and slowly turned as one. Surprise, anger and confusion jostled their way across Citar's face.

'Citar!' Rupert cried with relief while Lien shot behind Lord Jorge. Citar scowled at this amateur attempt at subterfuge.

*'You!'* The word leapt from Citar's tight throat, clawing its way through a year of anger, a year of grief, a long year of blame. Rupert looked taken aback.

'M-me?!' he asked.

'No not you Rupert, him,' she snapped, gesturing to Jorge. 'The idiot hiding behind your horse.'

'D-did you try to kill him too?' Rupert asked quietly over his shoulder. Lien frowned.

'Don't think so, we've never met,' he replied, peeping cautiously from behind Jorge's ample hindquarters to double check this was not in fact Jordan, the only other boy outsider he had ever met.

Citar went to snap back, but her brain made a flying tackle at her mouth, strangling the objection into a sort of inarticulate *humph*. After all, Lien was right: how could he possibly know this boy, this chevalier, to be the girl he'd met four years earlier? The glamour did its job well.

*A little too well*, a heretical voice whispered, sadly. Citar almost flinched at the regretful realisation; she tried to ignore it, but could not. Some denied part of her *wanted* to be recognised by Lien. Thought that maybe...maybe he'd see through the glamour. See that it was her under there. And be glad to see her.

Some treasonous voice in her psyche didn't hate him at all.

'No, we've never met. But you can come out, I *can* see you and talking to Jorge's rear end is frankly embarrassing.'

Lien obediently but regretfully emerged into the open: now he was in for it. Revealing himself to Rupert was a calculated risk; revealing himself to another chevalier was first clumsy and secondly dangerous.

'Hello. Could you pretend you *didn't* see me?' Lien asked, hopefully.

Citar felt her breath catch as she examined him closely. This was the real Lien, flesh and blood and grinning anxiously with strained desperation. This was not the handsome, stately future king of her dreams. He was older and taller but not remotely regal, no more a prince than Rupert, who was royal only in title. He now had three tattooed rings on his right arm, plus some partial inking around his left eye, as though the tattooist had started with the border of the art, become distracted and wandered off mid-job. Lastly, she took in the four pale scars running across his bare chest: the claws of Brynir, which had raked him as he saved her life four years ago.

Saved her because it was the right thing to do.

She had hated him so much this last year for not coming to her rescue again; for leaving Jordan to die under those same terrible claws.

Hot tears pricked the backs of her eyes. She blinked them back furiously.

'No, because I need your help. Or, perhaps you need mine.' Citar said stiffly, extending a rigid hand.

'Citar.'

She gave her assumed name forcefully.

Lien watched the hand curiously, just as he had all those years ago.

'Lien?' he hazarded. Citar cursed herself for forgetting and dropped the proffered hand.

'Lovely,' she said coldly then glared at the two of them. 'Now, did someone say something about dying?'

Miles ahead, while the remaining chevaliers were realising that they now numbered three, not five, Saul seemed to have attracted the company of a number of vagabond companions. They were just flitting around the boys – half-glimpsed through the trees, occasionally appearing on the trail behind, indistinct figures clothed in bland greys. There also seemed to be dogs roaming the area, always just out of clear sight.

Very large dogs.

'I have this nagging feeling. Like we should be worried,' Shiloh said quietly. 'You?' he asked Ben with a raised eyebrow.

Ben shrugged; he seemed content.

Shiloh had started out afraid of Saul's quietly threatening declaration – *I know your secret* – but not of the man himself, and he was desperate for water. But Saul's people were pressing closer now, so that the three remaining teenagers were surrounded. Shiloh could *see* this, and intellectually knew it was bad news, but he couldn't quite manage to be concerned about it. Something seated deep in his subconscious was frustrated by this paradox and it was giving him a headache.

'Saul. I can't help but notice that quite a few of your friends coincidentally seem to be passing this way,' Tryst finally ventured, also finding himself in a similar state of cognitive dissonance. The old man ignored him, but an answer was not necessary: he had indeed finally led them to a spring. But it was a spring backed by a sheer rock face, jutting up from the water. As far as dead-ends boded, this one boded badly. A number of lanky wolves were casually laying around the spring; when the horses approached - also unnaturally calm in the circumstances - the wolves looked up curiously. They did not seem aggressive, but Tryst heard the word '*Cuán*' whispered by Ben behind him.

Saul heard it too.

He finally turned around, his face twisted in a hideous excuse for a grin.

'Correct.'

His companions, all lean, wild looking men and women, pressed in around, and what the boys had assumed were large dogs travelling in their company were revealed instead as more wolves.

'We are all Cuán. And you are our prey.'

He growled, and it was an inhuman sound.

A chilling chorus of howls tore through the silence of the baking forest.

'Is that...?' Citar broke off, unable to finish. She had

accepted the existence of the nightmarish Cuán more readily than Rupert, who still occasionally muttered that they were stuff of legend, not real people who turned into wolves who actually lived in Leaverness and were planning to eat his colleagues.

'They will play first with your friends first,' Lien replied shortly, working feverishly. 'Then kill them.'

'How do you know so much about them?' Rupert asked, hovering around helplessly. 'And I thought they needed a full moon to change, or something?'

'There are many dangers in Leaverness. To live here, you must know them all. And the full moon is just a story.'

'Why did they follow him in the first place?' Rupert fretted.

'A spell. To make them not think of anything dangerous. They see Saul, they don't like him, but they don't feel "danger" when they should.'

'Blimey,' Rupert said. 'That's clever.' He thought a moment. 'So Jorge saved me, but how come Citar was immune?'

'Oh I wasn't,' she explained, a little embarrassed. 'I sort of knew it was a trap, but I couldn't feel afraid. It was really strange. But what I *could* feel was concern at you being left alone. So…I came back for you.'

Rupert managed to crack a wan, grateful smile. Citar frowned. Something different about the prince had been bothering her, and she'd just finally realised what it was.

'How come you're not stammering any more, Rupert?' she asked.

'I'm n-not?' Rupert blinked: he had been completely oblivious.

'Uh-uh don't start it again, it's way easier to talk to you like this,' Citar said warningly.

'I only s-stammer when I'm n-nervous,' Rupert explained. Citar frowned.

'But you are literally about to risk your life facing the Cuán. And you're nervous about it. You've just told us that a million times, but you haven't been stammering. Until I bought it up,' she added ruefully.

Rupert considered this, and concentrated on consciously speaking without his stammer.

'I think I only stammer when I'm with *people* who make me nervous,' he clarified.

Citar threw a glance to Lien.

'You're not nervous around *him*?' she asked, genuinely curious.

'Strangely, no,' Rupert said with an awkward laugh. 'I think it's because Jorge likes him.'

Of course the truth was more complicated: inspired by Saul, Lien had applied a simple calming effect of his own to Rupert's espréi. Yet as though to illustrate, Jorge now dropped his nose for an absent-minded stroke from Lien, who was sitting back examining his work. He had prepared a makeshift torch from a sturdy branch and many sticks, roughly bound together with a hardy vine around a centre of flammable tree gum. He shook it experimentally. When it failed to fall apart, he handed it to Rupert, who held it with his arm outstretched, as though expecting it might spontaneously combust.

'You understand what to do?' Lien asked, eyeing the boy off doubtfully. He did not exactly cut a heroic figure.

Rupert looked desperately to Citar, who shrugged helplessly.

'You really should let me do this, you know,' she said.

'Yes, we really should,' Rupert agreed fervently.

'Your horse will be afraid of the Cuán,' Lien insisted.

'Jorge – he is special.'

It was only a guess, but Lien was certain of it, and certain Rupert had no idea *how* special his mount was.

'*Just like his rider,*' Citar said under her breath, but not loud enough for Rupert to hear. He looked uncertain enough as it was.

'You're sure this will work?' the prince asked desperately.

'The wolf in the Cuán fears fire. It will work.'

'I still think you should be the one to do it…'

'You don't see me. Your friends don't see me.' Lien put one finger to his lips: *ssshhh*. 'Your time to be a hero.'

Lien was struck by déjà vu as he said it: it was like trying to convince Jordan to be the hero. This realisation was quickly followed by another.

'Also, do not drop the torch once it is alight! The forest is very dry, and will burn fast,' Lien warned. Unconstrained fire in the summer was absolutely forbidden. But he was already breaking the rules of the People today, and could think of no other way that he could use Citar or Rupert as a proxy to save the other chevaliers.

Rupert swallowed hard and wondered whether he should warn Lien that he ought to have a backup plan, since anything that could go wrong almost inevitably would; but in the end, decided to trust his horse's approval of the strange boy and hope for the best.

Naughty children across Altica might be told that they would be "taken by the People," to places unknown for punishment unspecified; but when they were *really* bad they might be told that they would be eaten by the Cuán. The consequences were more straightforward so it made a much more effective threat. The Cuán, or People of the Wolf, were not a natural race. They had all once been regular folk living ordinary but not blameless lives. At some point they had all wronged another and been held accountable to the witch Praxidice, who, as Vengeance personified, laid upon them a curse: she had simply enabled the beast within their souls to manifest physically. Thus whenever these unfortunates flew into a rage or allowed themselves to harbour cruel thoughts, they would shed their human forms, grotesquely transforming into wolves. Of course not your natural wolf, which is neither evil nor cruel, merely true to its nature; no, these were a vicious, relentless breed, capable of malice as only a human mind can be. The Cuán were nomadic, like the People, and did not often reside in Leaverness. There were stories told of them all across the continent, but as with Brynir, it was rare to find survivors to confirm such stories to be true.

Sky and Saul held an uneasy truce between their peoples, as part of which, each group hosted the other for one evening a year. Never for a meal, for the People were largely vegetarian and the Cuán ate almost exclusively in their wolf forms. But they were always tense, uncomfortable events. And Lien had come across the remains of victims of the Cuán often enough, and felt so viscerally enraged each time, that he wondered whether the truce was designed to protect the Cuán from the People, rather than the other way around. In any case, Saul and his people would not attack Lien. But while the youth of the People could think of nothing more fun than scaring the chevaliers, a pack of Cuán would think it equally good sport to slaughter every last one of them, and their horses too.

~

As Saul's companions pressed in around the three horses, accompanied by their growling and howling wolf pack, the old man reversed the half circle gesture he had made earlier, lifting the spell he had put upon the chevaliers and their mounts. The horses reacted immediately, bunching together, heads thrown high, nostrils flaring as they took in the rank smell of the Cuán. Tryst, Shiloh and Ben returned immediately to their full senses, horrifically aware of the danger they were in. As the dreadful howling of the wolves reached a frenzied peak, those People of the Wolf who had been in human form began to change. Grotesque as the transformation from human to wolf was, only Shiloh could bring himself to turn away; Tryst and Ben watched in mesmerised horror as the bodies sprouted coarse mangy coats and elongated, almost as though the wolf had always been on the inside of them and was now forcing itself out by folding the human skin back inside. Tryst was perhaps the least revolted; indeed, he found the whole gruesome process to be fascinating. This quickly turned to cold dread though as the pack of snarling, slavering wolves closed the ring around the terrified horses. Only Saul remained in human form, standing in the centre of the ring with his right hand held up in a closed fist.

'What's the plan Tryst?' Shiloh yelled over the canine din.

'Do you think we can charge them?' Tryst yelled back. Shiloh tried to kick his mare forward, but she only shrank back under him, wanting to be as far from the pack as possible; an impossibility, when surrounded from three sides and only the pool and a sheer rock face behind.

'That's a no,' he reported. 'Next plan?'

'Don't get eaten,' Ben growled, drawing his sword, trying to force his panicking horse forward. Before he could even begin a swing though, a streak of grey hurled through the air, and the sword fell harmlessly to the ground some metres away. Ben swore, and for the first time that the other boys had ever seen, looked afraid.

'I can't die here, torn apart by a - a *bedtime* story. I haven't even become a proper knight yet,' Shiloh wailed to the world at large.

'Saul! Can we negotiate?' Tryst shouted to the old man, who was watching their rising panic with great satisfaction.

'You three have nothing of value to offer the Cuán, son of Bane,' he replied, savouring the final three words. It was something in his earlier inflection that caught Tryst's attention though; he narrowed his eyes suspiciously.

'We three - but what of the other two?' he demanded.

Saul grinned, horribly. 'Smart boy. Pity. Dead boy, now,' he said, and with the opening of his right fist, Saul set the Cuán upon the chevaliers.

At once, several of the wolves launched themselves forwards, ready to savagely bring down the horses -

- and a terrified wailing suddenly echoed off the rock face backing the spring. Lord Jorge sprang powerfully over the circle of wolves, Rupert clutching on for dear life, pale as a sheet, but the burning brand clutched determinedly aloft. Adagio was hot on Jorge's heels, though in less bombastic fashion: even though Lien had had a word with him, in the language of horses, he was clearly spooked by the wolves and even the torch.

Not as much as the Cuán though: at the sight of the flame, the wolves started to slink back, tails dipped nervously between their legs.

Realising the effect he was having, and noticing the stunned relief on the faces of his fellow chevaliers, Rupert took heart. He shook the brand at Saul, who, alone of the Cuán, had stood his ground.

'Get back, monster!' Rupert roared, drunk on adrenaline. His wild eyes locked against Saul's furious glare; the prince waved the flame recklessly for good effect; and for a moment it looks as though he had a chance of pushing the old man back. But the prince waved the torch too quickly, and every human heart skipped a beat when the flame stalled – and then died.

'Ah,' Rupert said, feeling the adrenaline drain away under the overwhelming force of sheer terror.

'That wasn't supposed to happen.'

He flashed a shaky grin at the old man as the Cuán began to press forward once more.

Saul flashed a horrifyingly pleased grin back.

'Rupert, you *idiot!*' Tryst yelled. '*Now* what?'

'*Lien* – ?!' Rupert screamed with high pitched desperation as a wolf lunged forward at Lord Jorge. Its jaws snapped shut on thin air instead of Rupert's leg when the black horse half reared, striking the wolf across the shoulder, but though the wolf was thrown onto its side, it immediately leapt back up for a second assault. It paused though as Saul made a sharp whistle and held his right hand up, closed back into a tight fist. For a moment an uneasy stillness fell upon the panting humans, horses and wolves as Saul looked swiftly around. In moments he found Lien, partially hidden high in a tree above. Maintaining that cruel stare so deliberately that Tryst followed it and saw Lien himself, Saul slowly opened his closed fist, spreading his gnarled fingers wide, and permitting the Cuán to resume their attack.

Lien fully agreed with Trysts' assessment of Rupert. He'd given a foolproof strategy to a fool's fool, and his reward was disaster. He was frantically weighing up which terrible consequence he could best live with - revealing himself to try to extend Sky's truce to the chevaliers, or watching the chevaliers be ripped to pieces in front of his eyes - when Rupert had screamed his name and Saul had found him. Those oil black eyes bored straight through Lien, and the boy shuddered at the malicious sneer that ran across the old man's haggard face. And then with that bald stare, and contemptuous hand signal, Saul had dismissed him as a threat. That hurt, but Lien knew it was fair: what could he do against a whole pack of Cuán? Bravo could re-light the torch. Many of the People could use espréi to set it back alight. But he was an imposter amongst the tribe, an imposter containing a darkness that blocked the light of espréi.

While Rupert had been brandishing the torch at the wolves, Citar had drawn her sword and was swinging it at anything coming her way. When Saul had spotted Lien and paused his wolves, she had a moment in which to breathe, and to see, and to *feel*. And in the sudden stillness, what she thought she could feel was...

...Jordan.

Dear, sweet Jordan.

*Impossible.*

And then she shook sweat out of her eyes and squinted furiously because apparently she was also *seeing* things. It had to be a trick of the bright afternoon light, but she could have sworn she fleetingly *saw* Jordan behind Saul, like - like an after-image inside her eye lids, the sort you get after looking straight at the sun. She stared hard, but could now see nothing unexpected.

And then Saul had lazily opened his fist again.

The wolf that Jorge had struck down leapt again. Jorge shot back, but as he did, one hoof hit the unstable edge of the spring, which crumbled. The big black horse half fell back as that leg dropped into the water and then buckled. Three Cuán turned on him now, ready to drag down first the horse and then his rider.

Around the same time, a Cuán made a flying leap at Citar. She managed to block its teeth with her shield - the second time a knight's shield had saved her life in Leaverness - but the impact still pushed her back. This, combined with Adagio trying to leap forward into Tryst's horse, unseated her. She cried out as she fell to the ground. Adagio surged through Tryst's horse and plunged into the pool - the only route not blocked by wolves - past where Jorge was struggling to regain his footing. Citar was left with just a couple of feet separating herself and the bloody, snarling face of the wolf. Her shield had knocked it hard in the face, and it was enraged and ready to rip her face off in return.

Another wolf leapt at Jorge who, already unstable, was unable to evade or retaliate. The horse squealed in pain as the wolf clawed viciously down his shining black neck and shoulder, but snaked his head around to bite at the Cuán nonetheless, while Rupert, half un-seated, shouted and swatted helplessly at it with the smoking, blackened brand.

Lien was concentrating. He was concentrating so damn hard. He was fixated on the torch as Rupert flailed it around. He just had to do what any others of the People could do: open his soul eye and let the light flood in. Maybe then he would be able to see the energy of the torch, connect with the espréi in and around it, exciting it to the point of ignition –

– and even though the lives of five boys literally depended on his ability to do something he had been trained for since being a child, *still* it was the darkness he found, not the light.

**LET ME.**

What choice did he have?

The chevaliers died in front of him…or he let the darkness in.

Lien dropped out of the tree, landing in almost kneeling, head bowed.

Something that was not exactly Lien stood up from the ground, a little taller and a lot bolder, shimmering silver eyes fixed on the ghost of Jordan.

The little ghost looked back.

Lien started to stride out into the clearing around the spring –

– and was bowled down in a full body tackle by Bravo.

'Lien! You can't!' Bravo hissed, then sat back as he saw his friend's face.

'What's wrong with your eyes – ?' he started to ask, then both boys turned as one to look towards the spring, drawn by the *whoomph* of the torch as it spontaneously combusted, bursting into light. Not the golden-white light of a natural flame, no, this flame was a roaring pillar of power, purple at its heart, brightening to azure before flaring out to a brilliant amber.

# 8. JORDAN

As Citar stared bloodied, snarling death in the face, natural adrenal panic surged through her body, and she was prepared to try to escape the upcoming attack.

Until she saw Jordan again.

He was still unreal, an indistinct afterimage, but this time she was *sure*. He was standing next to Saul, and he was looking right at her.

He was terrified for her.

'Jordan – !'

From her half-sitting position on the ground, Citar reached out to him. He shook his head frantically.

She had thought she could only avenge him.

She had not realised she could be with him.

'It's okay. I'm coming – ' she whispered as the Cuán leapt for her. It pushed her down flat and stood on her chest, savouring the moment before the first bite. It was surprised by her lack of fear though, and its consequent pause was the first thing that saved her life. In that pause, she turned her tear-filled eyes from the slavering jaws above her face, to see Jordan again. But he wasn't looking at her now. He was looking towards someone who was stalking from the tree line towards him –

– and the second thing that saved Citar's life was the torch in Rupert's hand erupting back into flame.

Rupert almost dropped the torch in shock as the entire

wolf pack turned as one to behold the roaring flame. It razed the head of the Cuán sinking its teeth into Jorge's neck and blinded the wolf that was moments from biting off Citar's face. Jorge powered forward out of the spring, Rupert whooping wildly as he thrust the torch in every direction of the Cuán. A whimper spread across the wolf pack as, repelled, they backed off and slunk resentfully away from the unnatural blaze.

As the wolf that had been about to kill her fled, Citar sat fully upright again and looked desperately for Jordan.

He was gone.

Citar scrambled to her feet and took shaky steps towards Saul, who was staring so intently between Citar and the torch that he didn't even seem to notice the wolves fleeing past him.

'Saul!' Citar's voice shook. 'Where is he? What had you done to him?'

Saul had seen Jordan's sacrifice. He didn't entirely understand it though. How it was possible. He knew that Jordan's ghost had remained in Leaverness since the boy's death, a lingering shade that had refused to pass over. He was surprised, and a little impressed, that the little sprite had been able to transfer its remaining espréi into flame. But mostly, he was relieved that it had. Saul was obliged to keep Citar alive, and once the Cuán had tasted blood, they were hard to control, even by their leader. And things had definitely been about to get out of control.

'He is gone,' was all he intended to say before leaving, but found himself meeting Citar's enraged eyes.

'For you,' he added, as surprised at himself for saying

it, as Citar was confused by what he had said.

Shaking off the moment, Saul turned to leave, changing into a huge wolf as he did. Citar went to chase him even so, but was caught from behind and held back.

'Citar! Pull yourself together!' Tryst hissed. Citar struggled against him, and as she did, the massive wolf glanced back at her. She paused as she fleetingly saw its torn ears and scar cleft grizzled muzzle, before struggling harder as it loped away. Tryst was stronger though and held her until she finally sagged – for Jordan, Saul and all the Cuán were now gone.

*'Ow ow ow ow hot hot hot - !'*

Citar turned to see Rupert yelping at the torch, which he was holding at arm's length.

'Drop it in the water for goodness sake,' Tryst shouted, easily able to imagine the consequences of dropping it in a tinder dry forest. As though understanding, Jorge cantered back to the spring, without any urging from his squawking rider. As Rupert gratefully dropped the torch in the water, Citar felt a sudden, inexplicable pull towards the flame.

'*No* – !' she cried out, running towards the spring, but she was too late: the torch hit the water with a *plop* followed by a fizzing and bubbling. Citar waded in after it, tears pricking the corners of her eyes. The fire did not go out immediately, which it should have. Instead, it glowed a bright gold for several long seconds, ever so beautiful in its dying moments. Citar reached down and pulled the torch back out, but she was too late.

'C-citar?' Rupert asked, confused.

She couldn't speak. She just stared mutely at the dripping, smoking, blackened torch in her hands.

She felt like she had just lost something.

Like she had just lost her heart, all over again.

'I-it was b-burning m-my a-arm,' the tall boy added uncertainly, as though he needed to explain why he had dropped a blazing flame into water after it had done its job. He slid off Jorge and dipped his right arm into the water, right up to the elbow, biting down on his bottom lip as the cool water met his burning skin. No actual fire had touched him, but after the adrenal surge with which he had driven the Cuán back, he had realised he was being burned by the unreal heat output.

'He is *so* weird,' Shiloh said quietly to Ben, as they watched Citar stare numbly at the torch.

'Citar? You alright?' Tryst asked cautiously, wading into the spring towards her.

'We - we might have needed it again,' Citar forced herself to say. She had to cover her bizarre behaviour somehow. She couldn't exactly say *I just saw the ghost of my best friend and I think he was the flame that just saved our life and WHICH YOU JUST DROPPED IN WATER.*

'I-it was to-too hot, C-citar. N-no-one c-could h-hold it,' Rupert stammered, watching her worriedly.

'It wasn't a natural flame, that's for sure. Someone was looking out for us,' Tryst said.

*Someone was looking out for* me, Citar thought, and harshly wiped away a tell-tale tear before it could spill down her cheek.

Then they heard the shouting.

* * * * *

Bravo had woken in the late morning knowing in his gut that he needed to find his friend. He had been tracking

Lien from his pony when he heard the howls of the Cuán wolf pack. Bank had galloped hard through the heat to arrive in time for Bravo to see the first flame go out, and hear Rupert scream Lien's name, and see Saul find Lien in the trees. Bravo was initially enraged to see Lien interacting *again* with outsiders, and had been about to accost his friend there and then, when he had seen Jordan. At least, the *ghost* of Jordan, which shocked Bravo deeply. The sprite was hovering near Saul but reaching for a fallen chevalier, on whom the little ghost seemed singularly fixated.

Then Bravo had seen Lien dropping out of his lookout tree and literally going to walk into clear sight of the chevaliers. Now Jordan had turned to Lien - but Bravo wasn't waiting to allow Lien to reveal himself. He had run at and tackled his friend, and then seen it wasn't *entirely* Lien he was pinning to the ground. And then some insane amount of espréi had lit the torch, Jordan was gone, and by the time Bravo looked back down, Lien was himself again and was giving him the same astonished and questioning look.

*Did you do that?!*

They both shook their heads.

Bravo searched the scene closely, but, unable to see Jordan again, dragged Lien up and back into the trees and out of sight of the regrouping chevaliers. Lien fell to his hands and knees when released, while Bravo dropped into a squat, leaning back against the warm, hard and reassuringly real trunk of a tree. He needed a minute to sort through confused thoughts.

Jordan was dead. Bravo assumed it was Saul who had killed him, and that his ghost had become bound to the old man. Seeing a ghost in such an incidental manner was a very bad omen though, well known to the People. It was one thing seek a ghost, to be attuned to seeing ghosts, or to have a ghost manifest itself to you. But Bravo had not sought Jordan. He was not particularly sensitive to ghosts. And the ghost had not manifested itself to him - Jordan had been reaching for a fallen chevalier.

That Bravo had seen Jordan anyway meant one thing.

He was himself near death.

That was already a lot to think about, but then there was also whatever had been manifesting inside his best friend. He turned an interrogative look upon Lien. All of this was clearly his fault.

'What on earth was...*any* of that, Lien?' he demanded. 'You got involved with outsiders *again*! Did you learn nothing from the last time? You were seen by *three* chevaliers, and *Saul*. I mean...what were you *thinking*? And what happened to your *eyes?!*'

Lien turned from his hands and knees into a cross-legged position, and lowered his head into his hands, overwhelmed by the number of questions and accusations. He was still shaken from the encounter with his darkness. With his *surrender* to his darkness. He knew *he* hadn't lit the torch. Had whatever it was that was inside him done it? He didn't understand what had happened.

But Bravo was waiting furiously for answers, so Lien decided to start with the easier explanations.

'It's not my fault, Bravo. Aethon led me to them, just like last time, and who am I to deny my destiny?'

'Your *destiny*?'

Bravo was heavy handed on the sarcasm.

'Yes, you *know* Aethon leads people to their destiny,

well known mythology right there,' Lien insisted. 'And I was only seen by *two* chevaliers, one of whom had already seen me anyway and - admittedly amazingly - hadn't even told anyone. The prince from last year, can you believe it?'

'You were also seen by the boy on the chestnut,' Bravo snapped, standing up and approaching Lien. 'He followed Saul's eye-line, smart ass.'

Lien took a moment to remember which chevalier rode which horse, before landing on Tryst. He flinched.

'Oh boy,' he said anxiously, also getting to his feet. 'That's not good.'

'Lien,' Bravo said incredulously, '*none* of this is good! None of this is anywhere *near* good! And what did you do it for? What did you put the People - *our* people - at risk for? For *chevaliers*? For five boys who will grow up to be knights who will be enemies of the People? Who will chase us and kill us if they can? And you know why, right? It's not just about Lindahl and Sky.'

Bravo was wild eye to wide eye with Lien now, his voice rising with anger.

'They will kill us for looking after *you*!'

Lien was being so deeply sucked into the guilt Bravo heaped upon him, that he too was oblivious to the risk of Bravo's volume - until a movement in his peripheral vision pulled his attention. He glanced over to his right, and paled even more under his olive complexion.

'Don't you look away from me, Lien, this is on you, all of this is on you!' Bravo raged on. The passion was born of fear and love: love of Lien, fear of losing his friend and now added to an already volatile mix, fear of his own presaged death. And that rage was only just rising up, and so would have lashed Lien for much longer, but for an awkward cough from his left. Bravo's head twitched spasmodically to follow the sound, and he saw what had so startled Lien.

Bravo's red flush also blanched as he understood the terrible consequence of his outburst.

The cough had come from Citar, behind whom Tryst, Rupert, Ben and Shiloh were curiously gathered, drawn over from the spring to see what all the shouting was about.

Silence fell between the seven teenagers, eerie in the wake of the dying echoes of Bravo's outburst. Citar looked expectantly to Lien, knowing he was the only one who could speak to them all. Lien, however, could not find his tongue. His eyes ping-ponged between Bravo - also speechless - and the chevaliers. Finally, he opted for speaking quietly to his best friend, still in their own language.

'What do we do now?' he asked, wide eyes still fixed on the other boys. Bravo replied with a rare obscenity that perfectly encapsulated the quantity and depth of the shit that they were in.

It was Rupert who broke the silence.

'W-we d-didn't h-hear anything,' he stammered. 'W-we d-didn't s-see anything e-either,' he added, nodding urgently and encouragingly to his companions, who still had no idea what to make of the situation.

As usual though, Tryst caught on fastest.

'I take it we owe these two our lives?' he asked, taking in every detail of the two boys. His father had instructed him to look out for an Avenel boy living in Leaverness, and that was clearly Lien. But he was particularly intrigued by Bravo: he had never met one of the People.

Bravo returned the curious look with a furious glare.

'It was him,' Citar said, nodding to Lien. 'His friend doesn't approve of saving outsiders,' she added darkly.

It was said offhandedly, but caught both Lien and Tryst by surprise.

'You can understand their language?' Tryst asked.

Citar realised her mistake, and cursed herself. Cira of the Backwind knew Bravo and his dislike of outsiders; Citar of Avenel had never met him before this minute.

'No, of course not…it's just that the emotion of the argument seemed fairly…universal,' she hastily amended.

Tryst pondered this a moment before accepting it, far too easily, with a shrug. Lien managed to hold onto his suspicion for only a few moments longer before Citar's glamour pushed his whole attention to Rupert.

'L-lien s-saved us. A-and so the h-honourable thing t-to do w-would be to k-keep him s-safe in r-return. We m-mustn't t-tell a-anyone that we s-saw them,' Rupert continued, trying desperately to sound firm and making himself stammer more in the process. Lien, giving Rupert a grateful smile, wondered whether he had underestimated the prince. He was a coward for sure, but he had a good heart.

'Please,' he said slowly to the chevaliers, hands open wide in a supplicant gesture. 'Please do not tell anyone you saw us. Nothing. It was a great danger to us to help you, but now our lives are in your hands.'

'Look, I'm sorry, but I'm confused about all of this,' Shiloh announced, his brash tone clashing against Lien's impassioned plea.

'You,' he continued, pointing at Lien, 'look like you're like, you know, like us. And you speak Avenelese, although a bit crap, if you don't mind me saying. But then you're all –

weird and topless and tattooed and stuff. Nice scars by the way. *And* you made that magic flame, which was awesome, obviously, but seriously, what *was* that?'

Lien moved to say he hadn't made the magic flame, but Bravo stopped him with a light pressure on his wrist. He shrugged unhelpfully, instead. Citar noticed the interaction. She had her own theory about who had lit the torch, and this seemed to confirm it wasn't either Lien or Bravo, who were the only other likely candidates.

'Now *he*,' and Shiloh turned his attention to Bravo, 'is, like, I don't know. What *are* you?'

What Bravo was mostly was barely suppressed anger.

'He's from the People,' Tryst supplied. 'I'd guess they're both from the People.'

'No shit?' Shiloh exclaimed, delighted. 'I thought you were all long gone!'

'This is your big secret from last year, isn't it Rupert?' Tryst said, forgetting even to address the prince in an insulting manner. Rupert paused only a moment before giving a slight nod: there was no point in deception any more, the game was up.

'*Anyway*,' Citar cut in, 'the *point* is that yes, we will keep your secret. Right you lot?' and she glared at her companions. 'If it wasn't for them, we would be dead.'

'What happens if we don't?' Shiloh asked. 'Just asking!' he added defensively as the others all glared at him. 'I mean I thought they were hunted out of Leaverness until a minute ago, catch me up here.'

'The Order will hunt down the People,' Ben rumbled in reply to the question. It was his first offering to the conversation.

'Over the whole Lindahl thing?' Shiloh said, frowning.

'That was forever ago. Like, literally our whole lives.'

'Not because of that, you bellend,' Tryst said. 'Because *he,*' and he nodded to Lien, 'is from Avenel. If he finds out, my father will saddle up tonight and bring a group of knights down here to "liberate" him from the "savages" of the forest.'

'Well do you *want* to be liberated? I mean, you can come with us now, save an awful lot of trouble,' Shiloh offered.

Lien stared back at him, appalled at the idea.

'Your family is probably from Avenel. We could help you try to find them,' Tryst said thoughtfully, although he had his suspicions about the boy's parentage.

'And you are a danger to the People,' Ben said.

'Only if you tell of me!' Lien interjected.

'You could become a chevalier, like us,' Citar said, her heart jumping at the idea.

'B-but you d-don't have to,' Rupert added hastily, seeing Lien's surprise and Bravo's deepening scowl. Bravo turned a dangerous glare on his best friend, who was feeling flustered and overwhelmed by all the suggestions being flung around. They knew of Areté in Avenel, and they might be more likely to actually tell him things he wanted to know. He might find his family! He might –

– Bravo was gripping his arm now, nails biting into his skin.

Lien shook off the outrageous ideas.

'No, thank you,' he said, though the lack of conviction caused a painful increase in pressure from Bravo.

'I mean, of course not! The People are my family, and besides, I'd be a terrible chevalier,' he added, laughing it off now. The pressure on his arm released.

Citar looked disappointed.

Bravo glared triumphantly at Shiloh.

'Well no need to get your knickers in a knot, I was just making a suggestion,' Shiloh said defensively. 'I'm fine with whatever. I just like to have full disclosure, you know?'

'So we are in agreement? We ride back to Avenel, and say we had an uneventful trip?' Citar pressed, getting back to business.

'Have you *seen* Jorge? We're going to have to cover for him coming back with half his neck and shoulder missing,' Shiloh said. He was wildly exaggerating, but it was true that Jorge was injured and Rupert's right arm and hand were also bright red from the heat of the torch. As a pair, they made "uneventful" a hard sell.

'Does anyone actually know *how* to get back to Avenel from…wherever it is we are? You did lead us a merry dance chasing that damn unicorn, Citar. If you recall,' Tryst said dryly. Citar had the grace to look embarrassed, before looking hopefully to Lien.

'You know where we are, right, Lien?' she asked.

'The stream that feeds this spring joins the Willowbend River, which will guide you to the Willowald Trail. Aethon gave only a small chase today,' he grinned.

'Well thank goodness for that,' Shiloh said. 'Let's get everyone and the horses a good drink and then follow the stream to the river and get ourselves home. No-one will believe we're coming back mounted!' he crowed.

As the teens all headed back to the spring and horses, only two were unhappy: Bravo and Tryst. Bravo was because he was convinced one of the chevaliers would spill the truth, and Tryst because he was certain he would be that chevalier. Not intentionally, of course, but his father had specifically instructed him to bring news of Lien back to Avenel. Tryst was a superb liar, thanks to years of trying to learn how to lie to his father. He had honed it to a fine art, one that worked on everyone…except the one person he needed it to.

Bravo noticed Tryst's conflict, and, suspicious, dared to reach our his espréi to try to get a clearer picture of what the other boy was thinking. It was a touch that not many outsiders would even notice, so Bravo was shocked when Tryst not only felt it, but responded with a cold energetic push back and a sharp, hard look.

The boys held each other's challenging gazes for several long seconds, before Bravo closed the gap between them, eyes narrowed.

'You no tell?' Bravo asked, urgently.

'I will not tell,' Tryst replied coldly. And it was true. He wouldn't *tell*.

But that might not be enough.

The horses and teenagers all drank gratefully from the spring before Lien helped an anxious Rupert to wash Lord Jorge's wounds. The black horse's neck and shoulder were streaked with blood from a series of claw marks and the bite he had suffered right before the torch had been relit. He was tired and in pain, but remained as good natured as ever and was grateful for the gentle ministrations.

Lien and Bravo then lead the chevaliers to the little stream that fed the spring, and another thirty-minute walk to the wider, deeper Willowald River. Lien and Bravo walked on foot to rest their tired ponies; Rupert also walked the injured Jorge, while the other horses plodded wearily under the weight of their riders. No-one spoke, all were now exhausted from both the drama and stifling heat.

The mood of the chevaliers changed to relief though when the river came into sight: if as Lien said, the Willowbend would take them to the Willowald Trail, that trail, which ran through the safer outskirts of Leaverness, would take them to the Avenel Plain and then home to the city.

The chevaliers unsaddled their horses to take them into the river, where Lien and Bravo were already floating luxuriously while Jest and Bank, who wore no saddlery in the first place, happily cooled off in water up to their shoulders. Shiloh practically ran his mare into the clear, fresh water, whooping all the way. The relief of the cool clear water eased much of the tension and stupor in the group. Lord Jorge began to paw playfully in the river, splashing Citar and Adagio, who stepped back in surprise. Adagio snorted and pushed back with his nose, splashing Rupert, who grinned slightly desperately as he returned fire, using his shield from his back to scoop a torrent of water towards Citar.

'Prince or not, Rupert, you are going *down*!' Citar spluttered, releasing her own shield from her back, ready to scrum. In seconds, an epic water fight broke out amongst Rupert, Citar, Lien and Shiloh as they splashed, tackled and dunked one another, the chevaliers stumbling about awkwardly in their chain mail and armaments. Even Ben made the occasional half-hearted splash; but neither Bravo nor Tryst could shake off their concerns enough to join in. Instead, they ended up unintentionally sitting near each other in the shallows of the river, while their horses grazed on the bank.

'You know espréi,' Bravo said eventually, awkward in the unfamiliar language. Areté had drilled Lien relentlessly in Avenelese but Bravo had never made much effort to learn it.

'I don't know what you're talking about,' Tryst replied.

Bravo considered the other boy briefly, then reached out again with his own energy. He hit a cold, hard wall, and raised an eyebrow.

Tryst also considered the best way to respond. Magic was frowned upon in Avenel so it was important he gave away nothing in front of the other chevaliers. But a quick glance confirmed that they were all immersed in the water fight, and he felt an odd desire to connect with this strange, angry boy. Tryst had no-one but his mentor to talk to about magic, and even that came at a high price. It was a lonely and danger fraught vocation. But here was a boy around the same age who had grown up in a magical forest surrounded by magical people and creatures. What was forbidden to Tryst was second nature to Bravo, and Tryst was…envious.

He cautiously reached out his own energy to Bravo.

Bravo looked surprised, but accepted the contact. It was like they were gingerly holding one hand up to each other, palms touching, but energetically instead of physically. There was a curious synchronicity between their espréi.

Bravo slipped out an involuntary, shy smile, which Tryst unexpectedly returned.

'Bravo! Tryst! Come join!'

They energetically disengaged quickly, even guiltily, to look to Lien, who was wading towards them, panting and beaming. It was the happiest Bravo had seen him in weeks. He gave a sideways look to Tryst, who shrugged and got up to join in the fun. Twenty minutes later they were all stretched out to dry on the river bank, the horses grazing peacefully nearby. Lien flopped down contentedly next to Bravo, a little distance from the chevaliers, where they proceeded to speak in their own language.

'Maybe chevaliers are not so bad,' Lien grinned. Bravo wanted to contest this statement, but could not because, despite himself, he had also enjoyed playing in the river with them in the end. They were ridiculous in their chainmail of course - Citar had explained it was much too difficult to get out of and back into to warrant taking it off - but he had enjoyed the carefree laughter and play.

'Maybe,' he conceded, a ghost of a smile running around his lips. Then he thought further ahead, and sobered.

'But they are still a risk to us,' he cautioned.

'Rupert did not tell anyone about me in a whole year,' Lien pointed out.

'Rupert is one. Now there are five chevaliers going back to Avenel.'

Lien considered whether to make his proposal to Bravo now. Bravo, sensing his indecision, turned to look at him. His eyes narrowed suspiciously.

'No, Lien - no,' he said, rolling up to seated. Lien followed suit.

'Well it's just that I was *thinking* that maybe '

'Lien, I do not want to hear about your thinking. I think we'd all be a lot better off if you did no more thinking today,' Bravo growled.

'But Bravo, they know about Areté in Avenel,' Lien protested.

Bravo stared blankly.

'Of course they know about Areté,' he said, as though talking to a child. 'She lives most of her life in cities like Avenel!'

'Yes yes I know that - but they know she's *missing,*' Lien explained. 'Well, her friend Lady Selene Beckworth does. I think maybe she can help me work out where Areté is, and how to help her.'

'You're not going to Avenel, Lien,' Bravo said, getting to his feet and whistling to his pony, who ambled over. Citar, who had noticed the change in mood between the two boys, followed Bank. She paused next to Jest, who met her with a friendly whicker. She briefly wondered if he remembered her as she stroked his face and peered over his neck to observe the conflict.

'I need to meet Lady Selene Beckworth,' Lien insisted. 'If there's any chance she knows how to find Areté, then I have to take it!'

'Lien you'll stick out like a sore thumb in Avenel. Anyone will know you've been raised by the People!'

'I can talk Avenelese,' Lien protested.

'You have a *tattoo* on your *face!*'

Lien's left hand flew unconsciously to his left eye, gently running his fingers around the outside of his eye, though of course there was nothing to feel. In Leaverness there was little need for mirrors or glass and so he rarely caught sight of his own face. He had completely forgotten that, like Bravo, he had the beginnings of his tribal tattoo around his left eye. Teenagers of the People were tattooed around their left eye twice. The first time was when approaching their Kia'Oro, the trial representing the passage from childhood to adulthood. This marking was done physically by a tribe elder, like the rings the boys had around their arms. The eye tattoo would, at this stage, be incomplete, like an initial light pencil sketch upon which a drawing would be later completed. The full artwork would be revealed within the final trance at the closure of the Kia'Ora ritual. Every tattoo was unique. They sometimes represented something from the natural world - animals, seasons, natural phenomenon - but were often beautiful abstractions drawn from the soul of the wearer. Bravo's initial lines were all straight; Lien's were more cyclical. In the period between their initial marking and Kia'Oro it was common for teens to speculate on what their foundations would reveal; Lien had more than once worried he was getting a spider's web, even though he had no affinity with spiders.

Bravo's point stood though: no-one in Avenel would have a tribal tattoo on their face. It would be very hard to hide, and would definitely draw unwanted attention. And Lien's desire to go with the chevaliers triggered a deeply seated fear inside of Bravo: that he would lose his best friend to the city. To the outside world. Lien could not see himself so did not understand how much his skin colour stood him apart from the rest of the tribe. Bravo and the rest of the People saw his difference every time they looked upon him. They were reminded daily of this "otherness". And as Bravo had watched Lien playing in the river with the chevaliers, it was the first time his skin colour had not made him stand out. Instead, it was Lien who had fitted in.

It was Bravo himself who stood out in this group.

'It's time to go,' Bravo said brusquely. 'We will wait for Sky to return and consult with him about Areté and your dreams.'

'But that could be weeks, Bravo. Areté is suffering *now*,' Lien pleaded. 'Let me see Lady Selene Beckworth. *Please*.'

'*No* Lien!'

All of the chevaliers were watching now, drawn again by Bravo's increasing agitation and volume.

'This conversation is over. We're going home.'

'I'm not,' Lien insisted, holding his ground.

'You - are - not - going - to - Avenel!' Bravo said through gritted teeth.

'I'll come back, Bravo! I'll just go, find out what's happening, and come straight back.'

'Lien! You just don't get it, do you? If you go, you can *never* come back! They will think you belong there. That we *stole* you. Knights will follow you back. You will lead them to us, and you know what they will do!'

Lien initially had no reply for this. His resolve wilted under the furnace of Bravo's rage. He knew his friend was right. But he didn't feel that different, and he couldn't *see* his physical difference. He didn't understand why he should pose such risks to the People. To his family and friends.

It wasn't fair.

'You're right,' he eventually sighed, deflating. 'It's not fair. But you're right. I'll come home with you now.'

'If you were talking about Lady Beckworth, perhaps I can be of assistance,' Citar said conversationally, now that the argument seemed concluded.

'What's that Citar?' Lien asked hopefully, switching to her language.

'Lady Selene Beckworth is my sponsor,' she explained. 'I couldn't understand the finer detail of your argument, but I'm happy to try to help.'

Lien beamed.

Bravo looked suspicious.

'Thank you! I want to speak to Lady Selene Beckworth,

about Areté, but Bravo does not want me to go to Avenel,' he explained.

'Well that's to be expected, Avenel is far too dangerous for you,' Citar said, and Bravo understood well enough to look smug.

'What about Areté?' Tryst asked.

'She is in danger,' Lien said. Citar frowned; Tryst looked similarly dubious.

'There is not much on the continent that is dangerous to Areté,' he said.

'And she's probably just avoiding Avenel because they're making her the Marked Man. Marked *Woman,*' Shiloh chipped in.

'What is...the Marked Man?' Lien asked. He had not understood when he had been eavesdropping earlier and was glad of the opportunity to clarify.

'It's an Avenel tradition. The title is given to either someone who is wanted by the city but has not been caught, or in the absence of a suitably challenging criminal, it is Areté. Bringing in the Marked Man can get any boy or man into the Order, or, if they're brought in by a knight, that's a promotion, not to mention the kudos. The Marked Man is like the benchmark for skills at arms,' Tryst explained.

'What if they are not brought in by a boy or man?' Lien asked.

'Then by who?' Tryst asked, frowning.

'Well... you know. By girls, or women,' Lien prompted, unsure of why this wasn't abundantly obvious.

'Women aren't allowed in the Order,' Tryst said.

'It's a stupid rule,' Shiloh said, to everyone's surprise. The boy shrugged off the looks.

'I think women are underestimated. Just look at Areté,' he said.

'A-areté *is* im-mortal,' Rupert stammered.

'The Order is too dangerous for women,' Ben rumbled.

'Bollocks,' Citar said.

'*Anyway*, the title has being given back to Areté, so she's not likely to just wander into the city now,' Tryst concluded. 'I shouldn't expect to see her for a while.'

'I still need to see Lady Selene Beckworth,' Lien insisted.

'Well, if we can't take you to Avenel…I can ask her to come to Leaverness?' Citar suggested.

Lien looked triumphant; Bravo unconvinced.

'How to trust her to not tell of Lien?' he demanded, slowly and carefully speaking in Avenelese.

'Oh Selene already knows about Lien,' Citar started, before freezing in the widening stares of the two Leaverness boys. *Damn*, she'd done it *again*. Given away info that belonged to *Cira*, not to Citar.

'How?' Bravo and Lien said as one, giving each other fleeting side eye as they did.

Citar thought fast. She couldn't tell them any sort of truth. Explaining that she was Cira would break her glamour. Pretending Selene had told her as Citar would make sound Selene sound untrustworthy. She'd have to make up a lie, and not a very good one, because the truth was that if Selene held a secret for you, you knew there was nowhere safer for it, and she needed them to believe they could trust her sponsor.

'I heard them,' she said, trying to keep her tone even. 'I *over*heard them, Areté and Selene, I should say. I wasn't supposed to. I - er - I eavesdropped on them one night,' she finished, a little lamely, hoping that it came across as shame. Neither Lien or Bravo knew the word "eavesdrop" in Avenelese though, so she quickly explained that. Bravo looked shocked; Lien impressed.

'When?' Lien asked.

'Ohhhhh *ages* ago,' Citar obfuscated. She hadn't actually seen Areté since well before she left the Backwind.

'This is why you seemed to know me,' Lien grinned happily, some of his earlier suspicions about the chevalier dissolving in the face of this new information. Citar relaxed a little: completely by accident, she'd not only sold the story but also allayed his earlier suspicions.

'Okay,' he continued, 'you ask Lady Selene Beckworth. Where should we meet?'

Citar considered.

'Needs to be off the beaten path. How about a half mile along the Tanglewood Trail?'

Lien nodded; the unkept Tanglewood Trail broke off from Willowald and headed into more dangerous parts of Leaverness. They would meet no casual traffic along there - which made Lien think twice.

'It is not too dangerous for Lady Selene Beckworth, though?' he asked, worriedly.

'Nothing is too dangerous for Lady Beckworth,' Citar laughed. 'There's probably not much that's *as* dangerous as Lady Beckworth.'

Lien smiled uncertainly, even more curious to meet this impressive woman. She sounded a lot like Areté.

'You will come with her?' he suddenly asked, his smile widening. He liked this chevalier, and liked the idea of seeing him again. Bravo's expression darkened again, but Lien and Citar agreed the plan without him: a meeting at midday, in three days' time.

The earlier lethargy of the chevaliers was returning as the excitement of their near-death experience melted under the peak afternoon heat. As Lien prepared to say goodbye, he was surprised to find that he was a little sad to be leaving them. This encounter had humanised the chevaliers for him, for the first time, and he found he would have liked to spend more time getting to know them.

Ben gave him a curt nod and Shiloh a laconic salute.

Tryst extended a hand to shake; Lien glanced uncertainly between it and Tryst's face.

'Are you for real? You're supposed to take it,' Shiloh laughed. Tryst threw him a sour look, before returning to Lien with an apologetic look.

'You take my hand in yours, and we shake,' he explained. 'It's a gesture of friendship and respect, where we come from,' he added, aiming "respect" back towards Shiloh, who stopped laughing.

'Oh! Okay,' Lien said, relieved to finally understand, and grateful for the explanation. He carefully accepted the hand, then equally reciprocated the firmness of Tryst's grip. He allowed Tryst to lead the shake itself.

'This is right?' he asked, beaming. Tryst gave only a bemused smile though, and assured him it was exactly correct. He looked over Lien's shoulder to where Bravo was standing back with their ponies, looking sullen. Tryst gave him a short nod, which Bravo returned, his scowl softening briefly.

Lien retrieved his hand from the shake and turned to Citar.

'I know this will sound crazy, but I do feel like we have

met before,' he said. He still couldn't quite shake the feeling, even though it gave him a slight headache.

'But I've only met one other boy like you, years ago, and you are not Jordan,' Lien continued. His tone was conversational, but he and Bravo both clearly saw the sharp blink and disconcerted shadow that momentarily fled across Citar's face, before the chevalier caught herself.

'Not me,' she said, forcing a casual tone. She steadied herself to forge onwards.

'What was he like? This – Jordan?'

'He was really nice. And he was really loyal to his best friend, Cira,' Lien said, smiling at the memory. 'We had a great adventure! I would like to meet them again some time,' he finished cheerfully. And this was all true: Lien had liked Cira and Jordan very much, and would very much like to meet them again.

But Cira and Jordan had *adored* Lien, and *dreamt* of meeting him again.

Citar gave a small nod.

'I would too,' she managed, then turned back to busy herself with Adagio.

Bravo, well back from Lien but still in earshot, narrowed his eyes. He did not understand the whole conversation, but he knew Jordan's name, and he saw the effect it had on Citar. And he alone had seen Jordan's ghost, and his interest in the same chevalier. As he thought about it though, he felt an uncomfortable buzz in his head.

Lastly, Lien turned to Rupert. The prince was fussing Lord Jorge, whose wounds were clotted and already scabbing.

'He will be okay,' Lien said, pointing to the long thin

claw marks down his own chest. 'They will heal. But maybe we will have matching scars.'

'What did you get those from?' Rupert asked, wide eyed.

'Brynir the Cursed,' Lien said.

Off to his right, Tryst sidled closer to Citar.

'Weren't you keen to meet Brynir, Citar?' he murmured. 'Awfully big coincidence.'

Citar shrugged and indicated silence and then to Lien: *I'm listening.*

'Sounds awful,' Rupert said.

'Saul and the Cuán are worse,' Lien said, and grinned. 'You did good. You and Jorge get to be the hero of the story.'

'Well I w-wouldn't s-say that,' Rupert said, his stammer returning as he blushed a furious red. When Lien offered his hand, the lanky prince stared at it in such surprise that Lien initially thought he had misunderstood the rules of engagement. As his face clouded worriedly, Rupert hastily reached forward to grasp the offered hand and pumped it enthusiastically, forgetting his skin was tender and sore from the heat of the torch.

'S-sorry,' he apologised, 'people don't usually shake my hand willingly. You're doing it p-perfectly!'

'Friends?' Lien asked hopefully.

Rupert's face could have split, so huge was his smile.

'Of c-course. Thank you!'

'Thank *you*,' Lien countered. 'For not telling anyone about me last year. And this year.'

Rupert gave a shy nod at this.

'And – I am sorry for nearly killing you,' Lien added, taking his turn to blush. This time, Rupert gave an awkward shrug and looked back to his horse.

'Thank you all for your secrecy,' Lien said loudly to the group. 'I hope we will meet again!'

With a friendly and slightly pleading last look, Lien turned back to Bravo, still waiting with the ponies. The two Leaverness boys vaulted on easily; having seen the heights of the chevalier horses, Lien sadly realised they were outgrowing their beloved Bank and Jest.

Citar felt a chasmic emptiness as she watched Lien and Bravo ride away. Bravo's shouting had been a welcome diversion from her grief. She didn't know for sure, and she sure didn't understand how, but her heart told her that it had been Jordan who had saved them all. He had lit the torch as she had been about to be killed. And she *knew* that the flame had been all that was left of him, and now that it was gone, so too was he.

The subsequent departure of Lien and Bravo, the only people present who had also known Jordan, was like a double kick. She forcefully reminded herself that she would be seeing Lien again in three days' time. And in that time, she would have to work out how she felt about him now. Three years of imagining a divinely ordained princely version of the boy, followed by a year of – perhaps unfairly – blaming him for not being there when she had next needed him in Leaverness, had left her deeply conflicted about him. And then the Lien she had met today had been a blunt reality check, far divorced from the Lien of her dreams. Yet rather than being a disappointment, this version, she realised, was as fun as the boy she had first met.

She realised that she still liked him very much.

'I've just realised who Lien is,' Shiloh said suddenly, breaking Citar's line of thought. She looked around to his excited face, dread rising as she guessed what he was going to say next.

'He's totally the heir, right? I mean, think about it. He's the right age, and he's been hidden by the People. Sky must have stolen him from the Queen when she fled Avenel.'

'Yes,' said Ben, who had already come to the same conclusion. Rupert looked astonished; Tryst carefully impassive. He had worked it out when his father had instructed him to look for an Avenel boy in Leaverness.

'So…we *have* to tell someone, right?' Shiloh pressed. 'Avenel needs a king. And if he's the king, he's who we need.'

'I don't think he's the heir,' Citar said as firmly as she could. She absolutely thought he was the heir, after all. But all of Falric's warnings were ringing in her ears.

'Come on Citar, it's *obvious*,' Shiloh argued.

'I-it d-does m-make s-sense,' Rupert agreed.

'Even if he is though, he doesn't want to come to Avenel. He doesn't want to be a chevalier, much less a king,' Citar tried.

'Being an heir is not a matter of choice, convenience or enjoyment,' Tryst said.

'T-this is v-very true,' Rupert said, nodding fervently. 'I d-don't w-want to be an h-heir o-or a ch-chevalier b-but I m-must.'

'It remains true though that the Order will send all the knights to Leaverness, to raze it if they have to, to find Lien, if we come back saying we have found the heir,' Tryst said. 'And we don't *know* that we have found him. I'm not sure I'm willing to have the destruction of the forest and murder of the People on my conscience - are any of you?'

Tryst looked challengingly upon his colleagues.

Apparently none of them wanted that either.

Citar could have hugged him, and she didn't even like him.

'Then how can we find out for sure?' Shiloh asked. 'We can't do nothing.'

'I can ask Lady Beckworth? Maybe she will know, or will know how to find out?' Citar suggested. At least this stalled any rash action for a few more days. She was sure her sponsor would know better what to do next.

'This would be sensible,' Tryst agreed.

Shiloh looked unconvinced, but Rupert and even Ben were nodding their agreement also.

Shiloh surrendered.

'Okay. So Citar will report back to us after the meeting?'

Citar nodded and said she would.

'Okay,' Shiloh said again, in a tone which clearly said he was not okay with it but would reluctantly go along with it. 'Well, we need to sort out our story anyway. Who gets to be the hero of the day?'

'I think all things considered, that went splendidly,' Lien said cheerfully to Bravo as they rode home on their rapidly drying ponies.

'I mean I thought they were all going to die. Why would Aethon lead us all to Saul?'

'I don't know,' Bravo replied quietly. 'But I think something terrible is about to happen.'

Neither Lien nor Bravo could sleep the night after meeting the chevaliers. Bravo's mind had been in a swirling chaos of fear: fear of having seen Jordan, and therefore of the death he knew was coming for himself; fear of five chevaliers riding back to Avenel knowing a boy like them was in Leaverness, and therefore of a retaliation strike from the Order; and fear of losing Lien, either in a raid, or because his friend chose Avenel over the People. As he lay restlessly in the dark, running scenarios through his head, Bravo realised he was missing something important, something right in front on him, but which he couldn't quite put a finger on.

'Lien,' he whispered to the dark prone shape lying next to him. 'Are you awake?'

Lien immediately sat up.

'Completely. Can we talk?' he whispered back. When Bravo agreed, the two boys stole silently away from their tent and into the trees surrounding the clearing in which the tribe were currently encamped.

'I really need to talk to you – ' both boys started together, when they had settled down on a fallen tree. They stared, startled, at one another, then Lien laughed, and Bravo eventually followed suit.

'I need to apologise,' Lien tried again. 'I know you just worry about me. I didn't want to get involved with the chevaliers, I promise. It's just that I was led to them. By Aethon. And Aethon then led *them* to Saul. Which all seems damn suspicious to me. Because it was Aethon who also led Cira and Jordan and also us to Brynir, years ago. I mean...these can't all be coincidences, right?'

Bravo paused to take in this information: Lien's brain had obviously been as busy as his, but chasing different patterns.

'Bravo? Do you think I'm crazy?' Lien prompted, disconcerted by the long silence.

Bravo slowly shook his head.

'I don't think you're crazy, Lien. I've been trying to work some stuff out. But first, I have tell you something. Something bad.'

Lien's eyes widened as he waited for more information. Bravo took a deep breath, and told him about seeing Jordan.

Lien listened in shocked silence.

'I can't believe it,' he said eventually. 'I mean, he was such a nice boy. How can he be - gone?'

He couldn't quite bring himself to use the more definitive term.

'And you think Saul...did it?' he added. Again, he couldn't bring himself to say the sentence as it was in his head. He just couldn't reconcile his memory of Jordan with the concept of death. Of being killed. And as he thought that, Lien suddenly understood the terrible implication of Bravo's story.

'But - Bravo! If you saw Jordan, that means - ' he broke off, still unable to use the necessary words. Especially now that they also applied to his best friend.

'That means I'm going to die soon, too,' Bravo said hollowly.

Lien just stared. The news of Jordan had been bad enough, but the idea of Bravo dying too? He simply couldn't comprehend it.

'But - you can't. You can't go. You can't leave me,' Lien babbled. 'There must be some mistake. Maybe he was manifesting, and just - none of the rest of us noticed. Yes! That must be it!'

'There's no way you wouldn't have seen him, Lien.'

'But there was a *lot* going on, you know! Like wolves

and death and stuff, he was probably manifesting away and we all just missed him. So there. You're fine!' Lien concluded with a desperate shrug.

Bravo gave a resigned shrug.

'Maybe you're right,' he said dully, even though he was certain Lien was not. 'Do you think Jordan lit the torch? He disappeared after that,' he continued, wanting to change the subject.

'Can ghosts...do that?' Lien asked.

'They're basically residual espréi. Espréi lit that thing, you saw the flame, it was not natural. But I wouldn't have thought that sort of energy transfer was something that Jordan knew how to do. And why was he a ghost in the first place anyway? That's very rare. And speaking of weird stuff, what happened to your eyes back there?!'

'My eyes?' Lien asked, blankly.

'Yes, when I tackled you, your eyes were - silver. Really bright silver. You were...different. Like when you had that go at Brynir. It was like you were someone - or *something* - else. Don't you remember?'

Lien shook his head slowly. Of course he *did* remember surrendering to the darkness, but he didn't really know what had happened after that. And he didn't know how, or whether, to bring his darkness up with Bravo. He knew he did need to talk to someone about it eventually though.

'So...there's this...*thing*, inside me,' Lien said slowly.

'What sort of thing?' Bravo asked.

'I don't know. It's like a - a darkness. That's how I think about it. It's mostly a - a feeling. I experience it when I try to do anything with espréi. You know, when I try to use my soul eye. That's when I find it.'

Bravo digested this.

'Does it...speak to you? Is it like a - a person? A spirit?' he asked.

'No, it's just a presence. It's not like a person at all. It has only "said" one thing, but not with words, if you know what I mean. I *felt* what it was communicating. I didn't *hear* it.'

'And what was it - communicating?' Bravo pressed.

'Well, with Brynir, and then today, it said - without words, you understand - "let me".'

'Let me what?' Bravo frowned.

'Let me - you know. Take over. Deal with the situation.'

'And...you did? You let it?'

'I didn't want to!' Lien said. 'But in both cases...I had done all that I could. And I couldn't do enough. So...yeah. I let it. The darkness is what turned Brynir away.'

'And did *it* light the torch today?'

'I don't think so, you took me out before it could do anything,' Lien said. 'When it is in charge, I'm like a - a passenger. Like when I'm inside Areté actually, but then, I can think clearly. Funnily enough, this is more like being in a dream than that is. It's really disconcerting.'

'More questions for Sky, I suppose,' Bravo said after a short pause.

Lien looked panicked.

'I don't want to tell him!'

'Why not? He might be able to help you,' Bravo said.

'Bravo, I'm already a danger to the People. What if this is even more dangerous? What if...what if he has to exile me, because of it?'

'And what if he can help remove whatever it is?' Bravo countered. 'Although, to be fair Lien, it could be a useful -

presence. It's saved us, Cira and Jordan and then potentially it helped save the chevaliers today. That's pretty awesome.'

Lien hadn't thought of it like that.

'I guess so. I just wish it worked *with* me, instead of sort of, taking over,' he sighed.

'Is it inside you all the time? Like, right now?' Bravo asked.

'I don't know. I think so,' Lien said. 'Is this what anger is like?'

'No,' Bravo said dismissively. 'You have ownership over anger. The anger can take over, and sometimes it can feel like it has a life of its own, but it's fundamentally yours, part of you. This sounds like it acts *through* you, but isn't *of* you, if that makes sense?'

'I hope so. I hope it *isn't* part of me,' Lien said worriedly.

'I wish Sky was back,' Bravo sighed, laying back down.

'Me too,' Lien agreed. 'Where do you think he is?'

'I think he's looking for Areté,' Bravo said. Lien lay down too and closed his eyes. He wondered whether he should tell Bravo about his realisation about Areté saving Rupert - about how it was his fault she had disappeared. But it was so late, and he had already dumped so much on his friend this day and night.

'I feel like something bad is about to happen,' Bravo said after a long silence.

'Because of today?' Lien asked.

'Maybe,' Bravo said, noncommittally.

'Bravo, if the chevaliers do tell of me, perhaps I *should* go to Avenel myself? Then there would be no need for anyone to come here.'

'No,' Bravo said, this time forcefully, and to Lien's relief. He was curious about Avenel, and Areté had promised to take him there soon - before she disappeared. But he did not want going to Avenel to be a one-way ticket. Leaverness was his true home.

'We're worrying about nothing anyway, aren't we?' Lien asked, as much to convince himself as his friend. 'If they do tell of me, and knights are sent after me, the People are protected, right? I mean not if we show ourselves - obviously,' he added guiltily, 'but a group of knights who came looking wouldn't be able to find us, right?'

'Yes, I guess so,' Bravo agreed, but without the certainty Lien would have preferred to hear.

Lien tried to relax as silence naturally settled between them, but could not. He couldn't shake the feeling that he ought to go to Avenel though. If the Avenel boy in Leaverness came to the city, surely no knights would be sent to Leaverness? This, he felt, was the right thing to do, even though he had never had his long-promised trip with Areté and knew very little of the city and its people. And even though he took seriously Bravo's claim that he would not be able to return.

Bravo also tried to relax, but his brain was equally unhelpful. He knew his death was coming, after all. He was sure that Lien should stay in Leaverness though. If he went to Avenel he would have to stay there, for if he ever returned, he could be followed back. Knights could use Lien to find the People. But on their own, they should not be able to. There was a protection in place.

He just didn't know who the architects of that protection were, and that one of them was no longer able to provide it.

# 9. SKY

The late afternoon arrival of the triumphantly mounted chevaliers, including Jorge with bloodied wounds on his glossy shoulder and neck, attracted no small amount of attention in Avenel. The tradition of sending would-be knights off the beaten paths of Leaverness to face the wild forest spirits was a notorious and much celebrated event. The usual return of the riderless horses - and much later, their horseless riders - was an essential feature on the annual entertainment calendar. The return of mounted riders instead was a noteworthy skewering of tradition, and the chevaliers mostly enormously enjoyed the ride back to Voltanna through a sea of surprised faces and even the odd cheer.

Tryst alone looked pensive. Shiloh looked smug, Rupert relieved to be not only unharmed but conscious for this return, and even Ben dropped his habitual scowl. Citar fought the urge to beam at the crowd - that was hardly the demeanour to be expected of a male chevalier.

The five teenagers entered the city through the Leavensgate, the gate closest to the routes from Leaverness. They rode through and up and up the city to Voltanna, where they were met by a number of senior knights, led by Sir Bane and Sir Armitage, the Red and Blue Knights, and a team of grooms to take their tired horses. They felt like minor celebrities as they were asked to tell an assembly of senior knights of their adventures. They kept perfectly to the script they had agreed on the way back, because it was essential that there *was* a story to tell, and a way to explain the injuries to Jorge and Rupert. And it was mostly true, anyway. During their rehearsals on the way back, Shiloh had protested about Rupert being made the hero of the story, claiming it undermined their credibility. Citar had pointed out that technically, the story *was* true - Rupert *had* been separated, and he had carried the torch that had saved their lives, and his skin was red and sore to prove it. Shiloh had muttered darkly but failed to argue the matter further. With surprising patience, Tryst had helpfully explained to the prince how such a torch might be made, in case he was thusly interrogated.

To their seniors, the chevaliers said they had encountered an old man who had led them to the Cuán, but Rupert had become separated when Jorge refused to follow. The prince had made a torch with which to drive the wolves back, after which their horses had outrun the pack in the heat, although Jorge was injured in the fray.

Throughout the story, Sir Armitage was warm and congratulatory. Sir Bane however was cool and reserved, which was not unusual in itself, but made Tryst very uneasy. And he was correct to be concerned.

Because, but for his father, it all might have been okay. The chevaliers might have got away with their big secret, and kept their word to Lien and Bravo, and kept the boys and the People safe.

All but for Sir Bane.

The burly knight had listened with interest to the stories the teenagers told, watching his son with eagle eyes throughout. He was impressed with the performance - only Shiloh's resentment about Rupert's heroic role acted as a tell. So it wasn't the way the story was told that raised the Red Knight's suspicions; it was details of the story itself. He bought Lord Jorge separating Rupert from the group. He did not buy Rupert having the skill or sense to be able to make or light a torch alone. He did not buy Rupert having the courage to arm himself with only that torch and face the Cuán. He knew fire would drive the pack back, but he doubted it would have held them right back when they had blood in the air and on their tongues. And he definitely didn't buy the horses then outrunning the wolves, if they had been out for blood.

That night, Bane called his son into his study. Tryst, filled with dread and anger at what he knew was to come, nonetheless steeled himself and lied to his father with a straight face. He lied well, oh so well, which Bane acknowledged with a kind of twisted pride before striking his son hard across the face with the flat of his hand. Tryst caught his breath, blinked tears from his stinging eyes, wiped the blood from his nose, and repeated the story he had already told, his voice barely wavering even as his skin paled and sweat beaded on his forehead at the effort of trying to replace his true memories with the agreed fiction.

Bane was impressed at his son's resistance. He wanted a powerful heir, and had gone to unreal lengths to ensure he would have one at all. He was well on the way to making a strong heir of his son, but of course it was essential the father remained stronger still. And so he punched Tryst hard in the stomach. It was a dirty, cruel punch, one that lifted up into the ribs. Tryst doubled over in agony, then fell to his knees, gasping for breath. When he could speak again, he repeated his story a third time, his furious eyes holding his father's gaze steady even as his voice shook throughout.

The Red Knight knelt down to his son's eye level and calmly told him that he had brought what would happen next upon himself. Tryst flinched but it was too late: Bane had already placed his right hand firmly on the top of his son's head. Bane had needed to apply no coercion to trespass in Rupert's memories a year earlier: the prince had no reason to expect it and no ability to defend himself, even if he had. Tryst though knew exactly what Bane would do, and was years into the process of learning how to resist the mental violations of his father. He forced the false version of events to the forefront of his mind, in all the vivid detail he knew would be required to sell them to his father, while boxing down the real memories. For a fifteen-year-old boy, it was a remarkable feat of mental gymnastics, and again, Bane was impressed as he examined the created memories carefully before discarding them to search further for the real ones. Ultimately though, all Tryst's efforts achieved was to make the intrusion shockingly painful for himself. He was still not mentally strong or skilled enough to either fool his father, or prevent such transgressions happening altogether.

When Tryst tried desperately to pull away, Bane dug his fingers painfully into the boy's skull, ignoring the screaming and convulsions as he forcibly drew out the memories he required. When he was satisfied, he left his son collapsed in a silent, twitching ball on the cold, hard flagstone floor.

After exiting his study, Bane called for a maid. He told her that Tryst had suffered had one of "his turns" and required assistance getting to bed. Then he rode out, calling upon four men on his way.

Early the next morning, before light, three of those men rode out of the Leavensgate behind a wagon driven by the fourth. If the gatemen had inspected the contents of the wagon, instead of casually waving it thorough at the uncivil hour, they would have found it contained four sets of full armour, though the men were far from knights themselves.

Tryst watched them dully from a high window in his father's imposing manor, which was built into the mont under Voltanna. He had a devastating migraine, a bruised face and his chest was in a world of pain, but he knew that was nothing compared to what his failure would cost Lien and his people. He wanted so much to sleep, but the migraine prevented him. The migraine also complicated what he had to do next, but he felt he had no choice.

He slipped out of the manor and, with his bruising face hidden deep in the cowl of his robe, hitched an unsolicited ride on the back an early morning market wagon. When their routes diverged, he jumped off and ran, often falteringly, and stopping twice to be sick, to the blackened ruins of the Lethe Estate. This was his place of power. The manor house, Levithorne, had been burned down by a mob during the time of Du Romeau, and left as a grim, gaunt reminder of what happened to those who practiced black magic. Black magic was not Tryst's goal, but the energy of the estate was, for him, greater than even that of Voltanna, which was itself powerfully charged.

Tryst went into the charred, skeletal remains of the estate chapel and sat cross-legged on the hard floor, bathed in the cold illumination of the last of the starlight. The dawn was close, so he had little time. He slowed his breathing, steadied his mind as best he could with the migraine, and opened up a dream.

In the dream, he made a triangle shape with his right hand, index and middle finger raised, and called upon Callista. He was rewarded shortly after with the appearance of her psychic projection into his dream.

Callista crouched down before dream Tryst, who was cross-legged on the ground exactly as his physical self was.

'Take off your hood,' she commanded him, forgoing any greeting. The boy paused, and only reluctantly obeyed. In the physical world, Tryst remained still, while in the dream, he shrugged back his hood. Callista's face momentarily darkened when she saw the state of his face. She used her espréi to inspect him more closely. Tryst flinched violently at even the light touch.

'Tryst, shhhhhh, you know I am not your father,' Callista said gently. When the boy relaxed his guard a little, she finished her inspection.

'You have two bruised ribs,' she said gravely. 'And that's a shocking migraine, I cannot believe you have made it all the way here. It must be important.'

'It is,' Tryst said. 'I need to project into the dream of another.'

'That is very advanced, Tryst, I am not sure that you are ready for that,' Callista cautioned.

'I have to be,' he insisted. 'If I cannot do it through a dream, I have to do it in real life, and then…' he broke off, not wanting to complete the sentence.

Callista nodded, understanding.

'And then your father will know.'

'Or…can you do it?' Tryst asked, an imploring edge creeping unbidden into his tone.

'You know I can only *teach* you how to manipulate dreams, Tryst,' Callista said firmly, but kindly. 'Very few are gifted with the abilities you have, and I am, alas, not among them. First though, let me see if I can clear your head, it is a wonder that you could even summon me in such a state. You will have to allow me to…intrude.'

Tryst nodded stiffly. He was used to fighting off intrusion into his mind, so found it very difficult to allow anyone in. But he did, and because he had his eyes closed, even in the dream, he did not see that it was the golden eyed Cosmos, not Callista, who laid a translucent hand upon his head. The energetic sensation was warm, unlike that his of his father, which was always ice cold; and to his relief, the migraine soon subsided. By the time he opened his eyes again, it was Callista's bright blue eyes looking back at him, a contented smile upon her beautiful face.

'There we go. Now, we will try, and see what we might do. Whose dream do you want to project into?'

'Sir Armitage.'

Callista considered him with a raised eyebrow.

'I think you should start at the beginning,' she said.

* * * * *

Much later that day, which was the one following the encounter with the chevaliers, Lien was overcome by extreme tiredness after a restless night. Bravo had taken to afternoon naps anyway since starting his watches for Shah, and Lien joined him, literally unable to keep his eyes open. As early dusk fell, Shah finally returned, but bringing a completely different dream, one that felt like a normal nightmare. For Lien wasn't trapped inside Areté, but had an omniscient perspective. It was perhaps more like a vision, and what he saw woke him in a shouting panic. Bravo woke sharply too, quickly taking in both Lien's fear and the swirling smoke of the departing night-mare.

'Lien, what was it this time?' Bravo asked, grabbing his friend's sweat-slicked shoulders.

'It was different - it was just a normal nightmare - ' Lien started, trying to get his brain and breath under control. 'But it was so real - Bravo, I dreamt that there are knights riding for us. To attack us. I could see them, in the half light, just like it is right now. It was - *so* real.'

'It wasn't a normal nightmare, Lien, Shah brought it,' Bravo said, gesturing to where he had seen the mare disappear.

'What? Are you sure? It is not night!' Lien protested.

'Yes! I saw her.'

Lien's frantic mind screamed at him that what he had seen was real. There were more voices coming towards them now from the camp: Sindhe and two adults, alarmed at Lien's shouts.

'Do you think it was real?' Bravo asked urgently. Lien swallowed, decided to trust his gut, and nodded.

'Then we have to warn everyone,' Bravo said, springing to his feet. Sindhe, followed by elders Sade and Yael, came into sight.

'Knights. Knights are coming,' Bravo said, wasting no time on explanations. Sensing the boy's seriousness, Sade did not question the claim, but reached out a reassuring hand to Bravo's shoulder.

'Bravo, they can come, but they cannot find us. We are protected,' she said soothingly.

'By who?' Bravo demanded. 'Sky? He's not here.'

'Not *just* Sky,' Yael said, also unconcerned at Bravo's

announcement.

'Who else?' Bravo pressed, and his intensity began to unsettle even the elders.

'Areté,' Lien guessed, quietly, from behind Bravo. One look at Sade and Yael's faces told the two boys they were correct.

'Then we are not necessarily protected now.' Lien stepped forward, agitated. 'Please, we will explain later, but right now, we must prepare, they are very near. Please trust me,' he begged.

'Lien, we have been protected for many years, the Order has never been able to find us, not since – ' and here Sade suddenly paused, realising who she was talking to.

The tribe had not been found since Areté had brought Lien to them.

'Listen!' Bravo ordered, waving the others into silence.

Then they all heard it: the shouts of men, the drumming of the hooves of horses much heavier than those the tribe rode, and the clanging of armour.

Sade and Yael paled and Sindhe looked terrified, but Sade leapt into action.

'Yael, call in the herd. Sindhe, warn the children. Lien, Bravo, with me,' she ordered, hustling them all back towards the camp, but they were too late. As they ran back into the campsite clearing, four fully armoured knights swept in from the opposite side, torches aflame in the falling darkness. Their huge horses crashed through the site, scattering people and tents, while their riders set fire to every tent they passed. Shouts and screams rang all around as panic spread as fast as the fire across the campsite. Lien and Bravo froze, unable to do anything more than take in the horror. Everything was summer dry, tinder dry. Everything would burn, and not just the campsite: Leaverness would burn. In just brief minutes, all the structures of the camp were collapsing under the insatiable appetite of the flames.

'Help the children!' Sade ordered, breaking the boys' inertia. They obediently began to run into the chaos, but Lien stumbled on an unseen tent strut, poking out from its desolately fallen structure, pulling Bravo down with him. Throwing out their hands to break their fall, the boys smarted as their palms landed on stray ashes. Before they could scramble up, they felt a *thud-thudding* deep in the soft ground, vibrating up through their hands, wrists and knees.

'It's the herd,' Lien shouted to Bravo as they looked slowly up into what could have been certain death, or at least a damn good maiming, had it not been Jest leading the rush towards them. With Bravo clutching his back, Lien lurched to his feet, screaming his pony's name. Jest threw his fine head up high, practically folding his hind legs under to skid to a frantic stop, the larger horses scattering around him and the two boys he protected. Almost sobbing now, Lien reached out for Jest's taut face, running his hands over the wide nostrils and up to the frightened eyes. He whispered to the pony to be brave, and felt a shuddering sigh soften his tense body. Lien vaulted up onto the narrow back, pulling Bravo up behind him, and from this modest height, the boys finally gained a proper view of the source of the nightmare that had desecrated their lifetime of peaceful existence. Four monstrous metal men, the dancing flames mirrored on their armour, wheeled powerful horses through the carnage of the campsite. Avenel knights, men who had no business with the People, who ought not to be able to even *find* the People.

One knight threw down his burning torch and with a roar, pushed up his helmet visor and drew his heavy sword. His companions did likewise, briefly gathering their horses together to view the chaotic scene before them.

'Where are your protectors, Areté and Sky and the treacherous Lindahl, now?' the first knight bellowed, hefting his sword aggressively. 'The eye of Avenel is upon you. A reckoning is coming!'

The People all learned the language of Avenel, but it was spoken so rarely since they went into hiding that while the opening statement was easy to gather, most did not understand the second. But they all understood what came next.

'And where is the boy Lien?' the man roared. 'Bring him to us!'

Lien and Bravo both froze in shock at hearing Lien's name. Now, without a doubt, their responsibility for this horrendous attack would be known.

'No-one has to know you were there, Bravo, tell everyone it was just me,' Lien said urgently over his shoulder. He felt a crushing weight on his chest, a deep freeze in his soul as he realised that he had brought this nightmare upon the tribe.

'Jump down, I will ride to them alone,' he continued, tersely. Behind him, Bravo grimly shook his head, as did Sade, riding up next to them and using her horse to push Jest to the left, away from the knights.

'No Lien, we are sworn to protect you, and protect you we will,' she said firmly. Yael instead rode his tall black and white pinto mare towards the attackers.

'You dare to call yourselves knights,' he bellowed at them in their own language. 'You are nothing of the sort, and the boy is under our protection!'

Yael switched back to his own language as he wheeled his mare back towards the tribe.

'Mount up, my family, ride to Tauron'Est!' he commanded. While his back was turned away, the lead attacker snarled and kicked his horse forward towards the tribe elder, sword drawn, clearly setting out to make an example of the man.

'Yael!' Lien screamed in warning. Yael spun his horse back towards his attacker, but he did not try to evade the coming sword. Instead, he calmly spread his arms wide as the charger's great strides chewed up the yards separating them.

'Why isn't he moving?' Lien gasped, sure he was about to witness the man slain in front of them. But Sade was smiling and looking up to the night sky.

'Because he knows who is coming,' she said with relief and exaltation, as a dreadful piercing screech tore the air. An enormous falcon dived spectacularly down from the darkness above, swooping right in front of the charging horse, which braked and shied so hard that his rider was torpedoed off the side. The falcon continued towards the three remaining mounted riders; their horses scattered like birds from a thrown stone as the bronze bullet shot between them. While the men reached for manes, reins and slippery plunging necks to keep their seats, the falcon climbed back up on powerful wings to survey the destruction below. The fire was spreading through dry grass and into the surrounding trees, leaping up faster than even the most lithe children could climb. The tribe were all calling to and vaulting onto their horses, grabbing smaller children to sit in front and behind before galloping from the growing inferno.

'Boys, to Tauron'Est, *go,*' Sade urged one more time, before setting her horse off towards the falcon, her right arm outstretched. The burnished golden falcon swept down to perch upon her hand and they began a lap of the clearing at a flat gallop. Lien was unable to watch what happened next though, because Bravo had kicked Jest forward – towards the chargers. Both boys gripped onto the pony's slick sides as he bore down on the intruders.

'What are you doing?' Lien yelled back at Bravo, glancing back as he did, and seeing his friend's manic eyes. Lien's stomach flipped as he realised Bravo was going deep into a rage. He was momentarily distracted though by the realisation that they were not the only ones heading straight into danger: another charger, also carrying an armoured man, easily outpaced Jest. For a moment Lien thought the newcomer was a new enemy, but some instinct flagged the white horse and rider as friend, not foe. Yael had said the attackers were not true knights; Lien had never seen knights in action to know better himself, but it was immediately obvious that this man was superior in every way. The armour looked uncomfortable and unwieldy on the attackers; they yanked their horses around by the reins; their shields bounced around on their left arms; and they hefted their swords around wildly. This newcomer, this true knight, wore his armour like a second skin. He moved seamlessly as one with his white mare, without any contact on the reins. His left arm couched his shield into a tight defensive position, and he unsheathed his sword easily and held it effortlessly at his right side as he bore down on one of the fake knights. This target decided he'd rather have nothing more to do with any of this and tried to turn his frightened horse away, bellowing to his comrades. The one word Lien caught over all the chaotic sounds around them was "Armitage", and he grinned madly.

'You hear that? It's Sir Armitage!' Lien called back to Bravo, who showed no interest. Lien however knew from Areté's stories about the golden age of Avenel that Sir Armitage was a friend of hers, and the People. He was here to protect them, not to harm them.

The fake knight tried to parry Armitage's sword but his horse plunged forward wildly, almost unseating him, and he did not in any case possess the sword skill or strength of a knight. Sir Armitage's overhead strike met little resistance and threw the defending man's sword clean out of his hand, and threw his precarious balance off his horse's right side. He came down to the hard ground in a crashing, shouting heap and his horse took off. Sir Armitage immediately set his sights on another of the attackers. Bravo was pushing Jest towards the leader though, who was trying to set his horse towards Sade and the falcon, approaching them head on as they lapped the clearing. The clouds they were summoning were already starting to roll in around the burning clearing, lowering and thickening as they gathered in over what had, minutes before, been a perfectly clear dusk sky.

'Hey!' Bravo yelled, pulling the knight's attention. Realising who was approaching, he turned his full attention to the teenagers and their skewbald pony, who veered off, drawing him away from Sade as the first light drops of rain landed.

Bravo directed Jest out of the clearing, away from the

devastation, and they were chased by both the leader of the fake knights and by the ravenous fire. Lien was not so concerned about the fire now, for he knew the rain that was being summoned would intensify shortly; but he was worried about what Bravo planned for their pursuer. Jest flew with surefooted confidence through the forest; the charger was less confident in the unknown terrain, but the eerie orange flickering light of the fire illuminated the path enough for it to shortly begin to close the gap between them.

'Bravo! What's the plan??' Lien asked, and as soon as he had, Bravo changed his weight cues to bring Jest to a skidding stop. Lien was thrown painfully forward onto the pony's bony withers; the heavier charger required a longer breaking distance though and was forced into a sharp turn to the left, crashing off what passed for a trail and into the treacherous forest proper. The poor animal tripped almost immediately, falling heavily to his knees, throwing his rider over his shoulders. One of the man's feet remained caught in a stirrup though, half dragging the saddle off, and with the weight of his armour, he pulled the thrashing horse onto his side.

Bravo jumped from Jest and grimly approached, drawing his hunting knife from his belt. He put one hand out to the distressed horse, managing to speak relatively soothingly to it even while his hard eyes glittered with fury upon the undignified heap that was the attack leader. A few feet back, Lien hopped uncertainly from Jest, not sure whether he was going to need to help, or stop, his friend.

Bravo stood one foot on the helmet of the man - who was so tangled he could do nothing more than roar helplessly - and cut the saddle girth. Freed of his saddle and heavy fallen passenger, the foaming horse lurched to his feet and shot off into the forest. The man, presenting as a knight but without the strength of one, struggled against the enormous weight of his armour. Bravo furiously straddled his body. From the set and attitude of his body, Lien knew his friend had fully surrendered to his anger. To his rage. Bravo had never truly lost control of it before but here in the fire flickered darkness, while his people's encampment burned and facing what he thought was a real knight - representing the shame and abandonment he associated with his father - he had given it all the agency it craved. And knowing he was close to death ignited all of that ready tinder into rage. He would not die on this day though and he would not die at the hands of this man. Bravo pulled the visor up with one hand, drawing back the knife with the other. But before he could ruthlessly plunge it down into the exposed, terrified face below, Lien seized the hand in both of his own and held on with all the strength he had. Wrenched back, Bravo turned a shocked and then betrayed look upon his friend.

'He came to *kill* us!' he yelled. 'And to take you! He is a *murderer!*'

'But you are *not*,' Lien insisted, his eyes beseeching Bravo to regain his senses.

'It doesn't matter what I am Lien, soon I am going to die!'

'Bravo you are not going to die!' Lien said. 'I am not going to let you!'

'What do you think *you* can do about it?!' Bravo snapped. Failing to free his arm from Lien's grasp, Bravo turned upon his friend instead. He stood up from his straddle over the fallen man and threw himself upon Lien, their limbs flailing. Bravo quickly gained the advantage, and pinned helplessly below him, Lien found himself pressed down hard into the soft, wet earth, genuinely fighting for his life against his own best friend.

'Bravo - listen - this - is not helping!' Lien panted as he struggled to get free. The rain was torrential now: the fire was being extinguished as they fought.

'They *need* to be punished,' Bravo growled, painfully pinning one of Lien's elbows down with a sharp knee. 'Stay down, and let me deal with it.'

'Not - your - job - ' Lien gasped.

His darkness stirred.

He needed to end this conflict.

'And besides - it's - *my* fault! Let me - go - to try to - fix it,' he implored.

Bravo stiffened, his knee digging so hard into Lien's bicep attachment that he cried out from the pain.

'No, you're not going there. You're not leaving us,' Bravo snarled.

Deep inside, Lien's darkness snarled back.

'Come on - you *know* I can't - stay here,' Lien said, angry himself now, tears stinging the corners of his eyes as he said the words, acknowledging their truth.

'I'm a danger - to the People. To *you*. And the answer - is with Areté. I have to find her, Bravo. And maybe I can come back after - but right now would you *get off my arm*!'

Bravo's response was to kneel on Lien's other elbow as well, his face twisted with fear and denial, his dark hair falling forward with the weight of the rain so that it was impossible to tell if he was crying or not.

'You can't go, Lien, I won't let you,' he said, less forcefully, more fearfully now, but he nonetheless took his hunting knife and pressed it to his friend's neck.

'You can't stop me, Bravo,' Lien said through gritted teeth as he strained again to escape. The knife pressed dangerously into his throat: Bravo didn't let up a fraction. Lien felt a chill that had nothing to do with the mud and rain. His darkness was rising, trying to get to his muscles, to his voice. It wasn't even waiting for him to try to use his soul eye.

He tried to stamp it down.

'Don't make me hurt you!' Bravo snapped. 'Agree you'll stay.'

'I don't think – I'm the one – who is going to get hurt here – ' Lien panted, now both physically fighting his best friend and mentally fighting his own shadow.

'You need to get off me *now.*'

'Tell me you'll stay!' Bravo shouted, pressing the knife a little harder – just enough to break the skin.

'*No!*' Lien shouted back, bullishly lifting his head just a little more. He had to know for certain how far Bravo was prepared to go. The knife bit, and this time, Lien bled, and had his answer. But he couldn't fight on both fronts.

**LET ME.**

He didn't mean to. He really didn't.

But the darkness surged up anyway.

Lien closed his eyes, and when he opened them, he was just a passenger, watching through his own eyes but as though he were underwater. He saw Bravo flinch in shock at whatever it was he saw in the face, in the eyes, of his best friend.

The darkness pushed Lien's body upwards, *into* the knife. Bravo gasped as the blade drew a long red line into his friend's neck. He dropped the weapon onto the wet ground, and was about to scramble away from whatever was inside Lien, but it gave him up as quickly as it has taken him over. Bravo stared, confused, then looked back to the knife, then froze.

Not because of the trickle of Lien's blood, diluted with rain, sliding accusingly down the rough-hewn blade.

No, Bravo's eyes slowly rose up from the calloused, bare foot that had just landed next to the knife. Up long lean legs, a muscular torso and into the disappointed - no, sad - eyes of his grandfather.

Behind Sky, Sir Armitage's white charger steamed gently in the cool, easing rain, blowing damp clouds of air from her wide nostrils. Only the restless champing of her teeth on the metal bit broke an otherwise excruciating silence.

# 10. CALLISTA

Sky's only words with Bravo were to instruct him to ride immediately for Tauron'Est. Lien, however, he indicated to stay. Lien saw the shame in his friend's face but even more so, the fear in his eyes, as he reluctantly obeyed his grandfather. Lien also felt afraid. This whole attack was his fault. Was Sky angry? Was he going to exile Lien from Leaverness?

However Sky only gravely asked Lien to wait as he, Sade, Yael and Sir Armitage rounded up the four fallen and injured pretend knights. They were stripped of the armour they so badly wore, and Lien noticed that although they were generally unhappy and sullen about their capture, they all seemed relieved to shed the sheets of metal. Lien couldn't imagine why anyone would choose to cover their body in such awkward, heavy and cumbersome wear, although he did notice that Armitage wore it with considerably more ease. It still seemed mad to Lien though. Better to be lithe and agile and so able to avoid strikes, than heavy and slow and to be able to take them.

The horses the men had ridden in on had all long since bolted, so Yael brought forth four horses of the People. They were much lighter animals, built for speed and agility, and of course they wore no saddles or bridles, as was the People's way. The men looked incredulous as they were ordered to mount up. They hopped around hopelessly trying to throw a leg over to vault on, getting angrier and angrier as they repeatedly failed. Despite the severity of his own situation, Lien had to smother a giggle at the incongruous spectacle of these men, who had swept in to cause such harm, stripped of their armour and pride and reduced to such humiliation. Even Armitage, Sky, Sade and Yael were openly enjoying the show. They did not let the horses' backs get too pulled around though, but soon each stepped forward to leg the embarrassed men up.

Before escorting the men away, Armitage agreed to unmount them before they left Leaverness to let the horses return home, and have them cross the Avenel Plain on foot. He then had one more quiet, terse exchange with Sky. This one, to Lien's surprise, was in the language of the People, which Armitage spoke perfectly. He strained to hear what was said.

'How is it that they could find you?' Armitage asked. 'You have been protected for so long.'

'I believe Areté is…out of play,' Sky replied. 'We cannot rely on any protections she had a hand in being intact.'

'What can have happened to Areté?' Armitage asked, astonished.

'I am trying to fully understand it,' Sky said unhelpfully.

'When were you going to tell me about the boy?' Armitage asked, a little accusingly, after a pause.

'I was not. He is Areté's ward. But I have been encouraging Areté to take him to Avenel for some time, at which point, I am sure she would have introduced you.'

Armitage seemed unsure of how to proceed with his further questions.

'I don't suppose you will tell me whose son he is?' he tried.

'I will not,' Sky agreed.

'That is also Areté's job, I assume?' Armitage asked dryly.

'It is.'

'But she is - missing?'

'She is.'

Armitage gave a put-upon sigh.

'You know this will continue when word of tonight's events gets back to the city. You would do better for it not to get back.'

Here he looked meaningfully at the four men, waiting miserably on their horses.

'That is not our way,' Sky said. 'And somebody already knows. Somebody sent them.'

'There's a big difference between one person knowing and the whole city,' Armitage argued.

'They're not talking to us, so they may not talk to anyone else either,' Sky countered.

Armitage considered arguing further, but knew it was pointless. He nodded his reluctant concession.

'It is good to see you, my friend. It has been far too long,' he said, clasping Sky's forearm in the warrior's way.

'It has indeed. Perhaps better times lie ahead, once more,' Sky nodded.

Armitage took a long, searching look at Lien, a small forlorn figure standing with Jest. He gave the boy a short nod, then mounted up to take his prisoners back to Avenel.

As the five horses set off at a canter - the attackers yelping and grabbing for the horses' manes - Sky indicated for Lien to come and join him. They surveyed the charred remains of the campsite together. Lien felt his chest tighten as he waited for Sky to speak.

When he did not, Lien felt compelled to break the silence.

'Sky...I'm so sorry...' he started, his voice cracking, but the old man shook his head.

'This is not your fault, Lien,' he said.

'But look at what I have done,' Lien said, indicating the smoking ruins.

'You did not light the torches. You did not burn the tents.'

'But they did that *because* of me. I revealed myself to chevaliers, yesterday. I know I wasn't allowed to. But Aethon led them to Saul and the Cuán, and me to them, and I could not let them die.'

'Quite right,' Sky agreed. 'That would not be our way.'

Lien stared at the old man, astonished.

'I am...not in trouble?'

'I wouldn't say that. But the trouble is not with me, or with the People,' Sky said. 'We knew the risks when we took you in.'

'*Why* must I be a risk?' Lien asked wretchedly. 'Why can't I live here with you? I am happy. Why is it anyone else's business? Just because I look different? Why should that matter?'

'It is...a little more complicated than just the colour of your skin, Lien,' Sky said gently. 'Your path started in Avenel, even if you do not remember. It has had a lengthy diversion with the People, and I hope will continue to align with us, but it does not belong with us. This is a time of change for you. If you now try to force your life against your path, then the trouble you would further bring upon us *will* be of your doing.'

Tears brimmed in Lien's eyes. The words were said kindly, and meant kindly, but their meaning was devastating.

Sky was telling him he could not go to Tauron'Est.

He could not go home.

He no longer had a home.

'I want to stay here,' Lien said, his voice shaking.

'And I want you to also. But what we want for ourselves is not always what the world asks of us,' Sky said.

'Then what does it ask?'

'You have at least twice been pointed towards your destiny,' Sky reminded him, the smallest smile teasing around the sides of his mouth as Lien initially puzzled on his meaning.

'Oh - you mean Aethon? That's what he does, right? Leads people to their destiny?'

'Most of the time. Sometimes Aethon simply enjoys a chase. But two chases are a message that cannot be ignored. I believe you have had other messaging, as well?'

'You know about my dreams?' Lien gasped.

'Someone - or something - has created a bridge between you and Areté. You will not find her in Leaverness. Believe me - I have looked,' he added ruefully.

'So...you think I should go to Avenel?' Lien asked slowly.

'I think you would be safest riding for Tauron'Est. But safety is a luxury I fear we have granted you for too long. I do not regret that, but I am concerned that we have not adequately prepared you, and now with Areté missing, there is no time. But know this Lien: wherever you go, and whatever you do, it will always be with our blessings: hers, and mine.'

A tear ran down Lien's cheek.

Sky wrapped him in a firm embrace.

'Areté has hidden herself from us. There will be a good reason. But seek her, and accept help. You cannot do this alone,' he said quietly in the boy's ear. As he stepped back, and called his horse to his side, Lien remembered something he had wanted to ask.

'Sky – how did Sir Armitage know we needed him?'

Sky vaulted up onto Horse before replying.

'He said he had a dream,' he said.

Lien thought on this a moment.

'Could that dream have been sent by the same person sending mine?' he asked.

'There are very few who could do it, that is certain,' Sky said, and set Horse off at a gallop in the direction of Tauron'Est.

Lien walked numbly through the dark, smouldering campsite. The rain had made a slush of the ash, so that his feet sank into sooty blackness. He picked his way to the tent he had shared with Bravo, and by only the light of the moon and stars, rummaged through the wreckage until he found his staff. It was streaked with ash and the once bright feathers were but skeletons, but the wood itself was undamaged. It was made from a fallen branch of the borealus tree, and mere fire could not harm it. He walked next to the river, followed closely by Jest, who nudged him affectionately a few times in valiant attempts to comfort his bereft rider. At the river, Lien tore off the remains of the feathers, waded in and carefully washed the staff clean. With the chill of the rain now passed, the evening was still just about warm enough for Lien to strip and wash the mud and blood from the fight with Bravo from both his clothes and himself. He tried not to think about the fight. About the look in Bravo's eyes as his best friend pressed a knife into his throat. He knew the knife had gone dangerously close to cutting his neck too far; fortunately though he was left with only a thin red line to show what had happened. He also knew that his darkness had pushed his own neck into the blade. It had disappeared as soon the threat from Bravo subsided but in getting Lien out of danger, it had actually put him in more. The whole experience of being pushed down in his own body and mind - of being demoted to a mere passenger - had again shaken him deeply.

He forced himself to focus on what Aethon could have been pointing him towards. The unicorn had led Cira and Jordan to Brynir, and then himself and Bravo to them in their time of need. Jordan had later been killed - Bravo thought by Saul - leaving only Cira left to be part of his destiny. So where was she now? Did he need to find her as well as Areté?

Then yesterday, and years later, Aethon had led Lien to the chevaliers, and the chevaliers to Saul. And...the chevalier Citar had known Aethon, and wanted to chase him. To find Brynir! Lien frowned deeply - a headache was forming as he tried to see the connection he *knew* was staring him in the face. Cira and Citar. They had to be connected. They had to be - what? Siblings? Friends?

Yes! That had to be it!

The headache dissipated as quickly as it had started as the glamour successfully thwarted him making any closer connection. And so it was that Lien decided that Cira and Citar both had to be friends of Jordan. They both knew about Aethon and Brynir. Cira and Jordan must have told someone the truth of their adventure after all. Maybe it had been Citar who had been with Jordan when he died, not Cira? Or all three of them may have been there, or Jordan may have been alone - Lien had no way of knowing. He did know that Bravo had said that Jordan's ghost was intensely focussed on Citar. Jordan had wanted to be a chevalier, and what was it that Cira had said? The Order accepted only boys. So perhaps Jordan and Citar had been training together?

But then...why had Citar asked him what Jordan had been like? And said that he too would like to meet him?

There was only one thing for it: Lien decided he would have to ask Citar directly.

Which he immediately forgot that he had decided.

Instead, he found the remainder of the story easy to piece together. Clearly, he had been connected to and then revealed to the chevaliers in order to meet them and broker the meeting with Lady Selene Beckworth. Citar would be bringing his sponsor to Leaverness in another three days' time, but Lien was impatient. He could go to Avenel now, and find out everything there was find out about Areté. Lady Beckworth would surely know what to do. And as this was all the engineering of Aethon, this had to be his destiny.

Feeling much more optimistic now that he had a plan to focus on, Lien allowed himself to wonder that most unwise of questions: *how hard could it be?*

* * * * *

Lien rode only a few hours towards Avenel before exhaustion overtook him. It was not that late - the attack on the People had happened at only dusk - but it had been a traumatic evening and he found himself feeling drained. He stopped Jest for what he intended to only be a nap. Boy and pony lay down together, Lien snuggled up against Jest's warm back, and he fell deeply asleep until Shah visited him. She shared initially suspicious, then friendly wuffling breaths with Jest, before dropping her nose to deliver her nightmare into Lien's mind.

Lien had been in a blissfully dreamless state when he found himself suddenly dropped into a starving, stiff body. Every muscle ached and the manacles around Areté's neck and wrists had rubbed painful sores. Just the act of lifting her head on her frozen neck to see the face looming in front of her was an ordeal.

The long, narrow face belonged to Callista. Her bright green hair swept across one side of her face and her round, gold spectacles perched upon her head. Her bright blue eyes were examining Areté so intently that Lien felt like she was staring straight at him. But she was as oblivious to his presence as Areté herself.

She did not look pleased at what she was seeing though.

'This last year has not been kind to you, Areté,' Callista said eventually, and, to Lien's surprise, conversationally. Areté did not reply, and Lien could only imagine what expression might be on her pained, pale face. The visitor seemed unperturbed at the lack of response though.

'One moment, please,' she said, and left Areté's field of vision, though Lien heard only a few steps on the cell cobbles, meaning she had not gone far. Areté's head dropped back down, and Lien had a fleeting view of her bony, emaciated knees before her eyes mercifully closed. Lien shared the gnawing pain of her starvation, and felt enraged.

Returning footsteps suggested the visitor was close again, and with company, judging from the slower, heavier steps following behind. Areté's chin was gently lifted by a soft, unseen hand. She had not even the energy to open her eyes this time.

'Areté,' Callista said. 'I have water.'

Areté's eyes slowly opened and, after a few weak blinks, the green hair, spectacles and face swam back into Lien's view. Callista's lips were pursed in a severe expression.

'Really, this is not acceptable,' she said, while bringing a filthy, chipped cup towards Areté's dry lips. Lien wanted to *scream* at her, furious at the comment, but suddenly realised it was directed not to Areté, but to the second person, a large man hovering behind the speaker.

'You asked us to break her, Callista,' the man said, uncertainly.

'I did. Perhaps I should have been more specific about the methods employed – and excluded. I would never have condoned starvation.'

'We've tried loads of things,' the man said.

'I can only imagine. And do you believe any of it is working?' Callista asked coolly.

'Not really. But the lads have had some good sport,' the guard said, an unpleasant smile flickering across his face.

'I see,' Callista said. 'I am not sure "the lads" have thought very hard about this,' she continued, while delicately pouring a trickle of water into Areté's parched mouth. Lien, sharing her extreme dehydration, wanted to drink it greedily, but she could barely swallow.

'Areté is not a prisoner. She has surrendered herself to me as part of an Arrangement.'

Lien was shocked by this information. Areté *agreed* to be held here? Why? Why would she do this to herself? What Arrangement?

'There's…there's a lot of folk about who have beef with her though, aren't there?' the man asked guardedly.

'I should think there are, yes,' Callista agreed. 'And do they believe having her now have beef with *them* is a good idea?'

The man took a sharp inhale, and Lien saw it through narrowing eyes.

'You're not going to let her out?'

'She is here only until I have the Mandala. And *that* is only a matter of time,' Callista said.

The guard was visibly anxious now.

'I understand she also possesses an exceptional memory,' Callista added calmly. She returned her full attention to Areté, who had managed to take a few feeble swallows of water now. Callista sat back on her heels, the dirty cup held between her hands.

'If you please, Areté. Neither of us truly wants you here. At least, not under such circumstances. We can end your - visitation - at any time. Tell me. Where may I find the next Mandala?'

Callista's voice was warm and encouraging. Lien wanted Areté to tell Callista what she wanted to know. The suffering of her imprisonment was unbearable; he was ashamed of himself but he desperately wanted out - out of her body, out of the dream - but he wanted her to want out as well. The fact that she *could* get out, but chose to stay here, like this, was *infuriating.*

*Tell them, and then you can come back to us,* he begged her mentally, and he felt her flinch. Lien's heart leapt, and he was so energised by the possibility that Areté had heard him that he did not realise that Callista too had noticed the slight reaction.

*Areté!* he thought-screamed desperately. *Tell me where you are! How can I find you? How can I rescue you?*

This time Areté visibly stiffened, and Callista again took her chin, but more forcibly this time, and as she stared at Areté - no, *through* Areté - she blinked and when her eyes opened again they had changed. Her irises were a hard, glittering gold. Areté however did not meet the outward gaze, for she was looking *in*, she was feeling Lien's presence -

'No!' she gasped, involuntarily, out loud, while inside Lien felt her trying to force him out. It all happened so fast that he couldn't grasp *how* it was happening. Was she seeing him? Was she only feeling him? Was she angry? Was she afraid? He didn't understand -

I SEE WE WELCOME A VISITOR. LET US TAKE A CLOSER LOOK.

Cosmos' words were delivered directly into the minds of Areté and Lien, and the tone was deep, assured and cold after the warm congeniality of Callista. Lien met Cosmos' brittle, golden eyes through Areté's eyes, and felt seen. Exposed. Afraid. He also felt the physical changes in Areté: her heart pounded harder and a chill gripped her spine. *She* was afraid too in that moment, her lethargy vanished under surging adrenaline. Lien experienced her fear as terror, but before anything more could happen, Shah was there, translucent, galloping *through* Areté and collecting Lien. His dream self clutched at and cried into her mane as she galloped him through walls and far from the city in which Areté was imprisoned. He had no idea she was galloping him high in the air until she disappeared. Lien switched from crying to screaming himself raw as he plummeted towards the wide plain they had been above, which appeared to be rushing up to meet him far too fast -

'Lien! Wake up!'

Lien jerked awake to find himself on his back, heart

pounding and soaked in sweat. Jest stood over him on one side and Bravo, also sweaty and short of breath, was kneeling over him on the other. The close-up sight of Bravo's worried face caused Lien's confused brain to throw him a stomach-turning déjà vu of their earlier fight which. This, clashing against the horror of being seen by - whatever it was that had been inside Callista - and terror of the fall, all forced his body to roll onto his hands and knees and loudly empty his stomach on the damp earth.

'Lien - it's okay - you're safe now,' Bravo said, his words of comfort punctuated by gasping breaths of his own.

Lien's legs folded into kneeling and, groaning, his body slumped forward, his forehead resting on the soft, cool grass, as he succumbed to mental and physical exhaustion. Bravo would not let him rest though.

'Come on, sit up, you have to tell me what happened,' Bravo urged, physically trying to haul Lien's body upright. He found his friend to be a deadweight though.

'Bravo, I need a minute,' Lien mumbled into the ground. Bravo sighed and sat back in cross-legged to impatiently wait.

'What are you doing here?' came a muffled question after a few minutes passed, in which both boys' heart rates dropped and their breathing calmed.

'I've been trying to find you. All night,' Bravo said.

From his head down position, Lien gave him side-eye.

'Sky sent you to Tauron'Est.'

'I've broken enough of Sky's rules tonight, so I figured, why not one more?' Bravo said dryly. 'And - I wanted to see you.'

Lien let a questioning silence stretch out.

'To - uh - to say I'm sorry,' Bravo said, suddenly

examining his legs in great detail.

Lien slowly sat up to kneeling as he considered how to reply. He had been shocked by Bravo's violence in the fight earlier. He loved Bravo, and had always thought he could manage his friend's anger. But anger was one thing, and violence another. Even if that violence was born of love and fear. It had frightened the both of them.

'Okay,' he said eventually. It was not a helpful reply but he just didn't know what else to say.

'How did you find me?'

'Are you serious? You were screaming your head off,' Bravo said. 'I was half a mile or so back but Bank has never galloped so fast, we thought you were being ripped to pieces by wild animals or something.'

'I was…falling. My dream-self, that is. From really high,' Lien explained. 'From Shah. She rescued me but then she just…disappeared, and I fell.'

'That was a long fall,' Bravo said. 'There was a lot of screaming. And - how did she "rescue" you? From a dream? What was she rescuing you from?'

Lien rolled heavily over onto his back. The familiar sight of the tall trees reaching to the far pinprick stars comforted him, and gradually, he found the strength to tell Bravo the whole story. When it was done, he pushed himself up to sitting.

'So - Shah took you - well, your dream-self - *out* of Areté? Has that ever happened before?' Bravo asked.

Lien shook his head.

'I normally wake up from inside her,' he said. 'But this was so different. Areté has never known I was there; tonight, she did, and boy, she wasn't happy about it. And Callista - well, not Callista, there was something else inside her, it was so creepy the way she just switched off and this other *thing* took her place - this *thing* frightened even Areté. And it wanted to get to me, it saw me and I swear it wanted to just reach inside Areté and drag me out. I think, if Shah hadn't come, it would done it too, you know.'

'Have you ever experienced riding Shah before?' Bravo asked, too busy thinking ahead to be overly moved by Lien's account.

'No,' Lien said. 'I've heard her come in my dream, and I've seen her leave when I've woken up, but usually it's like she comes, and then I'm in Areté, and then I'm back in myself.'

'Well, now we know you *can* ride her. The question is whether we both can, and whether we can direct her. I will have to work on my astral projection, it might be that she collects you and I ride along with you.'

'But - she's not usually *in* the dreams,' Lien said, sitting up again, crossing his legs and leaning forward. His reticence around Bravo's recent behaviour was dissolving under his interest in this theory.

'That's okay, because I'd be astroplaning, and I'd "wake" you into what would basically be a lucid dream state. If we're both in the dream plane with her, then we might be able to interact with her directly as though we were all in the physical world.'

'And ride her back to the source of the dreams?' Lien asked. This is what he had initially proposed, just over a week ago and somehow also a lifetime ago.

'Well hopefully. I mean we don't know where she goes once she's delivered the dreams. Also we don't know if she'll let us ride her. I'll need to try a few things first and I don't fully understand how your link to Shah works. I think she is taking your dream-self into Areté. A form of assisted astro-projection, if you like. I can try to project myself into your dreams, which might mean when Shah takes you, I can hitch a ride. Or maybe I can open a dream between us, which Shah can enter, and again, I hitch a ride. But I could also be talking complete bollocks.'

Bravo grinned, and Lien returned a wan smile back at him.

'Only one way to find out,' Lien said.

'Exactly! Someone is directing Shah to bring you these dreams. That person wants you to know, and wants you to act. It would be much easier to just have a direct conversation with them.'

Lien's face clouded.

'They might not be trying to get me to act, Bravo. The dreams might be a…a punishment.'

Bravo frowned.

'Why would anyone want to punish you?'

'Because it's my fault that Areté entered the Arrangement. I'm sure that however it was that she saved Rupert was part of that. But what was required of her in return she won't give. And so it's all my fault, for chasing Rupert for that stupid feather.'

'So…she doesn't *have* to be imprisoned…but has chosen to be?' Bravo asked.

'Exactly. She doesn't *have* to be there, wherever "there" is. All she has to do is tell Callista who the next Mandala is, and she'll be free. I don't even know what the Mandala *is*, do you?'

Bravo shook his head.

'Never heard of it. Sky's the one to ask. Come to Tauron'Est, and we'll ask him.' Bravo's tone bordered on imploring.

Lien hung his head.

'Sky told me I can't come home,' he said sadly.

'He did what?!'

'He told me my path started and continues in Avenel. Someone there will be able to help. Selene Beckworth will be able to help. I'm sure of it.'

Bravo looked sceptical.

'Come with me,' Lien said suddenly, impulsively, surprising even himself.

Bravo turned a disbelieving stare upon him.

'Me? Come to Avenel?'

He looked appalled at the thought.

'Don't be stupid, I'd stand out like a sore thumb,' he continued. 'Which, actually, you will too, because of the tattoo around your eye,' he added. 'Bet you didn't think about that, did you? They'll not be welcoming you with the marks of the People, even if you're otherwise the same colour as them.'

'I don't know, Shiloh didn't even think the People existed anymore,' Lien pointed out. 'They seem very stupid in Avenel.'

'Not arguing with that, but I think you'll find more folk there know better than Shiloh,' Bravo shrugged. Then he looked pensive.

'What is it?' Lien asked.

'That – thing – took you over again,' Bravo said carefully. 'In the…the fight.'

Bravo had the grace to look ashamed. Lien only sighed.

'I know.'

'We need to find out what it is.'

Bravo had a suspicion, but he didn't want to say.

'I know,' Lien repeated, hollowly. He looked very tired now, so Bravo did not push the point. Not yet. One thing at a time.

They restlessly slept for a few more hours, back to back, Jest and Bank grazing or dozing nearby. When they woke in the morning, Lien mounted Jest and was steeling himself to say goodbye to Bravo, when he realised his friend was frowning deeply at him.

'Okay what's wrong now?' he sighed.

'There is *so* much wrong with this picture,' Bravo said, his hands making a circular gesture encompassing both Lien and Jest, 'but there's one thing which I am afraid you simply must fix before going on this foolhardy mission.'

Lien glanced down at himself and his pony. Thinking back on the outsiders he had encountered - knights, chevaliers and Cira and Jordan - there was indeed so much wrong with his appearance. But what of Jest? All he needed was -

' - oh no, Bravo - '

' - oh yes, Lien - '

' - we are not putting a - a *bit* - on Jest!'

'We don't need to put a bit on him, you nitwit. But we do have to at least put a bridle on him. You can't ride into any outsider place with nothing at all on your pony,' Bravo said, in the manner of one explaining the obvious to a petulant child.

'Well *where* are we going to *find* one, genius?' Lien demanded, indeed petulantly.

'We're going to make one, idiot. Honestly, you are never going to survive there. You'll be begging to come home in three days, I'll bet. Now help me find some vine so we can get on with it.'

The boys searched nearly half an hour to find a vine that looked sufficiently bland enough to pass at a glance as rope, and not the verdant plant it was. They then puzzled and argued for another half hour over what shape a bridle actually was. Eventually, after a number of fittings, removals and remakes, they stepped back to inspect a now-harried Jest, who had started to flinch and pull back from the four hands reaching around his delicate head to make adjustments.

The pony looked miserable.

'He looks miserable,' Lien complained.

'Then he's getting in character,' Bravo said briskly. 'If you want him to be an Avenel pony, he's going to have to get used to being miserable. They do terrible things to horses there. He's going to have to get used to living in a small box, and eating dry food, and you'll have to have metal nailed to his feet because the stone roads will wear his hooves down,' he continued relentlessly. 'You'll have to saddle him, and put a cold hard bit in his mouth, and – '

'Enough, Bravo! I'm just going to visit. I'm just going for information. I'm just going to find out where Areté is, and then I'm going to get Areté out of wherever the hell she is, and then I'm coming home. Okay?'

'I thought you said Sky said you couldn't come home…?' Bravo asked, gently now.

Lien lay his head against Jest's soft neck.

'He didn't say never,' he said eventually, voice muffled. Then he pulled back and looked Bravo square in the face.

'He didn't say never,' he repeated, firmly now. He then turned to his unhappy pony.

'Is that okay, Jest? We're both going to have to make sacrifices, but it's to help Areté. Can you cope with this - thing - ' and he gestured apologetically to the makeshift bridle, ' - and some of those other things, to help me find Areté? Because if you don't want to, you can stay right here with Bravo and Bank, okay?'

Lien stared seriously at his beloved pony.

'I mean it, boy. I don't want to ask you to do anything you don't want to do.'

Watching Jest's kind, chocolate brown eyes settling upon him, Lien realised the pony didn't really understand the intricacies of what he had just said, so he switched to the language of horse. Sure the horses understood the general intent and emotion of the human chat around them, whatever the language, but Lien needed to be sure that Jest truly understood what was being asked of him now. He asked again, in more broad, simple, emotive terms. Jest listened, and Lien's heart quickened and breath caught as he waited for a response. After seconds that seemed like miniature eternities, Jest rested his bridled face down against Lien's chest. Lien exhaled with gratitude and relief as he scratched his pony behind the ears, and Jest sighed contentedly. Lien glanced to Bravo, glimpsing a moment of disappointment before the other boy caught himself and manufactured a look that pretended he was pleased.

'Well,' Bravo said. 'I guess that's it. You're ready.'

Lien's relief faltered into a half smile, followed up by a short shrug.

'Guess so,' he said awkwardly. 'Thank you for helping me,' he added, genuinely. Bravo half rolled his eyes.

'Couldn't let you give yourself away *completely* at first

sight. And…you know the People are not protected anymore? Without Areté?'

Lien nodded mutely. How could he forget after last night?

'Which means, no-one in Avenel knows how to get to Tauron'Est. You cannot mention it, you cannot tell anyone how to find it. And you cannot come to us yourself, in case you are followed. You understand?'

Bravo was deadly serious now, and also sad, Lien realised. He suddenly felt the same way himself. Going to Avenel was a great adventure, but until Areté was rescued, it was a one-way trip from his home, his people, and from his best friend.

'And don't trust anyone you meet with why you are there. Find the chevaliers, find this Selene Beckworth, find Areté,' Bravo added. As if it could be so easy.

'I'll find Areté, and then maybe I can come home again,' Lien said, his voice a little thicker than usual even as he feigned normalcy. He tried not to think about what Sky had said about his path not lying with the People.

'And I'll help you. I'll find you, in your sleep,' Bravo said. He was not a natural hugger, but he hugged Lien now, in a firm bear-like embrace.

'Now piss off. And *be careful*,' he said, voice muffled by Lien's hair. Lien thought he felt a wet drop on his shoulder, but when Bravo disengaged, he turned abruptly so that his face was hidden. He stalked over to Bank and vaulted on his pony, his back still to Lien, and trotted him away, without as much as a backward glance.

Lien watched until boy and pony were completely swallowed by the trees, suddenly feeling terribly alone. A gentle nudge from behind reminded him that he was not completely alone though. Lien stroked his pony's soft, sleek neck affectionately.

'Well Jest, it's just us then. You ready?' he asked. Jest responded by rubbing his head up and down on Lien's shoulder so hard that he pushed the boy over in his effort to remove the bridle. But it was a nod of sorts.

'I'll take that. Let's be off then,' he said, smiling as he pushed the pony back. He vaulted on, then wish he'd asked Bravo which was the right way to hold reins.

# PART III

# AVENEL

# 11. COBI

Back in long forgotten times, by the long forgotten Aurealus, three towers were built across Altica, each on a different continent. They were all built on the intersection points of powerful ley lines, and both their locations and their construction were based on sacred geometry. These towers were called Voltarch, Voltane, and Voltaire. All three, breathtaking examples of architectural accomplishment, were severely damaged during the Occult Wars. While their original purpose was deemed so secret that this information too became forgotten, the decree never to fully rebuild them was faithfully passed down through the generations. Most people of contemporary Altica would be unaware that the towers numbered three, if in fact they even knew of any single one.

Voltaire's location was long lost, along with that of the fabled city of Phaedra in which it stood.

Fort Thantos was built around Voltane, and the city of Scyros around that.

The third tower, Voltach, was built at the top of a mount that was later terraced into the fortress Voltanna. The city of Avenel ran down the remainder of the mount to - and increasingly, across - the Avenel Plain. The plain was a vast, exposed expanse that to the north ran right up to the River Siena, which separated it from the forest of Leaverness.

While the fortress of Voltanna featured many towers, the original tower, Voltarch, soared highest, a multi-layered architectural marvel that could disappear into low cloud.

The fortress was the home of the Order of the Coeur and was also historically the seat of the king. Though the throne was currently empty, the Council of Voltanna also sat within its grounds, making Voltanna both the military and political centre of the Avenel Empire. The magnificent fortress was itself built in layers around the mount on which it stood, with every ring containing buildings, gardens and courtyards. It was a truly remarkable and beautiful construction, and those few who were permitted within its walls were the envy of those many who could only imagine what marvels lay inside.

The edges of Leaverness were well traversed and to the east and west established routes were heavily used by the constant flow of traders and travellers coming into and out of Avenel. These trails led to huge bridges over the Siena and then paths across the Avenel Plain, which was being gradually swallowed up by the inexorable spread of the growing city. The outer fortifications were rebuilt around every half century to reflect city's expanding circumference, essentially creating Avenel's very own geographic strata. Real estate inside the walls was precious, rare and well built, while the settlements outside tended to be more temporary in nature. Once these settlements were encircled in a new outer wall though, the land on which they stood became more valuable and built upon according to the current trends, giving the city rings of distinct architectural styles. Its geography essentially made Avenel into a three-tier society: the upper class lived on the mont under Voltanna; the middle class lived on the flats inside the walls, the wealthier the closer to Voltanna; and the poorer folk and new hustlers seeking their fortune in the big city settled outside. There were also larger estates and farms outside the walls on the far side from Leaverness, where families farmed much of the livestock and grain that fed the city. But as equally as Avenel pushed closer to Leaverness, it also encroached into the traditional farmlands, pushing them further and further back while requiring their produce more and more.

People from all over the continent, and even other continents, migrated to Avenel. The blooming science establishment routinely enraged the varied religious quarters; the monarchists insistently opposed the new wave of gentry politicians who had filled the power vacuum following the murder of King Du Romeau; and the ancient chivalrous Order of the Coeur argued with everyone as they defiantly held an increasingly tenuous grip of power over the city state.

By and large the royal family of Avenel had historically pursued the success of the city by ensuring the safety and success of its people. King Du Romeau had taken this ideology far beyond the city and kingdom he had inherited, trying to apply it across his expanding empire. However, the men and women vying for more power in the absence of a monarch were also interested in financial prosperity, but more so with their own than of others. They were focussed on their own short-term gains, where the preceding hereditary dynasty understood the importance of the long game. Concepts like honour, public service and civic responsibility were losing traction against the enormous opportunities for exploitative economic gain. After hundreds of years of relative internal stability and outside political and military supremacy, Avenel was destabilising from the inside out. To the average citizen little changed, but those who understood and paid attention to political intricacies were increasingly concerned about what the future held.

But at this time, Lien mercifully knew none of that. Avenel was a familiar view of course, but always from the comfortably extreme distance of Leaverness, which rendered the city's detail into soft pastel watercolour. The mountainous mass of Voltanna, stratified by dramatic towered and turreted walls of brick and stone that rose up grandly over the city below, was impressive from any angle and at any distance though.

While Lien found the prospect of entering the city daunting, he was surprised to find that he did not fear Avenel itself. He supposed that Areté had always spoken about it with affection, so he had known it as beloved to her. She characterised it as a living place, as though it was more than just a collection of buildings, in the same way that the People knew Leaverness was more than just a collection of trees. And she had told Lien many times that she would take him to Avenel one day and show him why she loved it so.

Lien and Bravo had twice been bold enough to ride all the way to where Leaverness met the River Siena and beyond it, the Avenel Plain. It was the closest they had been to the great city, and today, all the way to the river, Lien was happy to be in his beloved forest. But he knew that once he crossed the Siena, he would be in entirely unknown territory. He rode west towards the Willowald Trail, the largest trade route skirting Leaverness, figuring he could slip in with one of the huge merchant caravans heading to the city. As he approached it, the sun was two thirds towards its peak, relentlessly baking the plain and city again, and so he decided on one last delay. Jest eagerly followed Lien into the Siena until they found a depth at which the water closed over the pony's back and Lien could duck his head right under. Once they were fully cooled off, Lien led Jest back to the Leaverness side of the river, where the pony shook his whole body off like a wet dog. Laughing, Lien followed suit as best he could, shaking water out of his hair and from his vest and pants, but remaining deliciously wet in the hot late morning. All possible delays partaken in, he sighed, vaulted back onto Jest and rode him slowly towards the huge wooden bridge that represented the transition from Leaverness to the Avenel Plain. After about half an hour he began to hear the sounds of a caravan on the road ahead. Jest's ears flicked forwards and back as he took in the myriad sounds of voices, horses, oxen, heavy rolling wheels, the cracking of whips and the barking of dogs.

'Afraid that's our only way in, Jest,' Lien said, sensing his pony's uneasiness at the many unfamiliar sounds, and then continued to chatter away, as much to ease his own nerves as those of Jest.

'You know Erebus wears a bridle, *and* a saddle, and actually, he looks very handsome in them. Areté calls the bridle a *hackamore*, which is a bitless bridle, which is what we've made for you, Jest. Obviously Erebus doesn't need reins and so forth but Areté needs the saddle for the saddle bags and she says the bridle makes outsiders less bothered. We'll get you a proper bridle, made of the finest leather, and I'll clean it every day so that it stays soft and comfortable for you, I promise,' Lien said, stroking Jest's brown and white mane. When they reached the caravan though, they stopped in the trees along the trail. Lien knew they needed to join the line but the sight of so many people and carts, pulled slowly through the midday heat by hot horses and oxen, left him paralysed. The whole caravan rolled by until only a lone woman on a white horse was left. She was observant enough to notice the worried teenager and brown and white pony lingering in the tree line.

She drew her horse to a stop facing Lien and Jest, and watched them curiously. She was tall with a thick dark hair spilling over one shoulder and was of what men might politely call a "mature age". She wore a long blue summer dress and was riding side saddle, which Lien had never seen before. He stared at her, perplexed, as he tried to work out why she was sitting on her horse in such a manner.

'Are you headed to Avenel, boy?' she called to him. Her tone was guarded but not unkind. Lien caught himself staring and blushed.

'Yes,' he said, forcing his brain into Avenelese.

'First time?' she asked.

Lien nodded. It was unlike him to be speechless, but he felt very shy in this place, at this time, in front of this outsider woman.

'Come,' she said, reining her horse to face back along the track, inviting Jest to come alongside. Lien rode up next to her. He had to look a long way up, for she was taller than him and on a horse that towered over Jest.

'My name is Divinia,' she said as they started to walk together.

'I am Lien, and this is Jest,' Lien said, stroking his pony.

Divinia smiled.

'How remiss of me. This is Polly,' she said, nodding to her own horse.

'Polly is very beautiful,' Lien said, and it was true, Polly was a gorgeous mare. Divinia raised an eyebrow, and Lien blushed, realising he had perhaps made a faux pas.

'As are you!' he added, hoping this was the correct response.

Divinia laughed.

'That was unfair of me,' she smiled. 'It is good that you can admire a beautiful horse when you see one. Your pony is very good looking himself. He's much finer than the ponies I usually see though. Where was he bred?'

'In Leaverness,' Lien said unthinkingly, and bit his lip.

'Really? I hear the herds of Leaverness are very wild,' Divinia said.

'They are very - clever,' Lien said carefully.

'And where are you from, Lien?' Divinia asked, her voice light but her eyes betraying her interest. Lien realised now how utterly unprepared he was for Avenel. He didn't even know where to start with the lies he would need to tell.

'I am from - the Backwind,' he hazarded. He had at least been there once - well, *almost* been there - and it was the only place he could think of on the spot.

'The Backwind?'

The extent of Divinia's surprise, and hoisting of one of her fine eyebrows, told Lien he had already made a serious mistake.

'What a coincidence. I have just come from there,' Divinia continued. 'From the estate of Lord Falric,' she added, her tone cautioning him against making more wild guesses.

'When I say the Backwind I mean it was the nearest

town,' Lien improvised desperately. 'It was just – me and my brother. And our father. There was no-one else around. But I did meet Jordan, and his best friend, Cira, once.'

Lien used the two names to strengthen his claim, but as he did, Divinia's face clouded. At the last word though, her eyebrows knitted together thoughtfully.

'Just once?' she asked. Lien nodded. This was all true at least.

'Where did you meet them?' she pressed.

Lien chewed his bottom lip. Was it better to lie, or tell the truth?

He was not a natural or practiced liar.

'In Leaverness,' he admitted.

'You are the boy who saved them from the bear,' Divinia guessed, and from Lien's astonished reaction, knew she was correct.

'You don't have to pretend otherwise,' she told him. 'The children said you would have been in trouble for being in Leaverness alone. But it was years ago now, and much has changed since then.'

She fell into a troubled silence as she considered whether to tell this strange boy about the fate of the two children he had saved four years previously.

'Do you know what happened to them?' she eventually asked. Lien's heart gave a little conflicted flip: he did know enough of what happened to Jordan to not want to go down this road, but he also needed to know what had happened to Cira.

'I heard that Jordan...died,' he said, unable to keep a little shake from his voice as he finally said the word he had been unable to utter to Bravo the day before.

'He did. Nearly a year ago,' Divinia nodded sadly.

'What happened to Cira?' Lien asked, faster and more anxiously than he intended.

Divinia looked surprised.

'You didn't hear?' she asked. When he tentatively shook his head, wondering if he had made another error, she shrugged.

'Well. She was only a servant girl,' Divinia said, a bitter edge on her voice. 'The disappearance of a servant girl would not have been as big news as the death of the county lord's son, I suppose.'

'She – disappeared?' Lien asked.

'Well, we hope so. That would be better than the alternative,' Divinia said. 'Cira and Jordan chased Aethon into Leaverness again, the same as they did when they met you. Jordan was found, but Cira…no-one ever found her. We don't know if she is alive, or…'

She did not need to finish, Lien understood completely. But he was frowning deeply now.

'They chased Aethon again?'

Divinia nodded.

'It's a pity you weren't there for them this time,' she said. 'I know Falric wishes you were.'

'I would have been, if I had known,' Lien protested. 'I would have been there in a moment!'

'No blame was intended, Lien,' Divinia said quickly.

'Aethon did not lead me to them,' he said sadly. 'But Cira *is* alive.'

'You have seen her?' Divinia asked, hope lighting her eyes.

'No. But I know,' he said, touching his chest, over his heart. He couldn't explain it, but he was certain. Cira was his destiny. Aethon had led them to one another, after all.

'Well, I hope so,' Divinia sighed. 'Her mother, Flavia, is a good friend of mine. She has endured much hardship in her life, but this - I fear this is too much for her to bear. She and Lord Falric have suffered terribly this last year.'

Lien thought back on Falric - on his evident love of the children, and of his desire to help Lien for helping them. He had seemed a good man. He could only imagine how sad he must now be.

Divinia too looked so troubled that Lien wanted desperately to be able to cheer her up.

'I will find Cira,' he promised. 'I know she is out there. I will find her.'

Divinia gave him a wan smile.

'You seem like a good kid, Lien. What's a sweet country boy like you doing going to the big city? It will chew you up and spit you out if you are not careful.'

'I just want to - to see the city. And see Voltanna. I've only ever heard of it and seen it from a distance,' Lien said, and that was all also true. He did want to see Avenel, and its famous fortress.

'Well, if you want to see Voltanna, this is the time to do the looking, from a distance. Once we're inside the city, you'll just be looking up the fortifications,' Divinia said. 'The best views are from here on the plain.'

Lien obediently looked ahead, taking in the huge walls, turrets and wide battlements of Voltanna. The fortress consisted of numerous buildings built into each terraced level, above which soared Voltarch. Voltarch had been constructed in levels, each successive vertical tier narrower than the one before, and each section girded by elegant archways as tall as four or five men high. Lien proceeded to ask Divinia all about the city and fortress.

This was partly to get more information about Avenel, but mostly to stop her asking more questions to get himself into trouble with. As they crossed the plain he learned much about the city but nothing at all of Divinia herself. He had thought he was being evasive with her, but that was nothing compared to the way she seamlessly stone walled any of his questions about where she was from, where she lived and what she did with her time in the city.

They soon caught up to the back of the caravan and gradually overtook much of it, for like their merchant humans, the horses, oxen and donkeys were wearied by the heat, plodding along with their heads held low. Lien felt very sorry for them, struggling under such burdens, so preferred to look at the wares of the merchants instead. There were fabrics in a startling range of colours and materials, and wagons carrying grains, spices, fruits and vegetables Lien had never seen. Divinia helpfully explained whatever she saw him looking most curiously at. From his complete lack of knowledge of the wares, his slow, careful way of speaking and the tattoos on his left eye and right arm, she had drawn her conclusion about where he was really from, and knew it wasn't even the most isolated parts of the Backwind. But Divinia had enough secrets of her own to be respectful of those of the strange boy. She didn't know how to help him further though without more information, and knew she could not take him to her home, or even tell him where to find her, if he needed assistance. Which she was certain he would.

'You will need to use your hair to cover your left eye once we are in the city,' she said. Lien drew his hair over to the left side so that his fringe fell over his left eye.

'Like this?' he asked.

Divinia nodded, but her lips were pursed. This dealt with only one of Lien's two tattoo problems. She indicated they should draw their horses to a stop, and when they did, she removed a white and blue handkerchief from one of her saddle bags and tied it around Lien's right upper arm, hiding his three tattoo rings.

'Thank you,' Lien said, uncertainly.

'Least I can do,' she said pensively as they turned their horses back to join the caravan.

They would be entering Avenel through the Leavensgate. Of the four original gates of Avenel, this was the only one that had survived the generational expansions of the city walls intact. The others had long since been burned down or rotted from age and replaced over time, but this gate was made of the same huge doors it had ever been. As they approached, Lien felt its ancient espréi and frowned deeply.

'That is borealus wood!' he protested to Divinia.

She tilted her head to one side.

'There is much borealus in Avenel,' she said.

Lien looked shocked.

'But the borealus is the most beautiful and alive of all trees,' he said. 'It is a murder to cut one down.'

'These were all cut down hundreds of years ago, Lien. There is no new borealus wood in the world. There is only one tree left, in Leaverness, and they say it is enchanted.'

Lien nodded, wondering anxiously whether the charm that protected the borealus still stood, now that Areté was...wherever she was. That was another reason to find her as soon as possible, to restore her protections.

'And it is the strongest wood in the world,' Divinia

continued. 'It is in all the oldest buildings of the city. And it looks as though your own staff is made of it,' she added pointedly.

'This was made from a fallen branch,' Lien said defensively. 'I would never harm a living borealus.'

'Okay, but you might want to paint it another colour. If anyone gets wind of a new piece of borealus wood in Avenel, it will not be yours for long. That staff will be priceless here.'

Lien was astonished by this, and held his beloved staff a little tighter.

They were almost under the enormous gates now. Though weathered through hundreds of seasons, they still retained the distinctive red grain of the wood from which they had been made. Carved into the old wood was a half kneeling, bowed head man with wings outstretched behind him. He had both his hands on the hilt of an upright sword, its tip resting on the ground by his right foot. Set into these main gates were a smaller pair of doors, wide enough to ride 8 horses across through, and it was these that were open to allow travellers to pass into and out of the city.

'Who is that man?' Lien asked.

'That's the Patient Angel,' Divinia replied. 'He is an old legend of Avenel; a spirit of justice who kept peace with the Sinless Sword, which you can just see in his hands there, on the left door.'

'We have stories of him as well,' Lien said, eyes lighting up. 'Some of the earliest. But he did not have wings in ours. It was for him to stand equally in the darkness and the light; but this was sad for him, because he wished only to be in the light.'

'I think you know more about him than I do,' Divinia smiled. Then the explanation gave her an idea.

'Lien, if you - you know, get into trouble - go to the alehouse The Sign of the Angel. Ask for Cote, and tell him you are a friend of mine. He *might* help you. You can never quite tell with Cote. But he might also be able to offer you work, and lodging. I mean, you'll need *somewhere* to sleep. Have you thought about that?'

Lien shook his head, but he wasn't worried about where he was going to sleep, he assumed that he could sleep anywhere and would rather be outdoors than in a building. He was however worrying that he was soon going to be back on his own again. He sensed that Divinia would soon be parting ways with him, returning to her secrets as he pursued his own.

Lien could feel the heat radiating from the stone walls as they queued, waiting for their turn to cross through the Leavensgate. The guards, lethargic in the heat, remained in the shade of the towering gates, nodding each part of the caravan through with minimal observation. One guard however looked interested as Lien and Divinia approached. Lien initially assumed the interest was in himself, before realising the man was staring at Divinia. It was a hungry, slightly predatory stare, which disconcerted Lien. The guard then turned a suspicious look to at the boy. Lien slightly tilted his head so that his hair threw shadow over his tattooed left eye.

'He is with me, Brown,' Divinia said, surprising Lien with a sudden coldness in her voice.

'A bit *fresh* isn't he, Divinia?' Brown asked, smirking. 'You want to watch yourself with this one, boy.'

Divinia turned haughtily away from the man and rode

straight past him, under the threshold of the Leavensgate. Lien felt his hard stare following them as they entered Avenel.

'Don't worry about the likes of him, Lien,' Divinia said when they were well past the gate. 'But it would be - better for you - if we went our separate ways now. I thank you for your company on the ride and wish you well for your visit.'

The formality in her tone further surprised Lien. He frowned, unsure of what to say, much less do, next. Divinia, seeing his uncertainty, softened.

'Continue on this road. It is the Kings Way, and will lead you to Voltanna, the jewel of Avenel. It is always the first place that visitors go,' Divinia said, and with a distant smile, reined her horse away. She and Polly were almost immediately swallowed by the press of horses, donkeys, carts, pedestrians and all manner of livestock and poultry. The tracks across the plain had been wide with vast separation between traffic going into or out of the city. Within the gates though, both flows were pushed together onto a broad but singular cobbled road, which was becoming heavily congested. With his attention no longer focussed on the reassuring presence of his travelling companion, Lien now had no choice but to take in the city fully.

Avenel was the kind of city that assaulted the senses, at times overwhelming to even its own inhabitants. A teenage boy who grew up on the wilds of Leaverness had no chance of retaining his composure. There was so much just to *look* at, and that was before all of his other senses tried to process their own data. The eye-watering wall of smells, exaggerated and practically solidified by the stifling heat, intensified the further they rode into the city. Poor Jest fared no better, nervously drowning in scents and a sea of unfamiliar sounds: horse shoes on stone, the barking of dogs, the shouting of salesmen promoting their wares, and the continuous hum of bartering in the stalls lining the road.

And perhaps the worst of it was the espréi of the city: this was not the calm, ordered energy of the forest. The energy of the city was tense, loud and utterly chaotic. Lien and Jest alike felt bombarded by the alien feel of city life.

Only a couple of hundred yards within the main gates, the forest-bred pony stopped, legs locked out, his taut neck raised and a fresh sweat breaking out across his flanks. It took only a few seconds for the abuse to start as wagons behind them rolled to a stop. This caused Jest to swing around nervously and in doing do, block even more of the road. One carter brandished his thick whip angrily at the pony's quarters, an ox-cart pressed in from behind, a street merchant tried to shoo Jest on by waving a brightly coloured scarf in the pony's face, all while a large horse jostled in from the other side. Jest started to rear up nervously before backing into the protesting ox, his unshod hooves slipping on the unfamiliar, smooth cobbles.

Besieged by too much sensory information, and bewildered by the anarchic energy that surrounded them, Lien had no idea which way to direct the pony amongst the loud and angry crowd that now pressed in around them –

– when a gentle but firm hand took the loose reins and squeezed the frightened pony between two wagons and out into an alley.

'Don't want to stand around in the road like that, my friend,' the man grunted to Jest, stroking the pony soothingly. He was tall, almost as tall as Lien while mounted, and dressed in black leather trousers and a dark blue, long-sleeved shirt with a loose black silk necktie. That would have been more than enough to wear given the heat, but the shirt was topped with a battered, studded, black leather hooded vest, with the hood up. Despite his excessive wardrobe, the man did not look hot or even sweaty at all. And he looked only to the pony, not his rider.

Lien slid down to the ground, surprised to find his legs shaking a little. From the relative calm of the alley, the bustling thoroughfare beyond seemed like a bad dream. He leaned against Jest's shoulder while the pony tried to rub his makeshift bridle off on the stranger, relaxing at last. The stranger pushed back his hood and obligingly scratched Jest underneath the unfamiliar straps.

'Not used to wearing that, are you?' he asked the pony, his back still to Lien.

'How do you know?' Lien asked.

'He is a Leaverness pony, this is a terrible attempt at a making a bridle from vines, we are not speaking Avenelese, and you are somewhere you really should not be,' the stranger said. Lien was preparing a retort in Avenelese when he realised, with a start, that he had not only automatically spoken in the language of the People, but that the stranger had replied in the same. In fact, he was certain the man had spoken only in the language of the People from his first words to Jest.

'I do – speak Avenelese,' Lien said, a little stiltedly as he forced his brain to switch back to the less familiar language. 'And thank you for helping us,' he added, remembering his manners.

The tall man finally turned to Lien, inspecting him warily – suspiciously even, Lien realised. But before he could even get a good look at his rescuer, Lien quickly looked down and tried to shake his hair over his left eye. He was shocked when the man took his chin though and firmly forced it up and to the right, so that his fringe fell back, fully exposing his tattoo. Lien had a disconcerting flashback to Callista - or whatever was inside her - taking Areté's chin the same way, to see Lien behind her eyes. He tried to pull away, but found the stranger's grip to be painfully unyielding. Staring wildly back at the man's bright green eyes, Lien tried to read his expression.

He seemed - unsurprised. Certainly not alarmed, as Lien had expected. With a dismissive grunt, he let Lien go and returned his attention to Jest. Lien, however, stared openly at the man, for he required thorough investigation.

is skin was as pale as that of Areté and the People. It made a stark contrast to the olive of Lien's own skin, and the earthy palette he had seen everywhere since leaving Leaverness. The man's skin was also relatively unweathered, even though there was an aged, retiring aspect to his face, with deep wrinkles at the corners of his eyes. Lien unconsciously frowned as he tried to work out, amongst other puzzles, what the man's age might be.

'It's rude to stare,' the stranger growled, eyes narrowing.

'Like you can talk!' Lien parried, rubbing his chin.

'I see Sky has neglected to teach you to respect your elders,' the stranger said coldly. That froze Lien.

'Are you…of the People?' Lien asked, still staring.

'I am not,' the man replied.

'But…your skin? And you speak the language of the People,' Lien objected.

'I speak all languages,' the man said dismissively.

'Really? How many are there?' Lien asked, curiosity

fleetingly replacing suspicion.

The man considered a moment.

'For a reference you would understand,' he said, 'there are as many languages as there are trees in the Wyrd Wood.'

Lien's eyes widened.

'That's – ' and he paused as he searched for the right term in the unfamiliar language, ' – amazing – ?'

'Learn to be amazed less, or you will only be disappointed more,' the man replied curtly.

Lien frowned, for this was the opposite of the People's teachings. The tribe cultivated an attitude of amazement in their youth, encouraging them to see the beauty and marvels present even in everyday life.

He wondered what had made this man so bitter.

'But how have you learned all those languages? That must take a lifetime!' he pressed, still no less amazed.

'I suppose it would,' the man agreed blandly, as though he had never considered it and it was of no consequence.

Lien wondered how many languages Areté could speak. The Wyrd Wood was a dangerous area deep within Leaverness. While not large, it must have had a couple of hundreds trees within it. Did she know them all as well? She had certainly lived longer than most –

' – wait, how *long* a lifetime?' he asked, suddenly both suspicious and excited and unconsciously switching back to his native tongue. 'I mean, as achievements go, it kind of depends on the scale we're talking. Learning all languages in a lifetime that's say fifty years is completely different to a lifetime that's say five hundred years,' he continued. 'That's kind of cheating. Still impressive, of course, but it's an unfair advantage.'

'Long enough to have stopped counting,' the man said, still stroking Jest. The pony was making contented sighs and, with his eyes closed, looked close to falling asleep. Lien felt betrayed by the pony's trust of a man he himself found so unlikeable. His energy, his espréi, had Lien on edge. He tried to feel around the edges of it, but it was like probing a wall of ice, and earned him a narrowed side-eye look from the stranger.

'Are you part of the Order?' Lien asked, trying a different angle. The man had a warrior's bearing after all, and his leather vest wore many marks of violence. But his only response was a withering look.

'So - why did you help us?' Lien asked, brows knitting together. 'You don't seem at all surprised by me, and Jest. But you also don't seem...well...particularly *interested* in us.'

Jest heaved a sign of pleasure at the man's continued attentions.

'Well, not interested in *me*, anyway,' Lien clarified drily. He wasn't intending to be self-centered, but there was something about the whole encounter that felt off to him. He was grateful for the man's initial assistance, but was increasingly uneasy, to the point of even considering the heat and chaos of the Kings Way to be the better option.

'I am not particularly interested in you,' the man agreed.

Lien blinked. Perhaps he had overestimated the risk of being seen in Avenel?

'Others will be though, I am sure,' the man continued, as though reading his mind. 'Certainly you should employ discretion, particularly with - this - ' and he waved a casual hand in the direction of Lien's facial tattoo. 'Simpler minds are sure to over-react with breathtaking idiocy. However, this is not a chance encounter, I will confess. I know what happened in Leaverness last night, and I wanted to see what the forest might throw out today.'

'Leaverness didn't throw me out. I chose to come,' Lien said defiantly.

The man looked coldly amused.

'Is that right?' he said. 'Well, what would I know, waiting all this morning to see you cross the plain.'

'And how did you know about - last night?' Lien said, his brain catching up to his mouth, but with a small catch in his voice as memories of the night before arose unbidden.

'I know where to listen, and who to listen to,' the stranger said. 'Whether Leaverness has pushed you, or Avenel has pulled you, the result is the same. You are in the lion's den now, boy. I am not sure you are up to the challenge of surviving here, but I shall try to ensure you are not eaten on your first day.'

He untied his black silken necktie and, without asking permission, began to roughly fashion it over Lien's head so that his left eye was covered. Lien immediately found the change in depth of field uncomfortable.

'Is this really necessary?' he asked, squinting with his right eye.

'That depends on how quickly you want to find yourself in trouble, and shortly thereafter, dead,' the stranger replied coolly. 'How suicidal are you, boy?'

'I have a name,' Lien said, a little sulkily.

'I do not care,' the man said.

'Well, I do care,' Lien said testily. 'Who are *you*?'

He didn't really expect a reply, but he was getting annoyed with the dismissive manner of this man now.

'I am Cobi,' the man replied. 'You have an eye

infection. It is grotesque. You are from Hireath. It is a mysterious place, very difficult to find, about which little is known, so little can be asked. You are here to see your cousin, who is a chevalier. Play the idiot by speaking little, instead of, as you are now, speaking too much.'

Cobi stepped back to critically examine Lien, who now wore Divinia's handkerchief around his right arm and Cobi's necktie around his head and left eye. He did not seem pleased with what he saw.

'Do not remove the silk in public. Tell me where you wish to go, and I may take you there.'

Lien hesitated before answering - Bravo had warned him not to tell anyone but the chevaliers of his intention. But Bravo had also assumed Lien could easily find the chevaliers. Neither of them had appreciated how enormous Avenel was once inside, and how many people it held. He needed help.

His intention had been to seek Citar, to be taken to Lady Selene Beckworth, but perhaps he could now take a short cut.

He asked to be taken directly to the lady.

Cobi subtly tilted his head to one side. It was the closest Lien had seen to disturbance of the man's otherwise implacable demeanour.

'Of all the places in Avenel, you ask for the one to which I cannot take you,' was all he said though.

'Why can't you?' Lien asked, surprised that there was anything this man could not do.

'Selene and I are not on equitable terms. It would be most unfortunate for me to come to her attention,' Cobi replied.

'Well couldn't you just...point me in the right

direction?' Lien asked, frowning. Cobi shook his head.

'You should not approach Selene Beckworth without a mutual ally, boy. She is well protected. Who else did you wish to meet?'

'The chevalier Citar,' Lien said, 'but only so that *he* can take me to Lady Beckworth,' he added, with an accusatory edge.

Cobi frowned briefly over the name.

'I do not believe I know of this Citar,' he said. 'Tell me of another chevalier.'

'Uh, what about Prince Rupert?' Lien asked, figuring, correctly, that he would be better known.

'You believe Rupert will be of any assistance?' Cobi asked with mild surprise.

'He's got a good heart,' Lien defended the prince.

Cobi shrugged and closed his eyes, concentrating. Lien watched him curiously for several long seconds before experiencing what felt like a cold energy momentarily brushing past him.

'Are you...finding him? With espréi?' he asked, amazed anew. He had heard of the art of "casting" espréi - sending your own energy away to sense or find that of another - but had never encountered anyone actually doing it. The idea that Cobi could "find" Rupert in a huge and densely populated city like Avenel was breathtaking.

Cobi ignored his questions, instead holding up an irritable hand for what seemed to be an interminable time. As Lien waited, he briefly felt another distinctive espréi pass over him. It was powerful and masculine but a little wild - wild as in untrained. That was unusual: people who did not understand and manage their espréi really possessed such intense energy. Lien looked around, to the end of the alley, where he thought he saw a hooded figure disappearing over a rooftop far above them. He frowned, and watched until he was sure the man would not be returning. The he turned back to Cobi, who was still standing perfectly still with his eyes closed.

Finally, he dropped the hand, and his green eyes snapped back open, taking a moment to refocus on the physical world.

'We are just in time,' he said.

'For what?' Lien asked.

'Your Prince Rupert will be passing us shortly,' Cobi said. 'We can then follow him, and you can find an appropriate time to speak with him.'

'So...were you *finding* him, or *summoning* him?' Lien asked curiously.

'Finding, of course.'

'Still impressive,' Lien said.

'Summoning is immensely difficult. I would have had to start a few hours earlier to arrange events just so, that he would be passing just now,' Cobi continued.

'You mean - you *could* have arranged that?' Lien asked, wide eyed.

Cobi gave the smallest shrug, then listened intently. At a distance that only he could hear, the sound of the crowd on the Kings Way was changing.

'That sounds like them, let's have a look,' he said. He turned to speak reassuringly to Jest with a warmth that starkly contrasted with the indifference with which he spoke to Lien. It took Lien a moment to clock the language he used.

'You speak the language of horses as well?' he said, surprised. He had assumed Cobi was previously referring to the languages of all peoples.

'*All* languages, boy,' Cobi said, turning back to the bustling Kings Way, Jest calmly following at his right shoulder. Lien had to trot a few steps to catch up to his pony's right shoulder, again feeling a pang of betrayal by Jest's absolute trust in the unsettling stranger. He was soon, however, distracted by the change in the sea of sound coming from the crowded road ahead. Shouts to 'clear the way' came from the right, the direction from which Lien had already ridden, and shortly he could see why. Prince Rupert and Lord Jorge were approaching, with Citar, Tryst, Shiloh and Ben following, all dressed again in their light armament. On the far side of Tryst, concealed from clear sight, a taller adult knight in a full suit of armour escorted the chevaliers.

Lord Jorge was passaging his way grandly along the Kings Way, where all the other horses walked more calmly in the searing heat, though with their heads warily held high as the crowd pressed in on them. With his purple plume atop a helm that blindingly reflected the high sun, Rupert did indeed look princely from a distance; it was only as he came closer that Lien could see his rigidity and how flushed his face was, from both heat and his habitual state of worry. And worried he might well be, for the boys were receiving a mixed reception from the crowd. While generally being greeted with admiration and even a smattering of cheers on their ride to Voltanna, the subversive current turning against the Order was voiced in occasional crude shouts and jeers. One particularly bold protestor dared to throw a stone at Rupert with a holler of '*No more kings!*'

Fortunately his throw was wildly telegraphed and,

anticipating the man's intention, the knight escorting the boys leapt his white charger forward. With astonishing speed and accuracy, he caught the stone mere moments before it would have struck Rupert between his widening, terrified eyes. As Rupert hastily pushed his raised helm visor back down, the knight pointedly crushed the rock to dust in one gauntleted hand. His identity was now clear to Lien - whose eyes also widened, but his in wonder.

'Shame on you, John Fellowes, for a cowardly attack on a chevalier!' Sir Armitage bellowed. A small ring formed around Fellowes, a ferret-faced man, as those in his proximity sought to distance themselves from the wrath of the Blue Knight. Armitage swung a hard gaze across the whole crowd as he gauged their mood.

'We parade these chevaliers today to recognise their feat of returning safely from Leaverness manoeuvres,' he proclaimed, thrusting one fist into the air. About half of the crowd followed the prompt with a spattering of well-trained applause - even, from many women, enthusiastic applause. For however unpopular the Order gradually grew, admiration for a small number of its senior knights remained strong. Quite beside which, Sir Armitage was widely considered the very model of chivalry *and* the most desirable bachelor in the whole city.

The other half of the crowd remained sullenly quiet though. Lien thought perhaps the oppressive heat might be partially responsible, but a quick glance at Cobi's narrowed eyes and grim expression put paid to that.

Rupert's gaze restlessly roamed the crowd searching for the next stone, egg or tomato. He took a double take as his eyes passed over and shot back to Lien and Jest, standing in the mouth of their alley. The prince's eyes widened into a clear but unasked question, but Jorge was now passing the boy and his pony, and Rupert reluctantly had to turn his attention back ahead. Lien, who had eyes only for Sir Armitage, reining in his beautiful white mare so that he could resume his place next to Tryst, never even realised Rupert had spotted him. Armitage's gaze once swung in his direction but as it did, Cobi shrugged his hood up and in doing so, blocked the knight's sight of Lien so subtly that even the boy didn't realise what had happened. Citar and Shiloh meanwhile were happily enjoying all of the attention and did not see him at all.

Today Armitage wore a deep blue cloak over what Lien was sure was a different suit of armour. This one was more ornate and certainly cleaner and in better condition than the one he had fought in last night. Blue silk billowed between the plates of steel protecting his shoulders and elbows, and his horse wore a blue silken and silver stitched blanket over her hindquarters. There were even silk adornments hanging from her reins - which Lien thought very unnecessary - and she wore an ornately forged metal plate across her broad face, which Lien thought looked very uncomfortable. The blanket, cloak, face protector and Armitage's breastplate were all stitched or engraved with a dragon-like sea serpent. Keeping his visor up, the knight was constantly looking left and right, watching the assembled city folk carefully. The night before, he had moved with lethal fluidity; today, there was instead a grace and grandeur about him. The knight had a magnetic aspect. Rupert might be a prince, but it was Armitage who had the regal bearing.

Lien was so focussed on Armitage he did not initially understand the reason the knight was largely riding directly next to Tryst. But as they passed, and Lien lost sight of the knight's face, he looked to Tryst as well and saw that he looked uncomfortable on his horse. Armitage actually put out his left arm once to subtly steady Tryst in his saddle.

'Something's wrong with Tryst,' Lien said, on tip-toe as he strained to see the last of the chevaliers before they were swallowed by the crowd.

'I should imagine that he has had one of his unfortunate "turns",' Cobi said.

Lien looked on blankly.

'If you are to admire any knights, Armitage is more worthy of your worship than that boy's father,' was all Cobi would expand though. 'I notice you were very taken by *Sir* Armitage,' he added, managing to make the knight's title sound like a dirty word.

'I don't like knights generally, but Armitage is amazing,' Lien said, eyes alight. 'He saved us last night, he took on four men on his own, he was fearless. And he is a friend of Sky and Areté, which means he is a good man.'

Cobi looked momentarily as though he was going to argue this, but shrugged instead.

'Mount up and let us go follow your prince.'

Lien did so and Cobi stroked Jest reassuringly one more time before walking out of the mouth of the alley and into the veritable river of people, horses, oxen and carts that flowed towards Voltanna, the heart of Avenel. This time Lien was better prepared and steadied his breathing as people and animals pressed in and jostled around them.

'So what was that, just now?' Lien asked, louder now that they were back on the road.

'That was parading chevaliers like champions for not

falling off their horses in the forest,' Cobi said dryly.

'They were really being celebrated for not falling off?' Lien laughed. Although he was aware that the tradition of chevaliers walking home horseless from their first year Leaverness manoeuvres was in no small part his doing, actually celebrating them riding home seemed excessive.

'Indeed. The Order is losing its grip on the city. They will take any excuse they can find to parade chevaliers and knights around the Kings Way with fanfare, in the hope the people will obediently shout hurrah. And showing off the chevaliers, who used to be kept hidden within Voltanna until they proved themselves worthy, is suddenly all the rage since the reinstatement of the Commoner Trials. They think if they can make all boys dream of becoming knights, they can keep the common people on their side.'

'What are the Commoner Trials? And who are the common people?' Lien asked.

'You will need to find another to pose your endless questions to,' Cobi dismissed the query, and all others. Disappointed, but recognising a dead end when he hit one, Lien change tack.

'Citar was there too,' he said. 'Did you see him? Behind Rupert.'

Cobi briefly cocked his head to one side as he thought back.

'I saw him, but I did not *notice* him,' he said, surprised. He frowned.

'What do you know of him?'

'Not much really. Except that he knew the most about Leaverness of all of them. Well except maybe Tryst. But he knew of Aethon and Brynir - and all about glamours.'

'All about glamours? You don't say,' Cobi said, before

lapsing into thoughtful silence. Figuring they were done talking for a while, Lien allowed his attention to wander over his surroundings instead. They were still in the flats of Avenel, the newest parts of the city which were built over the Avenel Plain in the last half century. Here most of the buildings were one to two stories high, built primarily in stone with wooden girding, though not the wood of the borealus, Lien noted with relief. The Kings Way connected the Leavensgate to the fortress Voltanna, and its surface grew older as it went along, from large smooth blocks of stones at the Leavensgate to ancient battered cobblestones as they went further in. The buildings too changed, becoming older and taller as they proceeded. Every now and again an overhead bridge would cross the Way between buildings on either side, and many buildings had towers that partially overhung the roadway. The city felt endless to Lien, who couldn't understand how there could be so many people in the *world*, much less in one place. His neck soon hurt from craning to look up and around. All the stone, on the buildings and road alike, captured and reflected the heat of the high sun, so that Avenel was even more of an oven than Leaverness or the plains. Lien would have done anything for a light breeze and the shade of a tree. But there were no trees to be seen, until the terraces of Voltanna.

Divinia had been right about the best view of Voltanna being from the plain. The closer they got to the centre of the city, the less they could see of the fortress, beyond the sheer walls that fortified the terraced levels. The base wall was built in a hexagram shape of six walls cornered by six bastion towers. The Kings Way started to rise uphill and wind to maintain only a gentle incline long before they approached the enormous gatehouse. Voltanna had been built from the outset to both defend and also impress, and the original architects had obviously been given the term "imposing" in their brief and run with it. Huge flanking towers rose around an enormous, austere iron portcullis, which was currently raised to only half its height, yet still allowed easy clearance for the tallest man on the highest horse. The guardsmen here looked much more alert than those on the Leavensgate, despite the heat.

Lien was not only held enthralled by the sight of Voltanna. The fortress also pulled on him energetically. The espréi of Avenel was fundamentally dampened by all the stone that covered the earth below, and then jumbled up by the close proximity of so many people and animals. But Voltanna was different. The closer they got, the stronger became the pull of its espréi. It was a place of enormous power. It made Lien's spine tingle disconcertingly.

Lien was staring so intently at the gatehouse that he was surprised when Jest followed Cobi left, going around it. The unexpected movement dragged him out of the trance-like state the espréi had been drawing him into.

'You feel it too?' Cobi asked.

'Yes, I've never felt anything like it,' Lien said. He looked around, noticing no-one else seemed to be showing any interest in the intense energy of the place.

'Is everyone so used to it?'

Cobi shrugged.

'They cannot feel it at all.'

Lien gaped.

'But the espréi here is so powerful! How can they not feel it?'

'You were not brought up like these people. They

don't even know they have a soul eye, much less how to open it.'

'That's so…sad…' Lien said, but falteringly, because he could now barely open his either. Cobi noticed the catch in his voice and looked questioningly at him. But Cobi was keeping his secrets, so Lien felt it was only fair to do the same. Instead of responding, he looked to Voltarch, sailing up into the the bright blue sky. He had to use one hand to shade his eyes as the sun dazzled him from behind the tower.

'Voltarch was built here to channel the espréi of this place. To weaponise it. It is a monstrosity,' Cobi said, following Lien's awed gaze.

'Mon-strosity?' Lien repeated, stumbling on the foreign word.

'From "monster", which I am sure you know. There are three towers like this: Voltarch, Voltane and Voltaire. Together, they doomed a whole civilisation. But who remembers that now?'

'Areté does, and so do the People,' Lien said. 'You're talking about the lost city of Phaedra, right?'

'It was not lost. It was destroyed,' Cobi said darkly.

'You are like Areté, aren't you?' Lien asked impulsively, distracted from the most important part of the conversation.

'I am nothing like Areté.'

The quiet intensity with which Cobi said it made Lien doubt the claim.

'Do you know where she is?' he pressed.

Cobi drew Jest to a stop on the left side of the road and gave Lien a hard look.

'Don't know, don't care,' he said. 'You'd do best not to either.'

'That's not possible,' Lien said, frowning. 'She is my aunt.'

'She is not your aunt,' Cobi said.

'Well not literally, no,' Lien said testily. 'But in all the important ways she is. And...it is my fault that she is missing.'

Cobi gave him a sceptical look.

'You overestimate your importance.'

Lien flinched.

'Any trouble she is in, she has gotten herself into,' Cobi continued relentlessly. 'When a century of life is but a chapter, your entire lifetime is nothing more than a passing sentence. How very exceptional you must consider yourself, to believe anything otherwise.'

Lien stared, speechless.

'I should not be so hard on you though,' Cobi sighed at Lien's shocked face. 'Self-importance is a delusion you share with all these small people,' and he indicated the whole of Avenel with an elegant circle of his right hand.

'This is where I leave you,' he added, looking across the road to an old, grand, three-storey stone building built into the fortress wall. It was an alehouse and its name, The Sign of the Angel, was painted in elegant script above the door, and crowned by two interlocked rings.

This was the place Divinia had told Lien he could come if he got into trouble.

'You need to get over the wall, beyond which you will find the Order stables, and therein, your prince.'

Lien examined the wall above The Angel. If he climbed to the top of the alehouse, he would be over half way up the fortress wall. Even so, the rest of the wall would still be no easy matter to scale, but he could see that there were many indentations in the ancient stone, which a light, strong agile boy could use as hand and foot holds. He had climbed higher, smoother trees. Satisfied it was possible, he went to nod, then realised the issue with the plan.

'Problem? Cobi asked. 'I thought the People were excellent climbers.'

'What do I do with Jest?' Lien asked, dismounting and looking around the crowded street. Cobi nodded towards a rail on the side of the alehouse, to which a dozen horses were tied under the shade of a peaked wooden roof.

'Oh no – '

'What else do you suggest?' Cobi asked flatly.

'Isn't there somewhere – quieter – I can leave him? Are there… trees, and grass, in the city? He will wait anywhere I leave him.'

'He might be happy to wait, but there are plenty of folk in this city who will also happily help themselves to a loose pony.'

'He won't go with anyone else,' Lien said confidently.

'Then they will flog him until he does.'

Lien looked horrified.

'And then they'll take him to a knackers yard, since he'll clearly be too hard to train.'

When Lien looked blank, Cobi explained what the knackers yard was.

*'What?'* Lien exclaimed, outraged. 'Why would anyone *do* that?'

'Not a lot of meat on a pony like this, granted, but good glue to make from his feet, and there are plenty of uses for such an excellent thick mane and tail.'

Lien felt sick. He wanted to be away from this man, and this city, and its barbaric people. He needed to find Lady Selene Beckworth as soon as possible.

'But if I tie him up, they won't take him?' he sighed.

'Exactly. Any free animal is fair game. Do not leave this pony untied *anywhere* in Avenel.'

Lien exhaled heavily.

'I'm sorry Jest,' he said to his pony, who again tried to rub the bridle off on his shoulder. 'There's nothing for it. It's an indignity, I know, but I'm afraid we'll both just have to get used to doing things differently here.'

'The Sign of the Angel is a favourite haunt of the Order. You may find other people you seek here later in the day,' Cobi said.

'Is it named after the Patient Angel too?' Lien asked. 'Like the Leavensgate?'

Cobi nodded.

'You must know his whole story?' Lien asked, latching onto a more familiar and comfortable subject. 'What happened to him?'

'He ran out of patience, in the end, or so the story goes.'

'And then what?' Lien asked.

'And then there was nothing to separate the darkness and the light,' Cobi said.

'Oh. So bad things happened?'

'Very bad things happened,' Cobi agreed.

'Did he try to – to fix it?' Lien asked, frowning.

'He could not fix it. And he could not live with knowing what he had done.'

'So what did he do?' Lien asked, fascinated.

'He decided to forget it all instead.'

'That was clever,' Lien said, eyes now on the fortress wall he would shortly have to climb. 'If I did something terrible, and I couldn't fix it, I wouldn't want to remember it either.'

He suddenly realised that with all he knew, Cobi might know what the Mandala was. He turned back to his companion to ask, but found himself alone. Disconcerted, Lien tried to feel for Cobi's cold espréi, but he could not, for that was a man who knew how to keep his energy to himself. But as Lien tried fruitlessly to feel for Cobi, he encountered that wild espréi again, the one he had felt in the alley. Again, it came from up high - this time from the roof of The Angel, but there was no-one there to be seen, and as quickly as Lien felt it, the energy moved on.

# 12. DIVINIA

Lien offered Jest a drink from a communal trough and then, his hair sweaty under the neck tie, dunked the top of his head into the water to cool off. He wasn't quite desperate enough to drink from the dirty water himself yet, though he knew he may have to if he didn't find another water source soon. He next squeezed the pony into a tiny space on the crowded tie up rail between a huge bay horse and a smaller grey, apologising to his disgruntled mount all the way. He knew he could not leave his staff with Jest after Divinia's warning about its value, but also knew he could not scale the wall with it in his hand, and had no way to attach it to his body. He guiltily examined the saddlery of the horses tied up with Jest, and after some moral gymnastics, "borrowed" the neck strap from the bay horse. He didn't know if the horse would still be there when he returned, but he *intended* to return it, which he decided was the important part in the transaction. Besides, all the horses were covered in what he considered many unnecessary items of metal and leather, so he thought their riders really ought to try to make do with less.

Lien made a makeshift belt from the neck strap, tight enough to hold the staff against his back. He patted Jest goodbye, promising to return soon, and climbed up one of the wooden supports for the roof that ran over the tie-up rail. The roof was also made of wood, which was mercifully warm to run across; he knew stone, tile and particularly metal roofs were going to be painfully hot to traverse though. His bare feet were hardened to the heat of trees in the high summer but had no conditioning to any of the other materials used in the buildings of Avenel.

Vertical ascents were something of a specialty of the children and teenagers of Leaverness, but still required considerable skill and concentration, so Lien pulled the soaked black silk tie up above his left eye to restore his depth of vision. Scaling The Angel with its windows, ledges and drain pipes was relatively straightforward, however as expected, the slate rooftop was radiating such heat that he practically danced across the scalding tiles. The merely hot stone of the fortress wall was a relief to tackle after that. He swarmed up it, his strong fingers and toes finding holds all the way up. He did not look down until he was flat on his belly at the top though, and was glad he had waited. He had climbed higher trees, but their branches provided plentiful opportunities to save yourself on if you fell. The wall offered only a sheer drop to a hard rooftop, had he slipped. Lien caught his breath, and proceeded to look further afield.

The whole first ring of the fortress, the bailey, was where all the livestock and ancillary military services were located: blacksmiths, artisans, saddlers, armourers, carpenters and fletchers. The majority of it was taken up with the keeping and care of the hundred-odd horses of the Order of the Coeur though, and as Cobi had promised, this wall gave him immediate access into the stables of Voltanna.

Lien had never seen horse stables before, and so was curious to know what they looked like. Some of the stable blocks were built into the outer wall with the stables facing into the open air; some were in large, enclosed two-storey barns in which horses were stabled on the ground floor in two facing lines while their grooms lived above. There were three riding rings and an exercise track that ran all the way around the inner wall. Lien had few architectural reference points to draw from, but thought the stone and wooden barns looked grand, which pleased him. If horses were to be housed, he felt they should at least be housed well. He was uneasy at the idea of the horses being kept in such confinement though, and silently promised Jest he would be back in Leaverness as soon as possible.

A concentrated stench of horse manure drew Lien's roving eyes to a mountainous muck heap against the outer wall, which was stratified with a network of long planks of wood. While he was wondering what these were for, a groom emerged from the stables with a laden wheelbarrow. Approaching the heap, he rounded his shoulders and determinedly ran at it, aiming the barrow for one of the planks. It was a good start, but he ran out of momentum about two thirds up the mountain, resulting a great deal of huffing and puffing to inch the heavy load up high enough to finally, triumphantly, dump its contents at the very top - from which balls of manure ran all the way back down to the ground. Lien was delighted and immediately wanted to have a go at pushing a barrow up the shit heap himself, but was sidetracked by the sight of a striking black horse - also mountainous, within the scale of horse heights. This horse was tied up outside one of the outdoor stable blocks. He was being watched warily by a tall boy who was sitting cross-legged on the ground nearby. Lien grinned happily and jogged along the top of the outer wall as far as possible until he had no choice but to climb down carefully to the roof of the required stable block. He yelped quietly as his feet touched down on the hot tile roof and quickly trotted down the sloping roof before dropping down to the ground below.

Lord Jorge heard Lien before Rupert; the prince was following his horse's intent gaze when Lien dropped first to the roof and then to the ground.

'Lien!' Rupert said, surprised at the unexpected visitor, not to mention his unorthodox method of arrival.

'Hello Rupert! Hello Jorge!' Lien beamed, stroking the horse's glossy black neck.

'I was *sure* it was you I saw you on the Kings Way!'

'You looked very grand,' Lien said, kindly omitting the parts about Rupert also looking terrified.

'What are you doing here?' Rupert asked, face crinkled in confusion. 'I thought it was very dangerous for you in Avenel?'

'Someone told about me,' Lien explained, his face falling as he dropped down to sit cross-legged next to the other boy.

'Knights came and attacked the People. They burned our whole campsite. I - I couldn't stay.' Lien's voice faltered at the end as he felt a sickness in his stomach at the vivid memory of the previous evening.

'That's terrible! I'm so sorry,' Rupert said, before quickly adding, 'and it wasn't me, by the way! I promise. We all told the story as agreed. I don't know who would have told on you. I can't believe any of us would have.'

Rupert wasn't overly fond of the other boys, Citar notwithstanding, but he didn't believe for a moment any would have sold Lien out like that.

'Thank you. And I believe you, of course,' Lien said.

'So are you here to find out who betrayed you?' Rupert asked.

Lien cocked his head to one side, considering the word *betrayed*. He had not thought of it in that way before. He didn't like the feeling that came with the idea.

'No. I'm here to find Lady Selene Beckworth, to find Areté,' was all he said.

'Oh. Why did you come to me then? Surely Citar would be better? Lady Beckworth is his sponsor,' Rupert said, puzzled.

'I met a man who couldn't take me to Lady Beckworth or Citar, but could take me to you. He was really strange,' Lien replied, while closely scrutinising Jorge. Something was wrong with the beautiful black horse, patiently basking in the heat while his tail lazily swished at flies, but he couldn't put his finger on it.

'Why are we sitting here looking at Jorge like this?'

'Do you know how I got Jorge?' Rupert asked, staring blankly at his horse again.

Lien shook his head, although he had very strong suspicions about where - or who - Jorge had come from.

'He found me - he saved me - in Leaverness. Last year, after you - you know.'

He glanced awkwardly at Lien.

'I thought you would know that.'

Lien shook his head again, embarrassment and guilt over what he had done to Rupert the previous year lifting a flush to his cheeks.

'He's not a real horse, is he?' Rupert continued. 'I mean he's smarter than average. I mean *way* smarter. He's loyal to a fault, he never tires, he's never had an off day.'

'Special, yes. But still a real horse,' Lien said.

Rupert shook his head.

'A real horse - a normal horse - is wounded for weeks. I came here this morning before that stupid parade to tend his wounds, but...well. You won't be getting matching scars.'

Lien realised now what was wrong. He jumped up and ran his hands over the muscular shoulder he had seen furiously raked by wolf claws just two days before. But there was no wound to be seen. Not even a scab, not even a scar. Nothing but soft, shining, obsidian black coat. But where Rupert was clearly disconcerted by this discovery, Lien was delighted.

'Clever boy, Jorge,' he said fondly, scratching Jorge under his chin. The big horse grunted gratefully, his eyes still closed.

'You're not surprised?' Rupert asked.

'I did not expect it, but no, I am not surprised,' Lien said. 'I told you, in Leaverness, that he was special.'

'What *is* he?' Rupert asked.

Lien could not understand the boy's concern.

'He is a gift, from a friend,' he said.

Rupert was nonplussed.

'I wish I knew who,' he said, rising to his feet also.

'You don't know?' Lien *was* surprised by this. When Rupert still looked blank, Lien stood back and gestured to Jorge.

'What horse does he remind you of?'

Rupert thought.

'I had a tutor, years ago, with a big black horse. I mean, I think I did. Possibly I just dreamed it all. It's all a bit...foggy. But I do remember wanting a horse like it.'

'And here he is!' Lien beamed. 'What was the tutor's name? And the horse?'

'She was called...' Rupert broke off, frowning. 'That's strange, her name was just on the tip of my tongue.'

'What about the horse?' Lien asked.

'I do know it. I must. Give me a second...' Rupert screwed up his eyes with the effort of trying to remember. Lien watched the painful process curiously.

'Why can't I remember?' Rupert exclaimed.

'Can you remember anything about her? Without straining?'

'Only that she was the best tutor I ever had. I mean I can't even see her, in my memory, but I do remember how she made me feel. And that was - well, it's hard to explain - ' and he closed his eyes as he tried to put the feeling into words.

'She made me feel like I was worthy. Like I was brave. She's the only person who has ever made me feel like - like I'm not an embarrassment.'

Lien nodded, sure of at least one thing now.

'I think your tutor was Areté, and her horse Erebus, and that she was using a glamour, which has confused you. Although what you're experiencing isn't really how a glamour works, so I'm not completely sure about that part.'

'You're the second person to talk about glamours!' Rupert said. 'Citar was going on about them as well, in Leaverness. I'd never even heard of them before.'

'They're a powerful sort of magic, so they're not common,' Lien said.

'Magic isn't allowed in Mayana,' Rupert sighed. 'I mean my father says it isn't even a real thing.'

'How can you not think it is real?' Lien asked,

astonished.

'Well… I'd never seen anything magical. Until the Cuán turned into wolves. I mean they were supposed to be a *story*, not *real*. And then there was the torch thing. You did that, right?'

'That's…complicated,' Lien said evasively. Rupert gave him an initially questioning look, but decided to leave it alone.

'And then - this,' he finished, gesturing to Jorge's conspicuously uninjured shoulder.

'Well, I know for sure that it was Areté who saved you, in Leaverness. You don't remember?'

Rupert shook his head.

'I remember a voice I recognised, but I've never spoken with Areté - that I'm aware of. That I *remember*. How do you know?'

'She told me. Well, she told me off actually, for nearly killing you. Which I'm still sorry about, by the way,' he added hastily.

'You've already said that,' Rupert said stiffly. 'Was I really dying? I felt like I was dying. And sometimes I feel like - like I'm not supposed to still be here. Is that crazy?'

Lien considered how to reply. He was certain Areté had put herself into the Arrangement with Callista - or whatever was inside Callista - to save Rupert. He was certain that Rupert was supposed to have died in Leaverness a year ago - and thinking that, Lien suddenly realised he would have been responsible. Not for "almost" killing the prince, but for *actually* killing him, had Areté not intervened. The fact that the two of them were sitting together having a conversation was…literally miraculous. So Areté had saved Rupert's life, and saved Lien from having killed the boy –

'Lien…?' Rupert prompted, worriedly peering into the other boy's face. 'Are you okay?'

'Yes of course,' Lien said, breaking from his reverie. 'Sorry, I was lost in thought.'

'So – do you think I'm crazy? Am I…not meant to be here?' the prince prompted.

Lien thought fast. Knowing what Areté had done was a terrible weight he carried. Would telling Rupert the truth make it a worry halved, or doubled?

Looking upon the lanky boy's desperately worried face, Lien decided it would be the latter, and to proceed diplomatically.

'I think Areté was your tutor, and she wanted you to be here, so made sure you would be. And it sounds like she gave you Jorge, whose sire I bet is Erebus, to look after you.'

'Gosh.' Rupert looked awed. 'You think *Areté* was *my* tutor? And…and *cares* about *me*?' He shook his head in amazement.

'Well you're a prince, right? Princes are important?'

As Rupert's face fell, Lien realised he had made a mistake.

'I'm sorry, did I say something wrong?' he asked.

'No,' Rupert sighed, 'it's just that – the prince thing is just a title, you know? The *prince* is important, but not the person who is the prince. People aren't nice to *me*, they're nice to my title. They often don't even *like* me, but they pretend, because I'm a prince. If I wasn't, they wouldn't care about me at all.'

'Isn't it better they are nice to you though, and not mean, even if it's a show?' Lien asked thoughtfully. 'I mean it's sort of the opposite for me and Bravo: some of the People don't like us because we're sort of outsiders, regardless of who we actually are. It's so unfair. But I think I'd rather people were nicer to me than meaner!'

Rupert shrugged.

'That's a fair point. They'd probably be *awful* to me if I wasn't a prince. But if *Areté* cares about me...well, that's the question, isn't it? Does she care about *me*, or the title?'

Lien laughed at this. Rupert stared, puzzled.

'Oh Rupert! Areté doesn't care about *titles* and whatnot. She cares for *people.* Maybe there's something important about who you are, but she wouldn't have spent time tutoring someone she didn't care about, and she definitely wouldn't have given you a son of Erebus if she didn't like you. I've never even heard of her doing that before.'

Lien heard the astonished tone of his own voice and realised he was actually jealous of that particular privilege. As his eyes devoured the big black horse, he couldn't help but imagine what it must be like to ride such an incredible animal.

'So...will you help me find her?' he continued, to hide his envy.

'Of course!' Rupert's face clouded. 'Do you really think she's in trouble?'

'I know she is,' Lien replied.

'Okay. But...this is Areté.' He chewed his bottom lip anxiously. 'Lien...if something has managed to get the better of Areté...what makes you think you and I have any chance against whatever it is?'

'It's not just us though,' Lien said. 'There's Bravo too, and maybe Sky. And we're going to ask Lady Selene

Beckworth. And maybe Citar, he seemed to know lots of useful things.'

Rupert shrugged.

'Okay, I'm in,' he said, though his face betrayed his uncertainty. 'I mean, I don't know how much use I'll be, but she saved me, so I have to try to help her back. What do we do first?'

'We go and find Lady Beckworth!' Lien said. 'Where does she live?'

'Not far. But really, we need Citar with us to get an audience with her. I can find him during the afternoon and meet you after classes to go there together?' Rupert said.

Lien's disappointment was immediate and clear.

'Can't we go now?' he asked.

'I can't, I have sword next. If I'm not on the Loom five minutes after the bell, Master Reich will be very sarcastic.'

The lanky boy paled at the thought.

'Believe me, you do *not* want Reich being sarcastic about you. Besides, two teenage boys turning up uninvited will not get near Lady Beckworth.'

Lien thought only a moment before deciding his plan of action.

'I will meet you after classes, outside The Sign of the Angel. But I will explore the city first. It is my first visit, after all! Where does Lady Selene Beckworth live?'

Rupert reluctantly gave the boy vague directions, but warned Lien to wait for him and Citar before trying to meet Selene. They were interrupted by the sound of a long tolling bell, which made Rupert jump up to return Jorge to his stable, before racing off to class. Lien went to follow him. Rupert paused and looked at him in astonishment.

'You cannot be seen here, Lien, you're a stranger

inside Voltanna! Go the way you came. And cover your left eye!' He started to jog away with his horse, but paused, uncertainly turning back.

'Lien…about Lady Beckworth…' the prince started, then seemed to think twice.

'Yes?' Lien prompted, following to catch up.

'She's…' the boy dropped his voice as he finally charged on. 'Hers is a house of ill-repute.'

'It is a what?' Lien had absolutely no reference point for that statement. Rupert chewed a lip.

'It's a…a…place of scarlet women?' he tried.

Lien shook his head. Still blank.

'Never mind,' the prince sighed. 'Best if you find out yourself. But *not* without me, alright?'

'Alright!' Lien lied cheerfully. Rupert paused a moment longer, then shook his head and continued to run off.

Lien climbed back up the stable block, wincing as his hands reached the hot tile roof, then ran across it as quickly as possible. The roof of the single-storey stable was much lower than the three-storey Sign of the Angel, but also, the wall was higher on the outside than inside due to the terraced structure of Voltanna, so it was only half the distance again to climb up from this side. It was still a tough job to scale though, so again, Lien paused on the top, belly down, to catch his breath and enjoy the view. He didn't get to stay there for long though, as a shout came from an astonished lookout in the closest bastion tower. They had evidently missed Lien the first time, but now there were two guards looking and yelling at him. They were a long way up and reasonable way off though, so Lien didn't feel threatened; he just didn't want them to draw any attention to him. He got to his feet, gave them a cheerful wave and proceeded to jog back along the wall towards The Sign of the Angel. To his shock, a *thwip* sound momentarily preceded an arrow burying itself in the wall several meters ahead of him.

*'Hey!'* Lien bawled, turning back. He said nothing more though when he saw the two guards readying two more arrows. One landed between his feet. He leapt back, nearly losing his balance, and proceeded to sprint the remaining distance of the wall to the roof of The Angel. No more arrows followed him though, and he thought he heard some confused shouting from the tower, but he did not pause to look or try to listen. He did think he felt a whip-like touch of that wild espréi again, but still he kept his head down until he had scrambled down from the wall to the tiled roof of The Angel. Once there he still wasted no time, sliding down the far side of the roof from the archers. He did not slow down until he was safely in the shade of the horse tie-up. Here, he panted out his story to an impassive Jest. The pony only cheered up when removed from the horse sandwich in which Lien had left him. The huge bay horse was gone, meaning Lien was unable to return the neck strap, and had been replaced by a handsome but equally large chestnut horse, who had also been pressed up against poor Jest.

Lien had already decided that it was too hot to travel further by rooftop for the afternoon, so took Jest for another drink at the trough before setting off. He steeled himself to drink from it as well: he hadn't drunk since his last swim in the Seine, hours earlier, but had been sweating constantly since. The water of the rivers of Leaverness was crisp and clean; the trough water was warm and dirty and tasted terrible, but he had no choice. After drinking from his cupped hands, Lien again dunked his hot head and the silk scarf into the water before tying the latter back down over his left eye. Hoping this made him suitably inconspicuous - which of course it did not at all - he set off, following Rupert's vague directions to the home of Lady Selene Beckworth.

Jest was calmer in the roads now since his encounter with Cobi. Lien was grateful, but also curious as to how the cold man had managed to have such a significant influence on his pony. He clearly liked horses more than he liked people, but then, Lien could hardly blame him for that.

They were soon onto narrower, quieter streets free of market stalls and wagons and then onto the required road. Here Lien discovered that Rupert's specification of "the big house" was not particularly helpful. All of the houses on this road were huge: large buildings made of stone with intricate facades and often set back behind the road with manicured gardens ahead of them. They were very different to the tightly packed buildings of the Kings Way. As he halted Jest to ponder this dilemma, a man in the uniform of the Avenel Guard approached, his polished bronze breastplate dazzlingly bright in the sun. He carried his helmet under one arm and looked hot and harried.

'Can I help you, son?' he asked, shrewd eyes taking in every unusual detail of the boy and his pony.

'I am trying to visit my aunt, but I do not know which house is hers,' Lien said, trying to play it cool but producing a slightly forced, nervous smile.

'Well perhaps I can direct you,' the man said, guardedly. 'What's her name?'

'Lady Selene Beckworth,' Lien said.

The man initially frowned, then, when Lien's expression did not change, laughed.

'Someone's out to make a fool of you, son,' he grinned. Seeing the boy's confused expression, he expanded, somewhat.

'It's clear you're no nephew of her Ladyship, and if I might say, you're much too young to be seeking her – services – in any case. You'd best leave this endeavour alone.'

As none of this was remotely helpful, Lien remained politely silent. The guard squinted at him.

'Where are you from, son?' he asked. He was clearly suspicious but was not, Lien felt, an unkind man.

'I am from Hireath,' Lien said with barely a moment's hesitation as he recalled the script Cobi had given him.

The guard looked impressed.

'Hireath, huh? Don't meet many from there. How will you get back again? It's a right bugger to find, so I understand.'

'Those from Hireath can always find the way,' Lien hazarded, thinking of how Tauron'Est was unable to be found by anyone who had never been there before.

The guard seemed to accept this with a small shrug.

'And what's wrong with your eye?' he continued his conversational interrogation.

'I have an eye infection. It is grotesque,' Lien said, again verbatim. 'I have come to Avenel to have it healed,' he added in a moment of inspiration.

'You'll be wanting a doctor then, not the ministrations of Lady Beckworth,' the guard said, a smile twitching the sides of his mouth again. 'I can direct you to a good one, if you like. Won't charge you too much if you say I sent you.'

Lien was trying to work out how to politely wriggle out of the assistance of this inconveniently helpful man, when a number of city bells began tolling the hour. The guard pulled a pocket watch out of a trouser pocket and cursed. Lien only just stopped himself from asking what the fascinating device was for.

'Well I'm late, afraid I have to run, son. I hope you can get your eye sorted, but take my advice: leave Lady Beckworth well alone,' he said, and set off at a lope back the way Lien had come. Lien exhaled in relief, and nudged Jest to keep walking down the road, hoping he would find some clue as to which grand house might belong to Lady Beckworth. They soon came to a property fronted by a dense hedge, above which rose a high, elegant, wrought iron fence. The house, set well back above sloping manicured lawns and gardens, was a wide, two-storey building made of rose cream stone with ornamental white trim and enormous windows. Although Lien had never seen a house up close before today, even he recognised that there was an exceptional grandness to this one. While he paused Jest to enjoy the view, he was startled by the sound of someone clearing their throat noisily. Lien followed the sound to see a short man below him, his face lost amongst wrinkles and excessive facial hair and contorted into a sly leer. He was stupendously ugly. Both boy and pony stared at the figure with a mixture of curiosity, apprehension and lastly, on Lien's behalf, delight.

'You're a dwarf!' he said, thrilled. He had never met one, and understood sightings were rare.

'No shit kid,' the dwarf replied drily. 'Wouldn't be trying to spy on the young ladies, would ye?' he added, his leer restored.

Lien frowned, puzzled.

'No - sir?' he hazarded. 'I am looking for the home of Lady Selene Beckworth.'

The dwarf chuckled, inappropriately.

'You? You're a little *fresh*, don't you think?' he said with an inflection which made the whole sentence sound like a very rude statement. Lien frowned again, quite lost. It was the same term the guard on the Leavensgate had used, and led Lien to conclude he had misunderstood the meaning of the word.

'I think we have a misunderstanding...' he started, but the dwarf seemed to have suddenly lost patience for the exchange. Quick as a striking snake, he pulled a thick piece of metal pipe from the back of his belt and struck it hard against the iron gate, causing Jest to shy away from the reverberating crashing sound. Lien, grasping the pony's mane to stay seated on his slick back, glared indignantly at the dwarf.

'What was *that* for?' he shouted, stroking the tense pony.

'You've no business here, boy. Best to leave before my pipe takes away your youthful beauty,' growled the dwarf, as he proceeded to run the brutal piece of metal along the flanks of the iron gate. Jest backed away from the excruciating scream of metal on metal, and with one frustrated look back at the antagonist's face, distorted in gleeful malice, Lien turned the pony away to escape the dreadful sound.

He was not yet ready to do anything as sensible as wait for Rupert to finish his classes though. Finding the rear of the estate was only a matter of patience, haphazard Avenel geography and exploring a winding network of roads and back alleys. Soon enough, Lien was carefully standing on

Jest's narrow back, but even so, and straining to his full reach, he was unable to quite find the top of the tall and inconveniently smooth brick wall that backed the stately home. He considered, and eventually grinned. He had one, immensely stupid, possibility: the kind of prank he and Bravo would try for kicks when bored. Lien crept one foot right up to Jest's wither, the highest point of the pony's back. Softening his knees, he took a deep steadying breath, and gave Jest the cue to rear.

The People were, without exception, extremely accomplished horsemen. Their children could ride before they could walk and their horses were as much a part of their community as their fellow tribesmen. Their steeds could perform the most remarkable feats of obedience and agility. A little rear was nothing to ask of Jest, but Lien needed more. He needed the pony to sit back on his hind legs until his hocks almost touched the ground, and from there, push upwards to reach his maximum height. Jest made a few hopping preparations for the rear, during which Lien had to support himself against the wall to remain in his precarious position; and then Jest *sat* his hind legs down, before powerfully rearing his shoulders up to an extra metre in height. Lien *whooped* as he too bent his knees and launched himself from the pony, his fingertips scrabbling for purchase the top of the wall as he did. He had to desperately press his feet into the wall to push himself up and over, ending up flat on his belly at the top, panting and elated. He still had his staff strapped on his back by the makeshift belt, just in case he encountered the angry dwarf again.

'Who's the best boy?' he asked the pony. 'Just wait

there in the shade Jest, I won't be long,' he said, then, recalling Cobi's warning about not leaving Jest anywhere untied, cursed and added, 'I promise, I'll be really quick!'

The view from the top of Lady Beckworth's wall was magnificent. On one side, Jest gazed up curiously from the lane, beyond which a patchwork of houses and roofs spread up towards Voltanna. On the other, a broad lawn and further ornamental gardens ran out to a stretch of cloisters that took up the entire back width of the mansion house. Lien felt a brief and strangely familiar tingle and took a moment to realise what had caused it: the cloisters surrounded a tree, taller than they were, but not as tall as the mansion itself. This tree, Lien was certain, was the source of the strong espréi, but he could not place why it felt so familiar, when the tree itself looked to be an ordinary oak. Which was not to say that oak trees were ordinary, but they did not have an energetic feel like this. It would require further investigation, but not at a time when Jest was illegally parked, so to speak.

Ground level was considerably higher inside the wall and surfaced in soft grass instead of the hard stone that seemed to be everywhere in the city, so Lien took the opportunity to enjoy a flip on the way down. He tumbled elegantly through the air, landing lightly on his feet and relished the more direct connection to the earth. Stone had its own espréi but dampened the direct energy felt through natural surfaces. Reluctant for a closer encounter with the dwarf and his length of pipe though, Lien then made a swift dash across the exposed grass to a line of tall, identical trees separating the lawn from the gardens. Reaching the gardens, he flattened himself so dramatically behind one of trees that Lady Selene Beckworth, watching the whole affair through an eyeglass from the second floor of the mansion, giggled, accidentally spilling the tea she held in her other hand. As Lien peered around the side of the tree to plan his next move, she frowned though.

'Darius, pass me the binoculars on the bookcase over there, would you?' she asked, pointing to the bookcase without taking her eyes off the intruder in her gardens. 'Do hurry won't you, it's quite urgent,' she added as her companion, oblivious to the presence of the unsubtle adventurer outside, grunted at the effort required. He slowly fetched the requested item, which Selene quickly trained on the boy, just in time to watch his next dash in close up.

'Well I'll be damned,' she said, quietly now, her mood entirely changed. She watched until she lost sight of the boy in the cloisters.

'What is it?' Darius asked.

'I just saw something quite impossible,' she said slowly, carefully placing the binoculars on the window sill before resuming her seat. 'Areté has a lot of explaining to do. Anyway, the upshot is that a boy has just scaled the back wall and run into the cloisters, like a common thief. Do you think he means mischief?'

'If he does, Hector will be delighted,' Darius said, unconcerned.

'Given that he's just come over the back wall, I should assume he has already made Hector's acquaintance at the front gate,' Selene said, before lapsing into a thoughtful silence.

Darius was curious about her uncharacteristic sequence of mood swings. Selene had been severely chiding him until her attention switched to the garden. Seeing the intruder had initially delighted her, until she had seen him closer, when she abruptly changed to a melancholy he had never seen her display.

'You seem disconcerted, Selene,' he prompted.

'To be honest, Darius, I am quite so,' she agreed. 'I am reminded of a – a loss.'

A moment later though, she restored her usual bright and breezy persona with a winning smile.

'Which, I believe, brings us back to our previous topic.'

'I think it far more prudent to deal with your interloper than my misery,' Darius scowled. He thought he had dodged a dagger with the interruption, and did not wish the Lady to be allowed to resume berating him.

'I came to you with intelligence, not to be lectured. Do so and I may not bring you further such pieces of information.'

'It was very thoughtful of you, dear Darius, but I did already know about the dastardly excursion to Leaverness. I do always so enjoy your company though.'

Darius stared, then scowled.

'How did you know?' he asked.

'I don't believe there's much that happens inside – or outside – Avenel that I do not know about,' Selene said lightly. 'And it occurs to me that our visitor might well have a connection to those most terrible deeds. We should find out. Might you do so, and while you're at it, defend the honour of my girls, if required?'

'I see at least two oxymorons in that statement Selene – '

'Do you challenge the honour of my girls, dearest?' she demanded, a perfect eye brow arching dangerously.

'As equally as I challenge their need to be defended. They are quite ferocious all on their own,' he said with the fervour of a man who has personal experience of the women in question.

'Truly, chivalry is dead then, Darius. And you called yourself a knight! The shame,' Selene chided him, mostly playfully. The man sighed like a boy being asked to run an errand. He slowly raised himself from his seat, leaning heavily on his walking cane as he did.

'You can take one of those charming ornamental swords from the hall on your way down,' she offered. Darius grunted as he slowly limped his way towards the door. Selene shrugged and waved him out of the decadent sitting room with what Darius considered a very suspicious smile.

After the former Green Knight closed the door behind him - unnecessarily hard, she felt - Selene sat back deeply into her comfortable armchair and allowed herself the time to truly, fully experience the range of emotions she had just touched on, upon realising who Areté's ward in Leaverness truly was.

She permitted a single tear to run down an exquisite cheekbone.

Lien trotted silently through the cloisters to reach the house behind them. The baroque pillars were draped in a beautiful purple flowered climbing creeper and surrounded the magnificent oak, which was set in a square of perfectly cut emerald grass. The tree's espréi was practically a pull at this close proximity, and again, Lien knew he recognised it. He paused a moment to try to work out why, but felt a slight headache coming on, and found himself suddenly deciding it was absolutely essential that he get inside the house as quickly as possible. Which was technically true, in any case.

On the far side of the cloisters he arrived at the mansion itself. Lien had never been in a house, as such. The external structure of Tauron'Est, the ancient Leaverness fortress the People used as a winter home, stood strong, but the interior was largely a ruin and as such constituted what might best be called 'open plan' living. Lien was unaccustomed to closed or indeed locked doors, and decided he'd rather scope the internal terrain from a high vantage point instead. This is how he came to be peeking through a high, horizontal, inwardly opening window when he first came to understand something of why so many people had been so strange about Lady Selene Beckworth and her women. Who were less scarlet than hot magenta.

Lien was looking down into an indoor pool under a glass atrium roof. It was huge, with a vast fountain taking pride of place in the centre. It was full of, and surrounded by, beautiful women in various states of both repose and relative - but not complete - undress. Lien was so startled by the sight that as his widening eyes roved the chamber, he forgot how precarious his position was and smacked his head hard on the top of the window frame. Both that sound, and the *ouch* that followed it, made him the immediate object of attention of every woman in the atrium. Mortified by this unintended attention, Lien overbalanced and fell in through the window, twisting his body so that he at least ended up with both hands gripping the window sill and his chest facing to the wall, which was just too far away to be helpful. As his feet scrabbled for purchase, he heard various gasps and laughs behind him. Not wanting to hang around making a fool of himself for any longer than necessary, he decided to at least make a fool of himself from his own two feet.

He dropped, and although Lien usually had a cat's ability to land on his feet, in his fluster he stumbled the landing, banging one knee painfully against the rough stone. His staff, already loosened from his slip through the window, fell from the stolen belt and rattled loudly as it rolled across the stone floor in the sudden silence. A brilliant flush was rising as Lien turned to face his accidental audience. He swept up his staff and dropped an awkward half bow, trying to style out his graceless arrival, and was surprised when one of the women clapped enthusiastically, soon joined by a smattering of further applause.

'Wonderful!' said one woman in the pool, learning on her elbows over the edge. '*What* an entrance.'

'What little mouse is this, dropped amongst the cats?' asked a haughty woman from her recliner chair, considerably less warmly. As Lien stared dumbly, she swung her long legs off the recliner and strode the few paces between them to take Lien's chin in one hand and force his eyes up from the depths of her cleavage to meet her icy stare.

It wasn't that Lien wasn't used to seeing women's bodies - nudity was completely normalised in a culture in which men and women regularly bathed naked together. In fact, if these women had been naked, Lien might not have thought anything of it at all. What was scrambling his hormones was actually what the strategically designed swimming garments did to those bodies. Lien had never encountered cleavage of this size, or indeed depth, as produced by remarkable feats of undergarment structural engineering. For a teenage boy from the forest, it was an overwhelming experience. It was particularly confusing in the case of this woman, because until his eyes met hers, Lien had not realised that he already met her, albeit in completely different and innocuous circumstances, only a few hours earlier.

'You better have an extremely good excuse for your presence here, Lien,' Divinia growled, quietly enough that others could not hear.

Lien hunted around for brain or tongue but found both absent without leave.

'Nothing? How disappointing. You have exactly three seconds to at least make one up. One. Two. Thr – '

'Got-chased-by-small-angry-man-with-lead-pipe-need-to-see-Lady-Selene-Beckworth-please!' Lien gabbled, brain finally revving his frozen tongue into gear. By now he was surrounded by a press of women, wearing between them a vast range of expressions and not much else: curiosity, suspicion, amusement and resentment were all present and accounted for, along with a few eyes twinkling with sheer mischief and one face beaming with maternal affection. Divinia retained her sceptical expression, but the motherly woman shouldered in to take charge.

'Bless the child, look at him Divinia, he doesn't mean any harm. In fact, I do believe he's rather overwhelmed by us. Are you alright, dearie?'

The sight of her friendly, concerned face pulled Lien back to reality. Here was a woman who had been born with the mothering instinct already switched on, *and* she was wearing a towel over her swimsuit – he assumed she *was* wearing a swim suit – which helped enormously. Finally, he had somewhere safe to look.

'I'm not a child,' he protested weakly. She beamed.

'Course you're not my luvvie. So how old are you then?'

'Fourteen,' Lien answered promptly, but automatically giving the number in the language of the People. A couple of the women murmured appreciatively at the foreign word.

'Er…ten and four?' he tried again, unable to remember the whole number in the right language at that particular point in time.

'Oooo, he's not a local lad at all, is he?' another woman said, giving the boy a closer inspection. She spied the very top of Brynir's claw marks peeking out from under the V neck of his tunic, and to his shock, actually lifted his tunic up to take a closer look. She displayed his chest like a prize, to a mixture of admiration and concern.

'And would you look at these scars! What have you been grappling with, sonny boy?'

Divinia stared: she alone knew what she was looking at.

Lien pulled down his tunic sharply, blushing furiously.

'And what's wrong with your eye then, dearie?' asked the maternal woman, eyeing the black silk covering his left eye. Lien stepped back quickly, in case anyone tried to pull that up as well, but Divinia stepped protectively in front of him, knowing what was underneath it. He wasn't off the hook with her yet though: she needed to know why he had come to this place. When she had seen a boy spying through the windows she had immediately assumed he was a pervert trying to see the pretty ladies; when she had realised which boy it was, this suspicion was immediately followed by disappointment, for she had thought better of Lien. She was hoping her initial instinct was wrong though: that the boy had a genuine reason for his presence at Castelle Travers, and that crashing into the pool room was more innocent than it initially appeared.

She turned a hard look on Lien, who shrank back

slightly under its force.

'So, boy. What do you want with Lady Beckworth?' Divinia demanded.

'It is...private,' Lien said, glancing desperately around in a way he hoped communicated to Divinia that he could not speak freely in company. To his confusion, his statement instead elicited a series of giggles and sniggers from the ladies surrounding him.

'Of *course* it's private dearie,' the maternal woman soothed with a wide, knowing grin. 'These things always are.'

'N-no...I'm not sure what you're thinking but whatever it is, that's what it's not...' Lien stammered, the blush rising again. Divinia frowned, but given the options available - that Lien either genuinely did not understand what went on at Castelle Travers, or was an exceptional actor - decided that the former was more likely.

'I think the boy needs to be cleaned up, if he is to be presented to Selene,' she announced. 'Carla, would you help me take care of him? Privately?'

'I would be delighted,' said Carla. 'Come with me luvvie, we'll get you sorted, you'll be needing a bath if you don't mind me saying. I've nothing against the heady tang of teenage sweat, but we can't be having with it in front of her Ladyship.'

Lien was in the process of giving a sigh of relief - he was finally to meet Selene! - when a nearby door was thrown dramatically open to reveal Darius. The old man cut an initially impressive figure with a sabre in one hand, but this impression faltered a moment later when he revealed the cane hidden behind his back, and leant on it heavily.

*'Darius!'* Divinia bawled. 'When will you learn to knock, man? There are ladies in states of undress present!'

'Divinia, there's a teenage boy in your bathing room in case you hadn't noticed,' Darius replied testily, limping forwards with the the ornamental sabre pointed towards Lien's chest.

'Boy! Hands up!' he growled, stopping the blade's distance away. Lien complied immediately, his staff still in one hand.

'The boy is harmless,' Divinia snapped. 'What's that ruddy sword for? Someone could get hurt!'

'Intruder. Sabre,' Darius said exasperatedly. 'Why are we even having this conversation? And for goodness sake, put some clothes on.'

'You trying to give me orders, Darius? Because you know how I feel about – '

' – yes yes, everyone knows how you feel about men giving you – '

' – not in front of the innocent boy!' Carla shrieked, clapping two hands over Lien's ears. The "innocent boy" wriggled out of her hands, thoroughly flustered over all the fuss –

– and leaving Cobi's black silk tie in her hands.

At first he didn't realise, but a curious and then shocked silence descended upon the chamber as everyone strained to see what Lien had been hiding. He helped them all out by glancing around to see what they were all reacting to, until he saw the silk clutched in Carla's hand. While his heart skipped a beat, his left hand shot up to clamp over his left eye.

'It's nothing, it's not how it looks – ' he started, but Darius cut him off with a sabre blade to the neck.

'Explain yourself,' he growled. Lien scrambled for words, for an explanation, but found the bite of cold metal against his neck to be profoundly distracting, not to mention triggering after Bravo's recent attack.

'Oh *relax* you old fool,' Divinia said scathingly, pushing Darius' sabre away from Lien, who almost sagged with gratitude. 'He's been fooling around with his mates, clearly, we'll go wash it off,' she continued, taking the neck tie from Carla's unresisting hand, and passing it back to Lien, who took it gratefully. But just as it seemed that one disaster was averted, another naturally burst in, specifically in the form of the angry dwarf, sans lead pipe. The upgrade to a nasty axe more than half the height of its bearer did little to encourage though.

'Why hello Hector, why *don't* you join us,' Divinia roared, hands on hips, a tower of fed-up matriarchal rage. Lien and Darius shared a brief look of instinctive male terror before diving for cover in opposite directions as the dwarf launched himself and the axe right at the place they had been standing just seconds before.

'Hector! Not the floor...*oh*, never mind...' Darius groaned as the axe struck and then cracked a flagstone, burying itself half way to the handle. Even this barely slowed the dwarf down though: he easily wrenched it free and spun around for a second try. He hefted the axe over one shoulder, preparing a second swing at Lien –

'*Stand down,* you dreadful little man!' Carla commanded, pulling Lien behind her like he was nothing more than a ragdoll, and fixing Hector with a belligerent stare. Gasps and screams issued from the ring of women, and if he had been quicker, Lien would have tried to drag them both aside, but Carla didn't as much as flinch as the axe bore down on her. At the last moment, the dwarf engaged every muscle he owned to halt the axe a few short inches from Carla's impassive face.

'Not to kill the ladies,' Hector grunted, his tone suggesting it was a rule he only reluctantly obeyed. 'But intruder: dead!' and he glared meaningfully to Lien, clutching at the back of Carla's towel. Hector made to dart around behind the woman. Lien's developing sense of masculinity elected to make a run for it over hiding behind a woman's towel. He shot across the chamber, skirting the pool, the dwarf in close and destructive pursuit. Tiring now of being shouted at, threatened and chased, the boy glanced back, making a quick calculation in his head. Without warning, he suddenly checked his speed, spun around and thrust his staff between Hector's stocky, speeding legs. The dwarf's face registered first surprise, then fury, but he was a helpless victim of inertia. Stumpy arms waving like a baby bird trying to take off, Hector hovered for a moment on the edge of the pool - before taking an inglorious belly flop into the clear waters. The axe sank immediately, Hector only shortly behind it as his chain mail weighed him down. The women burst into spontaneous applause, which Lien, grinning from ear to ear, acknowledged with a quick salute of his staff, before legging it out the exterior door Hector had entered through minutes earlier. Darius went to follow but had his exit blocked.

'Divinia - !' he started, but she pointed imperiously towards the pool. Darius peered over the edge of the pool. Hector was lying face down on the bottom, arms and legs helplessly flailing.

'That is a truly beautiful sight,' the lame man sighed, leaning heavily on his sabre. Bubbles escaped from around the dwarf's helmet.

'Although. Uh. Do you think he can swim?' he added, slightly guiltily.

'Shouldn't think so, under all that armour,' Carla said, in a tone that strongly suggested Darius should be the one to do something about it.

'Oh no you don't, don't go looking at me like that,' Darius warned, glancing pointedly down at his bad leg. 'You don't get to wave all this women's independence business around only when it's convenient.'

Divinia shrugged.

'He's got us there, Carla. But really, can't we just leave him there – '

'Divinia, the very thought!' Carla exclaimed, removing her towel with a provocative flourish before throwing it at Darius. It would have landed on his head, had he not testily caught it in one hand. She was, as it turned out, wearing a swim suit underneath it.

'Come on Div,' Carla commanded, and the two women dropped into the pool.

'If it's any consolation, this is probably the cleanest Hector's ever been!' Darius called encouragingly from above, earning a drenching for his troubles. Behind, Lady Beckworth lounged in the door through which Darius had entered, observing the chaos of the chamber with the suggestion of a smile brushing the edge of her lips.

'What a jolly exciting afternoon,' she observed cheerfully, and laughed fully when the soaked Darius turned to face her. She noticed the shattered flagstone.

'I see that our intruder met Hector then,' she said. 'So where is the little devil?'

'Which one?' Darius asked dryly. He glanced down to the pool, where a couple of other women were now helping lug the dwarf plus his body weight again in armour towards the steps. 'Hector took a face plant into the pool.'

'Do him some good to be taken down a few notches. Where's the boy?'

'Legged it. No doubt vaulting over the back wall as we speak.'

'I think this is what one could call a comedy of errors,' Selene sniffed. 'But never fear, I have no doubt he will turn up again soon enough.' She grinned. 'Probably later today.'

Lien practically flew across the lawn, immensely relieved to be free of the confines of the atrium, the awkward attentions of the women, and of people trying to maim, if not kill him. Clearly he had much to learn about how Avenel and its crazy inhabitants worked.

Knowing the back wall was lower from this side, and driven on by adrenaline, Lien pulled a trick he had only tried a few times with Bravo - without a great deal of success, it must be said - while attempting to scale trees without low branches. He sprang powerfully from the ground, his bare feet finding scant purchase against the rough stonework, but just enough to almost *run* two steps up. The momentum carried him high enough that his reaching fingers skimmed the top of the wall. However he had made a grave miscalculation: in grabbing the top of the wall, he had to open his hands completely, such that his staff dropped down to the ground. He had not had the time or forethought to return it under the belt, and he cursed his error. Dealing with one crisis at a time though, Lien used a quick push from his left foot to force enough rotation into his body to swing his right leg up high enough that the side of that foot landed on the top of the wall, from which he could drag his whole body up horizontally. Ignoring the stinging grazes to his feet, shin, knees and thighs, he quickly moved into a crouch, from which, to his great relief, he could see Jest again looking curiously up at him. On the other side of the wall, a noisy crowd of women were spilling from the atrium and through the cloisters to watch his departure. Directly below on the house side of the wall lay his beloved staff, which Lien briefly considered dropping back down to retrieve, until a series of shouts preceded a bedraggled but enraged Hector pushing his way to the front to take up the chase. Lien swore again, but instead of going back for the staff, steeled himself for the joint-crunching drop back to the road level, the irate dwarf's bellow ringing in his ears.

# 13. The Sign of the Angel

Lien had no further leads to follow until Rupert emerged from classes, so after riding aimlessly around Avenel at ground level for around an hour, decided to take care of two hungry tummies: his, and that of Jest, who was used to grazing freely all day. Jest now hadn't eaten since they had started out across the plain, rendering the normally good-natured pony testy. Avenel seemed to have thoughtlessly buried all the grass under stone, or locked it up behind walls. Arriving back on the Kings Way, Lien surveyed the wagons rolling slowly along the road laden with, amongst other things, hay, and decided to test an idea. It was a resounding success, and after half an hour of standing to the side of the wide road and letting Jest snake his head out for strategic snatches of hay, the pony's kind temperament was restored. For himself, Lien rode Jest for a short distance along the Way behind a fruit wagon, surreptitiously lifting a couple of shiny red apples from a basket, which he then ate in a quiet side alley, sharing the cores with Jest. It wasn't a lot for a hungry growing teenager, but Lien was used to eating only erratically and the tart juicy apples lifted his mood as well.

The sun was making a slow late-afternoon descent when they arrived back at The Sign of the Angel. The tie-up rail was not as packed as it had been earlier at midday, but Jest looked put-upon nonetheless when he realised he was to be returned there. Lien shrugged helplessly to his pony and promised to sit with him until Rupert arrived. They first took a drink each at the trough - Jest much more enthusiastically than Lien - and then Lien dunked his head for the third time, before shaking it until his hair stuck out in all directions. He was giving Jest a thorough scratch under his sweaty bridle straps, his whole focus on the pony's contented face, when he felt the touch of that wild espréi again.

Lien's eyes snapped up and finally beheld the man who had been following them all afternoon. There was no mistaking which man in the area he must be: as seen in the alley with Cobi, he wore a light, slate grey, full sleeve hooded shirt that denied a clear view of his face. And beyond that, he was tall, broad and moved with athletic ease - exactly as Lien had expected from the nature of his espréi. Lien watched him openly, but the man simply walked past, just yards away from the tie-up rail, casual as you like, without even a sly sideways look in his direction. Lien was wondering whether he ought to go and speak to the man directly, when he heard another tolling bell from within Voltanna. Many bells rang the hours across Avencl and Lien didn't like the way they cut the day up into segments. The Voltanna bells however seemed to have no rhyme or reason, ringing out independently and apparently whenever they liked. This was the longest bell heard so far, and Lien hoped it might mean the end of the chevaliers' day. Sure enough, there was soon an increase in foot and horseback traffic from Voltanna, and eventually Rupert arrived, lingering awkwardly outside the alehouse, clearly unsure - or nervous - about what to do next. Lien called his name and gave him a friendly wave from where he was sitting on the tie-up rail. Rupert looked hugely relieved and headed over.

'Hello Rupert,' Lien said happily. 'Tell me, is everyone in this city crazy?'

Rupert considered before answering.

'Have you been getting in trouble, Lien?' he asked cautiously.

Lien's eyes widened innocently.

'Me? Of course not,' he assured his new friend.

Rupert sceptically ran his eyes over the many new bruises and scrapes on Lien's arms and legs.

'Are you sure? Only I heard someone broke into Castelle Travers this afternoon,' he said suspiciously.

'Never heard of that, Rupert, can't have been me,' Lien said cheerfully.

'Castelle Travers is Lady Beckworth's home,' Rupert said dryly.

'*Oh*. Well. I mean, *strictly* speaking I didn't know that, because you didn't tell me which house was hers, so really, I would say there just a series of coincidences and misunderstandings and actually I'm sure we could just head over and you could explain it all and – '

'Lien, *I* can't take you back there now,' Rupert interrupted him. 'I'm not what you would call an actual acquaintance of the Lady, and now they're looking out for you. We need Citar, I couldn't find him all afternoon. I'm sorry, I did warn you to wait.'

'Actually, speaking of warnings, I don't think I fully understood what you meant about Lady Beckworth's ladies – '

*'Lien?!'*

This time Lien was cut off – and Rupert saved from yet another awkward attempt to explain the business end of

Castelle Travers - by Citar, standing and staring at them from a few feet off. She had clapped a hand over her mouth, horrified that she had so been surprised as to call his name out loud. She was also horrified to discover that she was almost as happy, as surprised, to see the boy.

'What are you doing here in Avenel?' she asked, her voice dropping as she jogged over, glancing surreptitiously around.

'Hello Rupert,' she added shortly, her eyes glued to Lien though.

'Hello Citar!' Lien said, beaming. 'You're exactly who we needed to find!'

'Wait...did *you* break into Castelle Travers this afternoon?' she asked suspiciously, eyes narrowing. When neither boy answered immediately, she glared from one to the other.

'I *said* I'd bring Lady Beckworth to you! Going there was dangerous, hell, being *here* is dangerous, so *why* are you in Avenel at all?' she demanded. Lien held his hands up, as Darius had ordered him to earlier.

'C-citar, h-he h-had to come,' Rupert started but Citar shushed him with a glare. The prince weakly gestured to Lien to continue, but Citar shook her head exasperatedly.

'We're too exposed out here - let's get a table down the back where you can both explain to me what on earth is going on,' she sighed. When Lien donned his black silk tie over his left eye again, she stared, went to say something, thought the better of it and simply shook her head as she hustled the two boys into The Sign of the Angel.

If the pool chamber had felt enclosed to Lien, the crowded

alehouse felt utterly claustrophobic. Its usual clientele tended to be men of violence and breadth, many of whom stored a small arsenal of weaponry around their person. They were in fact like portable human armouries, with daggers, sheaths, swords and bows poking out at all angles, ready to trip up unsuspecting passers-by. This would immediately constitute an insult and lead to a fight of some description, which on a good day could potentially escalate into an all-out brawl. Women of even limited sensibilities tended to avoid the place, with its practically tangible, turgid cloud of testosterone hovering just below the exposed beam ceiling.

Lien made a valiant attempt at entering nonchalantly, but with his wet hair having dripped down his vest, Divinia's feminine handkerchief tied to his right arm, the black silk tie jauntily tied half across his face like he was a teenage pirate, and with his single visible eye wide as a saucer at the many unfamiliar sights, he failed completely. He drew dozens of curious and suspicious stares as he weaved his way lithely through the obstacle course of sweaty men and sharp and deadly objects. Citar chewed her bottom lip as she clocked the many stares but she missed the only important one: that of Sir Bane. But even if she had seen it, she wouldn't have known how dangerous it was.

Cira and Jordan had worshipped the Red Knight after meeting him as children, and had planned to come to Avenel to help him restore the king to the throne. But when Citar next encountered Bane, as a boy ready to participate in the Commoner Trials, he had not even spared a first look at her, much less a second. When she had then passed the Trials and been admitted to the Order as a chevalier,

Bane's disinterest had changed to an obvious dislike. He did not approve of the Trials being reinstated and he certainly didn't approve of common boys being allowed in, even if they met the required skills. She had reluctantly come to realise that he was a cold and manipulative man, and that the kindness he had shown her years earlier had been opportunistic only. Falric's discretion around him should have warned her, but Bane had had such a profound impact on the impressionable children, they could never have believed that he was anything less than the model of chivalry. Now older and wiser, she found it hard to believe that he could have Lien's best interests at heart.

If Citar had seen Bane's cool stare, she would have turned and marched Lien straight back out of The Angel. But she did not see him, or the lackey he summoned and sent away with lazy gestures. As Lien explained quietly what had happened in Leaverness and his plans to find Areté, Citar was unaware that four members of the Avenel City Guard were being reluctantly sent to The Sign of the Angel. They were reluctant because, being located at the foot of Voltanna, The Angel was generally regarded as the domain of the Order of the Coeur, whose mandate had, until recently, included maintaining law and order in the city. The knights were still resisting the jurisdiction of the state-empowered Avenel City Guard, and so The Angel was not a place any guard who cared for the condition of their reputation, face, or even life, would willingly attend.

While the guards made their way over, Citar, Rupert and Lien hunched over a small bench at the back of the alehouse for Citar to finish quietly interrogating them to her satisfaction. As they concluded, and she sat back to consider their next step, she realised she recognised a similarly shushed voice to their right. She glanced over to see the back of a male teenager and, facing him, an older girl. This girl was staring critically at her companion when she noticed Citar staring at her, and as their eyes met, the boy also turned around to follow her eye line.

It was Tryst, and he took a double take as he took in first Citar and Rupert, and then Lien.

'Lien - ?!' he gasped, his surprise and even shock clear. Lien responded with an open, friendly smile to the two people on the next table.

'Hello Tryst! Who is your friend?'

Lien intended to look only at Tryst but found himself unexpectedly transfixed by his companion. She would have been distinctive simply for being the only member of the fairer sex to be in The Sign of the Angel - Citar under her male glamour notwithstanding - but there was something else about her that held Lien's gaze. She was innately elegant, but also strangely austere. She was dressed in a faded green tunic and had her fair gathered into a loose bun. To Lien, she was the most beautiful woman he had ever seen, and he had just been in Castelle Travers with some of the most beautiful women in Avenel.

'Really?' Citar demanded, noting Lien's look with exasperation but also a little jealousy. Tryst scowled and his companion returned Lien's hapless stare with a very cold glare. Lien gave her a fleeting, embarrassed smile and looked back to Tryst.

'Gosh, you look terrible,' he said with unfiltered but genuine concern, upon seeing Tryst properly. The chevalier flinched, but there was no way of hiding the livid purple marks on one side of his face, and the raw grazing on the opposite temple. He looked drawn and exhausted after two sleepless nights.

'I was worried about you in the parade. Good thing Armitage was there with you,' Lien continued, completely failing to read the room.

'I'm fine, I didn't need any help,' Tryst said coldly, pulling himself together while the others looked awkward.

'Did your father do that to you?' Lien continued, remembering what Cobi had said about Tryst and his father.

Now everyone stared: first at Lien, then at Tryst, whose face darkened dangerously.

'Of course not,' he snapped. 'And it's none of your business anyway. Why are you here?'

'And who *are* you?' Tryst's companion asked.

'Hello! I am Lien, and I am from Hireath,' Lien said, a little proud at his obedient recitation. When the three chevaliers looked puzzled by this, the girl frowned.

'Hello Lien from Hireath. What's wrong with your face?' she asked suspiciously.

'I have an eye infection. It is grotesque,' Lien said, far too cheerfully given the subject matter.

'No, he doesn't,' Tryst sighed, shaking his head. 'Who have you been talking to, Lien?' He looked to his companion. 'He's actually from – '

'*Hireath*,' Citar interrupted, with a forceful glare at Tryst.

'We can trust Jessan,' Tryst glared back.

'Actually Tryst, I don't know *who* we can trust, given that someone sold Lien and his people out. That's why he's here.'

A silence fell on the small group while Citar and Tryst continued to glare at one another.

'I'm sure it wasn't Tryst,' Lien attempted to parlay

between the two. 'Are they always like this?' he asked Jessan, with what he hoped was a winning smile.

'I have never even seen them speak to one another before,' Jessan said slowly, looking curiously between Tryst and Citar. Then she looked suddenly away, towards the front of the alehouse.

'Trouble is coming,' she said.

'How do you know?' Lien asked, impressed.

'I can feel it, but really, you just need to look over there,' she said, nodding to where the four guardsmen were cautiously entering the alehouse. The presence of guardsmen here was an unusual event and so immediately drew attention. Cote, the proprietor of The Angel, made an immediate beeline to intercept them before his furniture started getting broken - most likely over the heads of the guards.

The leader, Sergeant Dedrick, had a quiet word with the barman before heading over to Sir Bane, Cote trailing unhappily. Dedrick tugged anxiously at the damp sweaty neck of his blue uniform as they approached the legendary Red Knight, who greeted them suspiciously magnanimously before quietly explaining why he had called them. News had spread quickly of course that someone had trespassed into Castelle Travers and assaulted the vicious dwarf who guarded the manor and its residents. Dedrick could not afford to make the personal acquaintance of any of the ladies in Lady Beckworth's employment himself, but he had seen Hector remanded for any number of felonies before his surprising turn to gainful employment, and was frankly astonished that anyone would - much less could - lay a finger on the wretched fellow. When Sir Bane explained that the perpetrator of such violence was present in The Angel, Dedrick swallowed hard, expecting to be faced with a hulk of a man.

Instead, he took a surprised double-take when Sir Bane pointed out the alleged criminal in question.

'But Sir – !' the Sergeant protested out loud, breaking the otherwise hushed volume of the conversation. Shortly after though he summoned over his three companions and they proceeded to weave their way to the back of the alehouse in the wake of the Dedrick's continuous stream of polite but increasingly tense mutterings of *do excuse me* and *would you mind sir* and *if you would be so kind as to remove your sword*. They fielded a barrage of stares, mostly hostile with an edge of curiosity, all the way.

The five teenagers watched their halting progression suspiciously; as they got closer, Tryst turned away and looked steadfastly down, indicating for Jessan to do the same.

The guards at least had the decency to look apologetic as they assembled awkwardly in a half circle around the bench at which Lien, Citar and a terribly anxious Rupert sat.

'Hello gentleman, how can we help you?' Citar asked brightly, but one of the guards was already sharing a look of mutual recognition with Lien.

'Didn't get yourself to a doctor I see, son,' the guard said, frowning, and wondering what bollocks Bane was setting them up for.

'You know each other?' Citar asked, surprised.

Lien nodded cheerfully.

'Yes, we had a very nice chat,' he confirmed, unsure of whether he ought to feel anxious or not. He could see that they were now the centre of attention of the alehouse, and that both Citar and Rupert were very nervous. Tryst remained turned resolutely away, while with occasional side glance, Jessan looked very taken by all the intrigue.

'I didn't catch your name though,' Lien added, politely.

'Corporal Cisco, Avenel City Guard.' Cisco looked uncertain, as did his three companions, and especially his Sergeant.

'I wonder if we could just go and have another of those nice chats,' Cisco continued, since he seemed to have inadvertently found himself taking the lead.

'Draw up seats,' Citar offered cautiously.

'Not here,' Sergeant Dedrick said.

'Then where?' Citar quickly countered.

'Down at the yard,' the sergeant snapped. 'Where do you think?'

'Are you arresting him, Sergeant?'

This cold question came from Tryst, who reluctantly pivoted around to level an imperious stare upon the guards. Realising he was now dealing with Sir Bane's son, defending the boy Sir Bane had instructed he arrest, Dedrick wondered what he'd done to deserve this ridiculous charade occurring during his watch.

'Yes,' the sergeant confirmed with a steely glare at Tryst.

'Kind of,' Cisco inserted, not wanting to see an unnecessary escalation between the guard and a scruffy teenager. 'Listen, I'm sure this is all a misunderstanding but really, we need to have a chat with - ' and here he indicated Lien, who helpfully supplied his name, ' - with Lien here to clear it all up. No need for any excitement. Just a - friendly - chat about where he's been this afternoon.'

'Oh, well I can't leave my friends right now, we have a very urgent problem to solve,' Lien said with a helpless shrug. 'I could come by later, if you tell me where to find you?'

'I don't quite think you understand what's going on here, kid,' Dedrick growled, tiring of this strange encounter. 'We're not *asking* you to come with us. We're *telling* you, and if you don't want to come, we'll *make* you.'

'They are arresting you,' Citar explained to Lien's blank face. 'They represent the law.'

When he still looked blank, she tried again.

'They think you have broken rules, which they enforce.'

'But I haven't done anything wrong,' Lien protested. 'I don't want to be…arrested.'

'It d-doesn't really w-work l-like th-that,' Rupert stammered anxiously. 'Y-you h-h-have to g-go w-with them.'

'And you can come the easy way - or the hard way,' Dedrick said, laying a suggestive hand on the sword sheathed at his hip.

'Then I choose the hard way,' Lien said defiantly, getting carried away with the machoism of the whole thing and pushing back his stool to stand up head to shoulders with the increasingly short tempered sergeant. Seeing Tryst's companion roll her eyes and Rupert frantically shake his head though, Lien suddenly wondered whether he'd made a strategic mistake. While three of the guards ignored Cisco's gestures to the contrary and tried to draw their swords - unsuccessfully given the enclosed space available - Lien leaned back into his friends to whisper 'But seriously, what *is* the hard way?'

Mere minutes later, the four sterling representatives of the

Avenel City Guard were running into problems. It wasn't as though the strange boy was persistently evading apprehension through any particular martial skill; it was simply that he was never where they needed him to be, in order to show their own. He had escaped their initial attempts at detention by leaping over tables, chairs, shoulders and even heads as required, and seemed able to anticipate their every move, variously slipping, skipping, ducking, dodging, flipping or cart-wheeling out of the reach of their hands and batons.

Every single time.

Had Sergeant Dedrick and his men tried to apprehend Lien almost anywhere else in Avenel, any present members of the Order would have delighted in intervening on their behalf, just for the sheer pleasure of embarrassing the Guard. But this was The Sign of the Angel, where it was unanimously understood that it would be more entertaining to allow the Guard to embarrass themselves with their inability to apprehend a dishevelled teenage boy, than to help them out. Thus the audience, able to gauge when they were on to a good thing, obligingly pushed back tables and chairs and shuffled themselves into a wonky circle, within which the attempted arrest could continue unobstructed. The Angel's owner, Cote, was standing stony and cross armed on the edge of the circle, grimly calculating how likely it was that damage would start to be inflicted on his property.

For his part, Lien was astonished at how slow and easy to evade his four adversaries were. Even with his depth and field of vision compromised by the necktie covering his left eye, he was always ahead of the guards. He was, if anything, starting to bore of the game, but was far too polite to allow it to show. Sparring of this type occurred regularly amongst the People, when the more experienced adults would slow a little, decreasing the complexity of their moves to better allow the younger generation to study and practice their martial and gymnastic skills. Here however, Lien found himself playing the role of the elders to these slower, less skilled adults. Actually hurting them did not occur to him: he had been raised to consider the injury of others as a sacred last resort, and Lien had never in his life physically harmed another person on purpose.

The rest of the crowd, on the other hand, were thinking that however gymnastically impressive Lien's evasion was, at the end of the day, it represented only defensive tactics and was thus proof that he did not really know how to fight. Unless someone managed to get hurt, and soon, the onlookers would lose patience and take matters into their own hands.

The chevaliers and Jessan had only been able to watch helplessly as Lien led the guards a merry dance around the inside of The Angel. Having started at the back of the alehouse, they had to force their way through the crush of spectators to get to the makeshift ring when it emerged. Restlessness at the lack of blood was spreading as Citar finally pushed her way to the front, just in time to see Lien easily ducking under a reach for his head; but the speed at which he dropped was so great that the tied-off section of Cobi's headscarf hung momentarily in the air above his head. Dedrick's hand closed onto this in a vice-like grip, so that the whole thing peeled off Lien's head to hang loosely in the surprised man's hand. That initial surprise however was nothing compared to that caused by the now exposed tattoos around Lien's left eye. The audience audibly inhaled, and Corporal Cisco stared.

Sir Bane suddenly looked less amused by the circus he had set in motion.

'That's not quite a hideous eye infection you got there, son,' Cisco said, coldly. Lien clamped a hand to his eye and reached with the other for the black strip of silk, but the sergeant jerked it back sharply.

'What is the meaning of this?' Dedrick growled, crumpling the silk and throwing it aside.

'He's from the People!' came a shocked shout from the gathering. The guards all looked spooked by this. The ring provided room to finally safely draw swords, which three of them now did. Cisco left his sheathed, for he considered three swords against one unarmed boy to be overkill. With the dangerous possibility of the arrest *becoming* a kill.

Sharing similar thoughts, Citar turned to the figure on her left, essentially risking suicide by unsheathing the swarthy man's sword with one smooth movement.

'Oi!' Citar yelled, and as Lien turned, she tossed the sword, hilt up, to the boy. This neatly represented about the exact amount of time the drunken victim of theft took to gather enough of his wits to gather Citar's collar in one ham fist, hauling the chevalier close enough to be almost anaesthetised by his stale alcohol-ridden breath.

'En-ter-tain-ment!' Citar spelt out desperately, nodding encouragingly to the newly recruited performance troupe. The drunken man paused, as the carefully broken-down syllables slowly penetrated his brain, and finally nodded approvingly.

'Yes, is good!' Citar agreed, monosyllabic with wild cheer, then coughed loudly as the big man dropped her back to her feet and gave her a massive approving slap on the back.

Back in the centre of the circle, Lien was looking down the length of the roughly hewn sword as though it were a foreign object. Naturally he had seen the ones the boys annually trophied from the visiting chevaliers in Leaverness, and he and Bravo had stolen into Sky's collection once to try them out, but given up shortly after as the damn things were too heavy and unwieldy for any real fun to be had. But he recognised that the game had changed as soon as he had grasped the braided hilt. The crowd cheered and the four guardsmen suddenly took the whole affair far more seriously, gathering together at a warier distance from their young opponent. Even Cisco reluctantly drew his sword, now that their opponent was armed. In such manner, the five circled one another guardedly for a few rounds, during which the crowd quietened down, enjoying the rising suspense. *Now* there seemed a better chance of someone getting seriously and amusingly maimed.

Lien was using the circling pause to learn, fast. He was watching exactly how the guards held their swords, and was feeling the weight of his own, trying to find the balance. He wasn't to know that Citar, with the best of intentions, had picked him a weapon as well-crafted and balanced as a shovel, quite aside from being far too long and heavy for a teenage boy.

One of the guards broke the stalemate with an enthusiastic forward thrust. Lien side stepped to block the horizontal strike with a vertical push but the move was laboured as he struggled to wield the sword with any of the elegance he had imagined he might. The guard, realising his opportunity, swiftly struck again from the other side and landed a glancing cut down Lien's right side as the boy managed only a clumsy half parry. Lien looked down in shock and astonishment at the red stain blooming on his vest, while the crowd went wild over the first blood. He had been cut and battered in training before, but only as a result of his own incompetence or genuine errors; never by armoured men being cheered on by a bloodthirsty crowd.

Three of the guards were buoyed by this first victory; Corporal Cisco was sickened though. He had joined the Guard to Uphold Peace and So Forth, not to cut up a clearly confused teenager for sport. He indicated to his companions to fall back, in the hope of resuming verbal negotiation, but they were stinging from the list of embarrassments Lien had so far heaped upon them. They rushed him, three to one. Citar watched in anxious disbelief as Lien struggled to defend himself with a series of awkward blocks and evasions - and no attacks of his own.

'You *do* know how to use it, don't you?' Citar demanded, making her way around the inside the circle to get close enough to speak to Lien. Lien flashed a desperate, helpless grin, barely managing to sidestep and block a heavy overhead strike. He was used to fighting staff to staff, where there was no distinction between a flat and edged side, and was getting too tired and overwhelmed to adapt quickly in the moment. He misjudged the next overhead block, which should have been angled to slide to the incoming blade off and instead simply met it head on, edge to edge, buckling him at the knees under the sheer weight and force of the older, stronger man's shoulders. Citar gasped audibly as the more bloodthirsty portion of the crowd - essentially everybody apart from her, Cisco, Tryst, Jessan and Rupert - *oooooooooed* appreciatively, anticipating the bloody finale.

Lien did the only sensible thing, under the circumstances. It was not something a knight or nobleman would ever do, but he was not and had no intention of being either of those things - although he was hoping to stay alive enough to enjoy *not* being them. What he needed now was not heroics, but a familiar weapon. One he was comfortable with. He dropped the heavy sword, rolled neatly out of harm's way and back onto his feet and, ignoring the protest from the cut down his side, legged it over to a slack faced man leaning on a broom.

'May I?' Lien asked politely but urgently, indicating the broom.

The man looked blankly from Lien to his broom and back again.

'No?'

'No, that should be yes,' Lien said as patiently as he could, under the circumstances. He could see the man wasn't quite all there.

'May I borrow your...thingy...?' he finished lamely, since the word "broom" had never entered his language lessons with Areté.

'No?' the man repeated simply.

'Oh. Er, please?'

At this point Tryst's companion, the tall, elegant and apparently quite bad-tempered Jessan, squeezed in next to the man with the broom. She rewarded Lien's rising blush with a highly unimpressed look that had "what*ever*" written all over it, but for reasons of her own, bailed him out nonetheless.

'Ant, give the stupid boy the broom please, love,' she asked, her tone warm to Ant even as her eyes remained coldly locked onto the still-gaping Lien. Ant shrugged and let go, allowing the girl to pass the broom over. This was exactly the moment when every young man needs a best friend at his side to provide a timely elbow to the ribs; without Bravo present to oblige, Lien simply continued to stare in that very foolish way any infatuated boy will.

The crowd quietened at this unexpected romantic turn, some of them now wondering whether they weren't actually watching a half decent display of street theatre. It was left to the rapidly mounting amusement of the guardsmen to drag Lien back to reality.

'You'll have more luck with us than with that one, boy,' one taunted. 'Glaciers melt faster than her heart!' and a rumble of approving guffawing laughter broke over the room. Lien's expression slid from entrancement to confusion. The girl's face, on the other hand, never changed.

'You going to just stand there, or you going to clean these jokers up?' she demanded. 'And I say that sarcastically, since you've exchanged a perfectly good sword for a *broom*.'

'Um...?' Lien tried. The girl rolled her eyes and physically turned him around to face his antagonists with an exasperated 'Oh do get *on* with it!'

As Lien faced the guardsmen once more, he consciously tried to pull himself together and regain his focus. Sky would not be having with such a distraction during a match. As for Areté...

Lien grinned, suddenly. Areté would have thought

him being rendered speechless by a girl was a cause for celebration, closely followed by merciless mockery. He took huge, unexpected comfort from this realisation. He then took a deep breath, centring himself in the moment and his purpose for being in Avenel. He was here for Areté. He was here for the People. The citizens of Avenel were all crazy, but they were only an obstacle and obstacles were for overcoming. He spun the broom handle twice, to get a feel for the dead weight on the end, and struck a defensive stance, inviting the commencement of the next round.

The guards, however, refused to engage. Lien raised one eyebrow and gestured them to attack, but they refused, to a man.

'Look, that's a broom, that is!' one pointed out, offended. There were knights present. This was too much. Lien glanced down at the ragged broom head and shrugged – it was indeed a disrespectful choice of weapon.

'Fair enough,' he agreed, placing one foot on the broom just above the head and with sharp leverage, snapping it off.

He heard a strangled whimper from behind.

'Sorry, I'll...um...find you a new one...?' he added apologetically to Ant, who looked genuinely distressed at the demise of his favourite cleaning aide.

Jessan just glared.

Lien experimentally spun his new weapon – spectacularly so, now that it was balanced – before readying himself, pole tucked securely under one arm. He grinned.

'We continue?'

The guards shifted uncomfortably, looking to one

another for moral support. The audience, by now spilling out of the alehouse and into the street and in the mood for more free entertainment, started to bait them rowdily. City guard reinforcements tried to enter, but Bane stopped them in their tracks with sharp hand signal. He looked less relaxed about the whole thing now, but was not yet ready to pull the plug.

As the chant of *Fight, Fight, Fight!* reached a crescendo, the match resumed. Mobile once more, Lien leapt and spun and danced around the irate guards, but in doing so, returned the fight to the stalemate at which it had started. Despite the heat and his growing fatigue Lien was, for his part, actually now enjoying himself for the first time since arriving in Avenel. Citar however was getting frustrated and crept around the inside of the circle, waiting for the opportunity to grab Lien and have A Word. When the chance finally came, the words were: 'This isn't a circus; finish this, before they finish you!'

Lien half turned, confused.

'They don't know the rules,' he complained.

Citar stared at him.

'This isn't a game!' she said. 'You've got to beat them, or get out of here!'

Lien frowned.

'You *want* me to hurt them?' he asked, puzzled.

'Well yeah, dumbass, if you *can*,' Jessan snapped from where she was standing with one arm comfortingly over Ant's shoulders. Lien shrugged. Clearly he did not understand the rules of Avenel, but he could see that he had drawn far too much attention to himself and needed to make an exit. And so he turned back to finish the match, exactly in the manner that he had always been taught not to do - for having been trained all his life to never harm another deliberately, he had thus far conducted himself with great restraint. Now given permission to let loose, Lien took a moment to centre himself and summon the spirit of the snake. His knees bent deeply, with the majority of his weight transferred to his back foot. He extended his right arm straight in front, the broken broom handle running from the forearm to over his shoulder. His spine lengthened. He inhaled.

The room quietened again.

Cisco realised he was actually holding his breath as he beheld this very strange sight. He quietly sheathed his sword, and stepped cautiously back while the other three guards advanced. Which is why he alone was left standing when, with the speed, accuracy and aggression of a striking snake, Lien disarmed and flattened the other three guardsmen in under thirty seconds.

A silence spread like a shock wave from the point of impact, out across the encircling crowd, and those at the back pushed and strained to see what had just occurred. Lien looked questioningly to Cisco, who shrugged and raised his hands in submission. Lien nodded, and turned to Citar.

'Like that is okay?' he asked, anxiously, panting from the exertion but bouncing lightly from foot to foot as the adrenaline coursed through his body. His voice rang out unexpectedly loudly across the hush.

Citar forced her jaw to close.

The audience was teetering uncertainly between lynching Lien and congratulating him, waiting for someone to take the lead in one direction or the other. It was Sir

Bane who took the lead with a few slow but powerful claps, which rippled from the front of the alehouse to the back, building into a raucous applause. Even Jessan was trying very hard not to look impressed.

Citar shook herself into action, leaping forward to grab Lien and propel him towards the exit. She realised a very large man was following directly behind her and turned to throw a dark, warning look at him, but took a surprised double-take that slowed her steps. His face was shadowed by a grey hood, under which he looked like a tramp: his face was covered in dirt, but his bright blue eyes were sharp and his face deadly serious. He first indicated *sssshhhh* with a finger to his lips before indicating she keep moving. Citar pulled her eyes back to the front, where she saw a new set of at least five guards pressing through the crowd towards them. Her breath caught in her chest because she knew Lien had been lucky with the first group: he had the advantage of surprise, and had turned it into a performance piece. These guards would be out for revenge once they realised what had just happened, and now, in the press of bodies, there was no room to move, much less for any of Lien's fancy footwork and gymnastics.

'We're in trouble now,' she said grimly over Lien's shoulder as, hands still on his shoulders, she manoeuvred him towards the door.

'Do we – fight?' Lien asked uncertainly.

'I'm not sure,' Citar admitted. 'I don't think so.'

Some of the patrons of The Angel obediently made space for the guards; others intentionally obstructed their progress. There was a cacophony of sound now – Dedrick was staggering back to his feet and yelling for the new guards to seize Lien; the new guards were yelling at people to get out of their way; those blocking their way were insisting they *leave the boy alone*. But all too soon they were on top of the two teenagers.

'Let go,' the man behind commanded quietly into Citar's ear. His low voice had such authority she surprised herself by doing as instructed, as she looked back over her shoulder. As soon as she had let go of Lien though, the man picked her up by her shoulders as though she weighed nothing, turned her and pushed her back into Tryst, who was pushing through behind. Citar bellowed in protest and tried to get back to Lien, but Tryst instinctively took hold of her.

When Citar let go of him, Lien had turned to see why. He too now encountered the huge man: the same man who had been following him all afternoon. He had been too flustered and distracted to even notice his espréi.

'Put your hands in the air,' the man instructed tersely. When Lien looked confused, he gave an impatient grunt.

'Put your hands in the air or they're going to kick five kinds of crap out of you,' he growled. Blanching, Lien turned back to face the guards with his hands in the air. Although he couldn't see it, the man behind him did the same.

'We surrender,' the man said, but now it was not with the clarity he had just used. Instead, he had suddenly acquired a drunken slur.

'Who the hell are you?' the first new guard demanded.

'I'm the boy's uncle,' the man said cheerfully, ignoring the surprised look his alleged nephew shot him. 'It's all a terrible misunderstanding.' He laid a friendly hand on the guard's shoulder. 'Let's go *talk* about it.'

The guard recoiled from the man's dirty face, shrugging his shoulder out from under the stranger's gloved hand.

'Chambers! Arrest that boy!' Dedrick yelled to the guard, finally making his way through the crowd. He and the other two guards Lien had taken out were all limping and various states of enraged as well as injured.

'He has just assaulted three members of the City Guard!'

Chambers looked in confusion from Lien – who looked unassuming and now increasingly perplexed about the situation – to the injuries of the first cohort of guards.

'This boy?' he asked doubtfully.

'Yes, he's very dangerous!'

'Does he *look* dangerous to you?' the stranger asked congenially.

'Not really,' Chambers said, looking Lien up and down with a raised eyebrow. 'Foreign. But not dangerous.'

'Exactly,' the stranger agreed jovially.

'*You* can shut up,' Dedrick growled at the huge man. He shrugged, putting his hands back up peacefully.

'We're coming, we're coming, just lead the way,' he said agreeably, though giving Lien a serious little nod as the boy looked questioningly to him. Lien didn't know what to make of it all, but sensed this man was here to help, and in the absence of a better plan, decided to go along with it.

'Well, let's go have that talk,' Chambers said, shaking his head, and turned with his men to head out of the crowded alehouse.

'Not *you,*' Dedrick growled, placing a restraining hand on the stranger's arm and manoeuvring himself between man and boy.

'We only want the boy.'

'To *talk* to?' the stranger asked, eyes narrowing

dangerously, letting the affable drunk routine slip.

'Right. To *talk* to,' Dedrick said, but his emphasis was chilling, and as he said it, and with surprising speed, he thrust one hand out, grabbing the side of Lien's head, and slamming it violently into the metal chest plate of a tall man standing next to him.

Quite a lot of things happened more or less simultaneously after that. The stranger swept Dedrick into a headlock and slammed his forehead into a wooden structural column. The patrons of The Angel who has seen Dedrick's dirty move broke out into protest at what had been done to Lien. People further back clamoured to be told what had happened. Chambers and the other guards leapt for the man claiming to be Lien's uncle. He threw them off like they were drops of water.

Lien meanwhile fell, dazed, into the surprised arms of the big man whose breastplate had just been used to assault him. As he felt his grip on reality slip, he felt the darkness surge forwards to take over.

'No – !' he gasped, trying to keep his hold on both consciousness and himself.

'You alright, son?' the man asked, as Lien stiffened in his arms.

'No, no no no – ' Lien panted, screwing his eyes shut and bringing his hands to his face as he tried to push the cold darkness down. Because his eyes were closed, he didn't see the guard – one he had previously taken down – pushing over towards him. The guard grasped his wrists, pulling his hands forward away from his face and wrenching him forwards. Lien's eyes shot open, startled, taking in the man's hard, angry eyes. Lien felt a different coldness as he realised, instinctively, that the guard was out for blood.

**LET ME.**

*No!* Lien thought back.

The guard who held Lien's wrists kneed him hard in the stomach. It was unprovoked and it was unnecessary. Lien cried out and doubled over -

- and let the darkness take over.

The stranger who claimed to be his uncle glanced over at the sound of Lien's cry. The guard holding Lien stood between them, so while he saw the boy sag around the knee in his guts, then snap back up, he could not see the reason the guard suddenly let go and stepped back. He did, however, see the distinct change in Lien's body language, and immediately shook off the guard he was fighting, to intervene.

'The hell - ?' the guard started when Lien's head came back up. He drew his knife but got no further because the boy launched forward at him. The guard went down, Lien's hands around his neck. Flailing, the guard punched his assailant in the left eye but the boy did not even seem to notice. Once again, a circle began to widen as The Angel's patrons also stepped back. Another guard went to pull Lien up but found the boy far too strong. Unnaturally strong.

The stranger pushed that guard aside and pulled Lien up, apparently without the issues the guard had experienced. Lien's struggling ceased though when his eyes met those of the stranger. But it wasn't Lien doing the looking. His pupils were liquid obsidian and his normally bright green irises were a metallic silver.

The stranger, not usually a man short of words, stared wordlessly. He kept his body blocking anyone's view of the boy's unnatural eyes. Guards were reaching for both of them, clawed hands grasping at arms and clothes; Citar and Tryst were pressing in too, trying to get to Lien. There was shouting all around.

With a grim, almost imperceptible shake of his head, the stranger made two fast strikes with the outside of his right hand, one on either side of Lien's neck. It was an expert, accurate carotid attack: risky but effective. Whatever it was that had taken over Lien, it could no more function during an interruption of blood to the brain than Lien himself. The boy crumpled. The stranger caught him, but as he did, he was stabbed with a knife in the right shoulder. He grunted and turned, Lien held in his left arm, his right arm catching, locking and breaking the arm of the guard holding the knife. The guard screamed; another guard swung a heavy fist which caught the big man on the right side of the face. Wanting to end the fight as quickly as possible, the stranger allowed the blow to take him to the ground. He tried to shield Lien's limp body as best he could with his own while feigning unconsciousness, as Dedrick and the guards proceeded to - as predicted only minutes earlier - kick five kinds of crap out of them until manhandled back by a grim Cisco, furious Cote and enraged Sir Bane.

And then a full brawl broke out.

# 14. KAI

A keen observer enjoying that evening's sunset might have noticed a magnificent bronze falcon swiftly crossing the Avenel Plain, before gliding austerely between the stone towers and turrets of the city, to finally alight on the crooked tin cockerel weathervane of a guardhouse. The setting sun bathed Avenel and the pale grey stone of the ancient fortress of Voltanna in an unusually peachy evening glow. It was a glorious sight Lien should have been denied, on account of being out cold in a small stone cell deep under the guardhouse. But although his body was sprawled out exactly as it had been unceremoniously dumped several hours earlier, his mind was active, though confused. As far as it was concerned, Lien - or something that looked a lot like him, minus all the physical ravages of the afternoon's exertions - was sitting cross-legged on a wide chimneystack atop the guardhouse. Despite the impossibility of his current circumstances, Lien felt no fear or even concern. He did however feel the piercing gaze of the regal falcon, perched incongruously astride the tin cockerel. Within a beat of his heart later, the falcon was gone, and instead Sky was serenely sitting cross-legged across from him.

'This isn't real, is it?' Lien asked, in his native tongue.

Sky smiled.

'It's real enough.'

'Have I - died?' Lien asked hesitantly, as disjointed memories of the afternoon presented themselves for inspection.

'No. But it was a close call.'

Lien nodded slowly.

'Sky, I'm so sorry. Again.'

Lien averted his gaze from those searching, intelligent eyes.

'Why now?' Sky asked gently.

'I have further endangered you, and the People. I am discovered.'

'You have lacked subtlety in your actions, it is true,' Sky agreed with a wry smile, 'but you were unprepared for facing Avenel. That is the fault of your guardians, not of your own.'

'I don't want to be here. I don't understand these people. I want to come home, to you,' Lien said.

'Home is a matter of perspective, Lien,' Sky said. 'Although you grew up with the People, remember that you were not born to us.'

The old man gazed around the rooftop panorama of Avenel, still warmed by the light of the dying sun. From up here, the city was a chaos of rooftops, plunging streets and open squares. Lien followed his gaze. He knew none of it.

'I was born…here…?' he asked, realising that he might finally get some true answers. He had been too numb to follow Sky's opening about his past the night before.

'You were,' Sky said. 'I kept telling Areté it was time for her to bring you here. But every year she would find another excuse not to.'

'Why?'

Sky considered how to answer, and took a roundabout

route.

'The People believe that ancestors are an inextricable part of the self. We would believe that, although you may not remember it right now, there is something of Avenel in you - and something of you in Avenel. But you have to understand that Areté has different ideas about legacy to that of the People, Lien. She believes that everyone chooses their own path, and that your past and ancestry can be irrelevant to your future.' He paused. 'I think this is what she needs to believe for herself,' he said thoughtfully, before turning a gentle gaze on Lien. 'And it is certainly what she would believe for you. So she wanted you to really find yourself, before you learned of your past.'

Lien went to ask for more - more information on his past, more about why Areté had withheld it, more about who he was - but Sky held up a hand, a small smile playing on his lips.

'For now though I am supporting Areté's position, however infuriating you may find it,' he said, kindly, but amused at Lien's exasperation. 'I do believe that in this situation, it is better that you are not told someone's else's story, to adopt as part of your own. You are more than your history, Lien. And I look forward to seeing what you discover, and decide, for yourself.'

Lien digested this in silence. He wanted so much to just have the answers he sought, and not more questions. But maybe Sky was right? Maybe where he came from *didn't* matter?

'I have never seen Voltanna look quite so beautiful as it does tonight,' Sky said as the sunset softened to pastel hues. The fortress did look magnificent with its pale stone turrets and ramparts painted in shades of pink and purple.

'But it is not a good place, and nor are its people,' Lien said, unmoved, and remembering Cobi's bitter words from that afternoon. To his great surprise though, Sky shook his head in disagreement.

'Voltanna is not evil, and nor are all the men and women within its walls.'

'But Sky, they attacked us, they – '

'The men who attacked us were not real knights, while the man who came to our aid was,' Sky reminded him. 'And I've seen the look in your eye when you behold Sir Armitage, Lien.'

'He is one good man among many,' Lien said quietly, but looking away, embarrassed that Sky knew how much he admired the knight.

'Then it seems to me that what the Order of the Coeur needs is more good men,' Sky replied lightly.

When Lien turned back to search the old man's eyes, to convince himself that he had misunderstood the sentiment, he found himself completely alone. As he looked around wildly for Sky, he saw only a falcon winging its way effortlessly towards the Avenel Plain and beyond it, Leaverness. Leaverness, where Lien wanted so much to go also. He watched Sky's graceful flight until he was lost in the distance and the failing light, a loneliness forming in the pit of his stomach. By the time Lien looked back to Voltanna, shadows were crawling across its walls. Now it looked less beautiful than gaunt and cold in the growing darkness –

– and then there was only darkness as the chimney stack, the city vista, and especially the clarity with which Lien had been able to think only moments earlier, all disappeared.

They were replaced with a crushing headache as Lien found himself making a slow and extremely painful return to the reality of his physical condition. The number of parts of his battered body screaming blue murder was overwhelming, so he focussed instead on the relatively straightforward matter of drawing shallow breaths through what appeared to be bruised, if not broken, ribs. Since it seemed that the pain from breathing was not going to improve, he turned to the next task: opening his eyes. Even this was difficult to do though, and he could open only one. He was in semi-darkness but even that initially felt too bright: his right eye stung and stars pricked around the edges of his blurry vision. Something was stopping his left eye opening, so he forced his left arm, which felt like a dead weight, to move enough that a couple of gingerly probing fingers could scrape off what turned out to be caked dried blood over a tender, puffy eye socket. It seemed he would have to remain single-eyed even without Cobi's silk scarf. He sent his fingers on a further reconnaissance mission; they returned with fresh blood from a gash on the left back side of his head – and thus, the pounding headache was explained. What was less obvious at that point in time was why he was laying sprawled out on his back, in half darkness, on cold hard stone. He continued to inspect his surroundings with his fingers, since sitting up was out of the question. Straw was scattered across the floor, but it was old, hard and spiky. He realised he was cold, possibly for the first time in weeks of baking heat. Part of that might be blood loss though, he groggily decided. He had a cold ache in his right side. His seeking fingers found a something tied around his waist. A cloth of some sort. The right side was wet with a warm, sticky liquid. This made sense: he remembered getting cut in the side. The rest of the damage he did not understand.

When did he get punched in the face?

He didn't *remember* getting punched in the face.

He tried to order the last things that had happened to him. Events and emotions permeated his concussion in a slow, disjointed manner.

He remembered Cisco, the broom, the permission to fight seriously, the cheers…

…and then Citar had got worried…

…and then the second set of guards had arrived…

…and then Dedrick had got nasty…

…and then the darkness had tried to rise…

…but he fought it down…

*…and then he had let the darkness go.*

Lien groaned out loud.

'Finally, it awakens.'

The gruff, male voice came from nearby. Lien automatically went to turn his head in the direction of the sound, and was rewarded with an explosion of stars across his single-eye vision. He gasped, audibly. What else had happened, that he could feel so terrible now?

'Don't try to move yet. I did say they would kick five kinds of crap out of you.'

'I don't…remember…?' Lien tried to say, but his voice was raspy as his dry mouth tried to make the words.

'Well. I don't think *you* were there at the end.'

*…and there had been that man…*

'*Are* you…my uncle…?' Lien tried again, licking his parched lips but with only a thick, dry tongue that made no difference. This was what it had felt like when last he was in dreaming inside Areté - but this time, it was his own body that was severely dehydrated.

'No, I am not. But I know you are Areté's ward, and therefore I felt an obligation to look out for you. Which, I might add, was considerably harder than expected.'

Lien heard the man get up as he said this, walk a few steps, then return to kneel behind his head.

'Areté…' Lien sighed, trying to hold onto her name as he said it, as though through it, he could hold onto her. 'You know her?'

'I have water,' the man said, ignoring the question. 'I'm going to support your head, only lift it a little,' he instructed. Lien gritted his teeth and strained to lift his head, gasping at the first painful effort. As soon as he managed a little rise off the ground, the man slid one hand under his head and neck and then one bent knee, so that between them, they shuffled Lien into an awkward semi recline. Every movement brought more blooms of pain for the boy, but he was desperate for the water and was eventually able to sip clumsily but gratefully from a dirty cup. The water was tepid and tasted even worse than that of the horse trough, but he didn't care, he would have drunk a lake of it.

'I think I'm…bleeding on you…' Lien mumbled, as he now distinctly felt the dampness on the back of his head against the man's chest.

'You're not the first and you certainly won't be the last,' the man said mildly.

'Where…are we?' Lien asked, trying to look around a little more from his propped up position.

'The good news is we're in the coolest place in

Avenel,' the man said. Lien couldn't see anything of him but a pale neck and long beard, since he was leaning back against him. What he could see though is that they were in a small, dark room made entirely of stone, and lit only by a flickering torch outside a line of metal bars. He noted just one detail at a time until his concussed brain registered what the whole picture reminded him of.

'This is a prison!' Lien gasped, and tried to sit right up.

'And yes, that's the bad news.'

The sudden motion made a wave of nausea surge through Lien's body, such that he sagged back against his unknown companion. The man supported him and gently laid the boy's head down into his lap.

'Easy there kid. You're going to have to take it slow,' he said. While Lien sighed and closed his eyes to ride out the nausea, the man used a dampened corner of his shirt to gently and carefully wipe more of the dried blood from around Lien's bruised, closed left eye. Lien stiffened, realising what else he would be seeing there.

'Don't worry, I've already seen it,' the man said, correctly guessing the boy's concern.

'You are not - afraid of me?' Lien asked.

'What is there to be afraid of? You bleeding on me some more? I have no quarrel with the People.'

Lien relaxed a little.

'Now that thing inside of you...that's another matter.'

Lien stiffened again and tried to get up. The man placed a firm hand to his sternum, holding him down.

'There's no hurry. You don't have to talk about it right now.'

'I don't - I don't even know what it is,' Lien said quietly.

'Has it taken over like that before?'

'Yes,' he admitted.

'When you were in danger?'

Lien gave a tiny nod.

'Handy. Some folk would be jealous of a little life-saving system like that,' the man said.

'They can *have* it.'

The man shrugged.

'You might want to understand what it is you have, before trying to give it away.'

'Who are you? And how do you know Areté? And…how are you here with me?' Lien asked, unable to get his aching head around that statement.

'I'm – Kai,' the man said, momentarily second guessing whether he ought to give his true name. It rang a bell, but there and then, Lien couldn't place where he had heard it before.

'Areté was…kind to me,' Kai continued. 'An aunt of sorts, I suppose.'

He met Lien's surprised, cyclops gaze.

'She collects lost souls like us,' he shrugged. 'And I'm here because Dedrick shot my attempt at a diplomatic exit. Since I knocked you out, I couldn't just leave you helpless.'

'*You* knocked me out?!'

'Believe me, you did not want to go around advertising that you have that thing inside you.'

Lien sighed and closed his accusatory eye. All the thinking and talking was making his head hurt more.

'I'm sorry. And…thank you. I can't control it, once it has taken control. I didn't mean to let it out.'

'It was an unfair situation you should never have been in,' Kai said. 'I would have expected Areté to have better prepared you for Avenel.'

'You know she's – missing?' Lien asked.

'I suspected,' Kai said. 'How do you know?'

'I have dreams,' Lien said, fainter now, too exhausted to consider how crazy this might sound. 'A night-mare takes me to her. I see through her eyes. Into her prison.'

'She's in prison?' Kai asked, apparently unfazed by this extraordinary claim. 'Do you know where?'

Lien vaguely shook his head as a catastrophic weariness broke over him. Talking was too hard. It could wait. There was nowhere to go, nothing to do, and he could barely move anyway. He would surely feel better after a sleep –

'Hey! Kid! You need to stay awake,' his companion ordered, realising Lien was lapsing into unconsciousness again. 'We don't have all night to hang around here.'

'But – where – is there – to go – ?' Lien asked, forcing the thoughts and words through the fog in his brain with difficulty. He heard the sound of something metallic being drawn across the stone floor and then a harsh clanging. He forced his right eye to open. A ring of heavy metal keys swam into focus. He stared at them blankly.

'You tell me,' Kai said.

'Is this – how – prison works?' Lien murmured, confused.

'Not normally, but I don't hold with being locked up, and I have very light fingers,' Kai grinned. 'We need to get you up.'

Lien sighed heavily but with Kai's assistance, and despite much pain from Lien's ribs and the wound on his right side, they got him into a cross-legged upright sitting position. Once he was sure Lien was not going to fall straight back down again, Kai got up from behind him and walked around so that he could now sit back down in front of the boy. For the first time, Lien was able to see more of his companion than his previously limited ground-up view of a bearded chin. Lit only by the flickering torch outside the cell, detail was limited, but there was a brightness to the man's blue eyes, even from behind his long dark hair. Lien's right eye squinted and his head tilted to the left as he tried to process what he was seeing.

The first thing that made Lien stare was the way sweat rivulets appeared to have run pale streaks down the sides of Kai's face. It was as though his companion's brown skin colour was actually an illusion produced by layers of dirt, under which he was so pale as to be practically white. Additionally, he had torn both the sleeves from his grey shirt, and the bare skin revealed was also pale. Like Areté, and Cobi – and the People.

'Are *you* from the People?' he asked, for the second time that day.

'Not according to Sky, but obviously, I had to wonder,' Kai said. 'I take it my dirt has run?'

'Uh…yes. Yes, it has,' Lien agreed, a ghost of a smile pulling around his lips. This was something he would normally find hilarious.

'Not to worry, plenty more where it came from,' Kai said, the shadow of a smile crossing his own face.

The second thing that made Lien stare was the bruising. Lien felt like he had been run over by a cart but Kai didn't look like he had fared much better. His face and arms were covered were livid bruises.

'What happened to you?'

'Some kid got himself into a fight with the city guard, and I tried to protect him when he ended up on the floor,' Kai shrugged carelessly.

'Kai I'm - I'm so sorry,' Lien said, appalled. He'd had no idea what this stranger had done for him in The Angel.

'I'm used to being kicked around. Dedrick would have killed you if he could. He's a nasty piece of work. Fortunately Cisco, Cote and Bane pulled him off us.'

Lien felt sick again. Kai reached an arm forward to steady his shoulder, which brings us to the third thing that made Lien stare at his companion: Kai's arms. He had been wearing a loose, light, long sleeved shirt all day as he trailed Lien. One torn off grey sleeve was now binding the stab wound on Kai's right shoulder and the other, Lien realised, was tied around his own slight waist to bind his side wound. The shirt was loose enough to conceal a massive chest but tearing off the sleeves had exposed broad, muscular shoulders that made him at least twice as wide as Lien. The man was *stacked.* Lien guessed Kai could throw a boy of his size over one shoulder and still outrun most anyone who chased him. This was not the lean wiry strength typical of the People; this had to be the sheeting of muscle required to wear and fight in heavy armour.

'Are you a knight?' Lien asked, also for the second time that day.

'Not according to the Order,' Kai replied dryly. 'Is it true the People were attacked in Leaverness?' he then asked, with a calculated change of the subject.

Lien nodded wearily.

'But the People are protected,' Kai frowned.

'By Sky and Areté. But Areté is - is gone,' Lien said, looking down at his lap.

'But where can she be that her enchantments are broken?' Kai mused. 'I mean there's gone and there's *gone.*

Perhaps I should have a chat with the men who went to Leaverness. Find out how they knew they could find you.'

'You know where they are?' Lien asked, a tiny surge of adrenaline lifting his eyes.

'I saw them being brought back into Avenel last night by Armitage. I've not seen such a sorry sight in years.'

'Where are they now?' Lien asked, head lifting fully up.

Kai regarded him intently before speaking.

'They're here. We're in the main Avenel guardhouse prison,' he said slowly, but speeding up as Lien started to try to get up at this news: 'But you can't even stand, so why don't you rest here while I pop out and beat some information out of them?'

'I can stand,' Lien insisted, contrary to all available evidence.

Kai cocked his head to one side and fixed him with a hard stare.

'Can you now?'

Lien thought to stand from where he was sitting cross-legged, but quickly realised he had wildly underestimated how difficult that would be. Instead, he put his hands down on the hard stone ground and adjusted his legs around until he was on hands and knees. From this position, he had a better chance of standing, but he was feeling so sick and weak he found himself seriously doubting he would make it up. He tried anyway, flexing his toes and pushing up with his arms as his legs drove his body up. He had to step his right leg forward and reach for Kai though as a head spin caused him to stagger. Kai, who had been watching this woeful progress grimly, caught him with a granite forearm. Even supported, Lien swayed alarmingly as his stomach and head turned.

'Lien. Be serious. Rest here, I will find them and come back for you,' Kai said.

'I can walk,' Lien said, through gritted teeth. He took his own weight evenly between his feet so that he could let go of Kai's arm. His legs shook. Lien had never been injured this badly before, there wasn't a part of his body that wasn't screaming for his attention, and he suspected he had lost a lot of blood. But he also knew he wasn't going to get to talk to the men who attacked the People with anyone except Kai, so he had a simple choice: walk, or miss the opportunity.

And there was no way he was missing this opportunity.

'I just – need a moment,' he muttered.

Kai went to argue, then paused, shrugged and stalked over to the cell door. He found the right key and reached around to unlock it from the outside, then turned back to where Lien was unsteady but still standing.

'Come on then. Let's go talk to these shitbags,' Kai said, holding an arm out to the boy.

Adrenaline is an amazing tool. The prospect of facing the men who had burned the camp, tried to kill his people and planned to steal him from Leaverness kicked Lien's system hard enough that he was able to slowly follow Kai's hulking shape through the wide, dank, flame lit corridor of the prison. The man ignored all the cries and entreaties of the other prisoners, some of who reached out desperately to beg for the keys, to beg to be freed. Lien flinched when arms reached too close, and carefully kept to the centre of the corridor, appreciating why it had been made so wide. They had not progressed far when, around a corner ahead, they heard the trundling of a cart and someone whistling a cheerful ditty between bouts of maliciously haranguing prisoners. Kai indicated Lien to be silent and still, and they waited until the guard was just around the corner from them. Kai then stepped out, and despite his instructions, Lien did too, curious to see what would happen next. The guard, a short and wiry man slowly pushing a food trolley, was taken completely by surprise as the huge prisoner loomed over him.

'W-what?!' he managed before Kai grasped him by the back on the head, smashing it straight down onto the top of the trolley. He grinned, humourlessly, as he dropped the guard into a limp pile on the ground. He bent down to take the guard's larger keyring, handed the smaller set to Lien, and indicated they were to continue. Stepping warily over the fallen guard, Lien felt very grateful that, so far, his dangerous companion seemed to be on his side.

After a few more twists and turns they came to a heavier, round wooden door, barred top and bottom.

'Special prisoners,' Kai grunted as he sorted through the larger ring he had stolen from the guard. He seemed to know what he was looking for, looking upon one thick metal key as though it were a prize of some kind. He had chosen well. The key grated home through the lock barrel, and the door swung open with the requisite groan of old wood and squealing of rusty hinges. Beyond were four cells, larger than those in the main prison, two on each side. There were two men in each of the first cells on the left and right. Four altogether, and Lien recognised all of them.

They all watched warily from their bunks as the man and boy entered.

'These your boys?' Kai asked loudly.

'That's them,' Lien said, his voice low.

Kai looked them up and down like they were something unpleasant on the soles of his battered boots. They all slowly stood from their bunks and approached the bars. They were various shades of injured, but nothing like Lien and Kai and they still looked like they would happily tear pieces off anyone who came too close.

'And what do you two want?' one asked, looking the man and boy up and down. To be fair, this didn't really help - there was only one torch at each end of the cell and with Kai and Lien standing in front of the nearest, there was little light on their faces from the torch at the far end.

'Kid wants to talk to you.'

Kai turned to Lien, who was feeling very out of place amongst these displays of adult aggression.

'Who's the kid, that we should listen?' another man asked. That was his first mistake. His second was stepping right up to the bars of his cell, and therefore into direct arm's reach of Kai. One moment he was leering unpleasantly, the next spluttering as strong fingers closed around his neck. Before his cellmate could react, Kai had pulled him forward which such force that he was knocked senseless against the bars. As he crumpled slowly to the ground, blood already running down his face and the bars, Kai glared around at the other three.

'Kai!' Lien protested, shocked at this second demonstration of what he considered disproportionate violence.

'Kai?' the first prisoner said, his confidence faltering.

Kai threw a sharp, dark look to Lien, who realised he had made a mistake naming his companion. As he shrugged apologetically, the name rang familiar again, but with his head still pounding, he still couldn't remember why.

'You should recognise the kid from your recent outing,' Kai growled.

The eyes of the man who was now alone in his cell narrowed with recognition. Lien had saved his life only the night before.

'It's the boy from Leaverness,' he said, glancing disconcertedly from Lien to his fellow prisoners.

'Correct, and you're going to tell him why you attacked him.'

'We didn't attack *him*. We went to *get* him,' the man Lien had saved said. He was looking Lien over as carefully as he could in the low light.

'Did you do all that to him?' he asked, his eyes flicking apprehensively between Lien's battered body and Kai.

'Don't be stupid. *I* don't assault children,' Kai said, so darkly that Lien realised the man who had gruffly cared for him in the cell was gone; the man in front of him was cold, distant and dangerous.

'Now listen and answer,' Kai continued, then turned a forceful but expectant glare to Lien. Lien swallowed hard. He could see that Kai was focussing on the lone man, the one Bravo had tried to kill, who was more likely to be the weakest link. Nothing in the world could have convinced him to swap place with someone who was so obviously a target for Kai's predatory instincts.

'Who ordered the attack on the People?' Lien asked, his voice thin in the tense atmosphere. The lone man remained silent, though his face betrayed his concern.

'I saved your life last night,' Lien reminded him urgently, his eyes imploring the man to cooperate. From his peripheral vision, he saw Kai's face slide between the stony mask to curiosity and back again.

'Answer him,' Kai snapped. The man shook his head. Kai started sorting through the keys, their clanging echoing ominously.

'You don't have the key,' the man said, but the waver in his voice betrayed his fear.

'You tell yourself that,' Kai said and Lien realised the big man was actually enjoying himself, in a twisted sort of way. He sorted through the set then held one up. To Lien, it looked like all of the others.

'I think it's this one,' Kai said. 'Shall we check?' and he advanced almost theatrically aggressively to the cell door.

'Don't say a word,' one of the men in the adjacent cell warned – standing well back from the bars.

'Easy for you to say!' the lone man returned, wide eyes never leaving Kai. 'You haven't got a psychopath coming in to say hello!'

'Don't worry, I won't leave them out,' Kai said, listening with satisfaction as the lock *clicked* open. He opened the barred door.

'Answer the question.'

'I can't,' the man said, desperately shaking his head.

'Why not?' Lien asked quickly, not keen to see more violence. Kai paused, looking back at Lien as though remembering his existence.

'Because it came from a man even more dangerous than you, Kai,' the man said, angry now. 'And a lot more powerful.'

'I don't know,' Kai said. 'I'm feeling pretty dangerous, and I'm the one who's about to walk into a cell with you. That's got to make me more powerful than the other guy in the here and now.'

He advanced a step into the cell.

'It came from one of the King's Knights!' the man said quickly, his hands held up in a pacifying manner.

'They are no more,' Kai growled, losing patience and closing the gap between them in impossible speed. He seized the man around the neck with an arm span such that, even at full stretch, the other man could not reach him. The stab wound in his right shoulder began to bleed anew through its binding, but he seemed not to notice.

'Two remain!' the man yelped. 'Come on - smart guy like you - you can - work it out - '

'I can,' Kai agreed. 'So, tell me *why* Bane ordered the attack.'

'Retribution. For the death of Du Romeau,' the man panted through Kai's tightening grip. Kai loosened it a little now though, allowing him to gasp gratefully for air.

'You're monarchists?' Kai asked, slightly dialling down the aggression. The man nodded as frantically as Kai's choke hold allowed, sensing the softening attitude.

'Why act against the People now though?' Kai asked suspiciously. 'It's been fourteen years.'

'Because their protection - is broken,' the man in his grasp said hoarsely. 'And because of the discovery of - the boy,' and he made a valiant attempt at nodding towards Lien. 'He had - no place being stolen - by savages.'

'I wasn't stolen, and they're not savages!' Lien protested angrily. 'You're the ones who attacked us, sacked our campsite. What had we done to you?'

'It's what your leader done, boy,' the man from the other cell said bitterly. 'He's dangerous.'

Lien moved to protest, but Kai silenced him with one warning hand, while releasing the other. The man gasped and clutched at his bruising throat.

'It's true,' Kai said. 'Sky *is* dangerous. He was certainly dangerous to Du Romeau, in the end.'

'How did you know the protection was broken?' Lien asked urgently. He had to know what they knew about Areté – *if* they knew anything about her.

'Bane didn't say,' the lone man rasped.

'Did he say anything about Areté?' Lien pressed.

The confused stare was honest enough for Lien to believe the man knew nothing.

'Did he say anything else?' Kai followed up. 'Any other – theories, or plans?' He threw a half look to Lien has he said it, and the man followed his gaze, understanding.

'He's interested in the boy,' he agreed. 'But I *swear* I don't know why. I mean – I can guess. We all guessed.'

'Guess what?' Lien asked.

Kai nodded thoughtfully, ignoring Lien's question. Studying him, Lien noticed two things almost simultaneously: the man in the cell with Kai looked much less compliant now that Kai had released him; and Kai appeared to have completely dropped his guard, going as far as to dismissively turn his back fully on a man he had just assaulted. Lien was thinking how unwise that was, when the man leapt at Kai's open back. But before Lien could even call a warning, Kai was already turning into the expected attack. He effortlessly caught the man into a headlock with his left arm and crashed his head again the cell bars. The metal bars were still reverberating as Kai spoke directly into the man's ear.

'That was a warning,' he said quietly. 'You know something more. What is it?'

The man gasped for breath, trying to blink a trickle of blood out of eyes.

'*You* - you and Lindahl - you turned the Order against commoners - you killed the chances of hundreds of other boys - and men - to join - ' he panted, but was interrupted by a second round of direct head-to-bars contact.

'Really? Are you sure that's all?' Kai asked, surprisingly calmly given the current violence. Glancing over at the men in the adjacent cells, Lien saw one of the men there was grim, the other openly frightened. This one looked down to their fallen companion, the man Kai had first knocked out, and his gaze stayed there. Lien followed it; the man was conscious now. Laying perfectly still, but watching the tussle.

'Kai - ' Lien started anxiously.

'Not now kid,' Kai snapped, tightening his grip on his prisoner's hair and neck, preparing for another knock.

'Kai! The other man!' Lien insisted, just as the man in question leapt up, launching himself at the intruder's back. But Kai seemed to be expecting that attack too, pivoting around with a knee-to-groin strike ready and a vicious circular right elbow strike to the temple to follow up. In the brief moments in which his prisoner was thrown to the left and the headlock loosened, the man attempted to lurch free. He never had a chance though. Kai twisted with his left arm.

The one around his neck.

There was a reverberating *snap* and the man fell limp.

Kai dropped his body to the ground.

'Oops,' he said, without even a pretence of regret.

Lien stared, horrified.

'You - you k-killed him?' he stammered, wide eyes dashing between Kai and the crumpled body that had, seconds before, been a living man who Lien himself had saved from Bravo. Kai ignored Lien though, turning instead to the moaning heap on the ground. The injured, concussed man was roughly hauled to his feet and pinned back against the bars, which again rattled their protest. His nose had been broken when Kai had initially dragged his face into the bars, and a gash on his forehead bled freely. His dazed eyes attempted to focus on the violent man who held him.

'What did that piece of garbage leave out?' Kai asked, still unsettlingly calm as one hand gripping his victim's throat painfully. The man tried valiantly to shake his head, but Kai grasped his chin and forced it around to see the corpse.

'You can join him, or you can tell me what I need to know,' he growled, very quietly, very close to the man's ear.

'Why tell you?' the man whispered, his voice hoarse from the constriction on his throat. 'You'll just kill me anyway.'

'Kai!' Lien protested, near tears. He was unable to bear such brutality, even against the men who had attacked the People. Sky had always insisted in the sanctity of life, all life, regardless of the way in which one chose to live it.

Kai shot a sharp sideways glance at Lien.

'You're lucky, the kid's soft and wants me play nice. You tell me what I want to know, you get to keep your life. Sounds like a fair deal to me.'

'You don't kill me, someone else will for talking to you,' the man managed, maintaining all the defiance he could muster.

'Maybe so, but I can make it a hell of a lot slower and more unpleasant.'

'Bane is setting a trap for Lindahl,' called a new voice. It was the grim man in the second cell, and it was the first time he had spoken. He was a tall, broad, bearded man, and he now stood right up at front of his cell, arms crossed, face set.

'That's assuming he's even alive,' Kai said slowly.

'Bane is certain that he is,' the bearded man countered.

Kai looked momentarily dubious, then realisation dawned.

'That's why the Marked Man is to be changed,' he said. As he did, Lien finally remembered where he had heard Kai's name before: in Leaverness, the chevaliers had been talking about Areté being made the Marked Man.

*Kai might be dead in a ditch, but a man like Lindahl does not just disappear.*

Kai *had* been a knight! And had spent years as one of the most wanted men in Avenel. No wonder he hadn't wanted Lien to use his name!

'The Order is pretending to have given up finding me and Lindahl, in the hope that he will return,' Kai continued, connecting the dots.

'And when they find out the Guard had their prodigal son in their guardhouse, there will be hell to pay,' the man in the adjacent cell said, smiling unpleasantly.

Kai shrugged.

'I never cared about the bounty, I've been here plenty,' he said dismissively. 'And it's a fun plan, but it won't work.'

'Why's that then?' the bearded man demanded.

'Because if I know Lindahl - and I know Lindahl better than anyone - if he's still alive, he's been here plenty too. You can't draw out someone who isn't actually hiding.'

'Lindahl will get what's coming to him - and so will you- ' the man in Kai's grip spat, but cutting himself off with a strangled gasp as Kai tightened his grip.

'Kai!' Lien protested.

The gasping became more desperate.

'Sky would never murder like this. And you say *he's* dangerous!'

'I never said that I wasn't as well,' Kai replied, his face an obscure, impassive mask.

But he did let go.

The man sank to his knees drawing shallow, shuddering breaths.

Kai left the cell in silence. He relocked the door, and indicated to Lien that they were leaving. But Lien didn't move, *couldn't* move. He was transfixed by the sight of the dead and gasping men. He had seen people *die*, but he had never seen someone *killed* before. Not by another person, and especially not by someone he knew.

'Kid!' Kai snapped from the heavy wooden door. 'Move it.'

Lien slowly dragged his eyes from the two men on the ground to Kai. He stared in a mixture of fear and confusion, and still did not move. Kai gave a sigh and stalked back towards Lien. Lien couldn't help himself: he actually flinched and stepped back.

Kai stopped, surprised.

'Looks like the boy's got you figured already, Kai,' the bearded man said, amused.

'I'm not going to hurt *you*, kid,' Kai said, a confused look displacing his scowl. 'I'm going to get you out of here.'

'But - you're a *murderer*,' Lien breathed, shaking his pounding head. The headache was being intensified by his fear and confusion, and he realised he was starting to have trouble breathing himself. He wanted to run, but he could barely stand. He stepped back again, shoulders hitting hard stone wall. His legs buckled and he slid down it, slipping into blessed darkness as he did. He was unconscious by the time Kai gathered him up and carried him back into the corridor and away from the jeers of the remaining two men. These were followed by shouts of 'Kai! Kai is in the prison!', which were picked up by other prisoners, who started to rattle their bars in fervour. Further shouts and clamour from ahead suggested that the guard Kai had knocked unconscious earlier had been found. Kai swore at the sound of footsteps running towards him, and the chorus of people shouting his name. He glanced down at the boy in his arms: Lien's eyes were open but glassily vacant.

Kai gently set Lien down on the ground, back to hard cool stone, gave him a last frustrated look, and left him.

This was exactly how Lien was found less than a minute later by Corporal Cisco. The guardsman crouched down to wave a hand up and down in front of Lien's blank, staring eyes. He gently pried his key ring out of the boy's fingers, re-holstering them on his belt.

'Well, can't blame a man for trying, eh?' he said sadly. 'Come along lad. You can't stay here all night.'

He scooped Lien up and carried the unconscious boy back through the network of the prison, now swarming with guards trying to find Kai, who appeared to have disappeared into thin air. When he arrived in the cell from which Lien had escaped less than half an hour earlier, he found Lady Selene Beckworth waiting. She was impatient at the outset and then fearsomely irate when she saw the condition of the boy she had been waiting almost all of her long lifetime to meet.

# 15. Castelle Travers

Lien lay unconscious for nearly two days, as his young body tried to recover from the physical and mental trauma of the previous three. In the early evening of the second day, as he transitioned from unconsciousness to sleep, Shah came to him. The translucent night-mare phased effortlessly through the wall and into the room, where she dropped her nose over the sleeping boy, nudging him with something that might have bordered on concern, or affection, before delivering the dream.

Lien found himself standing in a vast, rubble-strewn, ruined piazza, under a storming sky. A cold wind whipped at his hair and tunic, and looking down at his own hands, he realised he was in his own body, not that of Areté. He was faintly translucent and outlined in a thin, flicking purple light. This was not a dream like any of the others.

Lightning scythed through the roiling grey clouds, illuminating the remains of a high, pillared arch in front on him; the ornate centre section lay smashed on the ground below. Beyond was only a bruised, stormy horizon, but when Lien turned a full circle on the spot, he saw the piazza was otherwise surrounded by tall, ancient, elegantly crafted stone buildings: skeletons of a vast city, now damaged beyond repair by time and goodness knew what else. As he completed his 360-degree investigation, returning to face the broken archway, he leapt in surprise at finding himself face to face with Areté. Or at least, a projection of Areté, even more translucent than himself. She was not emaciated here, as was her physical body, but she was white as snow, her auburn hair swept into a wild mane in the high wind. In place of her usual armour, she wore a long light blue dress, woefully inadequate for the cold, the skirt snapping in the wind. She looked young, and vulnerable and lost - and even more shocked to see him than he was to see her.

'Lien?' she gasped, and as she did, she seemed to transform in front his eyes, morphing back into the older and armoured woman he knew so well.

'Areté!' Lien echoed, and then found a sob of relief catching in his throat. He reached impulsively to hug her, but fell straight through her. She stepped back quickly.

'You mustn't *be* here! How are you coming to me?' she asked, loud over the roaring storm.

'I don't know!' Lien shouted back. 'There's a night-mare, Shah, and she brings me these dreams, where I'm *inside* you. I don't understand! Where are we? Where are *you*? Why won't you give Callista the Mandala? Please! Come back to us!'

The questions he had pent up inside him tumbled out, one after the other, each more desperate than the one before.

Areté urgently shook her head.

'I can't, Lien. You have to trust me on this.'

Lien's face crinkled up. He reached out helplessly.

'Please, Areté! I did this, didn't I? Tell me how to fix it!' he begged, choking on raw sobs.

Areté's demeanour changed immediately.

'No! No, Lien, none of this is your fault. None of it, I

promise you,' she insisted, but as she stepped back towards him, the flagstones beneath their feet shuddered and a huge crack fractured the ground between them.

Areté shot Lien a hard look.

'You *have* to go. And you mustn't return,' she roared over a crash of thunder. In a flash of lightening she looked momentarily, frighteningly wild. She looked like someone – or something – else completely. Like an ancient and primeval apparition.

'Areté!' Lien cried, stumbling forwards. He tripped on a piece of loose stone and fell hard to his hands and knees on the shaking ground. Then the ground below him dropped away, down down down, and he screamed Areté's name as she disappeared far above –

'Lien! Come on, wake up!'

Lien sat up sharply with a gasp, causing the person shaking him to jump back in surprise.

It was Citar.

Lien fell back into soft pillows, staring uncomprehendingly at the chevalier, while his brain raced to catch up with this jarring intersection of the dream and physical worlds.

'Citar?' he managed, hoarsely, after several panting breaths.

'Yes!' Citar said. 'What were you dreaming? You were thrashing around shouting out Areté's name. It was like – like a fit or something. It was kind of scary, actually,' she finished, her tone sliding from worried to accusatory.

Lien tried to sit up again, causing the room to spin.

'Easy, easy,' Citar said, steadying him. 'You've been out for days.'

'Days…?' Lien muttered, sinking back into the pillows. The soft bed and pillows were unfamiliar to a nomadic boy raised in forests and mountains. It was an altogether different and better experience from his last waking though, on the cold, hard floor of a prison cell.

Outside, the sun was starting to set, but only a golden halo of light escaped around the heavy burgundy drapes blocking the towering windows. The appalling headache Lien had endured through the prison escapade was now just a background throbbing though, and the low candle light of the room was easy on his raw eyes. And he had two eyes this time: his left eye was back in use. A couple of determined blinks brought a ceiling decorated in elaborate floral friezes into focus. He closed his eyes again, trying to remember what had happened before the dream with Areté. He had a vague impression of Corporal Cisco. Then he remembered Kai, and the men who had attacked the People, and Kai's shocking and unexpected violence. And…there had been someone else. A woman…?

Lien tried to sit up again, which became an awkward struggle as the pillows and mattress both sank down under his weight, refusing to help him. He was a small shape drowning in pillows, sheets and duvets on a vast four poster bed.

'Selene! I need to see - Lady Selene Beckworth,' he tried to say, but the words came out as a series of dry croaks. He frowned, confused by what had come out of his own mouth.

'Don't worry, you just need a drink. And you're in luck, because you're in her house,' Citar said, padding over to a sideboard and returning with a glass jug and copper cup. While filling the cup, she laughed at Lien's third attempt to sit up before reaching out a hand for him to pull himself up on.

'Gosh, beds are hard work,' he panted, then sipped the water gratefully.

'I'll go tell Lady Beckworth you're awake,' Citar said when she was sure he wasn't going to spill the water over the expensive bedding.

'She was in the prison, I think? I can't really remember,' Lien said.

'She was,' Citar agreed, halfway to the door. 'And boy, was she angry when she saw the state you were in. I've never seen her so furious. She had Corporal Cisco carry you all the way here himself - in that heat! - and she dressed the poor man down the whole way. Tongue like a whip, she has. Cisco looked like he could have died of shame by the time she let him leave.'

Lien's foggy brain threw up an urgent red flag.

'Citar - wait! My pony! What happened to him?'

Lien couldn't believe he had taken so long to think of his beloved pony. If he had been asleep for days, anything could have happened to poor Jest!

'Jest is fine,' Citar grinned, turning back. 'Rupert told Lady Beckworth about him, and she had him collected from The Angel and given the best of care.'

'Oh thank goodness,' Lien sighed deeply in relief. Then he frowned a little.

'How did you know his name?' he asked, curiously. Barely a heart beat passed between Citar's face freezing and a reassuring smile spreading across it. It was Cira who had met and ridden Jest in Leaverness all those years ago, not Citar.

'I think Rupert must have known it,' she said breezily. Lien briefly thought on it, and nodded: he didn't remember telling either boys Jest's name, but a lot had happened in the last few days. Wait - the last - week - ?

'Lien...may I ask you something?' Citar asked uncertainly, pausing in the doorway.

'Of course,' Lien said, curious at her change of tone.

Citar walked slowly back in, and sat on one of the two seats against the wall.

'Back in Leaverness...did *you* light the torch?'

Lien's encouraging smile faded.

'Oh. Well. I don't *think* so. I mean I tried - I really tried, I promise. But I'm - I'm not very good at that sort of thing and...and there was a lot going on.'

Citar looked so pained that Lien realised the question had been even harder to ask than it had been for him to answer. He frowned, confused.

'Citar? What is it?'

'It will...sound crazy,' she muttered.

'Oh I'm really good with crazy,' Lien assured her. 'Really. Try me.'

She looked hard at Lien, but could see nothing but warmth and kindness in his eyes.

She exhaled deeply.

'I felt like there was...someone else there. I mean not physically, like you and me, but...like, a spirit. Or a ghost. And...I wondered if *they* lit the torch. Is that crazy?' she asked desperately.

Lien thought on how best to answer. *He* hadn't seen anyone else. He hadn't even been in control of his own body when the torch was relit - and that was *way* crazier than Citar thinking there had been a ghost in the clearing.

But he knew what Bravo had seen.

'I didn't see anyone else,' he started carefully, and

Citar's face fell immediately.

'But Bravo - he did see someone else,' he continued quickly, and Citar's eyes shot back up.

'Who?' she asked.

Lien chewed his bottom lip.

'It was a ghost. The ghost of a boy. Around our age. We knew him. We met him years ago. His name was Jordan.'

It took every ounce of control Citar could muster to not give herself away at this revelation. She *couldn't* show that she knew Jordan; that she cared for him. There was no way Citar could show any connection to Jordan, Falric or the Backwind, in case that led to connections to Cira. The glamour was designed to thwart association but if she gave info away directly, she broke its terms.

She forced herself to stay calm, and breathe normally, while she completely fell apart inside.

'Bravo said he seemed to want to protect you - and that after the torch was lit, he - he disappeared.'

Lien furrowed his brow as his weary brain tried to make the connection the glamour was pushing him away from.

'Did you...know Jordan?' he managed to force his voice to ask.

'No,' Citar forced herself to reply.

'Or - or his friend, Cira?'

Lien closed his eyes and put a hand to his forehead. Citar realised the glamour was acting upon him, which wasn't fair at any time, but especially while he was recovering from such trauma. She got up sharply.

'No, no I don't. And I'm sorry, I shouldn't have asked. I just thought...you might have known. I'll go and get Lady Beckworth.'

Lien closed his eyes as she slipped from the room, and when he re-opened them, his brain had found something completely different and much safer to focus on: he had made it to the first step of finding Areté! He had finally made it to Lady Selene Beckworth! She would surely know what to do next.

He realised also that the long sleep had done him the world of good: a quick bodily inspection revealed bruises to be receding, aches subsiding and the wounds on his side, temple and back of his head, although tender, to be well bandaged and clear of infection. He tried to settle back into the mountain of pillows to wait for his hostess, but again sank alarmingly into their soft embrace. After a few more false starts, he eventually turfed the pillows to the side and sat up with his back against the reassuring hardness of the headboard.

He did not have to wait for long. Lady Beckworth soon swept regally into the room, fixing Lien with such a calculating stare that he gulped nervously and felt guilty by default. He felt like she was examining him in unnecessary detail, and he couldn't read her conclusion. But while Lien thought their meeting to be of great importance, he had no idea how much more significant the moment was for his host.

'Well, the patient looks greatly improved,' she eventually announced, and finally smiled. 'Welcome, Lien. It took a whole day to get you to remain still and in one place long enough to find you, but it seems we finally achieved it - although it has literally taken unconsciousness to keep you out of trouble since.' She shook her head, making Lien wonder whether her tower of copper curls - arranged with a complicated network of pins, combs and flowers - might topple to one side, but it seemed tightly fastened in place, despite the vehemence of her subsequent ranting.

'The City Guard is manned by barbarians who aren't taught even the most elementary aspects of chivalry. Assaulting a child. Imagine it. Mind you, basic good manners ought to be bred, if not beaten into young boys by their mothers, but I am afraid one simply cannot rely on such standards these days.'

She softened slightly.

'Cisco's not such a bad sort, though. When Kai - ' and her voice hardened disapprovingly on the name ' - tried to steal his keys, he let him have them, so he could break you out.' She glared accusingly at Lien. 'He wasn't to know you'd prove so impossible to help. Would have been much easier for all if you had just introduced yourself in the first place, of course. Had Hector known you were Areté's ward, he would have let you in by the front door, instead of you skulking around the back and causing *such* a ruckus. That small - misunderstanding - ' and at this, Lien looked astonished, since Hector's verve with his axe had made it seem an extremely serious misunderstanding from his position, ' - combined with the dastardly attack on Leaverness, which I was absolutely horrified by - as would be all upstanding citizens of Avenel, I might add - must combine to make you think us all such barbarians. I assure you, it is not true, and you are safe now, under my protection.'

Lien blinked at the conclusion of the monologue, his disoriented brain trying to sift out the important facts in a stream of words in a second language he was not well practiced in.

Selene indicated with a nod of her head for Citar, waiting at attention for her patron's next wish, to sit on one of two chairs next to the sideboard. Selene herself swept her skirts under and sat on the side of the bed before turning back to Lien, her face sober.

'A night-mare just entered and shortly after, left my home. I can only assume her business was with you, Lien.'

Lien nodded, relieved to finally be able to make his ask.

'Yes! She brings me dreams of Areté. Lady Beckworth, I have come to Avenel only to find you. Do you know where Areté is? Do you have a plan to free her? I want to help!'

Selene frowned.

'Let us slow this down,' she said carefully. 'First, you may call me Selene. Second, how do you know Areté needs our help?'

Lien stared at her.

'You don't know? That she is imprisoned? Selene, she is being tortured! We have to help her!'

'Calm, Lien, calm,' Selene said, raising a beautifully manicured and be-ringed hand as she saw Lien's rising agitation. 'I have not seen Areté in nearly a year, it is true, but that is not unusual. She has many interests and responsibilities which demand her attentions, and all Altica is her domain. I have also had no alert to her being in any distress, which it would be in her power to send me.'

'She doesn't want to be helped, she's hiding from us,' Lien said.

'In which case we should respect that she has good reason to do so,' Selene countered soothingly.

'But she needs our help! She's a prisoner of a woman called Callista - do you know her?' Lien interrupted himself as Selene's face registered surprise.

'Not personally, no, but I know of her. Continue.'

'Well, if she tells Callista where to find the Mandala,' and here Citar shot a sharp look to Lien, and Selene a sharp look back to Citar, 'she can be free! But she won't tell, so she can't be free, and they're awful to her, Selene, they torture her. I experience it through the dreams from Shah - she's the night-mare - and it's terrible and we have to help her, if she won't help herself. And - and I think it's all my fault, everything that is happening to her is *my* fault...'

Lien's voice cracked as tears broke through. His face was a picture of desperation, and both this and his words triggered a similar feeling inside Citar. What had happened to Jordan had also been her fault. Not Lien's fault, for not being led by Aethon to save them a second time. *Her* fault. As the chevalier Citar, however, she did not have the liberty of expressing the grief and guilt of Cira. Citar tried to keep her face unflinching, but watching Lien's face crumple, she felt tears stinging the corner of her own eyes. She had to look up and sternly study the floral friezes on the ceiling as Selene leaned forward and wrapped Lien into a close embrace, holding him tightly as he cried out his guilt, fear, and confusion. Citar surreptitiously wiped her own eyes on her sleeve and had collected herself again by the time Selene pulled back and fixed Lien with a kind but firm look.

'Lien, I am going to call for food, you are still weak and you must be hungry. And then you will tell me *everything*,' she instructed, and swept out again, with a passing, worried look back at both her red-eyed patient and rigid, emotionally embattled chevalier.

Selene could easily have asked Citar to request food from

the kitchen, but she needed to allow herself the space to consider the situation. It seemed Areté's predicament was more severe than she had realised, but she could not share those concerns with the teenagers.

She had felt Shah's presence as soon as the night-mare had entered the protections set around Castelle Travers. She should not have been able to enter; that the protections had not stopped her had been worrying in itself. The sigil daubed in red on her quarters explained the intrusion, as Selene and the sigil's owner had an old and complex understanding, but this worried Selene further. It was in her power to strengthen the estate defences to ensure Shah could no longer reach Lien, and she knew that would be Areté's preference, but she was uncertain of the intended goal for sending these dreams to the boy.

Selene thought on the matter, her face troubled, while her kitchen staff prepared a light meal of fruits and bread. By the time she returned to the guest suite, carrying the tray herself despite the protests of her butler, she wore a reassuring mask of calm resolve that completely concealed the turmoil she felt inside. She watched Lien gratefully tuck into the grapes and slices of melons, licking his fingers clean of the sweet juices, then removed the tray.

'More soon, only a little to start,' she said. 'Let your body adjust slowly. Are you feeling better?'

Lien nodded; he was, and although he was still hungry, he could feel his tummy was confused by the foods after such a long time without. He had not eaten since stealing apples along the Kings Way some three days earlier.

'Now, tell us everything about Areté and these dreams, from the beginning,' Selene instructed seriously, sitting herself down on a chair next to Citar. Citar caught her eye and gestured to ask if she should leave; Selene subtly shook her head. And Lien told his story, from the start as he knew it to begin: chasing Prince Rupert to steal his purple feather for Sky.

Citar was delighted to learn the truth of the much-speculated story; Selene rolled her eyes at least once, unnoticed by Lien. Both sobered though as Lien, ashamed, admitted he had not realised the mortal harm the escapade had put Rupert in, resulting in Areté saving the prince's life. He explained that while Areté had made light of the cost, he and Bravo suspected it to be high. Selene grimly agreed that, to save a life, it would have to be. Lien explained Areté's subsequent disappearance and, many months later, the start of the dreams in which Shah took him into her body, where he experienced her suffering as though it were his own. Citar looked horrified and Selene concerned when he described the strangulation and drowning dreams, and how he had been choked and almost drowned himself. When he described the dream with Callista, and the thing inside her, Selene's face became dangerously blank; she dared not show her feelings. Lien tried to pause the telling to press Selene on what the Mandala was, but she ordered him to continue. He concluded with the dream Citar had just woken him from.

'And you just met Areté inside a - a shared dream?' Selene asked.

Lien considered the question. He hadn't had a chance to reflect on the dream since waking.

'Selene, have you heard of animus loci?' he asked slowly. Citar looked puzzled but Selene nodded.

'A psychic representation of a person's mind. Usually a

garden; sometimes a building.'

'Does everyone have one?' Citar asked, fascinated.

'Everyone has a way their unconscious mind organises memories, and as I say, this usually manifests as a garden. However, if the person is not consciously managing the space, it will be chaotic. The garden might be wild and overgrown with no clear paths, for instance,' Selene explained. 'It takes a huge amount of mental training to actually curate the space. It's incredibly powerful though. You can manicure your garden by tidying up your thinking; create trees, foundations or monuments from your achievements and traumas; and build pathways with focus and intention. You can learn to fully manage your mind by using your animus loci as a literal metaphor for yourself.'

'Can you do that?' Citar asked Lien, impressed. He blushed and looked down at his hands, clasped together on the luxurious turquoise silk duvet.

'I'm, uh - I'm not very good with magic, espréi, the subconscious and all that,' he muttered. He didn't tell them why though, and re-routed the conversation back to the dream before they could enquire further.

'So that's where I think it was,' he continued. 'I think we were somehow inside her loci. It wasn't a garden though, and that's what I've heard them described as too. And it wasn't a building. Selene, it was a city! It was huge, it went back miles, though we were on the edge, and there was nothing after the edge, just the storm. Is that even possible? For an animus loci to be a city?'

'Areté is very old. It would not surprise me if she had built something larger than a garden, but a city? That's impressive, and very rare. But she needs to know herself very well, so it makes sense,' Selene said thoughtfully.

'But the city was in ruins,' Lien said anxiously. 'I think that's what's happening to her mind, Selene. She's falling apart inside. And that's why, even though she won't help herself, *we* have to help her. We have to save her. So please, I have shared what I know: now tell me what the Mandala is, and how we find it. If we give that information to Callista, she will have no reason to keep Areté imprisoned, and I don't think she *wants* Areté there, she really doesn't. They are just…as stubborn at each other.'

'You are mistaken, Lien. No-one is as stubborn as Areté. Believe me, I would know,' Selene sighed. 'But. The Mandala is a…a spirit. A possessing spirit. It's like a partial Essene – you both know what that is?'

Lien nodded; Citar indicated that she only sort of understood. Falric had explained all sorts of mythology to the children but she was interested in Selene's take on the subject.

'The Essene are of what we call the Old World: ancient guardians of natural and emotional forces. No-one knows how many there are, but there are many.'

'Like – like time, and death, and love?' Citar asked.

'Not death as such, but endings. But you have the right idea,' Selene agreed. 'They represent those things, and they *are* those things.'

'Fal – my *father*,' Citar hastily corrected herself, unable to believe she had almost spoken Falric's name. It was a name Lien knew from meeting Cira, if he could remember. A name that belonged to Cira of the Backwind and had nothing to do with Citar of Avenel.

'My *father* told me, but he was not sure if they were real,' she finished lamely.

'They are *very* old, and not well remembered today, it

is true,' Selene said, flashing a raised eyebrow at Citar for her mistake. The girl chevalier looked down, mortified: her glamour would not protect her if she gave away her true identity herself. If she did that before her revenge against Brynir was complete, then the glamour would fall, she would be revealed as the girl she was, and punished as any girl would be for pretending to be a male chevalier. And if she even survived that, she would be unable to achieve her vengeance.

'Soooo...Mandala is...an Essene...?' Lien asked, dragging the sentence uncertainly as he tried to understand what had passed between the woman and chevalier.

'No, it is not,' Selene said in brisk, clipped tones. 'But it is a useful reference. Mandala is like a...partial Essene. Unlike Essene, it can only manifest from inside a mortal host. But like Essene, it has a purpose. And that purpose is to keep the balance between the Old and New worlds. Mortals - our humble selves - are of the New World; and the Essene, much of what you might call the supernatural and the Old Ones are of the Old World. They do not mix well, and Mandala ensures neither side can do serious harm to the other. Again.'

Citar, as always, wanted to know more, and opened her mouth to ask a number of questions, but Lien wanted to keep on topic.

'So Mandala is currently inside someone now, who even Areté cannot find?' he jumped in, before Citar could start.

'Under a glamour!' Citar said, changing gears gracefully because this she suspected from the conversation with the chevaliers in Leaverness and was excited to contribute.

'Indeed, a very strong glamour,' Selene agreed. 'And they cannot reveal themselves at *all*, or their glamour will fail,' she added, emphases aimed at Citar, although her eyes were on Lien.

'A glamour from...Praxidice?' Citar asked her patron, daringly. 'Is Praxidice Essene?'

'She is not. Praxidice is able to facilitate vengeance but she is not its ultimate arbitrator,' Selene said.

'How does Mandala decide on its next host?' Lien again pulled the conversation back on track.

'It is a hereditary line. The next host will be an ancestor of, or of the same ancestral line, as the current one.'

'So how many people could that be?' Lien pressed. 'How many ancestors can there be?'

'Lien. The Mandala has existed for thousands of years.'

'So...lots and lots of people?' Citar grimaced.

'Well yes and no. Generally, when a person realises they are of the Mandala line, they do not have children, or they encourage their children not to have children. But yes Citar, there are many branches from the original ancestor.'

'And who was that?' Lien asked.

'I am not thousands of years old, Lien, I do not know,' Selene sighed.

'Why do they not have children?' Lien asked curiously.

'Becoming the mortal aspect of the Mandala - being inhabited, or one might say, possessed by Mandala - is not a blessing,' Selene said. 'Mandala only manifests when the balance between the Old and New worlds is being disrupted. This process will culminate in what is known as The Call. There will be a point in the future at which Mandala will require its host to make a stand against dangerous forces. The Call is often sacrificial in nature.

Mortal Mandalas do not tend to have long or prosperous lives.'

Citar had even more questions now: what was it like being possessed? How did Mandala communicate with its host? What powers did it bring? But Lien was on a mission now.

'Okay so we can't find the current Mandala host, but if we can find the next person it will go to, we just have to hand that person over to Callista and then she will release Areté,' he surmised.

Lien was surprised to see Selene's face harden at this proposal. He shot a side glance to Citar, who gave an almost imperceptible shrug. An awkward silence fell in the candlelit room. There was a blood red halo around the heavy drapes as the sunset reached a glorious peak; it would be beautiful, but with the sudden deadly serious shift in mood, it felt more sinister to Lien, who realised he had made a terrible mistake, even if he didn't yet understand what it was.

'Lien, you are proposing handing an innocent person over to someone who considers them a threat. An innocent person who, because of some quirk of fate, has a destiny that threatens Callista, but who will be helpless against her. That is tantamount to murder. Are you a murderer?'

Selene's voice was grave and also, Lien realised, disappointed. He did not understand what "tantamount" meant but he understood enough of her question to look shocked.

'Of course not! I didn't mean - I hadn't - I hadn't thought of it like that,' he stammered.

'I would hope you hadn't thought it through, because the alternative would be that you thought an innocent life to be an acceptable trade for Areté's freedom,' Selene said.

Lien chewed his cracked, dry bottom lip. The truth was, he *did* think it was an acceptable trade. He didn't like that he felt that way, but it was true. He would trade anything – any*one* – to free Areté.

'And do you think she would thank you for that?' Selene asked quietly. Lien started: had she read his thoughts?

'Imagine the person you so cavalierly propose "handing over" to Callista is, say, Citar?' Selene pressed. Citar looked to Lien; her eyes widened when his set expression did not change.

'Or Bravo? Or Rupert? What if it was Sir Armitage? Or Corporal Cisco? What if it was *me,* Lien? Would you trade any of us for Areté? If you truly think you would trade someone else's life for her, you must be equally committed to trade a friend as to trade a stranger.'

Lien now could not hold her hard stare, or the slightly accusatory look of Citar. He looked down at his hands, fingers interlaced, knuckles whitening.

'Then how can we free her?' he asked eventually, in a small voice.

'*You* cannot free her. I cannot free her. Only Areté can free herself, and if she will not, then that is her choice and it is for us to respect that. If she knows who the next Mandala will be, and will not "hand them over" to Callista, you can bet it is because she has decided their life is more valuable than her freedom, and I believe she would be disappointed in anyone who took that decision away from her.'

'But it's not fair,' Lien protested, voice catching a little again at the helplessness Selene was proposing.

'Who ever told you that life would be *fair*?' Selene asked sharply. 'That implies there is an order and design to our lives; there is not. We live in a chaos where everyone's decisions can affect the lives of others. Callista does not care about *fair*. Mandala does not care about *fair*. Areté is *trying* to be fair, and look what it is costing her.'

The three fell into an uneasy silence, all lost in their own thoughts.

'Selene…tell me about Kai,' Lien eventually asked, desperate to move the conversation on. 'He followed me through Avenel, and then he tried to help me in The Angel. He got himself arrested to help me.'

'What actually happened there?' Citar asked curiously. 'It looked like you sort of – snapped? You attacked a guard, and then you were on the floor. Kai was way stronger than the guards but suddenly went down straight after you did…it was all really odd.'

'I don't remember exactly what happened,' Lien said, truthfully. 'But Kai said he let himself get taken down…to protect me.'

'He faked that? They kicked the crap out of both of you before they got pulled off,' Citar said. 'I thought they were doing to kill you both. It was so awful. I couldn't get to you.'

'And what would you have done, even if you had?' Selene asked brusquely. 'If grown men couldn't stop the guards, you would have had no more hope.'

Citar looked down angrily. The last time she couldn't help a friend, he *had* died. She had thought, there in The Angel, that she was going to lose Lien as well. She had to get stronger and more skilled if she was to be able to protect the people she loved.

'What happened in the prison, Lien?' Selene asked. Her voice was neutral, but she slipped an unseen, comforting hand over one of Citar's.

'He was - very kind, at first. He bound my side, explained where I was and helped me drink. Then he asked the about the attack on the People...and then he told me the attackers were in the same prison, so...I made him take me to them.'

'You *made* Kai?' Selene asked sceptically. 'No-one makes Kai do anything he doesn't want to do.'

'You know what I mean. He wanted to do it alone, but I said he had to take me.'

'Ah, you said you were going with him. There is a difference,' Selene said.

Lien grinned.

'Okay. I said I was going. We went to find them, and until that point, I liked him. I really did!' Here Lien sobered though. 'But once we were with them, he...he changed. He turned into a...a monster. He is a murderer, Selene.'

'He was a knight,' Selene said, unhappy about but unfazed by the claim. 'You'd be amazed how many people get killed in the execution of chivalry.'

Citar looked uncomfortable.

'Is he really a bad man?' Lien asked, chewing his bottom lip again. 'He seemed to care for the People. He was angry for us. But he was also *really* scary. And I think...I think he *enjoyed* hurting the knights.'

'Kai is...complicated,' Selene sighed. 'He is a good friend of Areté's, believe it or not.'

'He said that. That she was like an aunt to him, too.'

'Indeed. She trained him - and Lindahl, of course - to pass the Commoner Trials to join the Order. Not that Kai passed, he was always his own worst enemy.'

'Lindahl…who killed the king?' Lien said, surprised.

'The same,' Selene agreed. 'He was her protégé.'

Lien stared, unable to comprehend.

'But…the People are hated and hunted because of him!' he protested.

'Teachers are not always responsible for the actions of their students,' Selene said sternly. 'You have grown up in a uniquely peaceful time, even for the People, Lien. I am afraid life outside of Leaverness is much more complicated, and that you are to have a steep learning curve here in Avenel.'

Lien leaned more heavily into the wooden headboard. He was learning that he didn't know much about Areté at all, and it was an uncomfortable feeling. It was as though her life away from the People was a whole other vast, unmapped world. One he didn't understand, but worse, one he was realising he might not *like* to understand.

Selene sharply bought his attention back to the present situation though.

'In any case, if you find yourself with a choice between being Kai's friend or enemy, ensure you are the former and not the latter. He lacks both access to and interest in the more - shall we say, *subtle* - tools some of us are fortunate enough to enjoy. Consequently he employs more - how shall we say? *Indelicate* - methods to achieve his ends.' Selene sniffed disapprovingly, then glanced at the windows. The sun had set; no light crept around the blinds.

'Lien, I must get along. Citar should return to Voltanna, and you should continue to rest. I will say it was very brave of you to come to Avenel, and I greatly admire your desire to help Areté, even if I do not approve of your intended methods. However, I cannot stress enough that this matter is beyond your - and even my - ability to resolve. There is nothing more you can, or should, do, right now.'

'So I just keep dreaming of the terrible things happening to her, and do nothing?' Lien protested.

'No. Shah will not be able to enter my home again, I will see to that.'

'You can't do that! I need that connection. Someone is sending those dreams to me for a reason!' Lien protested.

'There will be no more dreams. You have done enough. Areté would not want you getting those dreams.'

'They are my only connection to her!'

'And they could kill you. You yourself said as much.'

'And she might die - because of me!'

'Did Areté blame you, in the dream you just had?' Selene asked calmly.

Lien hesitated. She had not.

'And even if she could, Callista will not kill Areté while she is withholding information she requires,' Selene continued.

'Can you be sure though?' Lien demanded. 'Why do her protections no longer stand? Why could the People be found? Being in prison shouldn't change that. That's got Sky really worried.'

'That - that I cannot explain,' Selene admitted.

'What could do that?' Citar asked.

'A magic stronger than Areté's, which is not insignificant,' Selene said.

'So maybe she does need us,' Lien insisted.

'And what do you think that you can do, Lien?' Selene's tone and face hardened for the first time. 'A boy from Leaverness who nearly got himself killed on his first afternoon in Avenel. What can *you* do to oppose a force greater than the most powerful person you know?'

'I don't know!' Lien almost shouted with frustration. 'That's why I came here! I came to you for *help!*'

He glared at Selene, betrayed.

'And I *will* help. I will keep you safe, which is what Areté would want.'

She glared back.

'If anything were to happen to you, Areté would kill me when she is finally free.'

'*If* she is ever free,' Lien muttered bitterly.

Selene ignored this.

'Now you may stay here another few days only, to complete your recovery, but then we must find somewhere else for you to stay, for this, I am afraid, is not a suitable house for a young lad,' Selene said brusquely.

'People would talk,' Citar agreed.

'Look, about that - ' Lien started, hoping to finally get to the bottom of what actually went on in Castelle Travers, but Selene held up a silencing hand.

'They would indeed, and they're already talking about you, so let's not feed the rumour mill. Fortunately, I have a solution. I have found you a guardian, who will try, bless him, to ensure that you do not get in any further trouble. Further, he will oversee your required community service on the Voltarch restoration.'

'...community service...?' Lien echoed, confused by this sudden turn of events.

'Yes. It seems Cote, the owner of The Sign of the Angel, was rather upset about the extent of damage caused by your fight with the Guardsmen. Naturally the Guard refuses to pay up, so I'm afraid you have to lump the bill.'

'What was damaged?' Lien asked in amazement. 'Apart

from me?'

'The guardsmen you flattened for one, but mostly, after you were - ah, *removed* - a very enthusiastic brawl broke our and damaged a lot of furniture.'

'But how is that *my* fault?' Lien protested. 'I wasn't even there!'

'But they were fighting over you,' Selene said. 'Over what happened to you. None of which would have happened if you had assisted the Guard in their enquiries, at which point I would have become involved and assured them I would press no charges,' she added pointedly.

While Lien tried to absorb this ludicrous situation, a polite but reluctant knock came at the door. Citar jumped up to open it.

'Ah, here he is, perfect timing as ever,' Selene said.

The tall, retiring gentleman with whom Lien had briefly engaged in the atrium limped in, with the aid of his cane, nodding courteously to both Citar and Lady Beckworth. The expression he reserved for Lien was considerably less warm.

'Lien, may I introduce your new guardian, Darius? You will find your pony happily installed in the fields of his home, where I am sure you will be equally content.'

Man and boy stared at one another, neither convinced by Selene's confidence, nor happy about the arrangement.

Once Lien had been left to rest - after another drink, piece of bread and an awkward exchange in which Citar had to explain the function and use of a chamber pot - Citar knocked shyly on the door to Selene's study.

'You must need to get back to Voltanna, Citar?' Selene asked from where she had been writing at her desk.

'Yes, but there's something I wanted to tell you first,' Citar said as she quietly closed the door behind her. 'Well, ask you first.'

'This is a Cira conversation?' Selene asked, laying down her quill.

Citar nodded.

'Years ago, you fixed my calf. But it was Shivaia who healed my knee.'

'I am aware,' Selene said.

'In a *dream*,' Citar continued. 'A dream I was absolutely convinced was real. And she sent Areté's stallion, Erebus, to fetch me.'

'Shivaia used a horse you knew, and had dreamed of riding,' Selene said calmly. 'Dreams are within her power, and this is how dreams work: drawing on elements of your own experience.'

Citar held her patron's eye contact, trying to detect any clues they might be giving her. She saw nothing, so decided to take the direct route.

'Is it Shivaia sending Lien the night-mare and the dreams?' she asked, chin pushed forward defiantly.

'That would seem possible,' Selene replied levelly.

'Then can't you find her, to find Areté?' Citar demanded.

'Do you not think, if it were that simple, I would not have already done that?' Selene asked, a little archly. 'One does not simply summon Shivaia. I have *requested* her audience. She has not been forthcoming. If she *is* sending messages to Lien, the method seems strikingly out of character.'

Selene looked upon her disappointed ward, and softened.

'I know you want to help him, Citar,' she said. 'I do too. But there are many pieces in play in this game and we are but pawns on the board. Until we know whose match it is, we are all somewhat at the mercy of the unknown players.'

A fleeting frown crossed Citar's face as she wondered whose game it was. Would Areté know? Would the Mandala know? And what role did they have planned for her, and for Lien?

'My Arrangement with Shivaia, in return for healing my knee, is to ally myself with the Mandala. Now Lien is also looking for it. Is that a coincidence?' she asked.

'Seems unlikely,' Selene said evenly.

Citar considered her next question. She was still avoiding the important one.

'Do you think Lien could join the Order?' she asked, hesitantly. 'You could be his patron as well?'

Selene raised a bemused eyebrow.

'Is that what you think he would want?'

'I'm sure he'd prefer it to labouring on the Voltarch restoration, and living with Darius,' Citar said fervently. 'I know I would.'

'It will do Lien good to get familiar with Voltanna, and I think the man and boy will be good for each other,' Selene said. 'And I would like to think he will get in less trouble on a building site than with a bunch of hormonal teenage boys messing around with sharp objects,' she added. 'Present company notwithstanding, of course.'

Citar nodded, but she wasn't smiling and her eyes were distant.

Selene frowned.

'Ask the question you are really here for.'

Citar paused to organise her thoughts.

'Lien said that Bravo saw Jordan. In Leaverness. His ghost. He was watching over me when the Cuán attacked. And then the torch was magically re-lit and then…and then Bravo says Jordan…disappeared.'

Tears welled, unbidden, in Citar's eyes.

'Oh Citar. *Cira*. My dear child,' Selene said, rising and striding over to the girl. Citar rose too, gratefully into a hug even warmer and firmer than that which Selene had given Lien.

'Cry it out, my girl, let it out,' Selene crooned, stroking Citar's short boyish hair as her body was wracked with sobs.

'Is he - is he gone?' Citar managed as the sobs subsided.

'I would think he is, yes,' Selene said softly. 'I'm so sorry.'

'It's not fair,' Citar whispered.

'It is not fair, no. This life is not fair. I wish I could make it so - for you, for Lien, for Areté, for all of us. But the only way to make it fair would be to remove choice and chance, and that would be no way of living at all.'

Citar nodded, took a deep breath and stepped back from Selene's embrace.

'Thank you. For letting me be - myself.'

'You have chosen a very lonely road,' Selene said. 'I alone know you are Cira of the Backwind. You can be yourself in our privacy.'

'Well, you and Praxidice,' Citar said weakly.

'Quite, but you will not get a hug and a cup of tea from her,' Selene said with a small smile. The she sobered.

'But you *must* be more careful around Lien, Citar.'

'I know,' she sighed. 'But it is…*difficult* not to reveal myself to him. I thought I hated him when - when he wasn't there for Jordan. But that wasn't his fault, I know that now.

But he's the only person I can share my memories of Jordan with, because he has them too. And…then when I met him again in Leaverness…' she broke off, unsure of whether or even how to continue.

Selene waited patiently.

Knowing that her patron understood these matters perhaps better than most, Citar forged clumsily onwards.

'It was like the years just - rolled back. I could again feel all the things I felt for the years after we first met. He was just the same. But I'm not. Everything for me is different.'

Citar's tone was relatively even but her face and body language told the real story. Selene had read and written the same book herself many times and knew it by heart.

'I see,' she said, walking slowly over to sit gracefully into her favourite armchair, indicating Citar do the same in another. This was a completely different sort of conversation now.

'And I understand. But he is not the ten-year-old boy you met in Leaverness either Citar, as equally as you are no longer the plucky girl he rescued. He's just been plunged, way over his head, into a completely foreign world. One in which he's going to make goodness knows how many mistakes. And you: you are, for all intents and purposes, a boy now. Whether Lien is to develop an interest in girls or in boys, there is no happy ending here. The longer you keep your secret, the worse it gets for both of you. But this is not a secret that will be easy, or even safe, to relinquish.'

Citar slumped down in her armchair.

'You will need to decide whether you want to keep your glamour intact and conceal yourself - and your feelings - from Lien; or whether you would rather stop being the chevalier Citar, and go back to being the girl Cira. You know you cannot have it both ways.'

Citar nodded, numbly.

'You also know the consequences of being revealed as a girl in the Order,' Selene said, though unnecessarily: the consequences were all that Citar could think of. She was not the first girl who had disguised herself as a boy to join the Order. The punishment was always the same though.

Selene waited until Citar reluctantly met her eyes again before continuing.

'Lien will need a good friend to support him through these trying times. You will need to decide whether that is a role you can fulfil, or whether you need to take a step back. To protect your own heart.'

Citar knew Selene was right. She hated it but, it was true.

Because the alternative - revealing herself to Lien, thus breaking her glamour and being discovered as a girl chevalier in the Order - was death.

# PART IV

# THE DREAMING

# 16. Tryst

Lien had been left to rest but could not possibly do so. The food and drink had revived him and now his mind was restless and his body ready to move. He could not stay in Castelle Travers if Shah was unable to reach him here, and besides, he wanted to stand directly on the earth, surrounded by nature, with a direct connection to the healing power of espréi – and not be kept on a luxurious bed inside a house built of stone. He also longed to see and hug Jest, but he could not turn to Darius either, for he suspected his intended guardian would be even less helpful and more strict than Lady Beckworth. And he had no idea how to find where Darius lived.

But Selene's instruction to do nothing infuriated him.

He was struggling out the of bed when there came a gentle knock at the door. Lien froze, mid thrash.

'Lien?'

'Yes?' Lien replied cautiously.

The door opened, and Citar poked her head around. When she saw him, she frowned.

'Are you trying to escape?' she asked.

'No, why would I want to do that?' Lien asked, one leg literally out of the bed.

'Because Selene is stopping you from doing anything and you hate it,' Citar said, slipping into the room and quietly closing the door behind her.

'Well, yes, okay, I am escaping,' Lien admitted, completing his exit from the bed. 'And don't even think of trying to stop me.'

He stood defiantly before her, but seeing the faint red of her eyes, he tilted his head.

'Are you - okay?' he asked.

'Yes, of course,' Citar lied.

'Has Selene said - or done - something to you?' he asked, his defiance sliding into concern.

'No! No no, nothing like that. Selene is very kind to me. She has my best interests at heart. Yours too,' she added pointedly. Lien shrugged, his defiance returning.

'I came here to ask Lady Beckworth for help. She won't help, so I must find someone who *can*.'

'And who is that?' Citar asked.

'Someone who will take risks. And action.'

Citar gaped.

'You're not going to find *Kai*?'

Lien shrugged.

'I'm going to try. If not him, maybe Sir Armitage.'

'I mean...aside from everything you told us about Kai - you know, the violence and murdering - he's impossible to find. Famously so. The whole Order has been trying for fourteen years,' Citar argued. 'And I don't know if even Armitage can do anything for you. I'm sure he would want to help Areté, but don't think iron and brawn are what is needed here.'

'Well, I'm going to try,' Lien insisted, hands on hips.

'Dressed like that?' Citar raised an eyebrow at his mostly naked brown body.

'Actually, no - uh, I don't suppose you know where my clothes are?'

Citar thought about pretending she did not, to delay his rash plans. But she found her eyes running down the scars on his bare chest. The scars Brynir left upon him because of her. Where would she be, if he had not taken rash action on that day? When Bravo and all the laws of his tribe said he must not?

She made her decision.

'I do actually,' she said, and retrieved his trousers, tunic and Cobi's black silk necktie from a sideboard. They had been washed - with actual soap - and then pressed, with an actual iron. Lien took them gratefully, then crinkled his nose.

'What has happened to them?' he asked as he smelled his clothes cautiously, suspicious at the heady rose scent.

'They have been washed. You're welcome,' Citar said dryly.

'Gosh. People will smell me coming,' Lien said.

'Hate to break it to you Lien, but they already could.'

'Ah but not when you are in the company of many people who smell,' Lien said cheerfully. He started to don his clothes. Citar wondered whether she should look away, then realised it was pointless. She had already seen him almost naked, there was no more to be seen in him getting less naked.

'Everything is so...soft,' Lien said, tucking the black silk into a pocket and stroking his tunic and trousers in wonder. 'And there are lots of marks missing. Is it magic?'

'I don't believe the laundry is magical, no,' Citar said, trying not to smile.

'I wonder what Jest will think.'

'He might not know who you are.'

'He is not in a stable, is he?' Lien asked, suddenly worried.

'No, Darius lives outside Avenel. Jest will be in a field - a big area of grass - and he will be well cared for, I am sure.

Rupert had to take him, you know. He would only follow Jorge.'

'Such a smart boy!' Lien said proudly.

'There's one more thing you're missing,' Citar said.

Lien thought a moment, and then his face lit up hopefully.

'My staff! You know where it is? I completely forgot to ask Lady Beckworth!'

Citar winked and rolled the staff across the top of the sideboard, where it had been lying, unseen. Lien beamed, taking it reverentially from her outstretched hands. Then he frowned.

'She had it painted,' Citar explained. 'She said it's made of borealus? You can't go carrying that around Avenel!'

'Ohhh, yes, Divinia said that,' Lien said, a little sadly. His beautiful red staff was now more of a gold colour. It wasn't unattractive, but it wasn't right.

'You should be grateful,' Citar prompted.

'Of course, of course I am,' he said hastily, lifting his head to meet her eyes. 'It's just...I have to hide so much here. My face, my language, my staff...but please thank her for me. Because *now* I am ready!'

'So – what first?' Citar asked hesitantly.

'Escape!' Lien grinned. 'Want to join?'

Citar cursed silently. He was *contagious.*

'Alas, my coming with you would only draw attention to your escape. Adagio is being brought around to the front for me and Hector will escort me out of the gate. But that will mean he's occupied, so it's a good time for you to make a run for it out the back.'

She pulled back the drapes blocking the tall windows,

which were revealed to actually be a pair of glass doors that opened onto the cloisters and the dusk lawn. They unbolted and opened easily. She stood between them, offering Lien his escape.

'I'm just not sure how you think you're getting over the back wall…?' she asked.

'Did it last time,' Lien said.

'You weren't bandaged with a stab wound, head wounds and four bruised or broken ribs last time,' she said pointedly.

That made Lien pause for thought.

'I'm sure I can work it out,' he said eventually.

Citar shrugged.

'I can meet you down the road? If you…make it?'

Lien shook his head.

'Thank you, but I do not wish to get you in any trouble,' he said. 'But I will see you soon!'

Citar smiled wanly.

'Yes. I hope so,' she agreed.

And Lien slipped out into the early evening with a last cheerful wave.

Citar closed the doors and drapes behind him, wondering whether she had made the right decision to let the boy loose again in Avenel. He could face down any horror of Leaverness, but was liable to get himself killed in the big city. He was lucky he wasn't dead already.

Lien walked silently though the cloisters, feeling the curiously familiar espréi of the oak tree again as he did. It was warm and energising. He felt as though, if he could just stop and rest beneath its vast branches, he would heal faster. But he had to take the window of opportunity during which Hector was distracted out the front. He wished he had thought to ask Selene about the tree though, and made a mental note to do so next time he saw her. *After* she had finished yelling at him for what he was about to do, of course.

He tried jogging across the long lawn, discreetly up against the side wall, but found Citar was correct: his physical condition for this escape was completely different to the last one. Jogging with broken ribs was not an option. He had to settle for walking swiftly and furtively, even then wincing frequently. Citar was also irritatingly correct about the back wall. There was no way he was going to be able to get over it unaided.

He cursed.

The end of a rope sailed over the wall, an arm's length away.

Lien stared at it, then up to the top of the wall. There was nothing to see.

'Hello?' he tried, as loudly as he dared.

Whoever was on the other side gave the rope a single, impatient tug, which made it jump on Lien's side. He felt a tiny brush of impatience from a powerful, uncontrolled espréi he recognised.

Lien shook his head in wonder.

He gave the rope a gentle experimental tug himself, and found it anchored. He pulled harder, to double check; it held his weight. He shrugged, took a high hold of it, tucked his staff under his arm, put his feet on the wall and slowly, carefully, painfully walked his way up.

'Stay low,' Kai, as yet unseen, commanded quietly as Lien approached the top of the wall. Lien obeyed, sliding onto his belly when he reached the top. His ribs protested.

The coolness of his room in Castelle Travers had belied the warmth of the evening; sweat lined his beautifully cleaned tunic already.

'Hello Kai,' Lien said, but without his usual brightness, because he was still feeling very conflicted about the man. Kai had saved Lien hunting for him, but the memories of his actions in the prison were fresh and raw.

Lien was also wondering how he was going to get down safely. The rope could only be climbed from one side.

'Toss me your staff,' Kai said, raising an arm. Lien obeyed. Kai caught it and propped it against the wall by a patiently waiting horse.

'How many broken ribs?' Kai asked.

'Four, apparently,' Lien replied, surprised by the question.

'Well, this isn't going to be as fun as it should be then, but there's nothing for it. You'll need to hang from the wall, then drop, falling as horizontally as possible.'

'You *will* catch me?' Lien prompted for the essential and missing part of the plan.

'Yes of course. Get on with it.'

Lien gritted his teeth. Such antics *ought* to be fun, but there is nothing fun about sliding your body down a wall, holding your bodyweight with your arms, and then dropping into the arms of a man far below, when you are covered in bandages, bruises and breaks. Good to his word though, Kai caught Lien easily in his powerful arms, and did so from a high reach all the way down to kneeling, to decelerate his fall as gently as possible. Kai allowed the wincing boy's feet to touch the ground and to lean against his own body as they stood up together.

'I've got you,' he grunted. Lien could only nod, trying

to choke down on various reports of pain from around his body.

'How - many ribs - did *you* break?' he managed.

'More than you,' Kai grinned humourlessly.

'Aren't you hurting too then?' Lien asked, clutching at his own ribs.

'I heal fast.'

'Like…fully healed?'

'Not quite. But well ahead of you.'

'That's very handy,' Lien said enviously. 'I like your horse,' he added, taking in the beautiful animal to distract from his pain. 'What is his name?'

The charger sauntered over, nose extended curiously. Lien breathed nostril to cavernous nostril with him, then the horse dropped his head. Lien scratched under his bridle straps obligingly. He was a dappled buckskin with the sandy gold coat and black mane, tail and legs typical of the colouring - which made him a kind of brown version of Shah.

'Apparently he likes you too, and his name is Chase,' Kai said, watching the exchange as he re-coiled his rope.

'Hello Chase,' Lien said happily to the horse, always happy to make a new equine friend.

Kai attached the rope to a ring on his saddle, then removed a hooded, long-sleeved top from a saddlebag and tossing it to Lien. It was a made of a light fabric in a dark pine green, which made Lien think of Leaverness with a pang of homesickness.

'Put it on,' Kai ordered.

Lien obediently slipped it over his vest. It fitted perfectly.

'Thank you, Kai,' he said, stroking the soft material with

delight.

'It's not a gift kid, it's a necessity. The tattoos are bad enough, but the head bandages are a dead giveaway. Hood up, eyes down anywhere around other people, understand?'

Lien nodded, and lifted the hood experimentally. Kai nodded approvingly, and mounted Chase. He offered a hand down to help Lien carefully up behind.

Lien loved riding more than anything else in the world, but realised even that was not going to be fun in his current state. Also because he was now sitting behind a saddle, he was much further back on the horse's spine than if they were both sitting bareback, which felt less secure - albeit more comfortable than being up near the bony withers.

'You should try riding bareback, it's much better,' Lien said, wincing as he arranged himself.

'We'll just walk, we're not in a hurry,' Kai said.

'How did you find me?' Lien asked.

'Everybody in Avenel knows both who, and where, you are,' Kai said.

Lien's eyes widened.

'I was supposed to keep a low profile,' he said anxiously.

'After your performance in The Angel? Hard fail on discretion, I'm afraid.'

'But...how did you know to find me *now*? And from the laneway?'

'I had a feeling,' Kai said casually.

'That's a very a specific feeling,' Lien countered sceptically.

'I often amaze myself.'

'How old are you?' Lien demanded.

'Thirty-something,' Kai shrugged.

'Oh.' Lien deflated. 'So...not hundreds of years old?'

'Not that I'm aware of,' Kai said, bemused by the boy's disappointment.

'Well...why did you come and find me?' Lien rallied. 'Which I'm glad you did, by the way, because otherwise I was going to have to try to find you, and apparently you are *famously* hard to find.'

'You would not have been able to find me, no. But I had a feeling our interests coincide,' Kai said.

'So you will help me! To find Areté?' Lien asked, spirits lifting.

'I'm not here to show you the sights, kid.'

'Thank goodness *someone* will help,' Lien said gratefully.

'I had a feeling Selene would tell you to be a good boy and do nothing.'

'Urgh, *so* boring!' Lien agreed.

'I'm disappointed she didn't warn you off me though,' Kai mused.

'Oh she did - in a way. She said you were... complicated.'

'Well that's not true at all,' he said. 'I'm very straightforward.'

'*And* that you were a knight!'

'Past tense, yes.'

'Why did you stop?' Lien asked, diverted by this new curiosity.

'My services were no longer required.'

'What did they call you in the prison? The Order's prodigy son?'

'*Prodigal* son. That's a big word and a long story.'

'How long is our ride?'

'Only long enough for you to tell me everything you know about where Areté is, and why,' Kai said in a tone that warned against argument. He was, Lien decided, like a less grumpy and more helpful version of Cobi - when he wasn't angry, that is. Lien had no idea if he could trust this hulking, violent man, but their instincts had guided them towards one another. And besides, Lien didn't have anyone else to go to. And although he knew he would be wise to be wary of Kai, he had sensed that Selene, despite her misgivings, still had a certain fondness for him. And Kai had shown him a number of kindnesses and considerations so far - not to mention more assistance than the woman he had come to Avenel to see.

'I'm looking for the Mandala too,' he said, keeping his tone casual.

Kai gave a surprised glance over his shoulder.

'Are you now?'

'Yes. Do you know who it is?'

Kai did not reply.

'If you want me to trust you, you have to trust me too,' Lien said.

'I know - who it *was*,' Kai said after another long pause. 'I don't know who it is now. But I have been searching for a long time. The Mandala is also very good at not being found.'

'Do you know who it might be next?' Lien asked, biting his bottom lip nervously at what the answer might be.

Again, Kai glanced around over his shoulder to look at the boy.

'I'm not aware it can be in two people?' he said slowly.

'Well I don't know either,' Lien said. 'But it's a – a blood line, right? If you know who is currently Mandala, you can guess who it is next?'

'I think you should start at the very beginning of your story, I'm clearly missing large sections,' Kai said.

Sitting behind, Lien could not see the deep, worried furrow in his brow.

Lien's story did indeed take the duration of the ride from the quiet roads around Castelle Travers through the heavier human, horse and oxen traffic of the Avenel early evening. Lien kept wanting to look up and around and gawk at the sights of the city, but forced himself to keep his head discreetly down, hood up, as he spoke. They walked for more than half an hour through the city until they ended up on a long, deserted road. This one was not maintained. It looked as though all the good cobblestones had been removed; the remaining ones were dirty and broken. A burned out, blackened manor house loomed ahead of them, reminding Lien of the damaged buildings of Areté's animus loci.

'What is this place?' he asked, disconcerted by its eerie energy.

'Levithorne. Old man Lethe was a black mark on the Golden Age of Avenel, so his manor was burned down and left like this as a warning to anyone else who might be tempted to dabble in the dark arts,' Kai replied.

A pair of heavy, rusted iron gates guarded the entry to the estate, locked with an old chain and padlock. The horse turned in front of them and continued parallel to a rambling stone wall and around a corner to a wooden door so overgrown by trails of ivy that it would not have been obvious even in daylight. Kai slid off Chase - swinging his right leg forward instead of back, so as not to kick Lien on the way down - and unlocked the door with a key hung around his neck. Lien expected it to open with a grinding of metal but it swung open easily and silently. Catching his surprised expression, Kai winked.

'First rule of trespass: do it discreetly, and oil all the hinges,' he said, leading Chase through the gate. Lien ducked low over the black mane to fit. As soon as he passed through the wall though he sat up sharply, for a thrumming, aggressive energy met him on the other side. His skin prickled, but it was the stirring of his darkness that made him flinch. It was only momentary, but in the warm evening air he suddenly felt cold.

'What is that?' he gasped.

'Thought you'd be able to feel it,' Kai said. 'Some can't at all; most experience it as an unsettling feeling. It's why almost no-one comes here; the energy spooks them. It's also why the estate is said to be haunted. It is, but that's not what they're feeling.'

'The espréi is…trapped, and doesn't like it,' Lien said, trying to analyse what he felt. Voltanna was a place of power but it was - structured. Channelled. This was not. The espréi of this place was wild.

'It is. There's a mirror realm here. You can't see it, and nor can I, but its espréi is reflected back and, I think, magnified. Lethe tried to tap it, and instead distorted it. It's a very powerful, but dangerous, place.'

Lien swallowed hard. He could feel that the espréi of Levithorne energised his darkness. He would not be able to use his soul eye at all in this place.

Kai led Chase to the stables at the back of the old manor

house. They had not burned with the house, but were in a state of neglect and disrepair, with gaping holes in the roof and some walls fallen in. They were tidy though; someone had cleared the rubble into just one stable, the floor was swept clean and there were no cobwebs in the wooden struts that held up what remained of the roof. There were twelve large stables in total, six each side. Kai had one set up for his horse, with hay and straw stacked in another. The stable between these contained a bed made of a cow skin laid over tightly packed straw in a low wooden frame. Blankets were folded at the end of it. Several glass hurricane lanterns, hanging on huge rusted nails, threw out a warm, golden light. The smell of sweet hay, straw and horse filled the air.

Lien inhaled deeply, and sighed happily. He preferred this makeshift living arrangement in every way to the luxury of Castelle Travers.

'You live here?' he asked.

'Only when I'm in Avenel,' Kai said, unsaddling Chase, who contently tucked into hay stacked into a metal rack in the corner of his large stable.

'I can't be found here, which means neither can you.'

Lien grinned. Finally, it felt like something in Avenel might be going right

'Tell me more about Areté? You have known her for so much longer than I have,' Lien asked as Kai brushed down his horse.

'If I had any friends, she would be one,' Kai said from somewhere down between Chase's long black legs. 'She's the person you want having your back in a tight spot.'

'Why don't you have any friends?' Lien asked. 'Must be awfully lonely.'

'If you insist on pursuing foolhardy missions like trying

to find the Mandala and free Areté, you are going to find out very quickly that "friends" are a liability,' Kai said, giving his horse a final stroke as he left the stable. Lien followed him through to the forge at the end of the stable block.

'But my friends will be helping me,' Lien said.

'And what exactly do you think your friends are going to be able to do to help either find a famously elusive mythical figure, or otherwise break a sacred Arrangement?' Kai asked as he lit the forge fire and prepared a canister of water to brew tea.

'Well to be honest, I don't know what *I* can do to help,' Lien shrugged. 'I just know that someone is sending me these dreams, and that must be for a reason.'

'Have you considered the dreams might be a trap?' Kai asked, crossing one leg over the other as he relaxed onto an old wooden chair. It groaned alarmingly under his considerable weight.

'Why would anyone want to trap me?' Lien asked, surprised at the suggestion.

'Not for you. For someone you will tell.'

'Like who? The Mandala?' Lien puzzled.

'Exactly,' Kai said. 'How better to get the word out then to use an intrepid child who cannot help but attract attention? *And* trouble.'

'I am not a child,' Lien scowled.

'Near enough, especially when you're dealing with ancient creatures.'

'Do you think Callista is of the Old World?' Lien asked, eyes wide.

'Not Callista. She's mortal, I'm certain of it. But you said there's a – a *thing* inside of her. That's going to be something old, powerful and very dangerous.'

'That's *why* it fears Mandala, right? Because Mandala separates the Old and New Worlds?' Lien said, remembering what Selene had said about it.

Kai nodded, checking the water. When it was boiling, he made two steaming mugs of tea. Lien was grateful – the air was finally cooling as evening turned properly to night.

'Tell me how you met Areté?' Lien asked, holding the cup between his hands.

'I met her when I was a few years older than you. Lindahl was about your age, maybe younger. He decided he wanted to be a knight. I was a bit old for it, but had nothing better to do. We were nobodies, and she mentored us to take on the Commoner Trials. We were so young,' he said wistfully. 'Now we're old and she looks half our age.'

'You're not old,' Lien protested, with the honesty of youth. 'You don't have any wrinkles or anything.'

It was true. Kai still had the wild beard but unlike in the prison, his skin was clean, and therein revealed as clear and smooth. With his piercing blue eyes, he looked much younger than Lien remembered – or than how he sounded.

'Flattery will get you nowhere,' Kai said flatly. 'You want to try that line on the nice ladies in town, not grouchy old men who take you to haunted houses.'

Lien yawned, involuntarily.

'I think that's enough talking for tonight,' Kai said. 'You need sleep, and lots of it, to heal.'

'I wish I could heal fast like you,' Lien sighed.

'You might find Levithorne helps. It's a very special place.'

Kai checked Lien's bandages, announced they did not need changing yet, and set him up a second, much smaller bed next to his.

Lien was nervous about sleeping on the grounds of Levithorne. He would usually have wanted to sleep outside the stables, on the ground, with a direct connection to the comforting energy of the earth - but not in this place. Any separation, even from just the brick floor of the stable, was welcome. The unruly espréi had become a background thrum but still had him on edge, and he worried it might amplify any dreams Shah might bring.

'I, uh, might have a nightmare,' Lien said uncertainly when he lay down on the skin and drew the thin blanket over his body.

'I'm counting on it,' Kai said. 'I'm right here, and I'll wake you up if you start to die or anything inconvenient like that.'

'Right,' Lien said. 'Thanks.'

The regularity and depth of Kai's breathing suggested he fell asleep almost immediately. Lien envied the older man as he lay wide awake. He was tired, but his brain was unsettled. The sounds of Chase eating hay and rustling straw in the next stable comforted him at least, as he looked up at the rotting timbers of the roof. Every now and again motes of dust would lazily saunter diagonally downwards, appearing when they crossed the shafts of moonlight that cut through holes overhead, before disappearing again. Lien started to relax as he watched the drifting dust, and as he did, he wondered whether the espréi here might strengthen his darkness enough to communicate with him. It was risky to even try to connect to it, but he felt quietly assured by the bulky presence of Kai next to him, not even an arm's length away. He slowed his breathing to slow his mind, closed his eyes, and gingerly extended his other senses to try to connect with the espréi of the estate. He felt its fizz, its convolutions, and felt like it *wanted* something of him...like it wanted to *connect* to him. Slowly, so cautiously, he tried to find his soul eye –

– and the cold darkness slid around the edges of his mind.

*What do you want?!* Lien begged of it.

But there was no reply. There never was.

At some point he must have fallen asleep, because he found himself sat cross-legged at a small campfire in a wooded clearing. It was still night. He looked down at his own hands and knees, and then at the forest around him, and felt his chest tighten.

He was in Leaverness.

He was *home.*

'Lien!'

The fire dropped height to reveal Bravo sitting opposite him.

He was, unusually, beaming.

'It worked!' he whooped, but remained seated and still, where Lien would have expected him to jump up and run around in his triumph.

'It worked! I've opened a dream for us to share. I've been trying for days, but I haven't even been able to *find* you – where have you been? And where are you now? You're on a ley line like nothing I've never experienced. Tell me everything!'

'This is – a dream?' Lien asked. He was not translucent, as he had been in Areté's devastated mind-scape. He could feel the palms of his hands with his fingers, but when he thought about it, he couldn't feel any air temperature, or smell the trees or smoke from the fire.

'It is! I've made it. I'm "hosting" it, if you like. You're asleep, and your consciousness is here with me. It's really hard to do: if I lose concentration, the dream can collapse and we will both be ejected into Aurebos.'

'Then what would happen?' Lien asked cautiously, unsure of whether he wanted to know.

'Well I can probably make it back to my body but you'd likely be stranded outside of your body, lost in Aurebos, never to make it back home,' Bravo said factually.

'But don't worry! I'm concentrating *really* hard,' he added when he saw Lien's shocked expression.

'That's – that's terrifying, but also amazing, Bravo,' Lien said, impressed as well as worried. Bravo had never tried such a thing before. And it was a really good dream – it felt very real.

'Thanks, I'm impressed myself! But it's mad hard to do, so tell me the important things quickly. I think I can only hold the dream together for another minute or two. I'm getting a boost from your location, but still, this is tough.'

'Ah, okay...well, I've been unconscious for a few days which is probably why you couldn't find me,' Lien started quickly.

'Gosh – you'll have to explain that another time, but yes, you need to be conscious for me to find you. Are you okay now?'

'Yes. I'm in a place called Levithorne – maybe ask Sky about it. It has a mirror realm, or something like that, under it. Or inside it. It's complicated. The espréi is reflected, or something.'

'That explains what I'm feeling from you. Did you find Lady Beckworth?'

'Yes, and she told me not to do anything. She tried to block Shah from even reaching me!'

'No way!'

'Yes! And, Bravo, we were right about the cost of saving Rupert: Areté made an Arrangement with someone called Callista. Callista allowed her to save a life, and in return, wants to know who is going to be the next Mandala. Areté won't tell, so because she can't fulfil her side of the deal, she can't leave.'

'Mandala?'

'Ask Sky about that too.'

The fire, forest and dark night sky flickered alarmingly. Bravo grunted with effort.

'Sorry - I can't hold it. Got to send you back.'

'But - Bravo - no - wait - !'

Lien sat up sharply. Kai was crouched next to him, watching carefully.

'You alright?' he asked.

Lien nodded.

'Yes - that wasn't Shah. That was my friend Bravo. He, uh, he made a dream. A dream to meet me in.'

Kai looked impressed.

'Does he often do that?'

'Never,' Lien said.

'Your being here probably helped. There's a kid who comes here to practice dream magic.'

'There is? Who?'

'Bane's son.'

'Tryst?'

Kai shrugged.

'Is Tryst Bane's son?'

'Yes.'

'Then yes, Tryst. Poor kid, wouldn't wish a father like that on anyone.'

'Why?' Lien asked.

'Awful man. Seems very grand and well to do, but there's a real darkness under all that,' Kai said. Lien frowned fleetingly, wondering how metaphorical Kai was being.

'Was Tryst one of the chevaliers you met in Leaverness?' Kai asked slowly. Lien nodded, then caught on, remembering what they had learned together in the prison.

'Ohhhhh,' he said. 'Bane sent the men to attack the People.'

Lien couldn't believe Tryst would have betrayed him though. But it did make sense. How else did Bane know about him being with the People?

'Tryst looked really bad when I saw him in The Sign of the Angel. I mean he had a bruised face and looked - just terrible. I wonder if Bane...you know...' Lien broke off, not wanting to say what he was thinking.

'If Bane beat the crap out of his son?' Kai supplied helpfully. 'Wouldn't put it past him for a moment.'

'And Sir Armitage said he came to our aid because he'd had a dream in which a boy told him about the attack on the People,' Lien realised out loud. 'Could that have been Tryst?'

Kai shrugged.

'We'd have to ask him. And by "we" I mean you, because he would be honour-bound to try to capture me and then I'd have to thrash him, which would just be embarrassing for the illustrious Knight Operis,' Kai said.

Lien stared.

'You think you could defeat Sir Armitage?' he asked, unsure whether to be impressed or sceptical.

'I have, many times. He's no Lindahl, and Lindahl is the only knight who could beat me - and *he* was cheating.'

'You are quite - violent,' Lien conceded.

'I told you. I'm just very straightforward. If you're getting into a fight with me, I'm going to win, whatever it takes. Morality makes things complicated. Armitage is a moral man. I am not.'

With this pronouncement, Kai hunkered back down on his bed, back to Lien, blanket drawn up over his shoulder. Lien lay on his back again, staring up at the ceiling, thinking about Tryst. Had the boy betrayed them by choice, or had he been forced by his father? Lien hoped the latter, though it meant Tryst had been beaten by Bane over Lien himself, which made his tummy knot guiltily.

Hours later, Lien woke naturally - which was frankly a huge relief after his last several awakenings. It was light, and Kai was gone, his bed left neatly made. Gentle equine sounds of chewing, tail swishing and rustling straw from the next stable indicated Chase was still here, so Kai was likely nearby. But Lien decided he needed to get off the estate and away from its unsettling espréi, at least for a few hours. He wanted to find Armitage and ask him who he had seen in the dream that sent him to Leaverness. He was also desperate to see Jest and, to his surprise, keen to see Citar again.

Lien tidied his blanket in the way Kai had and went to visit Chase, who came and put his head curiously over the stable door when Lien approached. He was huge, so much bigger in height and breadth than Jest, but his coat was as soft and he smelt just the same. In the daylight, Lien could finally see his true golden colour and the many concentric dapples that made up his shiny coat. Lien hoped Citar was right about Jest being free in a field. This horse seemed unconcerned by his captivity, but Lien doubted Jest would be so relaxed about being cooped up indoors, unable to stretch his legs and play with his friends.

Lien looked around the stables for Kai first before heading out into the fresh, dewy morning. The low sun shone through the skeleton of Levithorne, bathing even such blackened stone in warmth and beauty. Lien found himself drawn towards the old manor house, so skirted the side to get the front. He was fascinated by its fractured, fire-scarred facade. When he stood directly before the wide, cracked sweeping stairs that led to the front doors, he thought he imagined, between blinks, seeing it in its undamaged, gothic glory. But as quickly as he had thought he had seen it, the building was derelict once more, a brooding black ruin hunched against the bright blue sky. Levithorne had been destroyed long before Lien had been born, so there was no way the image in his mind had been a memory. And he had not seen enough houses in his short time in Avenel to be able to fill the detail in himself.

Lien began up the stairs, careful not to step in cracks or stumble on loose stones and shale. As he ascended, he started to hear *thud thudding* sounds, exhales and grunts of exertion. The blackened, heavy double front door was ajar, and slipping inside, Lien found himself in a vast reception room. The marble floor was cracked and grimy and stretched to the remains of what had been a grand staircase: the steps were gone, but the frame and bannisters remained. Lien felt the faint thrum of their espréi: they were made of borealus. In fact, as he looked around, he realised quite a lot the remaining infrastructure of the room was made of the wood of borealus trees. How many beautiful, sentient trees had been sacrificed for the construction of Levithorne? Lien shuddered, remembering the last borealus left in Leaverness was no longer protected by Areté and Sky's charm.

A shattered chandelier hung several meters too low and at a peculiar angle from the vaulted ceiling above, and in the centre of the space stood a bronze statue of a man. It had been disrespectfully wrapped in layers of padding and was now being used by Kai as a kicking post. He was roundhouse kicking it at various heights, without respite, and so hard that the floor shuddered with every impact. The stone base of the statue was deeply fractured and dust showered down with each blow. The statue was of a serious man in a robe with his arms crossed; the expression bled disapproval, as though it had been cast knowing this would be its fate.

'No night-mare?' Kai grunted. His whole body rotated powerfully with every kick, and the blows echoed through the empty building. His back was turned to Lien, who would swear he had not made a sound.

'No,' Lien replied.

Kai stopped, and turned to face him, his shoulders lifting and falling from the exertion.

'Who is that?' Lien asked, nodding to the statue.

'Old man Lethe. So arrogant - he made himself - the main feature - of his own house. But then - no-one else would have ever made a statue - to his monstrous ego - so

I guess - this is only way he would get one,' Kai said between panted breaths.

The detail of the statue was unreal. Only the crossed arms, shoulders and head were visible under the straw, hessian and ropes Kai had bound it in to convert it into a kicking post, but they were perfect renderings of a man, just in metal instead of flesh and bone. Lien moved in to look closer - and started when the statue blinked.

'And yes, he's in there,' Kai said, amused by the boy's reaction.

'What? *In* the statue?' Lien gasped.

'I told you the place was haunted,' Kai shrugged.

'But that's - that's terrible! Who put him in there?' Lien asked, horrified.

'He made a lot of enemies,' Kai said.

'Can we get him out?' Lien asked.

'We do *not* want to do that, believe me. There's nowhere safer for a man that dangerous than locked in his own statue,' and Kai gave it a last powerful roundhouse kick. The impact thudded satisfyingly.

'Right, let's grab something to eat and then go find our kingless champion.'

The morning was still early but already warm when they set out from Levithorne after a breakfast of tea and gruel. Despite the summer season, Kai still wore a light hood, long sleeves and gloves to hide his pale skin. Lien too wore his hooded, long-sleeved top, this time without his usual tunic underneath. The day would get hot even for just sleeves, much less a double layer.

They travelled first by foot until they could hop on the back of a passing wagon, crouched down out of the sight of the driver, before switching to what Kai announced to be his favourite method of traversing Avenel: rooftop.

Lien beamed.

'The city is so densely built in now, it's the safest way for a couple of fugitives to get around,' Kai explained as they used a drain pipe to scale the wall of an inn. If Kai still had any broken ribs, he showed no sign of them; Lien however made a slower and more painful ascent. He could feel that the one night at Levithorne had made a big difference, but not enough for what was about to happen.

Once they reached the broad, gently sloped top, the rooftops of Avenel spread out before and around them. Although the city had not been built with aerial travel in mind, Lien could see how easily a fit, lithe and clever runner could get around. The roofs were mostly made of tile, slate and thatch and although many were at quite steep angles, even these tended to have broad peaks that could be traversed by someone with excellent balance and no fear. The shallower angled roofs could be run along at any point, and many buildings had rooftop terraces, which were the easiest of all. Most of the streets were narrow enough to leap across effortlessly. This early in the morning, there was no issue with scalding surfaces either.

Kai set off at a light jog. Lien started to follow suit, grimacing at the objections from his ribs; but when his breath began to shorten, he gasped from the pain. Noticing the boy was struggling and falling behind, Kai slowed and waited for him to catch up.

'Ribs still giving you trouble?' he asked. Lien nodded, holding his left side and wincing with every breath. Panting hurt even more.

'Sorry, I forget the time it takes most people to heal,'

Kai said. 'Did Levithorne help?'

'I think so, but it still all hurts,' Lien wheezed. 'How long will it take?'

'To heal fully? Several weeks. But I think you'll find Levithorne shortens the process,' Kai said. It was supposed to be reassuring, but Lien stared.

'I have to stay at Levithorne? For weeks?'

'You don't have to,' Kai said, frowning. 'You can go your own way.'

'No, it's not that - it's not about you,' Lien amended hastily. 'It's - the place. It doesn't feel good.'

Kai considered the boy for several long seconds.

'Guess I've just got used to it,' he said eventually, and continued, but this time at only a fast walk.

'We must keep going though, as quickly as we can, or we'll miss him,' he said over his shoulder.

'Where are we going?' Lien asked, grudgingly jogging a few steps to catch up with Kai's huge strides.

'Voltanna.'

The fortress was unmissable from the rooftops, rising up and up in the centre of the city and crowned by the tower Voltarch, which climbed higher still into the bright blue sky. Lien could feel the espréi of Voltarch as they approached, like a gentle fizz in his blood, and so much more enjoyable than that of Levithorne. As the pains in his chest subsided, he was better able to enjoy the travel, far above the streets. They were above the rush, the crowds and the noise. They travelled a more dangerous but quicker and far more exciting route, and Lien felt a brief taste of the freedom he enjoyed in Leaverness.

They approached Voltanna from the far side of the

main gate, descending to ground level outside the wall.

'There's no way around it, I'm afraid, but generations of criminals have done work on this wall,' Kai said, looking up the pale stone defence. Lien grinned, for it was true: there were shallow indentations all the way up, perfect for hand and foot holds.

'I'm going up the guard tower over there to keep them out of your way,' Kai said, indicating a nearby tower along the wall. 'When you see me wave, climb up here and head to the tower. There's a bridge there that goes over the bailey and up into the second ring. In there, you will find the cemetery of the Order. There's a big old stone building in there - the mausoleum, you can't miss it - where the kings are buried. If we're lucky and not too late, you might find Armitage inside.'

Lien nodded his understanding, and waited as Kai swiftly scaled the wall. As Kai approached the top, he took a large rock from a pocket and thew it inside the wall, on the other side of the tower. When the guard looked out that way, Kai swiftly topped the wall, jogged towards and then entered the bastion tower. Less than a minute later, he appeared briefly in the lookout to wave, then disappeared back inside.

Hoping Kai had not seriously harmed the guard, Lien also climbed the wall, though he made both painful and slow progress. He used his legs to take his weight as much as possible because there was no way he could hang from his arms. He was feeling sick and exhausted by the time he got to the top of a wall he should have been easily able to scale in under a minute and enjoyed every second of. He collected himself and headed as quickly as he could towards the tower. Now he could see the bridge Kai had told him of: an arch of stone that connected the outer and second wall. There was no sign of Kai as he jogged across it, passing over the bailey. Below him were huge sheds containing hay and straw for the horses, and there was no-one to be seen. The second wall was higher than the first, as Voltanna was built on a hill, so the slope of the bridge, combined with the climb, caused Lien's breath to shorten, and then reluctantly, his pace to again slow.

On the other side of the second wall lay a serene oasis. The cemetery was full of trees, flowers, birds, grass and climbing roses. It was the most beautiful place Lien had seen so far in the city. He felt a calm emanating from it as he approached.

Some of the graves were marked only with simple stones; others had taller monuments and even statues of knights, horses and gentlewomen. The mausoleum was, as Kai had said, impossible to miss. The austere pillared stone monument was the only building in the area.

Getting down into the cemetery was a matter of carefully descending a helpful tree growing just back from the wall, followed by a short trot to the immense, heavily riveted door of the mausoleum. It was ajar. Lien looked around it cautiously, and saw a big man in the gloom, back to him. He was the right general height and shape to be Armitage, but as Lien had never seen the knight without a helm, he didn't recognise the long, wavy black hair spilling over this man's back.

'Sir Armitage?' he opened hopefully.

Armitage spun around, frowning, hand on the hilt of the sword at his side. Relieved, Lien drew down his hood and slipped through the door.

'Lien – ?' Armitage said, surprised. 'What are you doing

here? I thought you were with Lady Beckworth.'

'Sir Armitage - forgive the intrusion,' Lien stammered. Despite his best intentions, he was still awestruck at being in the great knight's presence. Armitage was not dressed in armour this time, but in an off-white shirt over dark blue leather trousers and black boots. This made him appear smaller than Lien had twice last seen him, but he was no less imposing. Like Kai, he was a huge man, but where Kai had a menace to his bearing, Armitage had majesty.

Lien thought he would make an excellent king.

The knight crossed him arms seriously.

'You should not be here - ' he started, but Lien held up his hands to stop him.

'I will be quick. Please tell me: how did you know the People were in danger? Why did you come to Leaverness?'

'I had - a premonition,' Armitage said, choosing the word carefully.

'You had a dream?' Lien prompted.

Armitage cocked his head to one side.

'A dream, or a premonition,' he conceded.

'Someone told you about the attack, in the dream?' Lien pushed.

'Yes, they did,' the knight agreed cautiously.

'Was it Tryst?' Lien asked, a tightness in his chest. He realised he wanted it to be. He wanted so badly for Tryst to have been forced by his father to reveal Lien and to have tried to help afterwards.

Armitage had been disconcerted for the entirety of the brief exchange, but was openly staring now.

'Yes... yes it was,' he finally agreed.

Lien sighed with relief.

'But it was...just a premonition,' Armitage insisted.

'You believed it enough to saddle up and ride to Leaverness,' Lien said.

'I went only myself, where I would otherwise have taken several knights. But it was…very real,' Armitage conceded. 'He was *very* insistent. But – it cannot have *been* Tryst. I do not know why the dream – the premonition – used him to communicate with me. I do not know him well.'

Lien naturally went to tell the truth, but was fortunately stopped by the sound of a stone bouncing off the top of the mausoleum. He glanced automatically out the door, then back to the knight.

'I need to go,' Lien said, turning to do so. Armitage had followed his gaze and now narrowed his eyes. With unexpected speed, he grabbed Lien's arm, turning the boy back to him.

'You're with Kai,' he guessed, his voice hardening. 'Lien, he is a very dangerous man, you put yourself at grave risk.'

'N-no, he's been good to me,' Lien stammered, taken aback by Armitage's unexpected intensity.

'He murdered a man in the prison, in front of you,' the knight said, astonished at this statement.

A second stone bound off the roof, harder this time.

'I know. But he's the only person who will help me. Please let me go, Sir Armitage,' Lien pleaded. Armitage had his forearm in a painfully iron grip. The knight realised he was causing the boy pain, and reluctantly let go.

'If only a bad man will help you, you need to think about what it is you need help with,' Armitage called as Lien shot towards the ajar door, but he was too late. Another man was coming through it, stepping sideways to pass through the small space Lien had walked straight through. Lien bowled into his broad chest and the man caught the boy by the shoulders as he reeled back. When the new knight then got a clear look at Lien's face, a shocked expression spread across his own.

'Cashan - let the boy pass,' Armitage called.

Cashan did not respond for a moment, only staring at Lien, who stared back, afraid of the man's expression. Then the knight let go of his shoulders and after a questioning look to Armitage, allowed Lien to slip out and flee from the building. Armitage quickly strode after him, stopping when he was outside the door. Kai, perched on the wall next to the tree Lien had climbed down, was helping pull Lien out of the tree and onto the wall. He gave Armitage and the still-shocked Cashan a cheerful salute, before man and boy dashed to the arch bridging the outer and second walls, disappearing down its slope.

'That's the Leaverness boy?' Cashan demanded when Armitage turned a questioning look upon him.

'Yes, what was that about? You looked like you saw a ghost.'

'I thought I did. He doesn't remind you of anyone?' Cashan asked.

'Of course he does. But it's not possible.'

Armitage shot Cashan a very hard look.

'Is it?' he demanded, suddenly suspicious.

'Of course not,' Cashan said stiffly. 'I was there, and Bane was…very thorough.'

'Of course he was,' Armitage said darkly.

Cashan ran a hand through his tousled brown hair.

'But yes - I did think for a moment that I had seen a ghost.'

*****

'Selene says I have to work on the Voltarch restoration, as community service for the damage to The Sign of the Angel,' Lien complained. He and Kai were sitting on the gently sloping rooftop near Voltanna, eating apples they had liberated from a merchant cart.

'What restoration?' Kai asked sharply, pausing mid-bite.

'I was hoping *you* would know,' Lien said.

They both looked across to the massive tower. They couldn't see its ground level, but they could see the scaffolding being built between its second and third levels.

Kai frowned.

'I assumed it needed some reinforcing or maintenance.'

'It needs fixing, the whole top is missing,' Lien said.

'It is not supposed to be fully restored,' Kai said. 'It is forbidden to do so. And before you ask why, I do not know the full story. I just know it was damaged in the Occult Wars, and there was an agreement made that it would never be repaired to its original state.'

Lien mentally filed that under the ever-growing list of things that were not urgent but he would like to understand more about, when he had time.

'But *how* can Tryst use dream magic? I thought you don't like magic in Avenel, and dream magic is rare anyway,' Lien mused, returning to their original subject of conversation.

'He must have a teacher. It might even be his father. I'm absolutely certain Bane has meddled in dark magic in the past. Not quite enough to get his house burned down though – he's a clever bastard.'

'How did you know where we would find Armitage?' Lien asked, wondering if Kai was able to cast his espréi, as Cobi had in finding Rupert.

'Armitage is a man of habit. He pays his respects to Du Romeau at the same time every morning.'

'The old king?' Lien asked.

'Yes. Since Du Romeau was murdered by Lindahl, Armitage has nominally been the Knight Operis - the king's champion. But there's been no king. He's spent his life in the service of the crown, only for there to be no-one under it when his big promotion came. So he goes to swear his fealty to the last king every day, in place of the next one.'

'That's sort of…sad,' Lien said.

'It's ritual, and it's stupid, but he's not the sharpest tool in the shed,' Kai shrugged.

Lien frowned.

'He worked out you had taken me to him, without me saying anything about you. I thought he was pretty on the ball,' he protested. 'And he's brave, and he's an amazing fighter. He took on the four men attacking the People on his own. I hope he gets a king to be the champion for.'

'Well, they do say there's an heir out there somewhere,' Kai said, and gave Lien a brief, odd look.

Lien caught it.

'You don't think it's me, do you?' he asked anxiously. 'I don't want to live in Avenel. I want to find Arete and go back to the People.'

'Let's hope it's not then. Bane seems to think you're valuable though, or he wouldn't have sent his thugs out to get you.'

'I don't like the sound of Bane,' Lien said.

'He's a real piece of work. Steer clear of him.'

'That's what Armitage said about you though,' Lien said pointedly.

'He's probably right too,' Kai returned, equally pointedly. 'But seriously. Keep clear of Bane *and* his son.'

'But Tryst might be able to help, if he can do dream magic too,' Lien said. 'And he was good to me in Leaverness. And he saved us from those men by sending Armitage.'

'Well you know his father can force information out of him, and you don't know who is teaching him. I would be very, very cautious, if I was you.'

But Lien was not cautious by nature, which is why, when he later met Citar and Tryst on top of the hay and straw sheds in the fortress bailey - arranged via throwing rocks at Citar to get her attention in the stables - Lien told him everything. Or at least, tried to.

Tryst had been reluctant to meet at all, and initially kept interrupting Lien's explanations with protestations that he didn't want to hear any more. His face only betrayed any interest when Lien got to Callista, the entity inside her, and their incarceration of Areté. This elicited a genuine look of shock, which Tryst quickly replaced with a fake mask of boredom. For Callista was Tryst's teacher, and it was also an Arrangement with which, in return for learning the secrets and methods of dream magic, he was taking himself deeper and deeper into her debt. Hearing how Areté's debt was working out made him feel sick. He was also puzzled by Lien's story of there being someone - or some*thing* - else inside his teacher. From that point, he listened very carefully and without interruption.

'I still don't know why you're telling me all of this,' Tryst said flatly though when Lien concluded. 'What is it that you want from me?'

The bruise of his father's hand on his face was just four almost invisible lines, unnoticeable to anyone who wasn't looking for it. He still looked drawn though.

Lien met his tired eyes.

'I know you told your father about meeting me in Leaverness,' he said, his tone even.

Tryst frowned; Citar looked shocked.

'You didn't? she gasped.

'I did not *tell* him,' Tryst growled. 'He knew we were lying. But I stuck to the story we agreed.'

'Then why was it your father who sent men to Leaverness to take me from the People? And why did *you* warn Armitage?' Lien pushed back.

Citar looked in wonder between the two boys as they tried to stare one another down.

'I didn't *tell* him,' Tryst repeated slowly. 'And I would appreciate any further - accusations - be made in *private*,' he added, with the meaningful glance to Citar.

'Me? I'm not weird about magic, I know it's real,' Citar said. 'I mean I think it's *amazing*.'

'Citar, would you give us a moment?' Lien asked, still holding Tryst's eye-line. Citar paused a moment, tempted to argue, but reluctantly sloped off to the far end of the shed, where she sat with her legs dangling off the roof.

Tryst glared at Lien.

'I know you can use dream magic,' Lien started boldly.

'And I don't think you understand how much danger that knowledge puts me in,' Tryst said, angry now. 'This isn't Leaverness, Lien. Magic is not a thing respectable people do here. You would be best forgetting what you know, and not having anything else to do with me. I knew it was a mistake to come here.'

Tryst stood up, ready to leave.

'Please, Tryst!' Lien begged, jumping up too and catching his elbow as he turned. 'Bravo and I need to help Areté, and the only connection we have is Shah, the night-mare who brings me the dreams of her. We want to ride her back to the source of the dreams, to find out who is sending them, and why. That person must know something that can help us to free Areté. There must be a reason they are sending her to me.'

'What makes you think that is even possible? To ride the night-mare?' Tryst asked, easily shaking his arm free of Lien's grip. He was older and bigger but even so, Lien was surprised at just how much stronger he was.

'Bravo does dream magic too,' Lien said.

Tryst looked dubious.

'It's true!' Lien insisted. 'His mother could as well. The People are teaching him the ways of Aurebos - of the dreaming realm.'

Tryst felt envious at this; on his face, the emotion was translated as a grimace.

'Lucky him,' he said, his tone brittle.

'Who teaches you?' Lien asked, curiously.

'No-one. I am teaching myself,' Tryst lied. 'As I said before, magic is not well regarded in Avenel. Now, do not tell me *anything* else. I won't tell...but that doesn't mean the things I know are...safe.'

Tryst immediately regretted the last sentence.

'Your father hurts you, doesn't he?' Lien asked quietly.

Tryst glared, his jaw clenched. He did want to tell someone though. And Lien, he suspected, was someone who might need to know.

'My father has - methods - of finding out what he

needs,' he said stiffly. 'Do not ever let yourself be alone with him.'

While the boys were staring gravely at each other, Citar jumped up from where she had been sitting and jogged over to them.

'Listen, I've realised who the next Mandala is!' she said excitedly.

Lien and - despite himself - Tryst, looked to her curiously.

'It's Rupert!' Citar announced proudly.

Tryst gave a dry laugh, but Lien frowned thoughtfully.

'Oh come on, he's useless,' Tryst said. 'You saw for yourselves in Leaverness.'

'No, think about it,' Citar insisted. 'Areté puts herself into debt to Callista to save Rupert, of all people? I mean, I like Rupert well enough but she could have saved anyone, anytime, and she chooses *him*, it *is* weird. So there has to be something really important about him. *And* she gives him Lord Jorge, who is no ordinary horse. *Then* she's asked who the next Mandala is and she shuts up. If that's all a coincidence, it's a pretty big one if you ask me.'

Tryst considered this, and shrugged.

'I disagree, Rupert is heir to a neighbouring throne, it might have been a tactical move on Areté's part. But let's assume you are right. What do you want to do - give Rupert to Callista, to eliminate her problem?' he asked.

Lien and Citar glanced guiltily at one another, recalling the earlier conversation with Selene.

Citar hadn't thought that far along.

Lien did not answer the question.

'Of course we don't,' Citar said firmly.

Tryst gave the pair a flat look.

'Seems to me the thing you need to do is find the current Mandala and send *them* to deal with Callista. Or - whatever Lien says is inside her. At least the Mandala will have a fighting chance against them,' he said.

The sincerity with which he said the last sentence caught Lien's attention.

'You say that but…we don't even know what Callista and her sidekick are capable of,' Lien said thoughtfully. 'They might not even be that powerful.'

'They're holding Areté,' Citar pointed out.

'No they're not; Areté is submitting to them, according to the terms of their Agreement,' Lien countered.

'She seems to believe she can kill the Mandala, and we don't even know the extent of its powers. I would assume she's a legitimate threat,' Tryst said, this time not allowing his personal knowledge to colour his words.

'Tryst, please will you help us?' Lien asked.

Tryst wanted to say yes. He wanted to get involved. He wanted friends, and he wanted a chance a find out more about Callista. But he couldn't betray her, and he couldn't let her - or his father - know what Lien and Citar were thinking and planning.

He kept his expression cold, melting the hope of the other two.

'I cannot help you,' he said. 'And I will ask you, again, not to involve me any further in your plans. It is better that way.'

This time Lien did not try to stop him from leaving; he paused a few strides away though, and turned back.

'And do not try to ride the night-mare, Lien. I'm serious. If something happened while you did, your consciousness would be stranded, disconnected from your body. Your body would likely die before you could find a way back – *if* you could find a way back.'

'How does he know that?' Citar asked quietly as she watched Tryst disappearing as he climbed down from the roof.

'He does dream magic too,' Lien said.

'What?!'

'Oh, but don't tell anyone,' Lien added hastily, remembering that Tryst had asked him not to share that information. 'Or he'll be in big trouble, apparently.'

'You bet he will,' Citar said. 'He'll be out of the Order and disowned by Sir Bane for starters.'

*Not if his father is also using magic*, Lien thought, but this time silently.

'I have to go too actually, break is almost over,' Citar said, noting a bell tolling further into Voltanna. 'You won't do anything stupid, will you?'

'Like what?' Lien asked innocently.

'You heard what Tryst said about Shah.'

'I did indeed,' Lien agreed.

'And?'

'And I will not do anything stupid,' Lien grinned impishly.

Citar went to argue, but paused, and sighed. He was clearly going to do what he wanted regardless.

'See you tomorrow?' she asked, hopefully.

'I hope so,' Lien said, a genuine smile on his face now.

* * * * *

In the late afternoon, after endless badgering and pleading, Kai took Lien to see Jest. Darius lived on a small farm outside the main city walls, on the side of the city opposite to Leaverness. It would take over an hour at a walk, which was all Lien was going to cope with after the morning's painful exertions, and he harangued Kai to take Chase bareback so that he could sit more comfortably up front and with the better view. But Kai refused, citing that riding around bareback drew too much attention, and set Lien up behind his saddle again.

They found Jest grazing in a field with an elderly black warhorse, a bay mare and a sway backed brown cow. Jest whinnied at the sound of Lien's voice and cantered straight over across the field. Lien hoped he would stop at the wood rail fence, but clapped his hands over his mouth in a mix of pride and dismay as Jest instead easily jumped over it. Lien slipped off Chase and ran to his approaching pony, who stopped only just in time, rubbing his face up and down Lien's scrawny body.

'Ouch ouch my ribs, Jest, stop!' Lien laughed, pushing the happy pony back and instead using his fingers to scratch hard at all of Jest's favourite places on his head. Jest then started frisking his pockets for the carrots he could smell.

'Are you happy? I've missed you so much! Who are your friends?' Lien asked as he fed Jest the carrots. The two horses and cow were ambling over, much slower than their new companion, to see what all the fuss was about.

'I hope you can get him back in that field, he's not coming with us,' Kai said, unimpressed with Jest's escape.

'Can't he come to Levithorne, Kai?' Lien pleaded.

'Only if he'll stand in a stable all day,' Kai growled.

Lien's face fell.

'Okay Jest you have to stay here with your new friends. You won't like the city and you definitely won't like being in a stable.'

Lien climbed through the fence and called Jest from inside the field. Jest snorted and jumped back in.

'Good boy, now you have to stay here,' Lien said, breaking the carrots into smaller and smaller pieces to make them last long enough to be able to share with the newcomers. The black horse's coat shone and was soft to the touch despite his age; he was obviously very well looked after, which made Lien dislike Darius slightly less. The cow's tongue was huge and so wet that she made Lien giggle as she took the proffered piece of carrot. Lien told Jest, in the language of horses this time, that he must stay in the field, and that he would be back as soon as he could. He then climbed onto the fence and took Kai's arm to remount. As they rode away he tried not to look back, but a forlorn whinny from behind made his chest tighten. He was relieved that Jest was safe and in a big field with friends, but he had no idea when he could get his beloved pony back.

* * * * *

Tryst was troubled by the news that Callista had trapped Areté into an Arrangement she must have known the warrior woman would not be able to fulfil, and that she had allowed Areté to be as abused as Lien had described.

Two years ago, Tryst had spent a night at Levithorne after running away from his father. It had been the first time Sir Bane had forcefully entered his mind to view his memories and Tryst, still just a boy, had been confused and frightened. He had always suffered nightmares and night terrors, and had been subjected to a difficult childhood as the son of the Red Knight, but that violation from his father had seemed liked a nightmare come to life. He had cried himself to sleep in the chapel of Levithorne, and Callista had come to him in his sleep.

Tryst's mother tried hard to love her son but he had always known that she had to make an effort to do so. This had installed a strong belief, early in his life, that there was something deeply wrong with him. Callista, in contrast, was warm and kind and believed that, far from there being something wrong with him, there was something *special* about him. She had initially offered only to teach him how to control his dreams - to defuse his nightmares - and this he had learned very quickly.

She had then offered him an Arrangement: she would teach him everything she knew about dream magic, and at some time in the future, she would require an undisclosed favour in return. She had told him that she was not allowed to teach him dream magic without a formal arrangement. Callista had been loose with her terminology and capitalisation though, and Tryst had not fully understood what he was committing to. But he was intoxicated with the prospect of being able to use dream magic, and of being able to stand up to this father. He could think then of no price that would be too high to pay.

And so he had agreed, entering a capitalised Arrangement, in which he would be required to do Callista a favour of her choosing, in a time of her choosing.

He had trusted her.

In his subsequent visits to Levithorne, they progressed from controlling his own dreams, to entering and influencing the dreams of others. Callista also started to teach him how to resist and fool his father's attempts to directly extract truths: dreams, she explained, are built on memories, and memories are the stories we tell ourselves about the things that happen to us. He could change the stories, which would change the memories. The smaller the required change, the easier it was to create a new story, or memory; the adventures in Leaverness required far more change than he could yet manage though. He had failed to fool his father. But Callista had not reprimanded or judged him. She had come to his aide, helping him project into Armitage's dream, sending the finest knight in the Order to thwart his father's plans.

She had only ever helped him.

But now he had to know what it was that she would want from him in return.

He was deeply afraid of what it might be.

That night, after speaking to Lien and Citar, Tryst snuck out after his parents and the household staff went to sleep, and jogged the twenty minutes it took to get from his family manor to the burnt-out shell of Levithorne. He had been avoiding Kai for several days now, and was careful not to pass anywhere near the stables where Kai and Lien would be sleeping.

Except Kai wasn't sleeping, and instead, discreetly followed Tryst to the chapel. There he watched the boy sit into cross legged against the central pillar, close his eyes and make the triangle sign with his right index and middle finger. When Tryst didn't move again for half an hour - even when Kai silently entered the chapel and walked all the way around him, crouched down before him and said his name - Kai returned to the stables. He washed himself with a bucket and water from the well, then washed and hung out his shirt after the day's exertions. He refilled the bucket and began to carry it to the stables to top up Chase's water, but as he entered the old building, his eyes narrowed. He proceeded to fill Chase's water trough up, chatting to the horse as he did, before making a show of walking back out of the stables, only to go around the outside to come back in at the forge end. He walked soundlessly back through, picking up his sword on the way, and stepped dramatically into the doorway of the stable in which he and Lien slept, sword at the ready.

Citar, sitting next to a sleeping Lien, jumped and yelped in surprise.

'Is everyone at Levithorne tonight?' Kai asked, one eyebrow hoisted high with disapproval.

'Hello! You must be - Kai - ' Citar said, and she had every intention of saying it in a cool and collected manner, boy to man. But she found herself unexpectedly overwhelmed in his presence, though in a completely different way to how Lien had felt in the presence of Sir Armitage. Lien admired Armitage. Looking on Kai, Citar was shocked to find her heart running faster, her breath a little shorter and a flush rising.

She had been told that Kai was dangerous and murderous. She was expecting some sort of monster. Some sort of strong, heroic monster who would put his own body between Lien and a vindictive boot in the guts, and could pick up her like she weighed nothing; but a dirty, dangerous monster nonetheless.

She wasn't expecting the man in front of her, and she especially hadn't been expecting him to be topless, with his exotically pale body on show. Wild beard, narrowed eyes and outstretched sword notwithstanding, her wide eyes drank in his youthful, square jawed face, bright blue eyes and broad, muscular chest and arms.

Kai was, without doubt, the most handsome man she had ever met.

'Can I - help you - ?' he asked eventually, as Citar continued helplessly to stare upon him.

'Oh! Yes! Very rude, I am so sorry. You just look - so *completely* different to how you did in The Angel,' she said, forcing her eyes to blink. 'I mean you were...dirty...and all...hooded and deep throated and menacing,' she continued, digging herself deeper into her embarrassment.

'It's Citar, isn't it?' Kai asked, dropping the sword. This wasn't the first time he had left someone breathless but it was more commonly girls and women, than teenage boys, who found themselves in this chevalier's predicament. Kai swung any which way, but he had age limits and thought it best not to encourage the teenager's interest in any way.

'Is anyone else here?' he asked, trying to focus the boy's attention.

'No - why, did you see someone else?' Citar asked.

'Yes, Tryst is in the chapel.'

'Why?' Citar frowned.

'I think he is dreaming,' Kai said, looking to Lien with a nod. 'Like he is.'

'Oh dear,' Citar sighed. 'I think Lien is doing something really stupid.'

'What a shockingly unexpected development.'

* * * * *

Callista had come straight into the dream Tryst opened to host her. It was, he realised, as though she had expected his summons.

'Tryst,' she greeted him warmly. 'You look better

tonight.'

'Thank you, I am,' he replied.

'So, what shall we work on now?' Callista asked, sitting cross-legged opposite him. The dream was also of the chapel, but in its original state - or what Tryst imagined it must have looked like before the fire pulled in its ceiling, melted its beautiful stained-glass windows and blackened its walls.

'Lien is looking for Areté, and has asked my help. He believes she is in danger. I wanted to ask you if you know where she is, or could help find her?' Tryst asked, his voice steady and calm.

'Now why would Lien ask for *your* help, Tryst?' Callista asked, and although her tone was that of polite curiosity, the inflection cut a little. Tryst realised she was as prepared to trip him up and he was her. His heart sank. He didn't want to play games with Callista. He loved her. He *had* loved her, in a deeply maternal way that he was now realising might be founded on deceit and lies.

He opted to open with the truth.

'He found out that Armitage saw me in a dream, and deduced that I can do dream magic. He is familiar with it, through his friend Bravo.'

'Ahhhhhhh yes, so it is Lien who dreams of Areté,' Callista said, a thoughtful smile spreading slowly across her beautiful, fine-featured face. 'This makes sense.'

'I didn't say that,' Tryst asked. In fact, he had very specifically *not* said that.

Callista put her elbows on her knees and leant her chin onto her interlinked knuckles.

'Let us be honest with one another.'

Tryst's mind raced under his calm demeanour. How

honest could he be? Callista evidently knew about Lien's dreams, but how *much* did she know? What might he accidentally betray?

'I will follow your lead,' he said, stalling for time and information.

'My wise boy,' Callista said fondly. 'Of course. Areté is in a mutually agreed debt to me, which she now refuses to repay. Until such time as she does, or the information comes to me another way, she must stay in my care. She does so willingly, as per the terms of our Agreement. But all of this you know, I believe.'

'I do. So please, tell me something I do not know. What is the debt you will require of me, as per the terms of *our* Arrangement.'

Callista smiled kindly.

'In all honesty, I do not know yet. But I think we can work it out together, now, if you wish to know with urgency. Tell me more about Lien. Tell me something *I* do not know.'

'I have nothing else to tell you,' Tryst said.

'I thought we agreed on honesty, my apprentice. I taught you to lie to deceive your father; not to deceive me.'

Callista gave Tryst a searching look, and when he remained blank, she briefly pursed her lips.

'It would be best, Tryst, if you tell me what I ask,' she said carefully. 'If you do not, there will be - consequences - beyond my control. And I do not wish to see you harmed.'

The juxtaposition between the sincerity of her tone, but menace within her words, surprised Tryst. He recalled Lien's belief that there was something else inside her.

'That sounds like a threat, Callista,' he said.

'I am afraid that it very much is, Tryst. But only if you lie to me. And I have only ever helped you, so it hurts that this is how you repay me.'

'Lien tells me that Areté is being tortured in your…care,' Tryst said.

Callista shrugged.

'I am patient, but she is ageless, where I am not, so I cannot wait forever to learn what I need to know. I allowed some agency to her keepers to motivate her to tell me what I need to know sooner.'

'You must have known it would not work.'

'There are other methods, it is true. But I do not think you would like them any more. I considered it better to try to motivate her directly before trying through…other methods. Other *people*.'

Tryst narrowed his eyes.

'You mean Lien.'

Callista smiled sadly.

'Last chance, my beloved boy. Please. Tell me what Lien plans.'

Tryst shook his head.

'I cannot,' he said simply.

'Cannot? Or will not?' Callista asked, a wry smile playing across her lips as she recalled Cosmos posing the same question to Areté. 'Or is it the same?'

Tryst nodded, steeling himself for whatever would come next. Surely, he reasoned, it would not be as bad as what his father could do to him.

'Then I am sorry, Tryst, surely I am, but we both serve a higher power, and now you must meet your true master. I am afraid you were never *my* apprentice,' Callista said, sorrowfully. She sighed, and closed her eyes, and when she opened them, they were a bright, cold, glittering gold.

YOU WERE MY IDEA. MY CREATION, TRYST.

Cosmos spoke into Tryst's mind, without the use of Callista's lips. Callista's body moved from cross legged to half kneeling, one hand on Tryst's head, with the speed of a striking snake.

I HAVE MANIPULATED YOUR FATHER FOR FAR LONGER THAN I HAVE TRAINED YOU.

As Cosmos effortlessly slid into Tryst's mind and watched his entire conversation with Lien and Citar play out, Tryst realised, dimly below the screaming but helpless protests of his mental defences, who had taught his father how to trespass into his mind.

*****

When Lien had fallen asleep in the stables of Levithorne, he had immediately found himself back at the campfire with Bravo.

'She's coming,' Bravo said tersely, eyes closed, from the far side of the fire.

'Who is? Areté?' Lien asked.

'Shah. I'm going to try to bring her into the dream too,' Bravo said.

'Bravo, I don't think we should – ' Lien started, but already he could hear the sound of galloping hoofbeats; although in the next moment he realised he could feel them in his chest and his head, not his ears. Bravo was suddenly, impossibly, at his side.

'You ready?' he asked, tense.

'No, definitely not, listen – ' Lien tried again, but then Shah was galloping into the clearing. In Bravo's dream, she looked like a real flesh and blood horse. She pulled up to an uneasy halt in front of the boys, nostrils flaring suspiciously.

'Calm her,' Bravo ordered, pushing Lien forward.

'Sh-shah. Easy, easy, beautiful girl,' Lien stammered in the language of horses. She threw her head up, eyes rolling to show the whites, but allowed him to approach.

'Get to her side,' Bravo said, following behind Lien, step for step like a shadow. Lien did as instructed, touching Shah for the first time, on the shoulder. Her dark dapple-grey coat was warm, and soft. She felt real. But she flinched under his hand. He spoke soothingly, and she allowed him to walk to her left shoulder.

'Well done. Now get on and make sure you get me up too!' Bravo said quietly and urgently over Lien's shoulder. Lien gulped. He knew Tryst's warning about the danger of riding the night-mare was true, but also, here he was *touching* Shah, as he had often dreamed of, like she was a real horse. Here he was able to vault onto her tall grey back and *ride* her, as he had imagined nightly as he had waited to fall asleep.

'*Now,* Lien!' Bravo hissed, and Lien stopped thinking about it. He vaulted onto Shah. As she shied violently to the right, his left arm held tight to Bravo's left arm and helped haul the other boy on behind. In the dream, he had no injuries, no pain. Bravo wrapped his arms around Lien's waist and Shah was off, galloping out of Bravo's campfire –

– and into the Lethe estate. There was a disorienting moment when she exited Bravo's dream and entered the physical world. Lien had perceived himself, Bravo and Shah as solid in Bravo's dream. When they entered the physical world, as their souls riding a night-mare, they all took on a shimmering translucence. Lien could look down through Shah's body to see the ground racing past below them.

Shah galloped straight towards the ruin of the Levithorne chapel. Lien was *pretty* certain they would phase through the walls with Shah but he still screwed his eyes hard shut as she ploughed full speed into what looked like solid stone.

Lien's eyes shot open again as he felt another disorienting lurch. They were solid again, but what made him gasp was the chapel itself. This was not the ruin he expected, but a beautiful, high, vaulted hexagonal construction. Grand decorative columns rose from each shallow corner and each wall was half stone, half tall stained-glass window. They were still in the darkness of night so the windows could not be fully enjoyed; instead the only illumination was the golden light thrown from a torch on each column. In the centre of the chapel rose up a huge column, itself made of six columns joined together, and in front of this stood Callista.

She had her hands buried deep in the pockets of her navy pleated skirt, floor length and the kind that a woman could ride a horse in astride, it contained so much material. Above this she wore a burgundy velvet waistcoat over a light cream shirt. Her golden glasses pushed back her emerald hair.

'This is a dream,' Bravo said quietly over Lien's shoulder. Aside from the miraculous reconstruction of the chapel, Lien would not have been able to tell: he could even feel cool air on his skin, which he couldn't in Bravo's dream. But *that* it was a dream wasn't what was important.

'The question is: whose?' he whispered back.

'Welcome, Lien and Bravo,' Callista said genially as the boys slid off the night-mare. Callista went to stroke Shah, but she skidded backwards on the stone floor, her grey head thrown high. Callista looked a little disappointed, but quickly shrugged it off.

'You are Callista?' Lien asked. Her eyes were cobalt blue, not the bright gold of whatever it was inside her that had sensed him in Areté.

'I am,' she agreed with a smile. 'It is a pleasure to meet you properly, after Areté has kept you hidden all of these years. Do you know why? I myself am desperately curious.'

'All of the People have been kept hidden,' Bravo said bullishly, saving Lien from a question he couldn't possibly answer. A question which cut straight to the uncertainty in the core of him.

'Well this is true, Bravo. Certainly *you* have needed to be hidden as well. Son of an Avenel knight and the daughter of the chief? *Very* controversial,' Callista said, eyebrows arched high at the drama of it.

Bravo made an aggressive step forward. Lien threw an arm out into his chest, holding him back.

'This is another dream?' he demanded, changing the subject.

'Yes! Isn't it good? *Such* detail,' Callista said proudly, her arms opening wide to encompass the chapel.

'You are no longer in Bravo's dream, of course – he could not hold a dream of this complexity for long, but it was a *very* good early effort, Bravo, and quite the innovative way to hitch a ride on the night-mare.'

Bravo stared at Callista, unable to decide whether he was being criticised or praised.

'Where is Areté?' Lien demanded.

'She is here with us,' Callista said calmly, and indicated to her right. A still figure lay on the ground by a wall, unnoticed, back to the group.

Lien ran straight over, heart in his mouth. He crouched down and gently took the shoulder of the prone person, rolling them onto their back.

It was indeed Areté.

She was breathing, but just only just. She was otherwise so, so still.

'Areté!' Lien said, the name catching in his throat. She was still dressed in her familiar armour, just as she had been when he and Bravo had said goodbye to her a year ago, but it was battered, dirty and blood-streaked. She was also still thin, and her auburn hair a wild unkempt mess. A little blood had dried around a reddening mark on the right side of her forehead.

'What's wrong with her?' Lien asked Callista furiously, as he tried to smooth Areté's hair back behind her ears, and helplessly stroked her white, drawn face.

*I'm so sorry, I'm so sorry* he sobbed in his mind.

'She is unconscious in the physical world. It would not have been - convenient - for her dream-self to be able to join us, but I thought it prudent to have her represented here,' Callista said.

'Whose dream *is* this?' Bravo demanded. 'Can *you* do dream magic?'

'No. I have extensive knowledge, but alas, none of your talent for it, Bravo,' Callista said.

'Then - whose?' Bravo asked.

'We are in the dream of my pupil,' Callista said proudly.

Bravo looked confused; Lien looked up sharply from Areté.

'You're Tryst's teacher!' he said, and as he did, his skin crawled at the realisation of what that meant. He stood up, astonishing even himself with the new depths of anger he felt towards Callista.

'I am,' she agreed. 'You should have listened to him when he told you not to tell him everything, Lien. You know I can only free Areté if she tells me, or I otherwise learn, who the current or future Mandala is. Now I'm not convinced of your Prince Rupert theory, but I'm certainly going to put it to the test.'

'Prince Rupert?!' Bravo asked Lien, puzzled.

'I feel the same, Bravo,' Callista confided. 'The Mandala is generally rather more - discerning - about where it chooses to go. But its options are potentially limited, and Areté did go to extraordinary lengths to save Rupert's life, so it is certainly worth investigating Citar's theory. Let us ask Tryst to bring him to us.'

Callista stepped to the side to reveal what her skirt had concealed from their perspective: Tryst, cross legged against the central pillar. His eyes were closed, face strained and sweat beaded upon his brow.

*'Tryst...'* Lien gasped quietly. The boy did not look like a willing participant in Callista's game.

'Where is he really?' Bravo asked sharply.

'Right here, in the chapel of Levithorne. We are in a dream he has created, within the same physical space. That makes it easier for him to maintain,' Callista said, kneeling down to inspect the boy. Her tone remained calm, but her face betrayed concern for her student.

'This dream is too big for him on his own,' Bravo said urgently. 'You're asking too much of him.'

'It is - a lot,' Callista agreed, looking up to Bravo

seriously. 'But I have trained him well, and here on Levithorne. It is built on a mirror realm. It makes him much more powerful.'

'It's still too much,' Bravo protested, appalled at what was being asked of the other boy.

'Shush Bravo, we are just players here,' Callista said, and turned back to Tryst's strained face.

'Tryst. Bring Rupert into the dream,' she asked him gently.

Tryst grimaced and semi shook his head. He didn't want to do it – or couldn't do it.

'Tryst,' Callista said, her voice hardening. 'Bring the prince, now.'

Tryst, eyes closed all the while, gritted his teeth and furrowed his brow deeper.

'Good boy,' Callista said, kind again, but also, Lien realised, unhappy. He hated her, but even so, he could see she did not want to be doing this to Tryst.

The dream shuddered.

The chapel flickered disconcertingly between the one of Tryst's imagination and the real ruin.

'He can't hold it alone,' Bravo said, angry now. 'And if he lets it go, we're all going to be lost in Aurebos.'

He turned to Lien, and gestured subtly with his head towards Shah, still waiting on the other side of the chapel. Lien gave Bravo a searching look which he hoped said *can she get us out?* Bravo gave an almost imperceptible nod. While Callista's attention was on Tryst, Lien and Bravo turned as one to run for Shah.

BE STILL.

It was Callista's body that stood up, but it was Cosmos who was driving now, their gold eyes burning. Lien and Bravo found themselves stopped mid turn.

TRYST. DESTROY THE NIGHT-MARE.

'No!' Lien shouted, instantly sick with fear.

DO IT NOW, TRYST, OR I WILL BREAK THE DREAM.

'Tryst, you can't,' Lien begged. Tryst was shaking his head as well, his eyes still screwed closed.

'The dream cannot be broken, Lien,' Bravo gasped.

'Shah, run!' Lien yelled to the grey mare

I WILL NOT ASK AGAIN, TRYST.

A single, glistening tear ran down Tryst's tortured face.

'Shah, *run!*' Lien repeated desperately, and the mare wheeled around to do so - but as she did, she disappeared. It was a near-instantaneous fade-out, unlike the way she would normally dissolve into tendrils of smoke after delivering a dream.

'Where is she?' Lien demanded, face blanched, chest tight. The force holding him and Bravo released them and they both fell forward from their semi-running freezes. As soon as they were recovered, they looked to Tryst. His head had fallen forward. He looked utterly spent.

SHE IS DESTROYED. MY APPRENTICE HAS BECOME LESS CO-OPERATIVE, BUT ULTIMATELY, REMAINS OBEDIENT.

Lien looked desperately to Areté, but she was as still as before.

NO-ONE CAN HELP YOU HERE, LIEN. NOT EVEN ARETÉ.

The words echoed dully in his head as tears for Shah ran down his face. He looked inside for his darkness.

*Where are you? I need you now,* he silently screamed.

Only silence answered.

# 17. COSMOS

'So Lien and Tryst are both dreaming?' Citar said, forcing her mind to focus on the important matters at hand.

Kai nodded.

'Do you think it's connected?' she asked.

Kai shrugged.

'Might be. But Tryst is here often, and Lien has nightmares often, so they might be doing their own things-' he broke off, listening carefully. 'You hear that?'

'There's a horse coming,' Citar said, jumping up. 'A big one.'

Chase moved to the front of his stable, snorting and banging his front leg on the wooden door.

'Stop that, you'll hurt yourself,' Kai snapped at his horse. Watching the restless movements, Citar had a sneaking suspicion, and hope blossomed in her chest.

'I think I know who it is,' she said, then as the distant sound of Rupert asking a horse if it could *please just walk now, because trotting is far too bouncy without a saddle, and why couldn't he have a saddle please?* also met her ears, she second guessed herself and expected Lord Jorge to make an entrance.

It was not Jorge though: as Citar had hoped, it was Erebus who came passaging into the stables. The magnificent sight was ruined somewhat by Rupert, dressed only in red and white striped flannel pyjama shorts, bouncing and protesting all the way.

'Holy shit, is that – '

'Erebus!' Citar agreed, delighted as he stopped in front of her. 'And Rupert, of course,' she added hastily, realising that was probably who Kai meant.

'Oh, hello Citar and very menacing looking stranger. This dream is just getting stranger and stranger,' Rupert said in the delirious tone of one who absolutely refuses to believe current events can be real.

'This isn't a dream,' Kai snapped. 'So what *are* you wearing, boy?'

'I think it *is* a dream,' Citar said, elated to find that Erebus seemed to remember who she was – who she *really* was. He dropped his huge nose into her hands in a familiar manner, and allowed her to stroke his broad face.

'This is definitely a dream, I wouldn't be caught dead in public without a top,' Rupert said fervently, glancing down at his long, scrawny torso. 'Which means you two are figments of my imagination.'

'I assure you, I am not a figment of your imagination,' Kai said. 'Citar, it can't be a dream, we haven't gone to sleep.'

'Not that we remember. But the last time I met Erebus, he came to me in a dream I had no memory of falling asleep into,' Citar said, completely forgetting that story belonged to Cira of the Backwind, not Citar of Avenel. 'And I really can't see Rupert getting on a horse without any saddlery if he was awake. Or in his jammies.'

'Absolutely not,' Rupert agreed.

'So what are you thinking? We're all in a dream together?' Kai asked sceptically. 'Why? Who would want the three of us?'

'Well, only one way to find out. After you,' Citar said, politely indicating to Erebus' back. Rupert looked, impossibly, even more worried; Kai raised an eyebrow.

'I'm not sure there's room for all of us – ' Rupert started, voicing the concern both males present shared.

'It's a dream, Rupert, I'm sure we'll all fit,' Citar said dismissively.

'Can I at least go get a bridle?' Kai asked dubiously.

'No!' Citar said. 'Stop fussing and get on the horse!'

'You first,' Kai said. Citar shrugged her agreement, and he legged her up behind Rupert. The two chevaliers looked down to him expectantly.

'You sure about this, old man?' Kai asked Erebus. The horse nuzzled him in a friendly manner then pushed Kai in the chest with his head.

'Alright alright,' Kai sighed, and vaulted up onto his back behind the two teenagers.

Somehow, they did all fit.

'Everyone shuffle up and hold onto – whatever you can,' Kai said. Rupert wrapped his hands in Erebus' mane. Citar gingerly put her hands on Rupert's waist and slid herself up so that she was right up against his back. That she was fine with; when Kai slid forward so that his body was against *her* back, and he put his big hands firmly on *her* waist though, she actually felt her breath catch a little again. After the event, she had thought often of being in Lien's arms on the ride back to the Backwind; but this was something else entirely.

'Alright Erebus, where to?' Kai asked over Citar's shoulder. 'Looks like you're the boss.'

'So sorry but – *who* are you?' Rupert asked over his shoulder as Erebus carefully turned under his three precarious passengers and walked out of the stables.

'Oh, this is Kai,' Citar said.

'What – *the* Kai?' Rupert yelped, looking around in fear and half sliding, half trying to jump off the side, unseating Citar with him. Kai grunted as he caught and manhandled the two chevaliers back into the middle of Erebus' back, shaking his head as he did. If Rupert really was the next Mandala, they were in even bigger trouble than he already suspected.

* * * * *

'Why would you have Tryst destroy her? She could do no harm to you!' Lien raged at Cosmos – but Cosmos was gone. He was shouting at Callista. But her cobalt eyes were no longer calm and warm.

'I'm sorry, but if she took you away before we had time to chat, that would be a problem for us,' Callista said stiffly. 'We do not like problems, Lien.'

Lien was processing Callista's use of *we* but before he could say anything, Bravo cut in.

'Look at Tryst, he's not going to be able to hold this dream for much longer, you must be able to see that,' Bravo said urgently. 'Say what you want and let us out while we can still all *get* out safely!'

Tryst looked very bad indeed. In fact, if not for the dream holding, Lien would swear he was unconscious. He thought of the effort it had taken Bravo to just hold their campfire dream for one minute. Tryst was holding the restored chapel, Callista, Areté, Bravo and himself in a dream that was now several minutes long, *and* he had killed Shah as well. He was clearly powerful, and no doubt Levithorne helped, but it had to be taking a terrible toll.

Magic always did.

The sound of hoofbeats turned everyone from Tryst though. Lien's heart momentarily leapt as he thought Shah might somehow be returning. But it was not his grey nightmare but her sire, Erebus, who came galloping through the walls of the chapel, solidifying with his three riders as he slid to a stop in front of Lien and Bravo's stunned faces.

'Lien!' Citar said with relief.

'Citar? Kai? *Rupert?*' Lien said, a little dumbly as he reeled them off. 'What are you doing here?'

'I assume we're crashing your dream,' Kai said. Unlike the teenagers, who were all focussed on one another, he was looking over the whole chapel.

'Not mine actually, we're all inside Tryst's dream,' Lien said, indicating to where Tryst slumped against the pillar.

'Oh my god, Tryst!' Citar gasped. 'What has happened to him?'

'He's holding this joint dream together, and it's much too big for him,' Lien said grimly, with a baleful look to Callista. She was staring at Kai though, frowning. Kai threw her a filthy look in return as he slid off Erebus and ran to the forlorn figure of Areté. He muttered her name as he crouched down to inspect her.

'You can't wake her,' Callista called.

Kai turned a furious glare on her.

'Callista, I presume?' Kai spoke her name with icy loathing.

'I see my reputation precedes me,' Callista said, evidently surprised by Kai's recognition.

'It's not anything to be proud of,' Kai growled, returning to his feet. 'What have you done to Areté?'

'She is merely unconscious,' Callista said. 'But I thought a physical representation would be helpful for us to all remember what is at stake, as we begin our - negotiation. Now that we are all present.'

'You've climbed the hierarchy of Scyros with suspicious speed. But I don't think that's all you. I think you've had some help, and I think I know what it was,' Kai said, stalking towards her. 'What are you, twenty-four, twenty-five years old? How old were you when it came to you? Twelve? Fourteen? Around the age of these boys here? When it offered you power and influence, if you would just do one thing? Just one thing, and then another, and then another? Exactly the same as you've done to Tryst here, I'll bet. *What did it promise you*, Callista, that you will trap and torture Areté, destroy the mind of a boy who had a gift you wanted to exploit, and intend to kill this buffoon - ' and here he waved towards Rupert, who looked startled, ' - because you think he's going to be the next Mandala? What could Cosmos possibly offer that would make you even consider, much less execute, any of this?'

Kai's furious monologue brought him to within a foot of Callista. He towered over her, and was twice as wide, but she held his glare gamely.

'Such big words from such an *ineffective* man, Kai,' she said coolly, but her face didn't quite match her tone. Kai snarled and thrust his right hand forward, but even faster, Callista stepped back and held up her right index and middle fingers. Kai's fingers froze in an open claw that had been about to close around her neck. She smiled, distantly, and stepped further back from his hand.

'It's always just brute force with you, isn't it?' she asked, circling around and away from the big man. 'Always reacting, never planning. Chaos, without order.'

She dropped her fingers, and Kai's hand closed on

empty air. He launched a punch; Callista lifted her two fingers again, and Kai froze again, his knuckles lined up with her calm but now cold eyes. Again she stepped back and to the side, out of range, and released him; the power of the punch pulled him a step forward but he swiftly recovered.

'We don't really have time for this, do we, Kai?' she asked, reasonably.

'What is it? What is it that's inside her?' Lien asked Kai.

'It is called Cosmos,' Kai said darkly. 'It possesses people, it seduces them with promises. *Good* people. It takes good people, and it corrupts them,' and he stared meaningfully at Callista. She looked momentarily disconcerted.

'You have met Cosmos before?' she asked, fully herself, then flinched, as though being reprimanded by an unseen force.

'I have been looking for Cosmos for a very long time, to right some old wrongs it did. But I'm not the only one looking, and you're lucky it's me who has found you first, Callista. You would kill Rupert to get to the Mandala; there are people who will kill you to get to Cosmos, and I am one of them, but I am the *least* dangerous.'

'L-listen, I'm s-sorry to interr-rrupt, but h-honestly, y-you're all t-talking about me b-being this – M-mandala – and h-honestly, I d-don't even know what that m-means,' Rupert said, loudly and nervously into the silence left by Kai's threat. He and Citar had also dismounted Erebus now and were hovering near the black horse.

'Thank you, Prince Rupert, for bringing us back on track,' Callista said brightly, turning from Kai's glowering glare to approach the prince. He stepped back nervously.

'I d-don't even kn-know what it is, s-so it's not f-fair to kkill me over it,' he stuttered, a little shrilly. Callista blinked and her eyes were gold when she opened them. Rupert stepped back; Kai lunged forward.

BE STILL.

Cosmos' instruction went straight into the minds of Kai and Rupert. Again Kai froze, as Cosmos put Callista's right hand onto Rupert's head. Rupert too could not move his body, but his eyes, wide with fear, rolled upwards to follow the hand. Then they closed and he gasped as Cosmos entered his mind. The intrusion took maybe only a minute, but one that felt like agonisingly long to everyone watching. Rupert's eyes blinked frantically behind his closed lids and he uttered a long, tortured groan.

When Cosmos released Rupert's head, Kai fell forward from his lunge, and Rupert crumpled where he stood. He would have fallen to the ground had Citar not caught and supported him into a slower descent to his knees.

Callista - for it was she again - shook her head as she knelt down in front of Rupert. He stared emptily at her, dazed.

'Something has been taken from you,' she said seriously. 'I do not know what it was, or why it was taken, or by whom. But you are damaged by it. And there is no sign of Mandala in you.'

The chapel shuddered again, shifting alarmingly between the ruin of the real world and the one of Tryst's imagination. Everyone glanced worriedly to Tryst, whose whole body was now slumped forward over his crossed legs.

'Why did you bring us all here, Callista?' Kai asked, eyes narrowed.

'You are an unwelcome interloper, Kai,' Callista said. 'I am not sure why Tryst has brought you to me. But the rest, I wish to inspect.'

'We are running out of time,' Bravo said angrily. 'And even if, by a miracle, we survive, you're killing Tryst with this. This is wrong.'

'I do not wish to permanently harm Tryst, so let us expedite our meeting,' Callista said. She closed her eyes, and Cosmos opened them, and spoke only to Bravo.

IF I LOSE TRYST, THEN I WILL SIMPLY HAVE TO FIND ANOTHER DREAMER.

Cosmos smiled benevolently as they stroked Bravo's cheek.

I CAN TEACH YOU SO, SO MANY THINGS, SON OF ENDORA.

'I don't want to learn anything from you,' Bravo said, recoiling from both the touch and unsolicited use of his mother's name.

EVEN WHAT REALLY HAPPENED TO YOUR MOTHER?

'Wh-what do you mean?' Bravo stammered, thrown by this.

WORK WITH ME, AND I WILL TELL YOU WHAT SKY WILL NOT.

'Don't listen to it, Bravo,' Kai warned, for although he could not hear Cosmos' words, he could see they were having a profound impact on the boy.

I CAN HELP YOU SEARCH FOR HER.

'She is dead,' Bravo said furiously.

HER BODY DIED. BUT ONLY BECAUSE HER MIND DID NOT RETURN.

Cosmos' golden eyes were luminous.

Bravo's eyes widened.

'What are you saying? That she was - that she is - in Aurebos?' he demanded.

YES. HERE IN THE DREAMING REALM, AS ARE WE, RIGHT NOW.

Cosmos smiled beatifically at Bravo.

TELL ME, BRAVO. HAS SKY EVER TOLD YOU OF YOUR TWIN?

'My - what - ?'

YOU REALLY MUST ASK HIM.

'Bravo! It will use you, like it's using Tryst,' Kai insisted.

Bravo's eyes darted between Kai, Tryst and Cosmos.

His face set.

'If my mother is in Aurebos, then I will find her myself,' he growled.

Cosmos shrugged indifferently.

YOU WERE MY IDEA, BRAVO. WE ARE CONNECTED. AND WHEN YOU DECIDE YOU WANT TO KNOW MORE, YOU ARE WELCOME TO COME AND FIND ME.

While Bravo stared, confused, Cosmos turned to Citar, still kneeling next to Rupert.

NOW LET US CHECK THE NEXT.

Citar and Rupert stood together, clutching one another. They backed off as Cosmos walked towards them.

STAND STILL, OR I WILL MAKE YOU.

Knowing the futility of trying to escape, Citar drew to a stop. Rupert stayed with her, but shook violently at Cosmos' approach. Citar watched breathlessly as Cosmos placed a hand on her head, terrified that the creature would see through her glamour. She didn't know what would happen if another person blew her cover; the glamour was supposed to be strong enough that none could. But whatever Cosmos was, they were clearly not a normal person.

Citar gasped as Cosmos entered her mind; it was like having a bucket of ice cold water thrown over her head.

NOW THIS IS INTERESTING.

Cosmos retracted their hand and tilted their head to

one side. Rupert held Citar as her breath shortened and her knees buckled, but she kept her eyes on Cosmos and her terrified faced *begged* for discretion.

Cosmos read the expression perfectly, and gave it due consideration.

And Cosmos gave Citar a sly wink.

'What is it?' Lien asked, trying to read the exchange between the two.

Cosmos did not answer, but turned to Lien. He instinctively stepped back as well. Cosmos waved one index finger in a "don't do it" warning.

WHICH LEAVES ONLY ONE. ARETÉ'S LITTLE PRINCE.

As Cosmos reached for Lien's head, he heard Kai shout *No!* and from his peripheral vision, saw him lunge forward. And then Lien felt like he was standing under a waterfall bringing ice water straight down from snowy peaks. His body and brain froze with the shock.

Lien had mixed emotions in the seconds before Callista's hand landed on his head. On the one hand, he wanted *someone* to tell him *something* about himself, and it seemed likely Cosmos would do that.

On the other, he was frightened of what he might learn.

The intrusion did not take long though, and when Cosmos stepped back, Lien fell forward to his hands and knees, shaking and breathless.

Cosmos' golden eyes inspected Lien critically. Kai, just behind Callista, had an unexpected expression: he looked *worried*. When Cosmos released him from the latest freeze, he detoured from attacking Callista to aiding Lien.

'Naught Giselle. How very disappointing,' Callista said

to Kai, as he knelt down to support the boy.

Kai looked confused as he helped Lien up to kneeling.

'Areté has been hiding a fake prince all this time,' Callista continued, thoughtfully. 'I wonder if she knows.'

Lien felt his stomach drop. He *wasn't* the heir! That was – good. He hadn't wanted to be the heir to the Avenel throne. But he had thought he was...*something*. But Cosmos thought he was nothing. They were more interested in Citar, and *Rupert*, and certainly Tryst, than in him.

He didn't matter.

The dream shuddered dangerously.

'Well there you go,' Kai said, pulling Lien back to his feet. 'No-one here is going to be the Mandala, so now *end* this. Let Tryst close the dream.'

'No! We can't leave without Areté!' Lien protested weakly.

'She isn't really here, Lien,' Kai said.

'And we *have* to go *now*,' Bravo warned from Tryst's side. He had drawn the slumped boy upright and leant him back against the column.

'I don't even know how he's holding this together.'

'That's because...he is not,' Callista said slowly, crossing her arms.

'Then who is?' Kai roared as the dream groaned. The ruin of the chapel of the physical world was reappearing for whole seconds now. Everyone looked alarmed and afraid – except for Callista.

She studied the group.

She frowned at Tryst. The boy was, as Lien had suspected, completely unconscious.

He had been for some time.

LET US FIND OUT.

Cosmos faced Lien with Callista's forefinger and middle finger raised.

STOP BREATHING.

Cosmos' instruction went straight into Lien's mind. Lien immediately felt his lungs stop working. He couldn't push air our or pull it in. His chest tightened and his eyes widened. As his brain started to panic, he *begged* the darkness to rise. Surely it would now? He had not been in danger when Cosmos had read him, but now - now he couldn't breathe. He couldn't *breathe*. He couldn't breathe, so he couldn't speak. He clutched helplessly at his throat and turned, eyes desperate, to his companions. The darkness was nowhere. Now that he needed it - *really* needed it - it had abandoned him.

'Stop it,' Citar said fearfully, even though she didn't fully understand what was happening to Lien. 'Cosmos, *stop it!*'

Kai's body was frozen again, eyes blazing with rage.

'Callista!' he yelled. 'I know you're in there. Is this what you want? To murder an innocent boy on behalf of that *thing* inside you?'

Cosmos turned a bland expression to Kai.

CALLISTA ISN'T HERE RIGHT NOW, KAI.

Bravo had his eyes closed, his face a mask of intense concentration.

THAT'S NOT GOING TO WORK EITHER, BRAVO.

Bravo's eyes opened, narrowed slits of fury. He stood aggressively.

YOU ARE ALL DEFENCELESS AGAINST ME. YOU ARE ALL HELPLESS AGAINST ME. BUT THIS MESSAGE IS NOT FOR YOU. YOU ARE MERELY THE MESSENGERS, AND LIEN IS THE MOST – EXPENDABLE – AMONGST YOU.

Lien fell back down to his hands and knees, unable to even gasp, as that would require air. He was so ordinary he was...*expendable*. The crush in his lungs was unbearable. He was becoming lightheaded, seeing stars, and he was going to die if Cosmos didn't release him.

Citar and Bravo ran to either side of him, clutching at his shoulders, but were equally helpless.

Lien knew he had seconds of consciousness left, and that there was absolutely nothing he could do about it. *And where was the darkness now? Now that he needed it?*

And...he had failed. Failed to rescue Areté. He managed to look up to where she was lying, meters away. He tried to reach out to her, but could not.

*Areté!* he cried in his mind, unable to make the words without air.

And Lien passed out, falling into the arms of Citar and Bravo.

'Cosmos!' Citar screamed, tears streaming down the sides of her face as she watched a second friend dying in her arms. Helpless again: as helpless as she had been when Jordan had died.

Cosmos ignored her, instead turning in a slow circle, arms held out wide.

I KNOW YOU ARE HERE. REVEAL YOURSELF.

The command seemed to be directed at the dream at large.

And the dream responded.

It ceased shuddering. From below Lien, a purple light began to draw a shape on the flagstones. Kai was released from the latest hold Cosmos had put on him, and a slow grin spread across his face as he realised whose sign was being revealed on the floor.

Whose sigil.

It was partially concealed by the bodies of Lien, Citar and Bravo, but it was huge and unmistakable, if you knew what you were looking at.

'Oh Cosmos, you are *fucked*,' Kai said.

Unperturbed, and arms still wide, Cosmos inclined their head grandiosely and addressed the glowing purple sigil.

SHIVAIA.

# 18. SHIVAIA

*Lien. Rise.*

Lien did so. He was standing in the centre of Shivaia's incandescent sigil, opposite the Dark Lady herself, although he did not know who she was. They were alone, bathed in a smoky silver and purple light. Outside the sigil lay only darkness.

Shivaia's eyes shone like radiant amethysts; her ageless skin was lily white; and her wild black hair was partially swept back with string and feathers. She wore the same flowing robe of blacks, greys, purples and blues that Cira had seen her in many years earlier; this was the first time Lien had met her though, and he was speechless, even though he was no longer starved of breath.

He suddenly realised he did not even need to breathe.

*You do not need air in a dream.*

'Is this – another dream?' he asked.

*No. This is a borderline. You believe you are dying in the dream though, and so, your soul will pass.*

'Pass to where?' Lien asked.

*If you wish to know, you need only leave the sigil.*

Lien looked to the darkness outside.

'Can I…come back?' he asked, already knowing the answer.

*No.*

Lien nodded. Seemed fair.

'So...I don't have to die? In the dream?'

***Not if you can open your soul eye and free your mind from the limitations of your body.***

'Oh. Well, that's not something I can do. Anymore.'

***You are alone here on the borderline.***

Lien's face showed his scepticism, but he closed his eyes - *do I have eyes in my mind?* - went to take a deep breath - *except there's no air in my mind* - and tried to find his soul eye.

***It is not your darkness. It looks through you, but it is not of you.***

Lien had been feeling his way to his soul eye when he realised the meaning of Shivaia's words. He looked to her, the eye forgotten completely as he went to ask her what she meant by that: what she *knew* of the darkness. She frowned at his distraction though, and impatiently placed her index and middle finger lightly on his forehead.

Lien might have been in his mind, not his body, but he nonetheless experienced the touch as ice cold, and he gasped - though reflexively, for there was no air - as his soul eye *opened.*

He experienced a blinding white light, and went to close his eyes, when he realised they were not what was doing the "seeing". It was his soul eye that was wide open, much more than it ever had been, and that was what was letting the light pour in.

Into what? His mind? His soul? Was there a difference?

The light was so far beyond just white that he saw all the colours playing around the edge in geometric kaleidoscopic arrangements. Lien felt ripped open, bare, vulnerable. The sensation was utterly overwhelming. He was starting to panic when Shivaia removed her fingers.

Lien's soul eye snapped shut as quickly as it had opened.

His legs buckled and he fell to his hands and knees for the third time that night. He felt utterly spent.

*Stand. You are not in your body. You are not only your body.*

'Who…are you?' Lien panted - even though there was no air - and still on his hands and knees - even though his physical body was not there to be exhausted.

He simply could not get his head around it.

*I am Shivaia.*

'The Dark Lady?' Lien said, amazement spreading across his face. She shrugged as she extended a cold hand to help him back to his feet.

*If you like. I stand in the liminal spaces.*

Lien frowned: he did not understand the word.

*Borderlines, or thresholds. Between waking and dreaming. Conscious and unconscious. Living and dying. These are my domain.*

As Shivaia spoke, she kept her hold of Lien's hand, and kept them moving. He was so preoccupied with pulling his sense of self together after the shocking opening of his soul eye, and following what she was saying, that he did not at first notice. He glanced down - and yelped, reflexively grabbing for her other hand as well.

*You will only fall if you cling onto your commitment to the rules of the physical world.*

They were floating, far above the sigil. Lien's brow furrowed as his fear was overtaken by recognition. He knew this sigil: he had seen it many times.

Daubed on the quarters of his night-mare.

'*You* have been sending Shah!'

*I have.*

'Why?' he demanded. 'I am...nobody. What did you want me to do?'

*Everything you have done. And you are best served - and in service - with Cosmos believing you are nothing. While they watch others, you will be free to act.*

Lien stared into the Dark Lady's brilliant amethyst eyes.

'What do I need to do?'

*First, you need to believe you do not need the air that you think Cosmos has taken from you.*

Shivaia looked down meaningfully, to where the sigil glowed far below their feet. Understanding, Lien steeled himself to believe he was not his body here. That the rules of the physical world did not apply to his...consciousness? Soul?

He let go of her hands.

He did not fall.

If he could have, he would have heaved a sigh. But he knew there was no air to release, and no body to release tension from.

Shivaia nodded approvingly.

*Then you need to find the current Mandala. Bring them to Scyros, to Callista. For forces like Cosmos are why it exists.*

And then Shivaia, the sigil and the surrounding darkness were gone.

*****

In the dream chapel, Shivaia appeared within her sigil from a swirling of purple mist and silver light. Her dramatic arrival was met with a range of reactions.

Cosmos was unsurprised and, despite Kai's grim pleasure, unconcerned.

Bravo had felt sick when he saw the sigil. He had recognised but not been able to place it when he saw it on Shah, but seeing it there on the ground awoke an old, buried childhood memory: of his mother drawing it obsessively.

Rupert had an unsettling sense of déjà vu: he was certain he had met this figure before, but could not think where or when.

Citar was shocked by the appearance. As Cira of the Backwind, she had been charged by Shivaia with finding and allying herself with the Mandala in return for the healing of her knee. Now she was Citar of Avenel - and did Shivaia know? Could *she* see through the glamour? Citar tried to catch the Dark Lady's eye, but her full focus was on Cosmos.

*Cosmos. You overstep your power, into mine. This is unwise.*

'Shivaia! Can you save Lien?' Citar cried out, before Cosmos could respond. She was not remotely interested in the posturing of the two creatures of the Old World - only in saving her friend.

*He does not need saving.*

Lien jerked in the arms of Citar and Bravo. He was on his knees, held between his two friends. They looked on in amazement and relief as he lifted his head to level a hard stare at Cosmos. He was no longer gasping or panting.

Cosmos cocked their head curiously, and lifted their index and middle finger again.

'That won't work again, Cosmos,' Lien said, allowing Citar and Bravo to help him back to his feet. 'I don't need air in a dream. You have no power here that we do not permit you.'

'Oh *now* you tell us,' Kai said, making another lunge forward. Cosmos froze him as easily as they had every other time.

Kai threw a dark look to Lien.

'It's...a little more complicated than it sounds,' he shrugged apologetically.

Cosmos went to speak again, but this time was interrupted by Bravo, who was jogging back to Tryst, now that Lien was out of danger.

'Shivaia: can you help Tryst?'

Shivaia looked upon the exhausted, unconscious boy, propped up against the central column.

'Will he...be ok?' Lien asked anxiously.

*Cosmos would have broken him completely, but I have been carrying the dream for some time. The physical damage will not be permanent.*

Everyone looked relieved.

*But I cannot speak for the mental damage. Tryst has been betrayed by one he trusted. And although I have helped him, he was still pushed beyond his capacity. This will not be without consequence.*

Bravo turned on Cosmos.

'I hope those consequences turn on you,' he said furiously. Cosmos looked unfazed.

I WEAPONISED HIM, BUT HE IS NO THREAT TO ME. NONE OF YOU ARE. NOT EVEN SHIVAIA. EVEN IN A DREAM CAST ON LEVITHORNE.

To demonstrate, Cosmos held up Callista's two fingers, and Citar, Kai, Bravo, and Rupert all stopped breathing. All believing they needed the air denied them, they each began to suffocate, as equally as Lien almost had minutes earlier.

Lien stared wildly to Shivaia.

Cosmos looked to her too with a serene smile.

IT IS ONLY A DREAM, AFTER ALL.

Shivaia gracefully stepped back into the centre of her sigil, keeping her eyes on Cosmos. Her face was a winters' midnight: beautiful, clear and ice cold, with the promise of snow.

*It is never only a dream in Levithorne.*

Shivaia spread her arms wide, and as she did, a brilliant heliotrope luminescence rose up from the sigil. It shone from the floor to the ceiling, and under its light, the whole dream shifted. No longer the ruined chapel of the physical world, or the beautiful version of Tryst's imagination, this was another chapel altogether. It was still a hexagonal shape, and it was still made of stone, but that was where the similarities ended. It was huge: the walls pushed back several meters on all sides and the ceiling rose so high it was lost to darkness. The central column became an enormous oak. Its stark, leafless branches grew up and out across the entire space.

Cosmos' hold dropped, and everyone gasped gratefully for air.

*You have over-extended, Cosmos, and you have done so in my realm.*

Cosmos' face showed first surprise and then delight.

IT IS **YOUR** MIRROR REALM UPON WHICH LEVITHORNE WAS BUILT! THIS IS IT?

Shivaia inclined her head.

*Nothing has happened in this dream, in this place, that I did not permit.*

Shivaia threw a sidelong glance to Lien as she said this. Lien frowned, unsure of her meaning. If she had been in control the whole time, why had she permitted Cosmos to go into the minds of all the teenagers? Why had she allowed Kai to be stopped every time he had tried to take action against Cosmos? Why had she allowed Cosmos to force Tryst to kill Shah? And allowed Cosmos to almost kill him?

*This is over.*

YOU CAN END THE DREAM, SHIVAIA. BUT ARETÉ IS STILL MINE, FOR THE TERMS OF OUR ARRANGEMENT ARE NOT MET. SOMEONE HERE MUST BRING ME THE

CURRENT OR NEXT MAND-

Calmly drawing a straight line in the air with her index and middle finger, Shivaia closed the dream, cutting Cosmos off mid-threat.

And everyone woke up.

Bravo started awake in Leaverness.

Rupert started awake in his bed in Voltanna.

Lien, Citar and Kai all woke in the Levithorne stables: Lien in his bed, Citar leaning against the wall next to him, and Kai flat out on the ground outside the stable, his sword fallen next to him.

The three looked confusedly to one another, but Lien caught his wits first.

'Tryst!'

They scrambled to their feet and ran for the chapel. At least, Kai and Citar ran. Lien quickly discovered all of his injuries remained in his body in the physical world and half walked, half jogged as smoothly as he could, falling far behind the others.

'I bloody hate magic,' Kai swore as he and Citar reached Tryst, collapsed on the hard ground in front of the central column.

'Tryst!' Citar said, dropping down next to the unconscious boy. He did not respond.

'Should we - try to wake him?' Citar asked anxiously. 'What if he's still dreaming?'

'He's not dreaming,' Kai said grimly. He swept the boy up into his arms.

'You need to get him to Selene. You can take my horse.'

Citar trailed Kai, who strode off magnificently, as

though Tryst weighed nothing at all. When they got to the chapel door though, they found both Lien and, unexpectedly, a big black horse waiting for them.

'Erebus!' Citar cried in delight. The stallion nudged her affectionately, then turned his side to them.

'Wait, are we still dreaming?' Kai asked suspiciously.

'Nope, my ribs are very real and still very broken,' Lien winced.

'Then I guess Erebus is taking Tryst to Selene,' Kai said with a wry shrug. He pushed Tryst up onto the horse's broad back and then legged Citar up behind him.

'Hold him tight, Citar,' Kai said.

'Don't worry about that. No-one can fall off Erebus unless he wants them to,' she said, but she wrapped her arms around Tryst nonetheless as the horse turned and galloped the two chevaliers into the night.

Alone now in the dark night, Lien and Kai walked slowly back to the stables. Kai lit the forge fire and made tea. They were both drained and exhausted by the events of the evening, and being thrown out the dream had left them a psychological hangover.

'Do you think Tryst will be okay?' Lien finally asked, as Kai passed him a steaming mug and settled down on the chair opposite with his own.

'I don't know, but he's in the best of care,' Kai said. 'What Cosmos is doing to Areté is bad, but she at least would have known the risks of entering into an Arrangement. But what it has done to Tryst...' Kai trailed off. His face was as frightening as it had been in the prison, when he had faced the men who had attacked the People.

'He's just a boy. There's no way he understood, and that's unforgivable.'

Lien listened silently. Tryst had been abused by his father, and then by someone he must have considered his mentor, perhaps even his friend. Shivaia was right: his injuries would be more than just physical.

There was something else bothering him as well though.

'Kai – who is Giselle?'

Kai was startled by the hesitant question.

'You heard that?' he said. 'I thought you might have been – you know. A bit out of it.'

'I heard. "Naughty Giselle." Callista said that to you. As though you would understand.'

Kai took a slow sip of the bitter tea.

'Giselle was the Queen of Avenel,' he said slowly.

Lien stared.

'Du Romeau's queen?'

'Yes. Do you understand?'

Lien bit his bottom lip and slightly shook his head.

Kai sighed.

'Callista seems to think the Queen was your mother…but the King was not your father.'

'Oh.'

They shared a long silence.

'I have a mother,' Lien said eventually, a little numbly.

'Had. Most likely. We don't know whether Giselle is still alive.'

Lien's face fell.

'And we don't know for sure she's your mother anyway. I'm sceptical, myself.'

'Why?'

The question was sharper than Lien intended, but he felt like Kai was trying to take something precious from him.

'Because I knew Giselle very well, and she was *very* loyal to Du Romeau. And I should know, I tried it on with her more than once.'

Lien stared.

'You tried to…to "get it on" with the queen? Who might have been my mother?'

'Lien, you weren't even around. And sure, she was an exceptional woman. She liked me, too. But she put me in my place, and I can't think of another man she wouldn't do the same to.'

'Tell me about her?' Lien asked.

'Giselle?' Kai sipped his tea again, but it was old memories that he was savouring. 'She was…remarkable. Kind. Courageous. Gorgeous. Fiercely intelligent. I hope she's still around somewhere, but Areté said your mother was dead, and while she doesn't always tell the full truth, I've never seen her lie. So if Giselle *was* your mother…'

Kai had the foresight not to complete the sentence, but the omission hung grimly in the air between man and boy.

'Did Shivaia tell you what to do next?' he asked, as much to change the subject as to satisfy his curiosity.

'She said to find the current Mandala, and take them to Scyros, to Callista, to deal with Cosmos,' Lien said.

Kai nodded thoughtfully.

'Then that's what we do. I'm not saying I know how, but *some*how, we must find the Mandala. And we must take them to Scyros, and let them deal with Cosmos. Shivaia wouldn't tell you so if they were not up to the task. And then we get Areté back, and then we have a *massive* piss up. Deal?'

'And then I can go back to the People?' Lien asked hopefully, which for him, was far more important than a massive piss up.

'Sure. If that's what you want,' Kai said, giving Lien a curious look. 'But why don't you leave that decision until we get there. A lot has to happen between now and then. This is not going to be easy. We have a lot of work to do - including working out this power of yours.'

Lien had never considered his darkness - *the* darkness - a power. But the semantics were irrelevant.

'What power?' he asked bitterly. 'When I actually needed it - *really* needed it - it wasn't there.'

'It's smart. Smarter than you, that's for sure,' Kai said. 'And Shivaia was running that dream. You heard her. Nothing happened that she did not allow.'

'Then why did she allow all of those other things to happen?' Lien demanded.

'Kid, you *will* learn, though I fear it will a long and painful process for you, that there are times to show your hand, and times to hold it. Shivaia needed to let Cosmos think they had control so they would show their hand. I think she also wanted to make a point - which she did very effectively.'

'What, that we were all helpless against Cosmos?'

Kai frowned.

'No, the opposite. You proved that yourself.'

'Only because Shivaia was there to show me. It was pure luck we met Cosmos in Levithorne, and in a dream. If we next meet them somewhere else, somehow else, we might not have Shivaia to back us up. I would have *died* if not for her.'

'You're making a bad habit of nearly dying. Let's nip

that one in the bud,' Kai said with a stern look.

'Better than *actually* dying though,' Lien pointed out.

'Well, can't argue with that,' Kai said with a wry smile. 'And I don't think we need to go looking for Cosmos again. That's what the Mandala is for. And…I don't think any of it was luck,' he added.

Before Lien could argue - which he was definitely going to do - the sound of Chase neighing and moving in his stable made them both look up. Kai was on his feet instantly, indicating for Lien to stay where he was, and be quiet. He swept up his sword and silently stole along the wall of the forge, before looking cautiously around into the stable aisle.

Lien watched breathlessly - he definitely needed air in the physical world - and let out a sigh as Kai relaxed. The big man turned and, with a puzzled smile, indicated Lien come over.

'What now?' Lien asked as he walked over.

'Have a look, and you tell me,' Kai said, and it was the first time Lien had ever seen him look - pleased?

But his surprise at this was nothing compared to his surprise at seeing the grey mare, neck outstretched inquisitively, standing outside Chase's stable.

*'Shah!'*

Lien went to run to her but Kai grabbed his arm and held him back.

'Hold up, you don't want to spook her,' he said.

'But - it's Shah! How is this possible?' Lien asked, looking wildly between the mare and Kai.

'I don't know but I'd go slow. She's not a night-mare anymore.'

'What do you mean?' Lien started, as he began a slow walk down the stable aisle: then realised Kai was right.

Shah looked as real, as solid, as physical as she had in Bravo's dream, but this was no dream.

Well, he *hoped* it wasn't a dream.

She whuffled angrily and shook her head at Lien as he approached, her eyes so wide the whites showed at the edges. When he was within an arm's reach of her, she stamped a foreleg and snaked her neck at him as though demanding an explanation.

'Shah - you're - you're a real horse!' Lien said in wonder, cautiously reaching for her. She shied away from his hand and pinned her ears back.

'Looks like it. And she is *not* happy about it,' Kai said bemused and keeping well back.

'Did Tryst do this? Or Shivaia?' Lien asked, stepping back as well, to make himself non-threatening to the irate mare.

'Cosmos told Tryst to destroy the night-mare. Maybe he did that - he destroyed the supernatural part of her, leaving her as a normal horse?' Kai speculated. 'Or maybe Shivaia did it.'

Lien gave a silent but heartfelt thank-you to them both.

'Want me to go around the outside and shut her in at the front?' Kai asked.

Lien shook his head with a little smile.

'No, she can stay with us if she wants, or she can be free if she prefers,' he said.

'She's going to be *really* unhappy when she finds out she can't just go through walls - and fences - any more,' Kai said. 'Tough for a night-mare to be relegated to being just a normal horse.'

'She won't be normal,' Lien said confidently as he went into the stable that contained the hay and straw.

'I bet she's hungry,' he called as he pulled off an armful of hay and lay it in the aisle. Shah stared at it suspiciously, legs wide, ready to run. But it smelt good, and she *was* hungry, for the first time in her life, so she tentatively stretched her neck forward, took a wisp of hay and chewed. She sighed with pleasure at the taste of it, took a step forward and plunged her nose deep into the pile.

Lien and Kai left her in peace to discover the joy of food, returning to the forge and their cooling mugs of tea.

'Don't know about you, but I'm beat as hell…but also reluctant to go back to sleep,' Kai said when they were settled back down.

'I hear you, but I need to sleep off these wounds and broken ribs,' Lien sighed, gingerly holding his left side.

'Yeah I reckon one of mine is still bruised,' Kai said, prodding his own ribs.

'Only one?!'

'Fast healing is a hell of a perk,' Kai grinned.

Lien grinned back.

It was the first time they had ever smiled at each other.

Was Kai a friend? Lien couldn't quite tell, but he hoped so. He was pretty sure Citar was, and, for better or worse, Rupert. Maybe Tryst too, when he recovered. Lien hoped they could be friends as well.

Lien sank back into the seat, allowing his eyes to close. As he relaxed, he remembered the searing light from opening his soul eye. He had to talk to Bravo about that.

Bravo, Tryst, Kai, Citar and Rupert. He felt like he had the right people together for the job. But he knew they would need more help too.

**LET ME,** said the darkness.

## ...TO BE CONTINUED...

And in the meantime, if you have enjoyed spending time with Lien, Citar and their friends, please help other people to find out about them by leaving a written review for *The Darkness Dreaming* on Amazon, Goodreads or wherever you go to find great books to read – with thanks from a new writer!

# AUTHOR'S NOTE

This photo is from 2011, when I asked my friend Sean Kelly to take me an "author's headshot". I was determined to *finally* finish my first book to enter in the inaugural Terry Pratchett First Novel Award. I had around twenty books partially planned or written, I was almost 30 and I needed to get a wriggle on.

My friend and comics writer Si Spencer agreed to mentor me through it and I worked very hard. But I did not finish. I don't know whether Terry would have liked this book, and I doubt it would have won, but I did win the inaugural (and sadly, only) Miss/Mister/It Discworld competition[1] the

[1] Judged and awarded by Sir Terry himself, and still the only competition of any kind I have ever won — though honestly, what could beat that anyway?

following year, which was nearly as good.

Eleven years later…I have *finally* finished that first book.[2]

And that sounds terrible, until you realise I actually started it twenty-seven years ago so…what's eleven years between drafts?

I'd like to share the influences and history of this book for anyone who is interested. You may have already made guesses if you've made it this far (and if you have, what's another thousand words between friends?).

In 1995 I was in high school when Xena Warrior Princess debuted: the greatest thing to happen to me since discovering Star Trek. I began developing a character, and her world and adventures, to get me through school. This character was Areté, and the stories I wrote about her actually come after the books centred on Lien and Citar and their friends (so may literally take another twenty-seven years to get to).

In primary school my father introduced me to Piers Anthony's Xanth series, which I devoured. But it was his Incarnations of Immortality series that I became obsessed with and learned to plot from (god help us all).

Also in primary school I discovered a local author, Helen Barrett, who wrote six beautiful, warm, funny and, at times,

---

[2] I am also widely assured I still look pretty much like this photo (albeit with the addition of professional makeup, hair styling, lighting and let's be honest, Photoshop).

heart-breaking books about horses, all set in my home state of South Australia. I loved these books more than I can say, and tried to track her down by writing to her publisher. It turns out she was her own publisher, and tragically had died less than a year before I discovered her. This was the nearest I had ever come to meeting an author whose books I loved, and I think it was Helen who gave me both the idea of trying to write books myself, and my underlying style. I wish so much that I could have told her what her books meant to me.

In primary school I made a habit of reading every book I found that had a horse on the front cover, but this proved more difficult in my high school library. I found one called Mort though, and this was my introduction to Terry Pratchett. That I later met the great man in real life and became involved in his fandom on the other side of the world would have astonished twelve-year-old me.

Anime was huge when I was in high school and my favourite was Rumiko Takahashi's Ranma 1/2 with its eccentric, hyperbolic characters, insane martial arts, gender switching love triangles (hello Citar!) and mistaken identities.

A friend of my brother then introduced me to something more serious though: Neil Gaiman's The Sandman. Oh boy. That opened all sorts of inspirations and further reading.

In a break year after school I went to chase equestrian dreams far from home. That went amazingly badly, but because it was pre-personal internet and I was lonely AF, I had nothing to do but read and write when I wasn't needed on the yard. The Fellowship of the Ring came out in cinemas that year and while reading The Lord of the Rings straight after, I set a lot of the framework for Lien's story. Which is *nothing* like LOTR, but the book and film really got me dreaming.

During university I started a new story intended for TV, which engaged me for the next few years. Then I moved to the UK and made a rather moderate effort to write for TV[3]–but I've never been what you'd call a finisher.

I came back to Lien while being a nanny in Italy. That was an incredible experience but I was so out of my comfort zone that I started getting up at 4am so I could start the day with something familiar: these characters and their stories.

Then I got into teaching fitness classes, which was supposed to leave more time to write. I did write, but not as much as I thought, and I spread myself safely across a lot of projects, so that nothing ever approached the danger zone of being finished (aside from the ambitious stint in 2011 when I wrote a lot of this book, then...didn't finish it...).

In 2012 I started working on what became the narrative fitness app Apocalypse Survival Training, and spent seven years learning that I'm a really crappy entrepreneur. I did

---

[3] The highlight was getting to pitch my time-travelling detective series at BAFTA, which was wild.

finish and release a whole ten episodes, which was a first, but ultimately AST spat me out tired and depressed and basically expecting to fail in anything else I tried.

2019 was a tough year, which turned me back to writing to find myself. I started this book again, and at the point that Lien leaves for Avenel, asked on Facebook whether anyone would have a read. At that time, I thought the book was around half way, but it was already 80,000 words.

Many people offered to read; only a handful came back to me though, which was worrying. My dear friend Bram, who has read everything I have ever asked anyone to read ever (which is quite a lot) finished it though, along with my friend Erika's young daughter Liv, and they were both very enthusiastic. And Rob Jackson, who I met briefly at a horseback archery session and friended on Facebook after because I thought he was cool, surprised me by going through it in huge detail, and urging me to keep going.

And my husband Ras, who by this time had suffered through many years of me claiming that all I wanted to do was write books and ride horses – while doing very little of either – never stopped encouraging me to keep the faith and make the time to keep writing.

It soon became apparent though that what I thought was Book 1 was at *least* two books, and if I broke the book in half, most of the really exciting stuff was in the second one. The new "first book" had no ending at all (or a title, and I've never really come to grips with what to call it). I sulked for a while, during which covid hit, and I spent 2020 transforming my fitness businesses while also trying to work out how on earth to turn half a freaking massive book into one coherent book with a decent ending. That was hopefully quite good – or at least, not shit.

I worked it out through 2021 and finished the first full draft in the only cafe I could find open on 1 January 2022.[4] Everything from Lien leaving Castelle Travers onwards was brand new. Tryst wasn't supposed to have magic until book 2 (which would now be book 3) and Cosmos didn't even recognisably exist. Which is mad. They were supposed to turn up much later, and in a different form, but became the backbone of this book and the ongoing series to fix my structure problems.

Then I moved house, and got busy, and let myself get paralysed over the dilemma of whether to try the bumpy soul-destroying multi-year road to traditional publishing…or just bloody self-publish it and get on with the next one.

My research was pushing me more and more to the latter.

At a Celebration of Life for a beloved lost friend, Nigel, I ran into Vicky Lear, who had read the full 2021 draft. She literally rounded me up while I was trying to eat all the cakes and told me – *ordered* me – to stop faffing around and publish the damn thing. She was *vehement* that I must do it, and do it now. I was shocked that anyone could care that much about my story.

---

[4] It was a Starbucks, of course, and the book was supposed to be finished before Christmas, but I'm rubbish with deadlines.

At the same CoL was Hannah Boron, a wonderful writer who has self-published her own book, and offered to guide me through the process and do the formatting for print and ebook. And with Hannah was Amber 'The Artful Nudger' Grundy, an amazing artist who did a gorgeous cover for Hannah's Tamzin and the Viper, and we discussed her doing mine as well.

This was 18 September 2022. If I was going to do this – if I was going to self-publish this book – I wanted to do it for Christmas 2022. Which was *very* tight. But with Hannah and Amber on my team, not impossible.

The 2021 draft was read to completion by a lot of people, far more than the 2019 version (and that was only half the length) and they had great feedback. Within a week Bram sent me back a ton of typos, and more notes came over the next two months. I acted on all the notes then printed the manuscript and sent it back to Rob, who went through it with a pen in October and found a lot more typos (how?!) amongst his other notes.

And then I did what no writer should ever do (and only self-published writers *can* do), which was to re-read it myself *while Rob had the "finished" version* and change a bunch more things – therefore any mistakes I've added in are entirely my own doing.

Now it is November 2022 and I'm sending this manuscript

to Hannah to format.[5] Amber completed the beautiful cover on time – which was not guaranteed, and for which I'm very grateful – and the first time I saw the full cover spread I realised this was really happening.

It's taken forty years, but I finished a book.
Reader, I am *terrified* to send it into the world. But here it is, in your hands!

These characters have been my constant companions since I was thirteen. I desperately hope that I have done them justice on the page, and that you too will care about what happens to them next.

If you've gotten this far, thank you so much for the investment of your precious time. I hope the hours feel like time well spent.

And...hurrah, here we are! One book down, nineteen to go...

*Adele Andersen*
*Berkshire, UK*
*22 Nov 2022*

---

[5] Hannah found a load *more* typos and I'm so fortunate that she read the whole thing as she formatted, instead of just checking margins and for widows and orphans — lifesaver!

Printed in Great Britain
by Amazon

14726984R00322